D0834537

A Dangerous Man...

A Perilous Desire

"You said once there might be wanted posters on you?" Mary Jo said.

"No recent one, not in the last ten, twelve years."

"What were the posters for?"

Wade's face tensed. "Shouldn't you have asked these questions earlier?"

"I want to know if there's any chance the sheriff might find them."

"Could be, if someone kept one, but I looked a lot different then." He didn't elaborate.

"You aren't going to tell me, are you?"

"No," he said softly. "But I'll leave if you want."

"You would like that just fine, wouldn't you?" she replied angrily.

"Ask me to leave," he invited her. They were no more than inches apart, and the heat between them could have ignited the barn.

Her hand reached up and touched his cheek.

His body shuddered at her touch and then his good arm went around her, bringing her close to him. "You're playing with fire, Mrs. Williams," he whispered in her ear.

Then he leaned down and his lips brushed hers . . .

Bantam Books by Patricia Potter
Ask your bookseller for titles
you may have missed

Defiant

Patricia Potter

BANTAM BOOKS

New York   Toronto   London   Sydney   Auckland

DEFIANT
A Bantam Book / August 1995

ISBN 0-553-56601-6

Published simultaneously in the United States and Canada

Bantam Books are published by Bantam Books, a division of Bantam
Doubleday Dell Publishing Group, Inc. Its trademark, consisting of the words
"Bantam Books" and the portrayal of a rooster, is Registered in U.S. Patent
and Trademark Office and in other countries. Marca Registrada. Bantam
Books, 1540 Broadway, New York, New York 10036.

PRINTED IN THE UNITED STATES OF AMERICA

OPM   0 9 8 7 6 5 4 3 2 1

Defiant

Prologue

El Paso, 1876

There was no uglier or sadder sound than the thud of dirt hitting a casket.

Mary Jo Williams had heard it before. She'd buried a husband two years ago, and now she was burying a friend, Tyler Smith. No, more than a friend. Ty had proposed to her several times, but she had always insisted she would never again marry a Texas Ranger.

Like her dead husband.

The tears in her eyes threatened to spill, and she blinked them back defiantly. She wouldn't cry, not in front of men who despised any sign of weakness. They were all here, Ty's fellow Rangers, except for Morgan Davis, who had been in the gunfight with Ty in a cowtown called Harmony. Morgan's girl had been wounded and he had stayed behind with her. Ty had been shot to death.

At least one man was getting out of rangering alive, Mary Jo thought with bitter envy. Why hadn't Ty?

Feeling Jeffry's hand tighten in hers, she looked down at her son. Only eleven years old and already he had seen too much death. He had campaigned for Ty to become his father, campaigned with the strategy and dedication of an army general. He had almost worn her down.

Ira Langford, the captain of Ty's Ranger company, spoke a few words at the graveside. Moving words, if you cared about honor and duty. Mary Jo used to care about those things, but now they were hollow words. What good was honor when you were so lonely you wanted to die, when grief nearly suffocated you every night and you awoke to emptiness? What good was duty when your son cried for a father who had always been gone? What about duty to the son?

Ira moved to her side. "I'm so sorry, Mary Jo," he said.

She stared at him blankly.

He looked oddly discomfited. "Can you come to my office?"

Mary Jo looked at Jeffry, who was bravely trying to hold back his tears. Rangers didn't cry. Mary Jo knew he was telling himself that. Over and over again.

"In a little while," she said stiffly. She hated Ira at the moment. She hated him for what he was, for sending men away to die.

He nodded. "Whenever you can." He hesitated. "God, Mary Jo, I'm sorry."

She bit her lip. "I'll be leaving here, you know. As soon as possible." She didn't know when that would be. She had so little money. Since her husband, Jeff, died, she had stayed on at the Ranger post earning a few dollars as cook and laundress and even tailor at times.

"I don't want to go," Jeffry said, and Mary Jo's heart nearly broke. He wanted to be a Ranger too, just like his father. Just like Ty and Morgan and so many others.

She would die first! She hadn't given birth to him to see him killed in a dusty street someplace. She had to get him away from here.

Ira's mouth worked. It was as much emotion as she'd ever seen from him. But he only nodded again, as taciturn as the men he led.

She stood at the grave as the others left, respectfully giving her a moment with the man they all knew had wanted to marry her.

She had brought a flower. It was not much of one. There had been a drought, and her gently nurtured flowers were almost all gone. The yellow burned stems seemed to symbolize her own life.

With Jeffry's hand still in hers, she stepped up. "Goodbye and Godspeed," she whispered. She tossed down the flower.

Jeffry took his hand from hers to wipe away his tears angrily. She put her arm around his shoulder and side by side they walked back to their small, bare, and ever so lonely house.

Two hours later, Mary Jo sat in Ira's office. Jeffry was at home, taking care of a new puppy one of the Rangers had brought him. Mary Jo had silently blessed the gift. Jeffry had been wanting a dog for a long time, and when the pup, which looked like a half-wolf, had greeted Jeffry with enthusiasm and a wet tongue, Mary Jo had taken one look at the boy's eager face and given her consent.

Jeffry had been so silent since learning of Ty's death, of Morgan Davis's decision to leave the Rangers and head north to Wyoming. He had worshiped both men. Now he had something special to love, and that was important. Mary Jo had had Jeff, and then Ty, and she swore to herself that was enough. She would never love a man again. She couldn't take another loss, not and survive.

"Mary Jo," Ira began slowly as he fingered an envelope. "Ty left this for you, in case—" He stopped, then just handed it to her.

Mary Jo looked at the envelope as if it were a rattle-snake. *He'd known he would die.*

Ira cleared his throat. "He'd already given me his resignation," he said, then commanded, "Open it."

Mary Jo finally managed to open the envelope. A legal-looking paper and a wad of bills fell into her lap. Woodenly, she picked up the paper and looked at it.

A deed. For a ranch. Five hundred acres in a place called Cimarron Valley in Colorado. And two thousand dollars.

She looked up at Ira. His blue eyes, usually so cold and watchful, were sympathetic. "An inheritance he received several months ago," he said. "He purchased the ranch just last week. That's where he had gone on his leave."

"I don't understand," Mary Jo finally managed to say.

"He was fighting his own battle with himself," Ira said. "He wasn't sure whether he could leave the Rangers or not. He had to be sure in his own mind. I think he made that decision the night before we left for Harmony. He was going to tell you when he returned. He knew how you felt about marrying another Ranger.''

Mary Jo closed her eyes. She knew how much the decision had cost Ty.

"He loved you, Mary Jo," Ira said. "Very much. He left this to you."

"To me?"

He nodded. "You can sell it, move East."

"I don't want it. I can't accept—" She felt terribly unworthy. She had turned down Ty's proposals repeatedly because he had been a Ranger. How could she accept this now?

"It's what he wanted," Ira said. "Don't fail him now. He wanted you and Jeffry to have some security."

Mary Jo rose and went to the door, opening it. She looked at the empty, burned plains, at the desolate, barren buildings. Two men were at the corral, saddling horses, their six-shooters strapped tightly against their thighs and rifles leaning against the fence. Dangerous men. Even cold-blooded men. God knew where they were going, who they were going after.

She thought of Jeffry, so young and so in awe of the Rangers. "I want to be a Ranger like my pa," he told her constantly. And she knew she would take Ty's gift. She couldn't let what happened to him happen to her son.

She turned back to Ira. "We'll leave Friday."

—⁓— *1* —⁓—

Cimarron Valley, Colorado, 1877

Wade Foster wanted to die, but the devil was being damned unaccommodating.

Wade decided a lifetime ago that living was a worse hell than any Old Scratch could devise. He should have died several times over if there had been any justice in the world. He'd courted death often enough, but then some demon always jerked him back from the final descent.

He stifled a groan now as he looked up at the sun. He might actually achieve his wish this day.

If only dying weren't so painful!

He had two bullet holes in him, one in his leg, one in his gun arm. The leg wound was no problem, except it bled whenever he moved, but his arm was a damnable mess. The bullet had ripped nerves and at least part of the bone. The arm was pure agony and hung uselessly at his side.

Not that it mattered. He was done for. He had no place to go, his leg wouldn't hold him, and he seemed to be in the middle of nowhere with his horse dead.

The pinto lay not far from him. It had been hit in the ambush, and Wade had used his last bullet to give it a merciful death. He'd loved that horse.

But everything else he loved was gone, too. He was used to loss. At least he'd thought he was. He thought he'd become immune to the terrible grief that threatened to swallow him whole.

This last act of his, this final vengeance, should have dulled that piercing, lacerating pain inside that never ceased, not even in his sleep—but it hadn't. Instead victory, if it could be called that, had made the pain sharper because now he had nothing to replace it: no one to hate, no one left alive to focus his rage upon. Only himself.

He closed his eyes, wishing numbness would take over, would wash away the hurt from his body and from his soul. Why did it take so long to die, for the blood to seep from his body, for the dehydration to drain what life lingered? If he had the guts, he'd use the knife to speed the process, but he would probably just mess that up, too.

He'd managed to ruin everything good in his life, from the time he'd stayed too long in town, sneaking a glass of whiskey at fifteen while his family was being slaughtered, to ten months ago when once more he'd indulged a whim while his Ute wife and son were killed. He'd avenged both acts. The last murderer of his wife lay dead just over a knoll.

Wade should feel some measure of satisfaction. But he felt so empty. He had nothing to look forward to, not here on earth, and certainly not where he was headed.

He moved slightly, and the pain in his arm was blinding. It crawled up his shoulder, the way fire consumed dry tinder. Finally, he was swallowed in its fury and the bright scarlet of pain faded into the blackness of oblivion.

"Jake!" Jeff heard the panic in his own voice and tried to control it.

But the wind was blowing hard now, clouds were frothing above, and he'd learned enough about the lightning-quick changes of weather to worry.

"Jake," Jeff called again. The dog had bounded after a rabbit and had been gone an hour. He swallowed hard. There had been reports of a big cat in the area, lured down from the mountain by livestock, and fear tugged at him. He couldn't lose Jake.

"Jake," he called again, and this time was rewarded by a series of barks. They were different from the excited, joyful sounds that usually poured from Jake. More urgent.

Jeff knew he shouldn't be this far from the ranch, not alone, not without his rifle. But then his ma too often treated him like a baby. He was twelve. Old enough to take care of himself, old enough to be called Jeff, like his dad.

The barking became more frantic, and Jeff's fast stride became a lope as he headed toward the sound. That inner voice kept warning him, but he disregarded it. Jake might be in trouble. A trap, maybe. There were still old traps around here, left behind by mountain men who had moved on long ago.

He reached the top of a hill and looked down. Jake was circling something on the ground, pausing now and then to bark again. Jeff wished he had his rifle, but he wasn't going to retreat now. His pa wouldn't have been afraid. His pa hadn't been afraid of anything.

Jeff approached cautiously. Jake looked at him expectantly, ran over to him and then back to his prize.

A body! Jeff hesitated, then took several steps forward. A man was lying on the ground, his clothes covered with dried and congealing blood. Jake sat down, put a paw on the man's shirt as if to declare ownership.

Jeff took another step forward. The man looked dead, but then Jeff saw a slight rise of the chest. He stooped down, touched the stranger's shoulder.

"Mister?"

No response came, not even a groan.

Jeff touched the skin. It was clammy. He looked toward the darkening sky and saw buzzards gathering above. His gaze searched the landscape, then he saw the still body of a horse not far away. He had to get help.

"You stay here, Jake," he ordered, not knowing whether the animal would obey. Though the dog tried hard to please, he, like Jeff, often ignored rules and instructions.

Jake seemed content to stay next to his precious find. Jeff hoped he would stay that way, keep the buzzards away from the stranger.

Jeff started running. Ma would know what to do. She always did.

·   ·   ·

Mary Jo looked up at the threatening sky and wondered whether she should saddle her mare and go looking for Jeff. She hated to do it. He had reached that age when he still needed mothering but resented it.

She didn't want to be too protective, but she had lost too much during the past few years to surrender her fears.

She looked toward the mountains. She loved this valley. Cimarron Creek flowed clear and fast several hundred yards from the ranch house, and nearby the Black Mountains rose in jagged splendor. She had been so beguiled by this place, she abandoned her plans to sell the ranch and take Jeff East.

It had also been a compromise with her son. He had fought bitterly against leaving the Ranger station, even more bitterly at the thought of going East. He still wanted to be a Ranger, and though he'd had to leave El Paso, at least he remained in the West and still had his horse and dog.

Mary Jo prayed every day she hadn't made a mistake, that she wasn't risking something more important than this piece of heaven. But it was such a good place to rear a son, open and free. She hoped Jeff would so love this land that he would forget his oft-stated desire to be a Texas Ranger.

Ranching was hard work. But she was used to hard work. She had worked from sunup to sundown at the Ranger station, but that had been for someone else. Now she worked just as hard, but this was for herself and Jeff, and she saw results daily. The garden was flourishing, and so was the little livestock they had.

The one problem had been hired help. The wealth of this land lay in cattle, and she needed hands to develop and run a herd. There were no fences, only open range, and a woman and boy couldn't handle the branding alone. She'd found few men willing to work for a woman who were worth their salt.

She looked toward the hill where she'd last seen Jeff and Jake playing. He had helped her finish mending fences around the chicken yard, and then she'd given him leave to explore with Jake while she cooked dinner.

But he had been out of sight now for a long while, and the sky overhead looked ominous. She was just about to saddle her mare, Fancy, when she saw Jeff running toward her, stumbling as he came.

She knew instantly something was wrong. Jake wasn't with him, and the two were constant companions.

She ran out to meet him, catching him as he started to fall. Winded, he couldn't speak for a moment, then stuttered, "A stranger . . . hurt real bad . . . about a mile . . . north of the old road."

"How bad?"

"He's unconscious." Jeff was regaining his breath. "His shirt and trousers are real bloody, Ma. He needs help bad. There's a dead horse nearby, and buzzards are circling."

Mary Jo didn't hesitate any longer. She couldn't leave someone to die, and she had a rudimentary knowledge of medicine. She'd doctored her share of Rangers over the twelve years she'd been married to one and the two years after her husband's death. She'd worry later about who the stranger was.

"I'll get the buckboard," she said. "You get our rifles, and that box of bandages and medicines. And some water."

Jeff nodded and dashed inside as Mary Jo went to the barn. She led two of their four horses outside and hitched them to the buckboard. Jeff joined her, placing the medicine box inside the wagon bed along with a canteen and one of the rifles. He held the other rifle in his hands.

"Where's Jake?" she asked.

"He's with the stranger," Jeff said proudly. "He found him."

"This man? You've never seen him before?"

Jeff shook his head.

A shiver snaked down Mary Jo's back. She wished there was a man around, that she had not let the last one go when she'd found him drinking in the barn. The fact was, no one else was around to help. The next ranch was hours away, and the only decent doctor was over a hundred miles away.

Her lips pressed together. Maybe Jeff was exaggerating the extent of the man's wounds. She felt a chill, a blast of suddenly cold wind, and she looked up. The sky was almost black. The storm wasn't far away. She urged the horses to a faster pace, looking frequently at Jeff for guidance. He gestured at a turnoff, and the wagon creaked and jostled in protest as she drove away from the road.

Mary Jo saw the buzzards wheeling in the sky, and she snapped the reins. She heard Jake's anxious bark, then Jeff's cry, "Over there."

She saw the horse, then the man several hundred feet away. The animal was obviously dead, and she gave it scant notice. She pulled up the wagon next to the still form on the ground and jumped down, followed by Jeff. Jake was running back and forth excitedly.

"Stay near the buckboard," she told Jeff as she leaned toward the back and retrieved the canteen.

"But—"

"If you want to help," she said, "get Jake."

"But—"

"Please, Jeff." He nodded reluctantly and whistled for Jake who reluctantly slunk over to him.

Mary Jo knelt down next to the man and felt the pulse in his neck. He was still breathing but just barely. Blood was everywhere, covering and stiffening what once must have been handsome deerskin shirt and trousers.

She'd seen men in deerskin jackets before, but none in trousers trimmed with rawhide lacing. And around his neck, he wore a rawhide string of black beads with a silver eagle inside a seven-pointed star. Mary Jo's gaze moved to his hips, to a well-used gun-belt. The holster was empty, but there was a knife in a sheath.

As her eyes skimmed over his body, she noted the lean strength of him, the corded muscles apparent under the shirt and tight trousers. His hair, longer than what she became accustomed to seeing at the Ranger station, was matted with sweat and dirt and blood. Pain had etched furrows in a face that was hard-looking and deeply browned by the sun. She had no time to notice more. She moistened his lips with water from the canteen, then she shook him gently.

A groan of protest escaped his lips.

Mary Jo swallowed. He was a big man. His present condition did nothing to eliminate the impression of strength. And the two bullet wounds did not recommend him as an upstanding citizen. Neither did the clothes, which looked more Indian than white. Did she dare bring him into her house?

Mary Jo quickly brushed aside the momentary hesitation. He was obviously too weak to harm anyone. She could send Jeff to the next ranch and ask that someone summon a marshal.

Getting him home was the first concern.

She had to be careful. Any jostling could start the blood flowing again, and he had already lost a substantial amount. She checked his arm. The wound was ugly, with the bone partially shattered. Particles of it mixed with the blood, some of it blackened, some glistening white amid the red.

She tore a piece of cloth from her petticoat, dampened it and washed around the wound. She bound it with yet another piece, then bound the arm to his shoulder to stabilize it.

Her attention shifted to his leg. There was a hole in his trousers, but she couldn't see the wound. She took his knife and, with the wicked-looking blade, cut the trouser leg. A quick examination showed the bullet had passed through without the kind of damage his arm had suffered. She bound that wound, too.

Then she eyed the man again, wondering how to get him into the buckboard. She splashed water on his face, tried to jar him back to consciousness, but nothing worked.

She looked up at Jeff. He was wiry and strong for his age; together, they might get him into the buckboard.

Mary Jo walked over to the horses and guided them close to the stranger. To her son she said, "Help me get him into the buckboard. You take his legs and be gentle."

He nodded. She leaned down, grabbing the man between his shoulders, and lifted. Dear Lord, he was heavy. Slowly, she and Jeff hauled him into the wagon.

"You cradle his head and shoulders," she told Jeff as she lifted her now bloodstained skirt and climbed up onto the wagon seat.

The wind had picked up, chilling the air, and she felt the first few raindrops on her skin. Big, thick, heavy ones. Mary Jo clicked the reins, and the horses started to move. She prayed that the worst of the storm would hold off until they got home. She'd seen these storms before, knew how vicious they sometimes became.

It was the longest trip she'd ever made, each minute seeming like an hour, with the stranger's pain-carved face vivid in her mind. She thought she heard him groan, but it was hard to tell for sure now that the wind was screeching through the trees.

Jake was running alongside, barking encouragement, oblivious to the rain beginning to pelt down, but Mary Jo felt it soak her dress and run in rivulets down her face.

The log ranch house had never looked so welcoming. She drove up to the door and hurried down from the seat to tie the ribbons to the hitching post in front. She rushed back to the wagon bed, wiping the rain from her eyes.

The stranger had not moved. Jeff looked at her with anxious eyes, his hands holding the man's shoulders. "He's awfully still, Ma."

She nodded. She ran to the door and opened it wide, paying little mind to the sheets of rain pouring on the wood floors. Lightning streaked through the sky, dancing in accompaniment to great roars of thunder.

Mary Jo and Jeff somehow managed to carry the man inside and into Mary Jo's bed. He was soaked. His blood was running pink over what remained of his deerskins.

Jake shook himself, showering everything with rainwater. Mary Jo sighed.

"Heat some water on the stove," she told Jeff, "and start a fire in here." She hesitated. "You'd better get the horses inside the barn, too."

Jeff paused. "Will he be all right?"

Mary Jo went over to him and placed a hand on his shoulder. It was the only sign of affection he believed manly. Hugs, he said, were for babies. "I don't know," she said. "He's hurt pretty bad."

"I want him to be all right."

"I know, love," she said. "So do I." And she did. She didn't know why this stranger's fate had become so important, but it had. Perhaps because she'd put so much effort into helping him. Perhaps because Jeff had already known too much death. "The water," she reminded him.

She lit one of the kerosene lamps and placed it on the table next to the bed.

Dear Lord, he was pale. There was something vulnerable about a man downed by illness or wounds, especially a man like this. The knife, the way he wore his gunbelt, indicated he was probably dangerous. She had seen enough of such men over the years to recognize the breed.

Who was he? And how had he gotten the wounds? She'd heard of no trouble around here. No outlaws. No recent Indian trouble. She swallowed hard. This man was obviously trouble. And yet . . .

She brushed aside a lock of her damp hair, and drew a chair next to the bed.

She started untying the thongs at the top of the stranger's shirt before realizing she would have to tug the shirt off over his head. She couldn't do that without jostling the wounded arm. She would have to cut the shirt off. The pants would have to go, too.

And then he would have no clothes at all.

She took the knife from his belt, then, holding her breath, she cut the deerskin shirt open. She managed to pull it off the uninjured arm but had to cut off the cloth pasted to the right arm with blood.

His chest was solid muscle, brown and dusted with golden hair that led down to the waist of his trousers. She noticed two scars, one at the shoulder, the other a jagged one on his side. Whoever he was, he was prone to violence.

She took the beads from around his neck, handling them curiously for a moment. They looked like something worn by an Indian, but this man was no Indian, not with his features and that dark brown hair. She put the beads carefully down on the table, then turned her attention back to her patient.

Now for the man's trousers. She hesitated. She had seen a man's naked body before, but this stranger was so starkly masculine . . . Even knowing how foolish it was, she suddenly felt very reluctant.

But he was shivering through the wet cloth. Taking a deep breath, she untied the thongs that held the waist of the trousers and pulled them down. He was wearing nothing underneath. Her throat suddenly tightened at what she saw.

Taken as a whole, he was magnificent. Sinewy and strong. She looked at the mangled arm, and thought of the injustice of it, like the marring of something perfect.

She heard footsteps outside the bedroom door and hurriedly placed a quilt over the lower half of the wounded man's body.

Jeff came in carrying a basin of water, steam rising from it, and clean towels. He placed the basin on the table next to the bed, then started a fire in the fireplace. Jake followed on his heels, taking up a sitting position on the other side of the bed, his head resting on the quilt, his eyes full of curiosity.

Mary Jo cleaned her patient's right arm as best she could. She didn't see an exit wound, which meant she had to extract the bullet. Praying he would remain unconscious, she found a pair of tongs in the medicine box and probed the wound. It started to bleed again. "Keep wiping the blood away," she told Jeff.

He moved quietly next to her and did as she asked. His face, when Mary Jo stole a quick look at it, was tense, and a tear hovered at the corner of his eye. He hadn't realized yet that compassion and being a Ranger didn't go together.

Sweat ran down her own face by the time the tongs finally found metal. She slowly, carefully extracted the bullet. What was left of it.

Mary Jo heard a moan coming from deep inside the stranger, and she sympathized with him. She also felt triumphant. Perhaps now he would have a chance.

She cleaned the wound some more, then poured sulfur powder into it and sewed it up. When she finished that, she sent Jeff out to find a piece of wood she could use as a splint. While he was gone she sewed up the wound in the stranger's leg.

His lower body was covered again when Jeff returned, holding a strong straight branch. He'd whittled off the knobs and rough spots, and intense pride flowed through Mary Jo. Perhaps because of where and how he'd grown up, he often seemed much older than most boys his age.

"That's perfect," she said, giving him a grin of approval. He beamed back at her.

"Can you hold his arm for me?" she asked. Again he moved quickly to her side, doing exactly as she told him, no longer smiling but intent on his job, almost willing the man to survive.

Mary Jo concentrated on tying the stranger's arm to the splint and then using a piece of sheeting to bind it to his chest.

"Will he be all right?" Jeff asked.

"I don't know," she answered. She finished and stood up, stretching. "But we've done all we can do. If he does live, it's because of you." She gave him a hug and held him close for a moment, surprised he allowed it in his newly discovered need for independence. That he wanted maternal assurance showed the degree of anxiety he felt for their unexpected guest.

But then he twisted away. "I'll get some more wood for the fire."

She nodded and sat back down next to her patient, studying his face once more. The lines appeared even deeper now, his face pasty. His breathing was shallow.

Dear Lord, let him live, she pleaded silently.

Thunder roared, lightning flashed just outside the window. She shivered, thinking how close he had come to lying out there in this weather. He would have been dead by morning, for sure.

She rose, lit another kerosene lamp, and sat down next to him.

She had done all she could do.

She could only wait now. Wait and pray.

2

The pain was so overpowering Wade wanted to sink back into oblivion.

He wasn't dead, he knew, unless hell was even worse than he'd imagined. But surely if he were burning in that place, as the preacher men always predicted, the agony wouldn't be centered in his arm.

He heard his own groan, then chanced opening his eyes. Closed them again. Then opened them. How in the hell had he gotten into a bed? He doubted whether such luxuries were standard in the netherworld.

He tried to move, to see more of the dim room, but the pain was too great and he sank back, closing his eyes as he did so.

Had he cheated death again, dammit? Why wouldn't he let go?

Something wet and rough, yet not unpleasant, nudged at him. He opened his eyes, and the earnest gaze of an animal that seemed part dog, part wolf met his directly. A great tongue hung out of one side of the mouth.

Christ. A dream? A nightmare? A hound of hell?

The tongue washed his cheek. He blinked, looking the animal over more carefully. Eager, inquisitive eyes stared back at him.

Memories darted in and out of his mind. Pavel. His dog when he was fifteen . . .

Pavel was the first thing he saw when he returned from town that hot day in July 1858. The body lay at the side of the road, still and bloody. Pavel always waited for him there at the crossroads, ever so patient, wanting only a word of welcome.

Wade had not been Wade then. He had been a reckless boy named Brad Allen. His rebelliousness had delayed him that day; he'd sneaked a bottle of rotgut from the saloon on a dare from other boys, and they'd spent the afternoon drinking and telling unlikely tales. It had been nearly sunset before he arrived home with seed, knowing that he would be facing harsh words and digging fence holes the next day.

But still, he was eager to reach home. The table would be laden with food, including an apple pie. It was his older brother's birthday. Drew would be eighteen today.

Perhaps that was why he'd lingered. He hated to admit it, but he was jealous of his brother, of his competence and the way his father trusted him so. He seemed satisfied with the small farm, not afflicted with Brad's restlessness to see more of the world.

Brad loved his family, his father who sometimes played the violin at night, his mother who was so quick with a hug, his sister, Maggie, who was thirteen and would soon be a woman herself. Already she was catching the eyes of the young men in their little corner of northwest Missouri. And he loved Drew, though he didn't understand his brother's reverence for the land.

When he'd seen Pavel at the side of the rutted trail, Brad stopped and dismounted. He knelt at Pavel's side, feeling for some sign of life, but there was none. The animal was cold, already stiffening. There were bullet wounds, many of them, and he let his hand linger for a moment on the large shaggy head before suddenly being seized with panic.

He mounted his horse again and rode toward the small farmhouse, spurring his horse into a gallop. But there was no plain farmhouse awaiting him, no smoke curling wistfully from the chimney into the sky.

The smoke instead was coming from blackened ruins of the house and barn. The fences had been torn down, and the horses were gone from the small corral. His eyes searched the trees that had surrounded the house and stopped, riveted by the sight of two bodies hanging from them.

Through blinding tears, he galloped over to them. His brother and father were hanging by their necks from a tree limb he and Drew used to climb. Their hands hadn't been tied but were hanging obscenely as the bodies swayed in the light breeze.

Brad slid down from his horse and cut the ropes with his knife. The bodies fell, and Brad straightened them out on the ground, trying to give them some dignity. Then he started looking for his sister and mother.

He found them several hundred yards from the cabin. Both were naked from the waist down. Both were covered with blood. Both were dead.

Brad sat down next to them. He took his mother's hand and held it for a long time, unaware of anything but over-

whelming grief. And then guilt. He should have been here. He was good with a rifle. Maybe . . .

The full moon was high in the sky when he started to bury all of them, including Pavel. It was dawn before he finished.

He looked out over the neat fields that had given his father and Drew so much satisfaction. The dawn was pink, soft, but something hardened in Brad that night. He didn't see the beauty of the sunrise; the only thing on his mind was vengeance.

He would never return here. He couldn't, not without seeing those bodies swaying in the wind.

He knew who had done this. The Jayhawkers, pro-Union guerrillas out of Kansas, had been raiding farms throughout the area, attacking every family they suspected of being pro-Southern. They had become so bloodthirsty, they needed little proof. Brad's father had been neutral, wanting only to mind his own business, but he would have defied someone trespassing on his land.

Brad felt the hate filling his heart, his gut, every corner of his soul. Its intensity wiped out every other human emotion. And he knew exactly what he was going to do.

He would find the antislavery irregulars. And he would kill every damned Jayhawker in Kansas.

His father hadn't wanted any part of this fight, but now it was Brad's . . .

"Jake." The name was spoken softly but authoritatively, and the dog moved away from Wade. He heard a swishing of skirts, then smelled something sweet, like flowers. He turned his head slightly, feeling a pounding behind his eyes as he did so, and swallowed a groan.

A woman. He hurt too much to notice more, to be more than mildly curious about how he came to be here.

"I'm sorry," she said in a pleasant, husky voice. "Jake seems to have sneaked in here. He's taken it into his head that you belong to him."

"Jake?" He barely managed to say the name. His voice was weak and shaky even to him.

"That huge beast of a dog," she said with a slight smile. "He found you."

Wade closed his eyes. A dog. He should have known. Perhaps it *was* a hound of hell after all.

"He didn't do me any favors," Wade said, unable to keep the bitterness from his voice.

"Don't," she said sharply. "I've lost a husband and a good friend, both of whom wanted to live very badly. Don't tell me I've wasted time and effort on a man willing to throw life away."

Wade opened his eyes and looked at her more intently. Her hair was auburn and pulled back into a knot at the back of her head. It was too severe for her face, which was strong but tired-looking. Her eyes were green, and bright with intelligence and, at the moment, a bit of anger.

But Wade didn't care about being polite. "I didn't ask you to. Why in the hell couldn't you leave well enough alone?"

Her lips tightened. "My son and his dog found you. I don't like the kind of lesson he'd learn if I left you there."

A kid! So he owed this ninth life to a kid. And a dog. His kind of luck.

He tried to move, and agony shot through him. "My arm?"

"In bad shape," she said frankly. "A doctor might have taken it off, but I . . ." She hesitated. "I got the bullet out and cleaned the wound the best I could. Put some sulfur in it. You might keep it if there's no infection, but I don't know . . ."

He stared at her, momentarily surprised out of his bitterness. "You took the bullet out?"

"There's no doctor within a day's ride, and the nearest is none too good," she said. "I couldn't leave you, and I wasn't going to send my boy out in this storm."

"Storm?"

"It's been raining two days."

"Two days?" Damnation. He'd been unconscious that long? The last miner? He almost panicked, thinking he might have lost his quarry. Then he remembered pushing his rifle to the man's throat and slowly pulling the trigger.

He glanced down at his half-covered chest, noticed for the first time it was naked. Taking mental measure of the rest of him, he quickly realized his lower half was naked, too.

He'd never been a particularly modest man, but now he felt vulnerable. Now he was weak as a two-day-old wolf cub, and he felt a flush rising in his face.

His left hand went to his neck.

"On the table, next to the bed," the woman said quietly.

He reached for the necklace, his fingers clasping it tightly for a moment before relaxing.

Then his eyes were back on her face. "Your man?" he asked, wanting to rid himself of those steady green eyes that studied him so carefully. She'd said a husband had died, but surely there must be another one, or a foreman or something.

She hesitated, and he realized there wasn't one here, and she wasn't sure if it was information he should have. He almost laughed. The thought of being a threat to anyone in his present condition was a joke.

Then he wondered how she'd gotten him here. She was of medium height but slender. Surely there had to be a man about.

She finally shook her head, apparently agreeing with him that he couldn't swat a fly if he'd been so inclined. At least she had the mind not to ask him how he was.

He became aware of a growing thirst. "Water?"

She nodded and reached down, pouring water from a pitcher into a tin cup. She again regarded him with that searching gaze of hers. It held a question but she evidently answered it herself because she didn't ask him anything. She merely lifted his head with one arm while bringing the cup to his lips with the other.

She was very patient, as he sipped slowly. When he finished the cup, she gently lowered his head. Clearly she was experienced at this, and he wondered about the missing husband. *I've lost a husband and a . . . good friend.*

So she knew loss, too. But at least she still had a child. His was buried on the side of a mountain. Bitterness and grief swept over him.

He closed his eyes, shutting her out. He hadn't thanked her. Not for saving his life. Not for the water. And he wouldn't. Why hadn't she just left him alone?

There was a silence, then that light swishing sound. The scent of flowers retreated, though a whiff remained in the air. He heard a door close.

Wade opened his eyes. He was alone in a dark room. No light shone through gingham curtains so it must be night. A low rumble sounded outside. She'd mentioned a storm. *She.* He didn't even know her name, nor apparently did she know his. She hadn't asked, and that was surprising.

He didn't understand why a woman alone had taken him in. For all she knew, he could be a murderer.

He was.

He hadn't been worth much before his wife and son were killed. He'd never been able to protect those he cared about. And now? Without his right arm, he was worth less than nothing.

He could even be a danger to this woman and her son. He'd just killed three white men. There was bound to be a posse.

Rain pounded against the roof. Thunder roared.

Then he felt sleep coming on, and he wondered if the woman had put something into the water, a touch of laudanum perhaps.

Thunder roared again and the room was suddenly ablaze with a flash of lightning. Then it was gone, leaving only blackness in its wake.

The door opened, then he felt a soft hand on his cheek. He wanted to shake it away.

It felt too good.

But it wasn't Chivita's touch.

He held himself rigid, and endured.

He heard a soft sigh, and then she was gone again, and he slowly commanded himself to relax. The drowsiness returned, taking him back to an empty, black place that had no joy, but no pain, either.

·   ·   ·

Mary Jo fingered the cotton shirt and denim trousers on her lap. They had been her husband's. Unwilling to give up everything he owned, she'd kept his clothes and was now grateful for bringing them here. The wounded man was disturbing enough. Having him naked in her bed was even more disturbing.

His pain-etched face and secretive gray-green eyes that were full of shadows haunted her. He hadn't wanted death just because he feared physical agony. Something deeper ran inside him, something so hurtful that it had taken away his desire to stay alive. Only an innate tenacity had kept him from dying, a core of steel that survived his best efforts to destroy it.

Laudanum had kept him sedated for two days during which he had mumbled on and off. She had caught only occasional words, but they had been enough to know he'd been to hell and back, and probably taken others with him. That should have frightened her, but it didn't.

Ruthless men didn't have consciences. But this stranger obviously did. Words of violence had mixed with ones of regret, phrases of retribution with those of grief.

And a name. Drew. Drew was mentioned over and over again in a tone harsh with sorrow and longing.

The sound had hit the chord of her own grief, brought back the sorrow of losing her husband and Ty. She'd felt linked to the stranger in ways she couldn't afford, didn't want.

Despite all the warning voices deep inside her telling her she shouldn't care, she worried about her stranger every minute. What would he do with a crippled arm? Where had he come from? Was there any family?

Mary Jo looked at the fire roaring in the fireplace, seeking answers. The stranger was trouble. The bullet holes in him were evidence of that. Someone had put them there, and for a reason. She couldn't allow her heart or mind to make room for such a man. But he was wounded and she was doing for him what she would do for any hurt thing.

Her attention returned to the clothes on her lap. They should fit, though the trousers would be a bit snug.

She had tried washing out his deerskin shirt and trousers, but they had been beyond saving. Unwilling to burn what didn't belong to her, she had dried them next to the fire and folded them neatly. They were pink with blood, ripped beyond repair, and part of her had regretted that as she had noticed the fine workmanship. Indian workmanship.

She had no sympathy for Indians. The Comanche had raided throughout Texas, burning and raping and killing. They had robbed her of her sister, her best friend, and her father. They were savages she'd been raised to hate and fear. Even the thought of them brought a cold terror to her heart. And the Utes, people around here said, were little better. Everyone had a horror story.

Why was he wearing those clothes?

She put the shirt aside and went into Jeff's room where she was staying while the stranger occupied her bed. Her son was sleeping on the floor, and she watched him from the door. He had been so anxious about the stranger, so excited about finding and rescuing him. She was glad he hadn't been awake to hear the man earlier; Jeff would be devastated to know his efforts were unappreciated.

She moved her gaze to Jake, who lay next to Jeff. She had scooted the dog away from the patient, and Jake had left the man's side reluctantly. It was strange the way the dog had attached himself to the man. His new allegiance disturbed her—but perhaps it was just his sense of protectiveness for something wounded.

Like hers.

Thunder rumbled again and she heard the crack of lightning. Much too close.

She decided to check her patient. She tiptoed quietly over to the bed, leaned over and felt his face. Cool now. No infection. She blessed the miracle.

The breathing, though, was not natural, and then she realized he was awake, only pretending sleep. She sensed the rigidity of his body, the tension in it. She wanted to say something, but she didn't know what. He obviously wanted to be alone.

Feeling uncertain and unexpectedly hurt, she turned around and left.

A noise shook Mary Jo from sleep. It was a low keening moan, a sound of such profound sorrow that it vibrated through her body and lingered there.

She sat up, tried to adjust her eyes to the darkness. She saw a movement where Jeff had been sleeping and realized the noise had disturbed him, too.

She reached for her robe, pulling it over her thin nightdress, and walked the several steps to Jeff. She knelt down beside him. "It's all right, Jeff. It's just the storm."

He shook his head. "I don't think so. It's the stranger."

So much for trying to fool a twelve-year-old, Mary Jo thought.

"Perhaps," she said. "You stay here while I check on him."

"I want to go," he protested.

"I'll call you if I need you," she said, then added, "Remember how you are when you don't feel well? You don't want anyone to see you that way."

He had started to protest, but the words died on his lips. She had chosen the one tactic that worked. He nodded reluctantly.

Mary Jo lit a kerosene lamp and walked out the door and down the hall. She'd left his door open so she could hear if he worsened during the night, and now she heard the moan again, a moan that turned into a shout.

"Not Drew, God, not Drew. Not again. Chivita! What have they done? Christ, what have they done?"

Mary Jo's heart stopped at the anguish in the voice, the utter hopelessness. He had kicked the covers loose and his naked body was jerking, fighting an invisible demon. He turned on his wounded arm, and pain shot through her own body in empathy.

She rushed over to him, sitting on the edge of the bed, trying to anchor his shoulders with her hand, trying to keep him still.

"It's all right," she whispered, knowing it wasn't all right at all. Whatever was deviling him was not all right. She feared it would never be all right.

When he almost toppled her to the floor, she slapped him across the face, trying to wake him. The blow quieted him. His body stilled, and his eyes fluttered open. A long breath escaped his throat, as if he had been holding it there, and sweat trembled on his face.

His gaze found hers, then shifted to his uncovered body. "Damn," he whispered, then tried ineffectively to pull the blanket over himself. Whatever nightmare had haunted him had drained the little strength he had.

Mary Jo reached over and covered him.

"Damn," he said again, clenching his teeth. Whether it was against pain or his obvious humiliation, she didn't know.

She looked away, picking up a towel and wetting it in the bowl of water she'd left on the table. She then washed the sweat from his face. His cheeks were rough with bristles.

"My clothes?" he asked.

"Beyond redemption, I think," Mary Jo said, trying to force humor into her voice.

"I can't . . . stay here."

"You can't leave, either," she said. "Not for a few days, anyway, probably longer. You wouldn't get to the door."

"I'll bring you trouble."

Mary Jo smiled wryly. "I've had trouble so long, the idea of a little more doesn't bother me."

"What about your boy?"

"I'll take care of Jeff," she said sharply.

"I have to have some clothes."

"You can have some of my husband's," Mary Jo said, "but later. The shirt won't go over that arm yet, nor the trousers over the bandage on your leg."

"I can't . . ."

Mary Jo suddenly smiled at the absurdity of the situation. It was the first time she'd known a man to complain of nudity. "I don't feel a whole lot better about it than you do, but right now there's no alternative."

"You haven't asked any questions."

"No," she agreed. "I didn't think you were well enough to answer any. But I have questions. And I *will* ask them."

His lips twisted slightly at the left corner. "I bet you will."

"I *will* ask one now, though," she said. "I can't just call you mister."

"Foster," he said with reluctance. "Wade Foster."

"Well, Mr. Foster, I'm Mary Jo Williams. My son is Jeff. I think everything else can wait."

"What time is it?"

"Near dawn, I expect," she said.

"I'm . . . sorry."

"Don't be. I've had nightmares of my own."

She wrenched her gaze away. His humiliation seemed to have disappeared, which had been her main intent. Men, she'd found, could live with a lot of things but rarely that.

"If you're all right," she said, "I'll leave you to sleep. That's the best medicine for you now."

"Is it?" he said softly, and she knew this nightmare had not been the first one.

"Who's Drew?" she asked suddenly. She hadn't meant to; the question just came.

His eyes turned so bleak that she wished she could take the question back.

"You weren't going to ask anymore questions yet," he said harshly.

"No," she said. "I just thought . . . it might help to talk it out."

"Drew is my son," he said, "and nothing will help." He turned on his good side, shielding himself from her, from her sudden intrusion.

Mary Jo stood there for a moment, stunned by the revelation, and then she noticed his shoulders were heaving. Suddenly she knew that Drew was dead.

"I'm sorry," she whispered. "So sorry."

He didn't answer. She blew out the light and retreated for the second time that night. She knew she wouldn't sleep. Nor, she suspected, would he.

3

Wade tried to stand, managed that feat, but no more. He collapsed back down on the bed.

The first light of dawn was leaking through the gingham curtains, and he didn't think the woman or her son would be awake yet, not after last night.

Christ, he hated the lack of clothes, the lack of dignity. He felt like a prisoner in this room, in this bed, and yet he knew the woman had been right. He wouldn't get far in his current condition.

Why had she gone to so much trouble on his behalf?

He cringed inwardly as he recalled his display of grief last night.

He hadn't mourned when he'd found his wife and son dead ten months earlier. Anger and hate had shoved out everything else and he'd focused only on avenging their deaths. He hadn't even mourned when he'd killed the last of the murderers he had tracked for months.

He hadn't allowed himself to feel. He hadn't, he realized now, even admitted to himself that his son and wife were really gone.

It wasn't until the woman had asked about Drew that he accepted the fact that Drew was dead, that his son had been brutally murdered. Those fine, dark eyes would remain closed forever; his lips would never grin again.

Wade was alive, and Drew was dead. History had repeated itself once again, and he didn't understand it. Why did he continue to survive when everyone around him died?

He resented the woman, by God. He resented her for saving what was no longer worth saving, for being kind, for reminding him of all he'd lost.

There was nothing left: not family, or peace, or self-respect, or love. He'd burned his own cabin, the one he'd built for Chivita in the valley she loved, along-side the river where he'd taught Drew to fish, the river that had lured greedy miners in search of gold, despite the Utes' claim to it.

The Utes would take him in, but he'd never been good at accepting charity, especially from people who had lost so much at the hands of the white man.

He had a past that shamed him, a present made unbearably ugly, no future.

Why hadn't he died?

Because he'd wanted it so damn bad?

He heard a whining, and he twisted his body around painfully. The dog was sitting there, its head cocked.

Jake. He remembered that name. Jeff and Jake. He wondered how old the boy was. His own son had been six. His fist clenched against the bed as he remembered the last time he had seen him alive . . .

"I want to go with you," Drew had said wistfully.

But Wade had planned to go up high in the mountains, after a herd of antelope. The route was too steep for Drew to ride his own horse, an old, fat mare unlikely to bolt. "Take care of your mother for me," he said instead.

And the boy had tried. Wade had found him near his mother, his head caved in, probably by a rifle stock, and his throat cut. He'd probably tried desperately to protect her, flailing small arms and legs. Wade kept seeing that picture in his mind . . .

The dog moved several feet closer, cautiously seeking a welcome.

"Come here, Jake," Wade said, inexplicably needing a touch of warmth. The dog wagged its tail tentatively and he approached Wade, resting his head on Wade's leg. Wade placed his hand on the dog's head, rubbing behind his ears as he'd once rubbed Pavel's. A growl of pleasure rumbled from the dog's throat.

"Backward, huh?" Wade whispered. "You don't know when to growl and when not to find someone."

A tail thumped happily.

"Jake?"

A boy's voice came through the door, and Wade lay back down, using the last of his ebbing strength to pull the sheet over his body. Jake took up a post next to the bed as a tall, thin boy appeared in the doorway. The boy paused there, looked toward the bed anxiously. Then he grinned, obviously pleased to find Wade awake.

Wade looked into the boy's hazel eyes, then noticed the cowlick of reddish-brown hair. The boy's face was freckled, the grin infectious. In five or six years, Drew would have been this tall, this full of energy and life.

"Jake found you," the boy said.

Wade wanted to will him away. He couldn't bear reminders of what could have been, of the emptiness that lay ahead.

He also remembered Mary Jo Williams's explanation of why she hadn't left him to die. *I don't like the kind of lesson he'd learn . . .*

Wade tried to sit, but he fell back on the pillow, and the boy's grin disappeared. "I'm sorry. I shouldn't have bothered you. I'll take Jake . . ."

Wade fisted his fingers underneath the sheet. He couldn't believe that this thin boy and his mother had managed to bring him here alone. It must have taken immense effort, immense will.

"I hear you had some part in it, too," he said, trying to smile.

The boy flushed with pride. "Can I get you anything?"

"I think you can go start the stove." His mother spoke from the doorway.

"Aw, Ma."

"Unless you want us all to starve?" she said.

The boy looked rebellious for a moment, then retreated reluctantly.

The woman approached the bed. Her auburn hair was held back in an untidy knot. She was dressed in a practical high-necked blouse and simple skirt and wore no jewelry except for a plain gold wedding band.

"Thank you," she said simply.

He narrowed his eyes in question.

"For not throwing his efforts back in his face."

"As I did to you?"

She smiled. "I don't expect much."

He was inexplicably sorry about that. "You should," he said, shocking himself that he cared.

She tipped her head. "Have you changed your mind about dying?"

"No," he said flatly.

"Why?"

"You don't want to know, lady, believe me."

"Mary Jo. Everyone calls me Mary Jo."

Wade was silent. He didn't want to think of her as Mary Jo. He didn't want to think of her at all. He especially didn't want to think how appealing she looked with that slightly challenging smile on her lips.

"Is anyone after you, Mr. Foster?"

He hesitated, then answered because he owed her, even if he hadn't wanted her help. "I expect so."

"The law?"

"Could be."

She didn't shy away as he'd expected, but then not once had she reacted as he expected since he'd first seen her. But her gaze did sharpen. He could tell she was every bit as adept as he was at staring down men. Or she was a good actress.

"Are you going to tell me why?"

"I killed three men," he said.

"Did they deserve it?"

No comment could have surprised him more. He had told her the bold truth, half expecting, half hoping perhaps, she would dump him back out in the rain.

"Well, did they?" she prompted.

"You would take my word for it?"

"I'm not sure until I hear it."

"You're either a damned confusing woman or just plain foolish," he said rudely.

"I'm neither, Mr. Foster. I just believe in my instincts. You didn't want to hurt my son's feelings, and the dog likes you. That makes me inclined to trust you. I've always thought children and animals have more sense than full-grown folks."

He just stared at her, not knowing what to think. He'd never met a woman like her, Indian or white. Living alone with a young son. Trying to run a ranch or farm on her own. And then pulling a foolish stunt like taking in a gun-shot stranger. Asking, for God's sake, if he was dangerous.

He muttered to himself.

"I didn't hear you, Mr. Foster."

"Hell, you don't want to," he said a little louder than he intended. He thought she would flinch at his profanity, but she merely looked amused.

"You keep telling me what to think," she said with exasperation and just a trace of humor. "Let me make up my own mind. You still didn't answer my question. Did those three men deserve killing?"

"Yes," he snarled.

She smiled at the strength of his reply. "You must be improving," she said with some satisfaction.

Damn, she was stubborn. "I hurt like hell," he said, wanting to cut off the conversation.

The smile disappeared. "I know you do. I wish I could help more. I do have some more laudanum."

"No," he said. "But . . ."

He felt like a fool. He needed to relieve himself, but he was too weak to go anyplace. And then there was the matter of his lack of clothes.

She understood immediately, and just a touch of

humor was back in her eyes. He sensed it lurked there more often than not, and he resented that it was now aimed at his embarrassment over his bodily needs and nudity.

"There's a chamber pot under the bed," she told him. "If you need any help, Jeff—"

He shook his head. He just wanted her gone.

"I'll have some broth for you shortly," she said. .

"Don't you ever sleep?" Wade heard himself ask. He hadn't meant to prolong the conversation, but he couldn't help wondering. She'd been with him half the night, and then again when he'd had the nightmare.

"I don't need much," she said. "I never slept well when my husband was away."

Don't ask, something told him. Yet he did. "Your husband was a rancher?"

"A Texas Ranger," she said somberly.

Wade was stunned. A Ranger's wife! He'd been running from lawmen since the war.

The news made her efforts on his behalf all the more bewildering, particularly the fact that the law wasn't standing by his bed at this very moment. He wondered about the husband who had married this independent and determined woman. And felt immediately disloyal to Chivita. Gentle, giving Chivita.

Her image was suddenly in his mind's eye. The dark hair that flowed to her waist, the deerskin dress she had made so carefully to please him. Everything had been to please him. It had been that way since he'd been taken in by the Utes ten years ago when he'd had no place to go, when he was a pariah among decent people, his name a curse in Kansas.

He had changed his name, thought he'd changed the man, but the last few months proved he hadn't.

And now he was trapped here. No strength, not even enough for a few steps. No clothes. No horse. No money. And a liability to the Utes, the only people who would accept him if he were to return.

His gaze met the woman's, held for a moment. He was the first to turn away. He heard her retreating foot-steps, then the closing of a door. He had a few moments' privacy.

He started to get up off the bed. There were things that had to be done before she returned. He'd be lucky if he could manage them.

I killed three men.

He'd said the words so matter-of-factly, yet Mary Jo knew he had been watching her, waiting, perhaps even hoping she would give him some clothes and toss him out.

Well, she'd known the moment she set eyes on him that he was dangerous, that he was all too familiar with guns.

Three men. When? Where? Why?

The law could be after him. Why was she not afraid? Or repelled?

God knew she'd loved men who loved the law. In the twelve years she'd been married to Jeff Williams, she might have spent a total of three with him. The remainder of the time he was out riding down outlaws, Comanches, Comancheros, renegades.

She wondered secretly if her acceptance of the stranger wasn't a rebellion from that, from the neglect and the deaths of two men she'd loved.

The fact was she just didn't fear this wounded stranger. She even appreciated his mild words to her son. Whatever he was, he wasn't mean-spirited, despite the deep bitterness that haunted his eyes, his dreams, his words. He had conquered it enough to be kind to her son, and that meant a lot to Mary Jo.

His modesty had also been appealing. He was a gentleman, had been raised to act like one. She wondered what else he had been.

And who might be after him?

She glanced at the rifles on the wall. Both she and young Jeff were crack shots. Her husband and Ty had made sure of that. Texas was not a safe place to live, and no one thought less of a woman if she knew how to protect herself.

Mary Jo went to the door and opened it. It was still raining hard and Cimarron Creek was close to overflowing. Since the house was on a small hill, it was safe, but what few crops they had were endangered.

Mary Jo closed the door and went into the kitchen. Jeff had fueled the wood stove. She put some chunks of ham into water along with pieces of vegetables. Then she started some biscuits.

Jeff was restless, frequently looking toward the closed door to her room. He'd been like a caged wolf these past few days, unable to go out in the storm except to milk the cow and feed the horses and chickens, and he didn't consider *that* going out at all. And he'd been so anxious about the stranger he'd found. "He'll be all right now, won't he?" he asked.

Mary Jo nodded. "I think so. At least, I think he'll live. I don't know about that arm."

Jeff frowned. "Do you think he might be a lawman?"

"No," she said gently, "I don't think so."

"He wore his gun tied down."

"A lot of men wear their guns tied down."

"Did he say anything to you?"

She shook her head. She hated lying to her son, but she didn't want to tell him his new acquaintance had so coldly said he'd killed three men.

"Maybe he's a marshal. Or an army scout. He was wearing Indian beads."

"I don't think so, Jeff," she said. "He could just be a drifter."

"Then why did someone shoot him? Did he say?"

She shook her head, telling herself it wasn't a lie. Wade Foster hadn't explained exactly why he'd been shot.

"Can I go see him?"

"I think he needs a little privacy right now," Mary Jo said. "But as soon as those biscuits are done, you can take some in and see if he can eat them." She paused. "I'll go see about his gear."

Jeff's eyes opened wide. "In this storm?"

She grinned at him. "I won't melt, I promise. He might have some other clothes with him."

Jeff grimaced and she knew why. Buzzards would have gotten to the horse already. But she had done more gruesome things in her years on the plains; once she'd helped bury a neighboring family massacred by the Comanches. Her best friend, Betsy, had been scalped, her older brothers tortured. Their parents had a dozen arrows in them.

The only sight worse than that was her sister being taken by Comanches. Mary Jo was seven then, and she and her eight-year-old sister had been playing with a ball, moving farther and farther away from their ranch house. The Comanches appeared out of nowhere. Mary Jo yelled and started running toward the house, sure that her sister was right behind. Then she heard the terrified scream from her sister and shouts from her parents as they raced toward her. Her mother scooped her up while her father chased the riders and shot at them. But the riders were soon gone and with them her sister. None of them had seen her ever again. Her father had searched for years, and the search had eventually killed his spirit. Only a shell of him remained by the time he died.

Mary Jo wondered once more about Wade Foster's necklace and deerskins. Why in God's earth would he wear the heathen things?

Jeff was scuffing his shoes on the floor, waiting impatiently for the biscuits. She sought a way to expel some of that energy. "Why don't you get some wood for the fireplace?"

He nodded, fetched his oilcloth slicker, and disappeared out the door, eager for some action, even if it was only doing chores. She was hoping there would be a school next year; currently, there weren't enough families to support one, and she'd been teaching him herself from the few books she'd been able to find.

She stirred the broth as she kept her ears open for sounds beyond her bedroom door. He should be finished with his personal needs now. He would need a wash and a shave.

She'd occasionally shaved her husband. It was one of the few personal things he'd enjoyed having done for him. But she hesitated to offer that service to the stranger. It had been an intimate thing between her and her husband; they had even occasionally ended in bed, though he usually preferred night for lovemaking. In some ways, he had been prudish about lovemaking, feeling there was a time and place for it, while Mary Jo thought any place or time was right between husband and wife as long as the desire was there.

The thought brought a hot blush to her cheeks and a yearning to her womanly place. It had been nearly three years since she'd been last loved. Hard work had subdued the need, but now she felt the rush of heat deep inside.

She shook her head in disgust at herself. She couldn't believe she was having such feelings for the first stranger that came limping along. Especially this stranger.

Jeff would be turning over in his grave. So would Ty.

But she just plain couldn't get Wade Foster out of her mind, not those intense eyes, nor that strong, lean body under her bedclothes. Perhaps because of his grief over his son. She'd known grief, but she had never lost a child. And she'd never seen a man so consumed by sorrow.

He was a very disturbing man in many ways, and she was foolish to harbor him without checking with the law.

Perhaps when the storm ended, she would ride to town and make inquiries. If she could ford the stream. If—

The door banged open and Jeff plunged back inside, rain flying in with him. Jake stayed outside, barking frantically.

"Men coming, Ma," Jeff said. "A lot of them."

Is anyone after you?

I expect so.

Almost without thinking, she made a decision.

"Jeff, don't say anything about the stranger."

"Why?" It was his favorite question, and she always

tried to give him answers. This time she didn't know if she could.

She looked at her son, wondering what kind of lesson she was teaching him now. But she had to protect the man they'd rescued. She didn't understand why she felt so strongly about it, but there it was.

She tried the truth. "I think he's in trouble, but I don't think he's a bad man."

Jeff thought about the answer for a moment. It was *his* stranger after all. He had found him. Well, Jake had found him. And Jake liked him. That made the stranger all right in his book.

He nodded.

Mary Jo hurried toward her bedroom, giving only a brief knock before entering without invitation.

Wade Foster was on the side of the bed, the sheet obviously pulled quickly in front of his privates. His face was drenched in sweat, the color pale, his lips clenched together.

"Men are coming," she voiced aloud. "Could be a posse."

He tried to stand, but couldn't. He fell back against the pillow, swearing softly. "I don't want to bring you trouble."

"No one could know you're here. The rain would have erased any tracks," she said. "I'll turn them away."

He stared at her. "Why?"

"I don't know," she said frankly.

"I don't want you or the boy involved."

"We already are, Mr. Foster. Now just stay here and be quiet."

"I don't understand you."

Mary Jo smiled. "Not many people do."

A loud knocking came at the front door, accompanied by Jake's renewed barking. She wished she'd had time to hide Wade Foster; she would just have to make sure no one searched the house. Thank God, everyone in this area knew she was the widow of a Texas Ranger and the heir of another. She would be the last person suspected of harboring a fugitive.

Casting a reassuring look at Jeff, she hurried to the door, opened it, and faced the sheriff and six of her neighbors.

"A man was found dead, killed some four miles to the west," Sheriff Matt Sinclair said. "We're checking all the ranches and farms." She gave him a warm smile. Since the day that she and Jeff had come to Cimarron Valley, Matt had been kind, attentive, and concerned that she was trying to run a ranch on her own. Others had been contemptuous.

"In this weather?" she asked.

"The dead man appears to be a miner from his clothing, though God only knows what he was doing here." He cleared his throat, then added reluctantly, "He was shot once in the leg and then in the throat at close range. Cold-blooded killing if I've ever seen one. Just wanted to alert everyone, check if they've seen any strangers around."

Mary Jo slowly absorbed the news. Wade Foster had tried to warn her, but she hadn't been prepared for the details.

"Do you have any idea who did it?"

"That there's the devil of it," the sheriff replied. "No one's seen or heard anything. Could be just plain robbery, and the killer's long gone, but I want to be sure everyone's warned."

"Thank you," Mary Jo said.

"I don't like leaving a woman and kid alone," he said. "One of my men can stay with you, sleep in the barn."

Mary Jo shook her head. "My husband taught me to shoot as good as any man, and I wouldn't be reluctant to do it," she said. "Jeff here is just as good. And Jake would warn us of any trespassers. But I thank you for the offer."

"Well, then, if everything's all right . . ." His voice trailed off.

"Thank you for coming by, Sheriff." Mary Jo knew she should offer them something, particularly coffee, but it was too risky. She started to shut the door.

The sheriff added, "I'll send someone over every couple of days to check on you."

"No need."

"Just to make me feel better," he said with a slight smile.

Mary Jo tried to smile back, but couldn't. She felt terribly deceitful.

Tell him, something inside her demanded. Tell him about the murderer in your bed.

But no words came. She merely nodded her thanks. As she watched him and the others mount their horses and ride away, she wondered if she had just made the worst mistake of her life.

4

"You don't think he's a killer, do you, Ma?"

Jeff was looking up at Mary Jo with pleading eyes.

Mary Jo hesitated.

A cold-blooded killing if I've ever seen one. The sheriff's words rang in her head. *Shot once in the leg and then in the throat at close range.*

Wade Foster had admitted killing three men.

Her reply: *Did they deserve it?*

She couldn't believe she'd asked that. Did any man deserve to be killed that way?

But Wade Foster rattled her brain. Part of her wanted to run after the posse. Instead, she looked down at Jeff. "I don't know," she said honestly. "But he's too weak to move or be moved."

"I don't think he killed anyone," Jeff said.

Mary Jo wished she shared his certainty. She felt

suddenly chilled, and it had nothing to do with the cold wind blowing in the door. She closed it, setting the bar in place.

It was time to get those answers to questions she'd hesitated to ask.

She sniffed the air and smelled the distinct odor of something burning. The biscuits!

Mary Jo moved swiftly to the iron stove. Smoke came pouring out when she opened it. She plucked out the biscuits, most of which were blackened and hard. Two looked less black than the others.

She bit her lip, feeling more than the normal exasperation. She looked down at her hands and saw them shaking, and she knew it wasn't because of the biscuits. She could make more easily enough. It was not as if she had more important things to do, not in this weather.

Except see to the stranger's horse. The posse must not have found it, or Matt Sinclair would have said something, would have been more insistent about searching the place.

What was she doing harboring a murderer? A man who had shot another, not just in hot anger, but with cold-blooded intent. Shot in the throat. And still she worried about the posse finding the stranger's horse and returning. Finding him!

Why was she protecting him? She was jeopardizing her son, herself, everything she was trying to build here.

Mary Jo set down the biscuits and turned to Jeff. "There might be a couple you can salvage."

"What about the stranger? He needs to eat."

"I'm making some broth for him." She heard a note of impatience—or was it fear?—in her voice. She regretted it immediately when she saw Jeff's face.

"I'll take him a cup of milk in the meantime," she said. "You eat what you can of the biscuits, and I'll cook some ham." His face instantly brightened. She had to buy the hams, and she used them sparingly.

There was fresh milk from their cow, Circe, one of their first acquisitions on the ranch. Mary Jo poured a cupful from the pitcher and walked to her bedroom, knocking on the door before opening it several seconds later.

Wade Foster was once more sitting on the side of the bed, the bedclothes pulled over his lower half. Sweat stood out on his face, which was white with strain. His mouth was a tight, grim line. He must have been up, probably standing by the door, listening.

"Why didn't you tell them?"

She closed the door and leaned against it. "I don't know."

His eyes narrowed as he scrutinized her. A muscle in his jaw tightened.

She had to ask. "You said you killed three men."

The set expression of his face didn't change. He waited, not saying anything.

"The sheriff said he found a man, shot in the throat. Did you—"

"Yes," he answered flatly.

"Why? Was he going to kill you?"

"He was begging, lady," he said coldly. "And I walked up to him and put a gun to his throat and fired."

His eyes became alive with anger and pain and defiance. She could see all of those emotions warring with one another, crosscurrents in a violent storm. "Send your son after that posse, lady," he said.

"I never met anyone who wanted to hang before."

She tried to keep the tremor from her voice. *Don't show any weakness.* But she knew he wasn't telling the real story. He didn't get those wounds *after* he'd killed the man. He'd been wounded, almost fatally himself, and it must have taken the last strength he had to level a gun and fire it. Why was he trying to provoke her, challenging her to call back the sheriff? Did he *really* want to die that much?

"I'll bet you never met a cold-blooded killer before, either." His voice rang hard and cold. "That's what the sheriff called it."

"What do *you* call it?" she asked.

"Just as he said, Mrs. Williams, cold-blooded killing. That miner shot at me, but that didn't make any difference. He was going to die, anyway. He'd emptied his gun, and he was on his knees. And I walked up to him and put a gun to his throat and pulled the trigger. Is your curiosity satisfied now?"

"No," she said. "I want to know why."

"What difference does it make? A killer is a killer."

"It makes a difference to me," she said. She couldn't be that wrong about someone.

Mary Jo saw that muscle moving again in his cheek. She saw his body tremble with the effort of sitting, of controlling all those violent emotions that had suddenly taken over.

She felt his pain. It seemed to vibrate between them. No one, she thought, could be immune to his agony.

"What did he do?" she asked in a whisper. But deep in her soul she knew, and that was why she hurt for him. *Drew.* His son. The killing hadn't been cold-blooded. He may have thought it was, but it hadn't been.

He had lowered his eyes to the floor. Now, he raised them, meeting her gaze.

"You're a fool to harbor me, Mrs. Williams," he said. "I've never been good for anyone. Death is my middle name."

Clearly he wasn't going to say any more. She willed strength into legs that had gone rubbery and she took the few steps over to the bed. "I didn't ask you for anything, Mr. Foster. I don't need anything from you." *Dear God, let that be true.*

She thrust the cup down at him. "Drink this milk," she ordered. "You need it, if you're going to get well enough to leave," she added grimly. "That's what you want, isn't it?"

"I don't understand you," he said.

"Let's just say I have a weakness for strays, and you don't look in any condition to hurt me or mine."

"My just being here can hurt you."

"Not if no one knows."

"Doesn't anything get through to you, lady?"

"If you think you can leave, go ahead," she said calmly. He was angry and that was a good sign. Anger was much better than resignation.

He tried to move, and the bedclothes started to fall away. He grabbed them, pulling them back in place. He glared at her.

She was still holding the cup of milk. "If you don't take this," she said, "I'll remove those covers. At the moment, I'm stronger than you."

"Hellfire. Don't you ever give up?"

"Not usually," she said.

"Give me that damn milk."

She handed it to him, watching as he sipped and then greedily finished the cup. He placed the cup down on the table and slowly sank back down on the bed. "You said there were some trousers?"

She nodded. "I'll check your leg wound later. If the bleeding's stopped, I can make the bandage less bulky and you can wear something of my husband's."

"Your husband?" he repeated.

"I kept some of his things after he died," she said softly.

He looked down at the eagle necklace on the table. He'd burned everything else at the cabin. He hadn't wanted reminders, or memories. Even the good ones had been killed by that last blood-soaked scene. It clouded everything, every memory, with red mist. He probably would have destroyed the necklace too if the miners had not stolen it. He'd found it on the first one, before he'd forced out the names of the other two. It had become his talisman for revenge, not for protection.

The woman was looking at him with an understanding that bewildered him. "I don't want a dead man's clothes," he said rudely. "I want my own."

"They're nothing but rags. Unless you have something in your gear."

He shook his head. He hadn't taken anything but food. He hadn't thought beyond finding those miners.

"Your horse. Anything on it that would identify you?"

He was startled again. She could have been a lawman herself, he thought wryly. "The bridle. It's beaded. I don't want the Utes blamed." Christ, he hadn't even considered that until now. "I have to get—"

He tried to sit again. And managed it only with

supreme effort. Then he swallowed his pride. "I . . . will . . . take those clothes."

Mary Jo was fascinated with the contradictions in him. He had just admitted to cold-blooded killing, yet he was ready to risk his life and the pride that appeared even more important to him, so someone else wasn't blamed for his crimes. She didn't know anyone who cared an owl's hoot over what happened to Indians.

"How far do you think you'll get?" she asked.

"As far as I have to," he said. "And I'll go naked if I have to."

He *would* try, she realized. He wouldn't get much farther than the door, but he would try. And she and Jeff would have to drag him back.

"I'll go," she said. "The posse apparently didn't find your horse. How far is it from the man you killed?"

Man you killed. How easily she'd said the words. *Forgive me, Jeff.*

"A couple of miles. After I was shot . . . after I killed him, I didn't realize my pinto had also been badly hit. He just kept going, bleeding to death, and I wasn't even aware . . ." The lines in his face seemed to deepen. "He was . . . so gallant. And now he's dead. But I won't be responsible for more, dammit." He stood, uncaring now if he were covered or not, then swayed as he took a step.

Still, he was magnificent. Taller than she'd thought, with a rider's lithe grace and tightly muscled thighs.

"All right," she said. "I'll get you those trousers." Just putting them on would sap what strength he had. She wouldn't help him, and he would discover on his own that he would never reach that horse. Even if he did he could never manage to remove the riding gear, not with that arm.

He wasn't listening to reason. Sheer will and determination were driving him, but neither could be sustained. He'd lost too much blood, had been too badly injured.

She ached for him. Something inside her didn't want him defeated. He had called his horse gallant, but she was seeing the man's gallantry now.

She didn't want him dead. All thoughts of sending for the posse had disappeared from her mind. His urgency became her urgency.

Only for a fleeting second did she question why. The answer came even quicker. He needed her. No man had ever needed her before. Not Jeff. Not Ty. They'd wanted, but they'd never needed. Even her son needed her less now.

She hadn't realized how much she wanted that need.

But she mentally thrust away that idea. She couldn't afford that kind of thinking.

She fetched the trousers, throwing them to him. Wade Foster caught them with his good hand, and she left once more, pulling the door closed behind her. He would have to discover his weakness on his own. She wouldn't increase his humiliation by watching.

Jeff looked at her anxiously. "How is he? Did he say anything about the posse? He didn't kill that man, did he?"

Mary Jo closed her eyes for a moment, trying to decide what to say. She had already lied to him. She couldn't do it again.

"Yes," she said, "but the man was shooting at him, and Mr. Foster . . . well, he had good reason."

Jeff's frown smoothed out. "Like when Pa had to shoot someone?"

"Something like that," Mary Jo said, hoping it was the truth.

"I knew it," Jeff said, a smile coming to his lips. "But why doesn't he just tell them?"

"He's too sick," she said gently. "They would have taken him to jail while they checked, and I don't know if he would have survived the trip."

Jeff accepted the explanation. Because he wanted to, she knew.

"Would you go saddle my horse for me?" she asked.

"Why?"

"I need to retrieve some of his things from his horse. I want you to stay here and look after him."

He nodded and flew out the door, calling Jake to follow him. Jake cast a woebegone look at the closed bedroom door, then followed. The stranger had two advocates in this home. Two good ones, in her opinion.

Wade damned his weakness and the trousers. They wouldn't go past the bandage on his leg. He swore and just looked at them for a moment. Then he tried to pull them once more, automatically using his right arm. The pain nearly annihilated him. He breathed slowly, one deep, steadying breath at a time.

How long since he'd last eaten? Four, five days except for that milk. Now he was paying for that neglect.

He used his left hand to untie the now rust-colored

bandage on his leg. It took him a very long time, but finally it came loose and he unwrapped it. The wound was raw and ugly, seeping a yellow-reddish discharge. The skin around it was red and puffy.

He needed part of the bandage to remain. If only he could cut it. His knife. Where was it? He couldn't find it, and he was damned if he was going to call her. He had seen the doubt in her eyes, knew she thought he would fail.

To hell with her. He used his teeth to tear the bandage, then he had difficulty wrapping the smaller piece back around the wound. Finally, he just threw it on the floor, and stuck his wounded leg in the trousers. He stood, pulling up the trousers with his left hand. He swayed. He was so dizzy.

He got the trousers over his hip, but buttoning them was another problem. He sat and then tried to button them as despair flooded him. What if he never regained use of his arm?

He finally managed to twist the last button into the hole. The trousers were tight. A dead man's clothes. Fitting, somehow.

Wade stood. Dizziness assaulted him. The world was whirling around him, or maybe *he* was whirling. He didn't know. He tried to take another step. He had to retrieve the halter, the beaded halter that his wife had given him.

The dizziness increased. He tumbled to the floor, falling on his right arm. Agony stabbed him. Damn, he could still make it. He had to.

But as he tried to rise, he admitted defeat. Once more, he couldn't protect the people he cared about.

．　　　．　　　．

Jeff had not yet come back when Mary Jo heard the noise from the bedroom. She opened the door and her gaze quickly found him on the floor. He was trying to sit. His breathing was labored and harsh, but he wasn't giving up. He kept trying, even as pain-filled eyes looked up at her.

"Say it, dammit." His voice was raspy.

Why did she understand him so well? She kneeled down, offering her hand to him. "You had to find out for yourself," she said, keeping sympathy from her voice.

He stared at her hand as if it were a poisonous snake. She wondered whether he had ever accepted help in his life.

"Take it," she commanded. "Unless you want to wait until Jeff gets back."

His eyes were full of frustration, but he finally held out his left hand and struggled to his knees. A groan escaped his lips, but he immediately cut it off. Giving him her shoulder to lean on, she managed to get him back to the bed.

"I *will* get your gear," she said.

He turned his head away from her.

"Jeff will bring you some broth in a little while," she said softly. "Eat as much as you can."

He didn't acknowledge her words.

She returned to the kitchen and finished frying ham, then set a plate for Jeff, and watched him eat. She had no desire to hurry. The task before her was nasty at best.

"I don't know how long it will take," she said, ignoring the bites he sneaked down to an eager Jake. She should lecture him on dog food and people food, but

Jeff had been so good these last few days, so grown-up in his attempts to be helpful with the stranger.

Part of her was proud. The other part hated to see him grow up, knowing he would leave one day. She swallowed her rebuke and looked away as if she hadn't seen.

"Take Mr. Foster a bowl of broth," she said, "in about an hour. It should be ready then. Check first, though, and see if he's sleeping. If he is, let him sleep. He needs the rest."

He nodded. "You sure I can't help you?"

She shook her head. "Someone needs to watch him, all right? And if anyone comes by . . . ?"

"I know," he said impatiently, but his eyes were full of excitement. It was heady for him, this small conspiracy they shared. Or was it so small? Her son had watched her lie to a lawman, protect a man who confessed to being a murderer. She must be crazy.

A tingle of apprehension ran through her. Dear God, she prayed silently, let me be doing the right thing.

She put on her long coat and a floppy felt hat. It was still raining, and she wondered whether it was going to rain forever. At least no one else would be out in this mess, only the posse and it was gone. She hoped.

Mary Jo had no problem finding the horse. As she thought, there were no tracks. Despite her brave remarks to both Jeff and Wade Foster, she had to force herself to dismount and approach the animal.

The birds had been at it, and the stench was strong, even with the rain. She immediately saw the halter. It was elaborately braided, colorful and distinctive. Undeniably Indian. She already wore gloves, but she wrapped a thin rag around them before taking the halter off.

She knew she couldn't get the saddle off, not with the horse lying on it, but she could retrieve one of the saddlebags. Using the knife she brought with her, she cut the leather strap between the bags, taking the one not hidden by the horse's body. She then eyed the dead animal one more time for anything that looked Indian. That seemed to be Wade Foster's greatest concern. The saddle blanket looked well worn and ordinary. The saddle and stirrups were the same. Satisfied that none of the items could be linked with Utes, she mounted her horse. She hoped the cold rain would wash the smell of death from her.

She wondered whether it would ever wash off her patient, or even whether he wanted it to.

She looked down at the halter. Why did Wade Foster care so much that Indians not be blamed for his actions? Comanches had taken her sister, massacred her best friend and family. The Utes here in Colorado had been accused of similar atrocities, including the setting of numerous forest fires to kill settlers. Feelings against Indians ran as high here as they did in Texas.

What connection did Wade Foster have with Indians?

Chivita. Was it a Mexican name? It couldn't be Indian. She'd heard of white men who took up with Indian women, but she'd never met one. And he'd said his son's name was Drew.

Mysteries. So many mysteries surrounded him.

.   .   .

Jeff poured a bowl of soup and buttered a piece of bread, then carefully placed both on a tray, along with a glass of milk and a spoon.

He went to the bedroom door, knocked lightly so as not to wake the stranger if he was asleep. There was a grunt in response.

Jeff opened the door cautiously. He had seen little of the stranger in the past few days, and he couldn't quite forget the sheriff's words, despite his brave words to his mother.

The stranger was lying on the bed, wearing a pair of trousers. His face was rough with bristle and he looked tired. But he seemed to relax as Jeff entered.

"I've brought you something to eat," Jeff said hesitantly. "Ma's gone out to see about your things." He paused. "You're wearing Pa's trousers."

The stranger's eyes flickered slightly. He tried to smile, but he wasn't very successful. Jeff set the tray down on the table next to the bed. "It's real good, Mr. Foster," he said with no little pride. "My ma was the best cook in Texas. She used to cook for the whole Ranger company down there."

Wincing, the stranger struggled to pull himself up and lean against the pillow. His eyes never left Jeff, and Jeff felt a little disconcerted. They seemed to be searching for something, and Jeff didn't know what.

Jeff picked up the bowl and spoon and sat on the side of the bed. "Can I help you, Mr. Foster? I know that arm must hurt a whole lot."

A hardness suddenly gleamed in the man's eyes, but then it was gone. His chest rose with a small sigh. "I would be grateful, boy," he said. "If I tried, I might just ruin these fine trousers of your pa's."

But despite the soft words, Jeff saw the fingers of

the stranger's good hand ball up in a tight fist. Jeff understood. He was a man too, and men didn't like needing help. He sure didn't, when he'd been sick last year.

So he didn't say anything, just spooned some broth and carried it steadily to the man's mouth. They finished the broth in silence and then the man closed his eyes. Jeff started to go, then hesitated. "There's some milk and more bread too, when you want."

The stranger opened his eyes. "Tell me about your pa," he said unexpectedly.

Jeff began to fidget. There was nothing he liked better than to talk about his pa, but his mother had warned him not to wear out the stranger. Jake had moved over to the bed, and put his head on it, obviously waiting for the stranger to acknowledge his presence. "Jake likes you," Jeff said. "He doesn't like all that many people. He's part wolf, you know. I think he believes you belong to him, since he saved you, like the Chinese people do." Nervousness made the words all run together. It was exciting to have a man to talk to, especially one he had helped save. "Ma told me about the Chinese. She read it someplace. She's always reading when she can."

The stranger looked confused by the rapid flow of words, but one side of his mouth turned up slightly, and Jeff felt his chest expand with pleasure. He remembered the man's original question. "My pa was a Ranger, one of the best there was. So was Ty." Suddenly his pride seeped away, gone in that sense of loss he'd had since Ty died.

"Who's Ty?" the stranger asked.

"He was courting my ma. He was killed last year. He left this ranch to us. I miss him real bad, just like my pa. I'm going to be a Ranger too someday, just like them. Ma doesn't want me to, but—"

"But Mr. Foster needs some rest."

Jeff turned around sheepishly at the sound of his mother's voice. "But Ma, he asked about—"

"I know," she said. "I heard." She was still wearing her coat, which was dripping water. She took off the floppy hat, and her hair fell down her back. She used one arm to wipe rain from her face; the other carried a braided bridle and a saddlebag. A strong stench accompanied her into the room.

Jeff's gaze fastened on the bridle, then he looked back at the patient. "I've never seen a bridle like that."

The stranger's eyes had moved to meet his mother's. Jeff felt an odd presence in the room, like electric tension in the air before a storm. The stranger wasn't smiling, nor was his mother.

"My wife made it," he said simply, his eyes glinting with challenge. Then he turned away, facing the wall, closing off Jeff and his mother as readily as if he'd slammed a door in their faces.

Jeff looked up at his mother. She was biting her lip as she sometimes did when she was uncertain about something. But then she put her arm around him and guided him out of the room, gently closing the door behind her.

5

Hours later, Wade was still thinking that he owed the woman thanks, but he couldn't force the words from his mouth. There had been disapproval in her eyes as well as questions as she'd fingered the bridle. What would she think if she knew he'd had an Indian wife? That might cause her to throw him out when murder hadn't.

But then why should he blame her? Almost everyone in Colorado despised Indians. Hell, it was probably everyone, what with all the newspapers screaming about atrocities and moving all Utes to Utah where nothing but starvation awaited them.

He sickened whenever he thought about it. The Denver papers had been particularly virulent, accusing the Utes of everything from burning down forests to massacres that never happened. Wade had heard all the charges from miners and hunters traveling through Ute territory. Justification for stealing more land.

And the Utes, hoping for peace under Chief Ouray despite broken government promises and treaties, had steadfastly tried to appease the whites by giving up more and more land. The whites always wanted more, though, particularly the minerals in the Utes' shining mountains. And then they took other things that didn't belong to them, like Ute women.

Even his son had been considered less than human because of his Indian blood. So easy to kill. Nits make lice. That's the way many soldiers put it.

Wade couldn't withhold a groan. Drew had been the one good thing in his life, the only thing that had made any sense in the past seventeen years.

He had cared for Chivita. She'd been gentle and kind, and she had given him a son, but he'd felt no passion for her, only gratitude that she had soothed some of that fierce anger he had turned on himself.

She had been so accepting, so eager to share with him the simple pleasures of a mountain sunrise or a bud on a tree. She had asked for so little in return for teaching him, in her quiet, innocent way, how to live again. And now he'd turned away from all her lessons.

Wade reached for the beaded necklace on the table. It had belonged to his son, a gift on his name day. Chivita had patiently carved the beads from buffalo horns, and Wade had traded for the silver eagle, which had been fashioned by a Navaho craftsman. It had been Drew's prized possession.

There were still traces of blood on it. Drew's blood, he supposed. Ignoring his pain, he dropped the necklace over his head. He could care less what the woman or her son thought. He wondered whether he was actually challenging them.

It galled him to owe a debt to a woman who, like so many others, held Indians in contempt. It galled him even more to be imprisoned here by his own weakness.

Unable to sleep, he tried to sit. The lamp beside him was still lit, and he put out the flame, then looked toward the curtained window.

He wanted it open. He wanted to feel fresh air. Maybe then he wouldn't feel so trapped.

He managed to get to his feet and stumble over to the window. He pushed aside the curtains and tried the window. It opened halfway, and he leaned against the wall and breathed deeply.

The rain had stopped, but the sky was dark, unlit by any star or piece of moon. He couldn't see the mountains. Black Mountains, they were called.

But they weren't nearly as black as his soul.

Mary Jo wasn't sure when the rain had stopped. She woke to the stillness of the night. It was eerily silent after the nearly constant sound of thunder and the pounding of heavy drops against the roof.

She might as well get up, walk around, do something. Once she woke up at night, she always had trouble going back to sleep. Years, she supposed, of waiting for the sound of a door opening, of boots approaching her room. She'd spent nearly all her married life waiting.

And now she felt as if she were waiting again, but this time she didn't know for what.

She stood in her nightdress. She'd made it herself several years ago before Jeff had been killed, and he had loved it. She'd spent hours sewing lace to the thin cotton. It had been a luxury, and she had not worn it since he died. She had no idea why she had put it on. A need to feel like a woman again?

She nibbled on her lip as she tried to deny the longing that had been stirred inside her. It kept bubbling, no matter how hard she tried to stop it. The fact that it had started with the stranger's arrival terrified her. He was everything she should run from, should keep young Jeff from.

Air. Fresh air should restore her reason. She tiptoed through the room, careful not to wake her son. She crept quietly to the front door and opened it, standing in the doorway.

A fresh breeze seemed to be washing away the heavy, sultry air that had clung around the ranch house for many days. It felt good brushing through her hair, cooling her hot face.

She relished the sight of clouds rushing across the dark sky. Rushing away now to plague someone else with endless days of rain.

And yet she was grateful to the rain. It had helped the stranger. It had washed away his tracks.

The stranger.

Her thoughts kept coming back to *him*. And her protectiveness toward him, regardless of how rude he was, or how ungrateful.

Jake came out on the porch and sat, cocking his head to one side. He whined for attention, and she stooped down, her hand running absently alongside his ears. The whine changed into a growl of pleasure.

"Ah, Jake," she whispered. "What do you see in him to like?"

He growled again.

"You're just as troublesome as he is," she told the dog. He wagged his tail and then, as if to prove her charge, he darted down the steps and into a yard that was now mostly mud.

Disregarding the dampness of the steps, she sat down and leaned against the post, too tense to go back inside. Somehow the vast darkness around her was comforting.

Why wasn't she afraid of Wade Foster? Because she had already endured much in her life? She had gone hungry as a child when crops wasted away, and she had huddled in hiding with her mother during those times the Comanches were raiding. She had waited in fear with her mother for her father to come home, and years later waited in fear by herself for Jeff to come home.

Now she *was* afraid again, not of Wade Foster but of her own emotions, of her need and her loneliness. They had been tolerable until he came.

My wife made it. She knew she hadn't been able to hide that moment of shock. She still couldn't believe it. An Indian bridle. And the necklace was Indian. The necklace that he had so frantically sought when he'd first awakened.

Jake bounded back up the steps, shaking himself and covering Mary Jo with mud. How nice to be so indifferent to niceties. How nice to have nothing to worry about but a good roll in the mud.

But now he would have to stay outside the rest of the night.

She finally stood. "You can be a watchdog tonight," she told Jake.

He looked dejected.

"It won't work this time," she said severely.

He whined, and she almost gave in.

"No," she said. Before she could change her mind, she went back inside, closing the door behind her. She wished she didn't feel guilty, though she knew that in moments Jake would be out exploring, sniffing, and having a good time.

She wouldn't be granted the same pleasure. The same perplexing questions about the mysterious Wade Foster would only continue to whirl around in her head.

Wade's window looked out onto the porch and he had seen the woman. He'd told himself he should retreat to his bed, that he shouldn't invade this moment of privacy she apparently sought. Yet he hadn't been able to take his gaze from her, from the slender form that moved gracefully, that leaned wistfully against the post.

What do you see in him to like? she'd asked the dog.

Nothing was her insinuation, and he didn't blame her. So why did she continue to care for him? Why hadn't she told the posse he was here? Why hadn't she just let them take him away? Why had she taken the trouble of retrieving his bridle?

His good hand clenched. He knew his body's ability to recover. Two days, and he should have enough strength to leave. But how? No horse. No money. No place to go. How far could he walk? Not to the Utes' shining mountains.

And he had no way to repay the woman. God knows how he hated debts. Especially to someone who would have looked down on his wife and child.

He'd watched her bend her head, her hair tumbling down across her shoulder as she hugged the dog.

She puzzled him, interested him in ways he didn't want to be interested. He had nothing to offer a woman like her, would never have, now that his right arm was smashed. He accepted that. Punishment for the past.

He limped away from the window and back to the bed. Her bed. It even smelled of her, flowery and fresh. Something in him ached at the thought. He would move over to the barn tomorrow, and then leave as soon as he could.

He closed his eyes, but he kept seeing her there, on that porch. Almost ethereal in the white gown.

"Goddammit," he whispered. It was as if the devil weren't finished with him yet. He'd just devised a new torture.

Birds were singing when Wade woke the next morning to a soft knock on his door. The sun was streaming through the window, and a light breeze was ruffling the curtains.

All of which meant the posse would probably be nosing around again.

But he felt better. The food and rest had helped. How much?

The knock came again.

"Yes?" he finally said, convinced now that whoever it was—mother or son—was not going away.

The door opened, and Mary Jo Williams came in. A delicious smell wafted in with her. His stomach grumbled.

She smiled, that tentative, searching smile that he'd never seen on a woman before. He'd seen the type that lured, that seduced, that was coy. And he'd seen the kind that sought so hard to please. But never this kind that challenged yet showed compassion. The kind that indicated tolerance but not surrender.

"You look better," she observed. "And sound better."

He was instantly embarrassed but didn't know what to say so he just waited and watched. She wasn't beautiful as much as she was interesting. Her eyes were alive with intelligence, spirit, and curiosity and yet she had learned to hold her questions. Her hair, gleaming red in the streaming sunlight, was plaited in a long braid that fell halfway down her back. The part of him that was still very much male wished he had seen more of it last night, and he felt the strongest desire to run his hands through it. No. His hand. *One* hand. The other was useless. He frowned at the harsh reminder of reality and lowered his gaze.

She was carrying a tray with a bowl of steaming hot water. He also saw soap and a razor.

"I thought you might like to wash before eating," she said. She hesitated a moment. "I could shave you if you like."

He wasn't sure he would like that at all. He didn't like the dependence. And he sure as hell didn't know if he wanted her hands on him again. They were too soft, too tempting.

Yet he hated to think how he looked. He had let his beard grow during the war. He had thrown away every semblance of civilization during those years.

After a Yank had begged him for his life and Wade had turned on a fellow guerilla, he'd wandered off to the mountains and simply existed. He'd understood what he'd become and had nursed his self-hatred, remembering as if it were yesterday the faces of men he'd killed.

His left hand touched his cheek, feeling the roughness again. Had he reverted to that animal that didn't deserve to live among decent people?

And then he became aware once more of the woman's searching gaze on him. He nodded.

She moved closer to him, sitting in the chair that touched the bed. He wished she didn't always smell of flowers. He closed his eyes at her first touch, kept them closed through the washing and soaping of his face, and finally the scraping of the razor against his skin.

He almost winced at the longing her touch stirred inside him. He felt disloyal to Chivita, because she had never aroused this need in him, had never stirred his heart.

It was suddenly all he could do to keep from pushing her away. He felt just as naked now as he had without his trousers, as if she were peeling layers of defenses from him, rather than whiskers.

But he held himself still, tolerating. After what seemed hours, the razor left his face, and he felt a cool towel against it.

"You can open your eyes now," she said, her voice carrying a tiny bit of amusement. "I didn't slit your throat."

He opened them. His left hand felt his face. Smooth and clean. It felt good. "I didn't think you would," he said.

"Then why . . . ?"

She'd been honest with him right from the beginning. It was time he was honest with her, as honest as he could be.

His gaze met hers. "It felt too good. Better than I deserve."

She tipped her head slightly, studying him. "It's an improvement." Then she hesitated. "Are there wanted posters?"

"I doubt it," he said. "At least not current ones."

Her eyes narrowed in question.

"I don't think anyone saw me," he said. "They're probably just looking for any strangers, especially those with a hole in them."

"How did you kill . . . that miner when you were shot that badly? He couldn't have shot you after—"

"I managed with my left hand," he said, biting off each word. "You can do anything if you want it bad enough. And he was out of ammunition. And scared." That, he thought, should silence her.

But it didn't, although her face paled slightly. "He killed your son?"

"And my wife," Wade said. "He was one of three, and he was the last to die." He watched her, then said deliberately, "And you can stop being polite. My wife was a Ute, my son a . . . half-breed. He was six years old when those men slit his throat after raping and killing my wife. Of course, most would say that it was no great loss. Two less Indians." He couldn't keep the bitterness from his voice.

"I'm sorry," she said softly.

"Are you? Are you, really? I saw your eyes when you brought that bridle in."

"I don't say things I don't mean, Mr. Foster," she said defiantly. "I'm sorry whenever a child is killed. But I've also seen white children killed by Indians. My friend was killed, and my sister was taken by Comanches when I was seven. We never found her though my father never stopped trying, not even ten years later."

She snapped her mouth shut and rose. "Breakfast will be ready shortly."

Wade watched her leave, regretting his angry words, regretting the flush he'd brought to her face and the old grief to her eyes. He was so good at hurting those around him. So damn good.

Jeff finished washing off Jake with pails of water from the well. Jake shook himself, dousing Jeff, then gave him a lick as if to forgive him for the indignity of a bath.

"Now don't do that again," Jeff scolded him. Jake slunk away dejectedly.

Jeff quickly dried himself with a towel, then skipped up the steps to the porch. His stomach was growling, and he wanted to talk more to the stranger.

His mother was frying eggs on the stove, and he smelled ham again. Golden biscuits already lay on the table, and Jeff's nose wiggled with delight. He'd told the stranger the flat-out truth. His mother was the best cook in Texas. And Colorado, too.

She plopped a piece of ham on a plate. "Cut that up for Mr. Foster," she said, "and butter those biscuits. You might put some of those apple preserves on them."

Jeff was glad to do it. It was good to have another man in the house. He loved his mother, but he missed the Rangers and all the attention they had given him. They had taken him fishing and hunting, and talked to him as if he were a grown-up. Treated him like one too, giving him responsibilities in caring for the horses. He knew a lot about horses.

Jeff wanted the stranger to stay, wanted Wade Foster to share things, man to man. His mother still treated him like a child. Worried when he was gone too long, when he got lost in his own thoughts while meandering down along the stream or riding his horse.

He didn't blame her. Jeff understood that he was the only person she had. Ty used to explain it to him when he'd complained about too many hugs. She needed a husband, Ty had said.

Jeff didn't want just any old father. But he was impressed by the stranger, by the way Jake liked him. Jake didn't take to just anybody. And Mr. Foster didn't talk too much or try to make anyone like him. He wore his gun right, the way Jeff's pa had and he'd been sad about his horse dying.

Those things added up to a lot for Jeff.

He'd completely disregarded the sheriff's words about cold-blooded killing. As his mother said, if the stranger killed anyone, he had a reason, and Jeff was not a stranger to that line of thinking.

It made him wonder, though, if the stranger had ever been a lawman. Or in the army. Jeff had so many questions, but his ma had warned him against pestering their guest.

Jeff didn't think he would be pestering, though. Just a few tiny questions, like about his son. Jeff had been surprised to hear about the son. Mr. Foster said it real sad but angry like, too, and Jeff had guessed something awful had happened. The stranger had hurt, just as Jeff had hurt when his pa died, and then Ty.

Jeff finished cutting the meat while his mother prepared the tray, adding a glass of milk along with a cup brimming with coffee.

"You take it in to him," his mother said. Jeff was a

tad surprised, but then she had been stiff and tight-lipped since she'd come out of Mr. Foster's room a little earlier.

Jeff picked up the tray and was halfway across the room when his mother spoke again. "Tell him to eat as much as he can, Jeff. And don't ask him any questions, please. I think he's had a bad time, and he doesn't need reminders."

He turned around to face her. She looked worried, and she hardly ever looked worried. "I won't," he said, thinking, though, that it wouldn't hurt if he just sort of stuck around a few moments in case the stranger *wanted* to talk. Maybe he was lonely, the way Jeff sometimes was.

He entered the bedroom and was amazed to see the stranger standing. He was wearing trousers, but his chest was still bare and Jeff saw scars. Though clean-shaven now, the stranger still looked dangerous.

But not mean, Jeff thought, as Mr. Foster's mouth quirked a little when he spied the food-laden tray.

He sat back heavily on the bed, as if he could no longer hold himself up. His eyes didn't leave Jeff, and Jeff felt like dropping the tray and running from the intensity of his gaze.

But he didn't. He held himself straight and looked straight into the stranger's eyes. "Ma said for you to eat as much as you could."

"I'm obliged," the stranger replied hesitantly, as if unused to the words.

"Ma fixed it," Jeff added. He put the tray down and started to leave.

"Jeff."

He turned back to the stranger.

"Tell your mother . . . tell her . . . hell . . ."

Jeff could see the clenched muscles in the stranger's face. "Tell . . . her I'm . . ."

Jeff grinned. "I'll tell her you said thanks." He spun out the door before the stranger could protest Jeff's liberal interpretation of what he was trying to say.

6

Wade ate half the food on the plate. Christ, but it tasted good. He hadn't had those kind of biscuits since that morning he had left his family farm for town.

The reminder sickened him, but he forced himself to drink the milk. He needed to get strong. He needed to get the hell out of here.

His gut twisted at the thought of the danger he was putting these people in. It twisted even more at the thought of their discovering who he really was. That his real name still brought curses in two states, and that a noose had hung over him for more than fourteen years.

He hadn't missed the beginning of hero worship in the boy's eyes. Jeff might as well look up to a rattlesnake. Wade had seen the same light in Drew's eyes, and he had failed his son completely.

Wade stood and walked to the window. The heavy rain had washed away some of the vegetable crop. A wheat field to the side was all but gone.

The corral fence needed fixing. He wondered how many horses the woman had, whether he could borrow one. He had one asset in this world: twenty horses he'd rounded up in the mountains and carefully bred with those of Chivita's Tabeguache band. The Utes were superb breeders of horseflesh, and he had learned much from them. His own stock was now being tended by Chivita's brother, Manchez, in a high mountain valley.

Wade had to get there.

And then?

What would he do with one usable arm? He couldn't rope wild horses. He couldn't even break them.

Thoughts tumbled over in his mind. He would give the animals to Manchez. He owed his brother-in-law for failing to protect his family. Perhaps he could give several of the horses to Mary Jo Williams. And then there would be no debt at all. Then he would disappear.

He took a few more steps, trying his legs. The wounded one ached, a dull throbbing that would grow worse the more he tried to use it. How far could he get on foot? To the fence if he were lucky. He was as much a prisoner in this room as he would be in a jail cell.

He needed a horse. Would the woman loan him one? Why should she, for God's sake? He was a man who had admitted to killing.

He could always steal one. Wade Foster knew a lot about stealing horses. But then in his mind's eye, he saw Jeff's face and how crestfallen he would feel if Wade did steal a horse.

Damn the kid, and those eager eyes and hopeful smile. He didn't want to be trusted.

He took a few more tentative steps. The wound in his leg pulsed. Riding would open it again. Just how much blood did a man have to lose before dying?

A knock came at his door. He stiffened, then grunted his permission to enter. He couldn't very well forbid the woman to come into her own room.

The door opened and she stood there. He studied her closely: the dark red hair that smelled like flowers, the smooth skin, the high cheekbones, the slim body that held so much determination and too little fear for her own good.

She smiled when she saw him standing. "You're better!"

He nodded curtly. "Well enough to give you your room back. I can stay in the barn, if that's all right. Just a day or so, until I can move on. I've been enough trouble."

The smile disappeared, and her eyes became cautious, almost as if a curtain had fallen over them. "I doubt you'll be strong enough to get far, and the barn is damp, ripe for infections. I would prefer that you stay here. Jeff and I are fine as we are."

"I don't—"

"If that posse comes back, you're safer in my bedroom," she said. "They won't look here. They might search the barn."

Wade clenched his teeth. She was right, dammit. He couldn't imagine anyone invading this woman's bedroom against her wishes. She would quell them with a simple look.

Hell, she was quelling him.

He sighed in surrender. Then knowing he was

about to fall down and not wanting to do that in front of her again, he retreated to the bed. He sat stiffly, holding himself rigid by sheer strength of will. "Another day," he said. "I should be able to—"

"Maybe walk to the gate," she interjected. "Not much farther than that."

"A horse. If I could borrow . . ." He was determined to leave this place, one way or another, even if he had to beg, something he hadn't done in twenty years. "I have some horses in the mountains. If . . . I can get to them, I could repay—"

"You wouldn't get far on a horse, either," she said softly, even regretfully. "And we don't have any extra, just Jeff's and mine, and the two wagon horses which double on the plow."

Frustration flooded Wade. Frustration at his helplessness, his dependence. He wanted to strike back at fate, except fate wasn't handy. The woman was.

He glared at her. "What would your neighbors think if they knew you were harboring an Indian lover?"

Her steady gaze didn't waver. "Same thing, I guess, if they knew I was sheltering someone who killed that miner."

"It doesn't matter to you? My living with the Utes."

She hesitated, troubled eyes meeting his. "I don't know. I can't say I understand it."

"I'm too good to marry an Indian?" he asked mockingly. "It was the other way around. Chivita was much too good for me."

"It's none of my business," she said.

"It *is* your business," he disagreed. "If I'm found

here, I'm very likely to . . . contaminate you. And Jeff."

A flicker in her eyes told him she had already considered that. Again, he felt reluctant admiration. He wondered what her husband had been like.

"Tell me about your son," she said unexpectedly.

Wade hesitated. "He was just a boy," he finally said, his voice breaking. "Just a boy with hopes and dreams . . . and feelings like yours." He didn't want to talk about his son with anyone, with her. Yet the part of him that wanted to keep Drew alive urged him on. "I think he was trying to protect his mother when he died. His body was near hers."

"And you?"

"Hunting," he answered bitterly. "I should have taken him. He wanted to go."

"I can't tell you not to blame yourself," she said. "Sometimes you can't help it. I've blamed myself for Ty's death."

"Ty?" He didn't want to be curious, but he was.

"He wanted to marry me. I kept saying no because I didn't want to be widowed again. Perhaps if I'd agreed, he wouldn't have gone that last time."

So that accounted for some of her sadness. Grief was bad enough, but guilt kept it burning longer.

"He was a Ranger, too?"

Her eyes widened in surprise.

"Your son told me."

"Jeff. His name is Jeff." She said it so sharply, she must have guessed what he was trying to do. Keep himself distanced from them.

"You should turn me over to the law," he told her.

"If I did what I should," she said, "I wouldn't be

here in the first place. Everyone told me I couldn't run a ranch by myself, that I should go East.''

"Why didn't you?"

"Jeff, mostly, I guess. But partly me. I grew up in Texas. My father was a small rancher during the war. He was stubborn, and he taught me to be stubborn. After . . . my sister was taken, he made sure I could take care of myself. I can ride, and I can shoot a rabbit from five hundred yards, but I don't think I can be an Eastern lady. I was willing to try, for Jeff, but then he made me realize it would break his heart. It was bad enough leaving El Paso and the Ranger station. This ranch was a compromise with him. And then everyone told me I couldn't." She looked chagrined. "I got my dander up."

"And you had to show them all?"

"And myself."

"You need help."

"I know," she said. "But I haven't been able to find anyone worth their salt who will take orders from a woman. Last hand got liquored up and nearly burned down the barn." Her gaze suddenly turned speculative. "You know anything about ranching?"

Wade couldn't believe what he was hearing. She shouldn't trust him. Besides, he would be as good around a ranch now as a campfire in hell. "Don't even think it," Wade said, forcing a hard edge in his voice. "I'm gone as soon as I can put one foot in front of the other." She kept standing there, and he felt the need to put his intention more forcefully. "You sure as hell don't need a one-arm killer around here."

A curious light came into her eyes but she changed the subject. "I'll get some fresh bandages," she said.

He had the unsettling feeling that his protest had made no impact at all. What kind of woman was she?

What kind of idiot was she? Mary Jo wondered as she walked around the main room of the ranch house. And yet she couldn't quite reject the idea that Wade Foster could possibly be the answer to some of her problems.

He was finally sleeping after her painful nursing of his wounds. The wounds that he claimed rendered him useless. But she didn't need his arm or leg. She needed intelligence and leadership to lure workers to the ranch.

He could help her while he healed. She could provide food and lodging until he was well enough to leave. And she could throw in a horse.

But a killer? A man who had taken an Indian as wife? From his nightmarish ramblings, there could be even worse. She and Jeff had been safe because he was so weak. But as he improved?

On the positive side, though, he'd not hidden the facts from her. There was his thoughtfulness toward Jeff. Jake liked him. And there was the undeniable fact that she had little choice.

The ranch was not mortgaged, but she and Jeff couldn't live here forever without cash coming in. They needed to develop a herd. They needed wheat for feed for the cattle come winter. They needed more horses, and they needed men. They needed someone like Wade Foster to find them. Once things were going well, she could take over, and Wade Foster could leave.

But how to get him to stay? She could blackmail

him, of course. Threaten to go to the sheriff, but she wouldn't. She would lose the ranch first.

A simple trade, perhaps? A horse and wages for three months of his time. He would be well enough then to leave, go wherever he wanted, hide wherever he wanted. That, she suspected, was his objective.

She had no doubt he would balk at the idea, but it made so much sense, Mary Jo knew he would see reason. Eventually. Before he was capable of walking out of here.

Mary Jo had reservations. A million of them, not the least of which was Jeff's fascination with the man and the disappointment her son would feel when Wade Foster left. Another was the kind of example the man would set for Jeff. Did she really want someone who lived with Indians, someone who had killed, someone who obviously had other secrets, to influence her son?

A third reservation, of course, was that he really could be dangerous. But then he had a bad arm, and she and Jeff both knew how to defend themselves.

And dangerous in other ways? Wade Foster stirred feelings in her she'd thought she had laid to rest. Her breath grew shorter when she entered his room, her heart thumped harder. She was fascinated with the contradictions in him, the violent emotions that thrashed around inside. Her husband and Ty had been stoic, showing little emotion, suspicious of those who did otherwise. She'd learned to harness her own feelings for them, to keep from putting a hand in theirs in public, or saying words that might embarrass them.

And tears? Never.

Yet she had known they both loved her. In their own way.

She swallowed hard. She didn't want to care again,

not about any man. She couldn't stand to bury another one, and Wade Foster had trouble written all over him.

But she had so few choices. It was already midsummer. The rain had washed away most of her vegetable crop. She had a few head of cattle, wearing the brand of the former owners of the ranch, wandering out on the range. They could die this winter if no one were to look after them. She would lose everything she'd worked so hard for these last nine months.

Wade Foster could be the answer to a prayer.

She hoped he wouldn't be the inspiration for a nightmare.

"Ma, rider coming."

Jeff's voice carried throughout the ranch house as he opened the door and yelled out his message.

Mary Jo finished wiping the last dish and hurried into her bedroom. Wade Foster was sitting on the bed's edge, trying to put on the shirt she'd left on the chair for him.

His frustration was evident as he shrugged the shirt over his shoulders, then tried to get the left arm in the sleeve. She wanted to help, but he wouldn't appreciate it. And he'd have to learn to do it by himself sooner or later, especially if the right arm didn't mend.

Veins stood out on his forehead, and his mouth was clenched tight as he tried for the fourth time. He succeeded, a glint of triumph shining in his eyes.

"You heard," she said.

He nodded. "I don't want you protecting me. I'll give myself up, say I forced you to help me."

"Who would believe you?" she asked. "You can't take more than a few steps."

"I can't stay here," he said.

"You would rather hang?"

"You don't understand, Mrs. Williams," he said through gritted teeth. "I don't want any more people on my conscience. Particularly not that boy."

"There's no time now to argue about it. We'll discuss it later."

She went out the door, closing it behind her, hoping he would heed her words. He was too unpredictable, but she didn't think he would do anything to hurt her, and revealing himself now could well do that. It would be obvious she had harbored him.

She moved swiftly to the front door. Matt Sinclair was dismounting. Jeff stood awkwardly nearby, placing himself between the sheriff and the front door. Mary Jo felt a little sick; she was teaching her son deception by keeping information from the law.

She hated it. Yet she had made up her mind.

"Sheriff," she said. "Have you found your man yet?"

He shook his head. "We found a horse, but nothing else. We figure there must have been two of them, riding double now. Probably long gone from here. Rain erased any tracks. I'm just checking once more. I don't suppose you've seen any strangers around?"

"No," she said. "Would you like some coffee?"

He nodded. "That would be appreciated."

"Jeff, why don't you water his horse for him?"

A frown bent her son's mouth, but he nodded and took the reins. Mary Jo led the lawman inside. "I have some biscuits left from breakfast."

He smiled crookedly as he took his hat from his head. He was a nice-looking man with intelligent brown eyes, friendly and not as laconic as the Rangers she'd known. "That sounds good, Mrs. Williams. I've been riding since sunup."

"No one has seen anything?"

He shook his head. "That's why I think they're gone. Probably some drifters." He stood while she poured a cup of coffee, then put several biscuits and a big spoonful of preserves on a plate. She set cup and plate down on the table, giving him a chair that put his back to her bedroom.

This was risky, she knew, but hospitality was expected out here. She hadn't offered any the first time, and she worried that he might think that unusual.

She poured herself a cup of coffee and sat down across from Sheriff Sinclair. "Any problems from the storm?" she asked after he'd finished a biscuit.

"The Berryhills lost a calf. Drowned. Some crops gone," he answered. "Looks like you suffered some damage."

Mary Jo nodded.

"Still no luck in finding hands? If there's no more trouble, I can come over next week and give you some help."

She hesitated, then plunged in. "Ty's brother promised Ty he would help me if anything happened to him, and I wrote him for help. He's had an accident, but he's coming here to recuperate and hire some men." Mary Jo held her breath, but the sheriff seemed to accept the explanation. Everyone around here knew about her husband and Ty.

The sheriff nodded. "When will he arrive?"

"I don't know. Any day."

"Well, I'll check with you in several days. See if you need help until he comes."

"Thank you," she said, trying not to see the interest in his eyes. Sheriff Matt Sinclair was a good man, and she tried hard not to encourage him. He was a bachelor, and she was one of the few single women in the area; his interest was natural, but she didn't want entanglements ever again. Wade Foster was different. He would move on; he had made that very clear.

"You're a good cook, Mrs. Williams."

She smiled. "I appreciate your looking in on me. I know you have other ranches to visit."

He shoved his chair back. "You'll let me know if you see any strangers?"

"I will."

He hesitated. "There's a dance next week. I was kinda hoping . . ." The invitation dangled in the air.

"I'm sorry, Sheriff. It's just too soon. I'm still mourning."

He nodded respectfully. "Maybe later."

She nodded noncommittally.

"That's a fine boy you have."

Mary Jo winced. The sheriff knew how to get to her. "Thank you," she said quietly. "He's had a lot of grief."

"So have you, Mrs. Williams." He put his hat back on.

She opened the door to let him out. Jeff had watered his mount and tied it to the hitching post. Now he sat anxiously digging his hands into Jake's fur.

Mary Jo smiled at him, and the worry lines in his face eased. "Take Jake inside," she said, "and feed him." She winked at him, and he grinned.

She stood on the porch as the sheriff mounted his horse and trotted out the gate. She watched him until he disappeared, trying to figure out how she was going to convince Wade Foster to become Wade Smith.

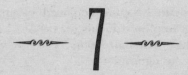

7

Wade Foster glowered at her as she entered the bedroom. He was at the window, standing to one side
where he couldn't be seen if the visitor glanced back.

"Who was that?"

"The sheriff."

"What did he want?"

"You," she said. "The man he was hunting the
other day." She avoided telling him what was probably
the real reason, that the sheriff had started his court-
ship.

"Why didn't you tell him?"

"Why didn't you come out?" she countered. "Give
yourself up? Tell him you're the killer?"

He frowned; his voice grew harsh. "Maybe I agree
with you that no one would believe I held you at gun-
point. But they will in a couple of days, when I'm bet-

ter." He paused. "I *could* kill you then. You and the boy."

"Like those three men?" she taunted him, calling his bluff, knowing he was only trying to frighten her.

A muscle flexed in his cheek. He didn't answer.

"Is it over now?" she asked. "Your . . . vengeance?"

His insolence faded, replaced by an even more frightening emptiness in his eyes. "Am I going to kill again? Is that what you mean?"

"Yes," she said quietly.

He shrugged, leaving her to form her own conclusions. He had retreated inside himself.

"Mr. Foster." Her voice was suddenly sharp. "I want an answer."

"Or else?" he said coolly. "You had your chance to give me up." He took a step toward her, and Mary Jo had to will herself not to move away from the heat suddenly raging in his eyes.

"I might kill again, lady. If this arm gets better. Even if it doesn't. I'm damned good at killing. One of the best, they used to say. I can't even remember how many men I've killed, and a few more don't matter."

Mary Jo held her ground. She had learned long ago not to retreat in front of a man.

"Who used to say?"

He stared at her in amazement. "Doesn't anything faze you?"

"Women don't last long out here if they're easily frightened."

"Easily frightened?" His brows furrowed together. "What in the hell *does* it take to frighten you?"

"Someone I care about dying," she said softly.

His gaze fell, and he walked to the bed, sitting

down heavily. His left hand trembled slightly as it rose to his wounded right arm, rubbing it, as if to bury his thoughts in a sea of physical pain.

"What about your son? You're putting his life in jeopardy."

"Am I?"

"You don't know what I'm capable of."

"You're capable of worrying about the feelings of a twelve-year-old."

"That doesn't cost me anything."

"And my feelings?" Her hands clenched, and she buried them in the fold of her skirt so he couldn't see them.

"That does cost," he said with a direct honesty that surprised her.

"Why?"

"I don't understand them. I keep wondering about the price. What do you want, Mrs. Williams? Why did you take me in? Why did you doctor me? Why are you feeding me?"

She swallowed. Now was not the time to present her plan, not when he was in this suspicious mood. But it would be worse if she waited, if she lied to him.

"There was no reason in the beginning, Mr. Foster, except the one I told you. My son found you. I couldn't leave you out there to die."

"And when the sheriff came by? Why didn't you tell him about me?"

"I don't know," she said honestly. "I just . . . couldn't. You were still so ill."

"And now?"

Mary Jo decided it was time. She had to be honest with him, or he would never trust her. "I . . . need you."

His frown eased, as if he were pleased that his cynicism was proving true. "I'm sorry to disappoint you, but I'm not what anyone needs." It was obvious he wasn't sorry at all. His mouth was twisted in a mocking smile that held no humor, only bitterness.

"You said I needed a man."

"I'm not a whole man anymore, lady. I haven't been for a long time, and I'm even less now with this arm. Hell, I can't even earn my keep. Can't chop wood. Can't hold a gun. I can't help anyone."

"Not if you keep indulging in self-pity."

"It's not self-pity, dammit, it's common sense."

"You still have a mind, don't you?"

"So do you. At least I thought so. Now I wonder."

"I have a mind, all right," she said, suddenly furious herself. "But no man seems to think so. They won't take orders from me."

"Lady, everyone who's ever relied on me is dead. I don't particularly care to add to that list."

"I'll risk it."

He rose and walked to the window. He still limped, and he wasn't all that steady, but at least he could cross the room without falling flat on his face.

"I won't," he said, looking out over the ranch.

Mary Jo wasn't going to invoke the obvious: gratitude. It was clear he had none. He'd stated that from the beginning. But she did have something he wanted. "Not even for a horse?"

He turned, his one good hand clenched.

"You won't get far without one," she added quickly. "You have no money. It would be difficult for you to steal one now."

"Not yours," he spat back. "You make things real easy."

"But you won't, will you? Not because of me, but because of Jeff."

"Don't make the mistake of thinking you know me," he warned. "You don't know anything about me. Where I came from. What I've done. What I'm capable of doing."

"Where *did* you come from?"

He shook his head in frustration.

"A horse," she offered again. "Stay here three months. Hire some men for me, someone who can stay on as foreman. A horse is yours plus a hundred dollars."

It was a generous offer. More than generous. She knew it. And the surprise that flitted in his eyes indicated he knew it, too.

"Why do you think any man would take orders from me?"

Why? Mary Jo couldn't explain it, but she knew he was the kind of man others respected. Maybe it was the toughness. The innate assurance that couldn't be bought or taught. Though torn and battered now, pride was there in his stance, in his reluctance to accept help. But she couldn't say any of that.

"You're my only option," she said. "Without help, I'll lose the ranch. Without the ranch, I'll have to go back to the Ranger station, and Jeff—"

"There's worse things than being a lawman," Wade Foster said. "That's your worry, isn't it?"

"I've already buried two. I won't make it three."

"So you'll take up with the likes of me?"

"I won't be taking up with anyone. I'll be hiring you."

"And what will your neighbors say?" He grinned wolfishly.

"I'll say you're Ty's brother come to help. They know about Ty and would understand that. It will also give you more authority than a hired foreman."

"You have it all figured, don't you, lady?"

"No," she said. "I just need help."

"Any way you can get it?"

She nodded.

That magnetism that had flickered between them from the very beginning flared again, its flames licking at every nerve in her body. She felt heat all the way to the ends of her toes.

"I'm trouble, Mrs. Williams. How long do you think any hand would stay here if they knew I had an Indian wife?"

"They wouldn't know that."

His mouth tightened. She knew he was going to say he wouldn't repudiate his wife and child, wouldn't hide them.

"It won't work unless the neighbors believe you're kin of some kind. I told the sheriff . . ." She hesitated.

"You told him what?" His voice was sharp.

"I was . . . expecting Ty's brother. That makes your presence here natural. They would never guess you were involved with the killing."

He sent her a chilling look. "Blackmail, Mrs. Williams?"

"No. You can leave here anytime you want, and I won't say anything. But until I get help, I can't spare you a horse. It's simply a matter of helping each other."

"And where would I stay?"

"The barn. There's a small room in back. I'll clean

it up. As more men are hired, we'll need a bunk-house."

"I think I prefer your bedroom." There was a nasty tone in his voice, and she knew he was trying to frighten her again. She knew she should be frightened. He was dangerous; she'd recognized that from the beginning. But she wasn't afraid. At least not of him. Maybe . . . of her own feelings.

"That's not included in the bargain," she said firmly.

"What if it's a condition?"

"What about your wife?"

It was an agonizing blow, but they were striking out at each other now, both fully aware of doing so, yet unable to hold back.

His lips pressed together. "Don't even mention her, Mrs. Williams."

"Why? You seem ready to forget her. How long has it been? A few weeks?" She wanted to wound as he was wounding her by suggesting that she would sell herself.

"Ten months," he said flatly.

Ten months? He'd been hunting her killers for that long? She understood hot-blooded revenge, but nearly a year . . . that spoke of cold-blooded, planned murder.

"Changing your mind, Mrs. Williams?"

She ignored his latest challenge and the fact that he could easily read her mind. "Yes or no, Mr. Foster? And no, my bedroom is not included in any arrange-ment," she reiterated.

She saw him hesitate a moment, and it surprised her. He was considering her offer at least, and that was a major victory.

"I'll think about it," he finally said.

Mary Jo nodded. She knew she couldn't push any further; she was lucky to have won that much.

Or was she?

Mary Jo waited two days for an answer, and then she couldn't wait any longer.

Wade Foster was walking around, and she saw all the telltale signs of restlessness. She had seen them in her husband when he'd been idle for a few days. She had to find out now what Wade Foster intended to do. And she wondered about her own intentions, whether she could go through with her plan, whether she wanted to convince Wade Foster to stay.

She'd never reacted to a man the way she reacted to Wade Foster. She'd loved her husband. She'd admired him ever since he rode up to her father's ranch, hunting down an outlaw, when she was fifteen. He'd been a hero to her then and had become a friend over the next few years. They'd married when she was eighteen, after her father and mother died within months of each other. But Jeff had never made her senses tingle, never made her face flush or her blood run hot just with a glance.

It should scare the devil out of her. But the devil seemed determined to remain. The fear, however, wasn't enough to dissuade her. If she didn't get help, and get it soon, she might have to sell the ranch, and either return, defeated, to the Ranger station or travel to a new city and start all over again in a place she didn't know or understand.

She could marry again, but that was just as sorry a solution to her troubles. Loneliness was better than that life-draining fear she'd endured with Jeff and Ty.

Independence better than reliance on a man who might die the next day.

But, dear God, she ached for a gentle touch, for sweet words. She wanted to be brave, but not forever brave alone. Sometimes, she wished . . .

But wishes were for fools. Reality was something else.

A lock of hair fell across her face, and she brushed it back, feeling the roughness of her palm against her skin. She glanced down at her hands. They were brown from the sun, and callused by hard work.

She was thirty-two and felt, at this moment, fifty. She must have imagined that flash of desire in Wade Foster's eyes, conjured that soul-deep attraction between them.

Wade Foster was disturbing. But he was her only hope.

He had been prowling around the house, stopping occasionally to rest, obviously testing his strength. He'd said little, and his face revealed even less, but she felt the storm brewing inside him, and she didn't know what to do about it.

She waited until after dinner. For the first time, he sat with them, and it hurt to watch him struggle to eat with his left hand. She had made stew with chicken, cutting it into small pieces before putting it into the pot. She did not want to give him anything that had to be cut, realizing he would hate to be reminded of his handicap.

She kept a steady conversation going with Jeff, hoping that their taciturn dinner guest would eventually join in rather than glower.

Jake was sitting between Jeff and Wade Foster. Mary Jo saw Jeff's hand creep down occasionally, and she knew he was sneaking bits to the dog. Wade Foster was conspicuously ignoring the dubious activity.

After a particularly loud gulp from Jake, her son glanced around innocently. "Didn't I tell you that Ma's the best cook in the world?"

Jeff had just uttered the last word when Jake emitted what sounded suspiciously like a burp. Jeff flushed.

Wade Foster smiled. It was the first smile Mary Jo had seen touch his face, and it was wondrous. The harsh lines seemed to fade, and the tanned skin around his eyes crinkled. And then those same eyes focused on Mary Jo, watching, waiting, glinting with a hint of amusement.

Mary Jo found herself holding her breath. She should scold Jeff, but she was too charmed by Wade Foster's indulgence of her son's disobedience.

"If you're going to feed Jake at the table," she finally said with pretend exasperation, "you had better teach him some manners."

"Does that mean that I can—"

Mary Jo cut off his eager words. "No, it doesn't. But I think it's time you started teaching that animal to behave."

Jeff's face fell. "But I don't know how—"

"Like a horse," Wade Foster said unexpectedly. "Patience and firmness. He's a smart dog. He'll learn quick. He just needs to know what's expected."

Jeff looked at him. "Will you help me?"

Wade Foster's smile faded, replaced by caution, then something like resignation. He nodded, and Mary Jo knew she had her answer. He would stay. For a little while, at least.

He turned his gaze on Mary Jo, and she was careful to keep her expression neutral. One flash of victory on her face, and he might change his mind. They had struck a bargain. An impersonal exchange of services for goods. Nothing more. Yet her heart thumped so loudly she was afraid he could hear it.

"When?" Jeff asked enthusiastically.

"We'll start tomorrow," Wade Foster answered.

Jeff grinned happily. "You're staying then?"

Wade Foster hesitated. "Maybe a few days. I don't want to take your mother's room any longer."

"Can we go fishing?"

Mary Jo nearly winced at the longing in her son's voice. She knew he'd missed the Ranger station, the occasional fishing expeditions with Jeff and then once with Ty. Ty had even offered to teach her son to swim after Mary Jo had expressed fear about Jeff going fishing alone, but he'd never had the chance. Jeff wanted badly to learn, and Mary Jo couldn't help. She didn't know how to swim; neither her father nor Jeff had approved of women swimming. Indecent, her father had called it, though he hadn't hesitated to teach her how to shoot.

Tensely, she waited for Wade Foster's answer to Jeff's question. He had glanced at his bad arm, and she knew he was thinking he wouldn't be much good at fishing. She prayed silently that he wouldn't dash her son's hope.

"Let's just concentrate on Jake now," Wade Foster said.

Jake whined at the sound of his name, his tail thumping up and down on the floor like a military drum tattoo.

Jeff looked slightly discouraged. But the response wasn't exactly a no, and Mary Jo relaxed.

•   •   •

After she finished the dishes, Mary Jo took a lantern and went out to the room in the barn. She had cleaned it thoroughly when they first moved here. It was small, more fit for a hired hand than a foreman.

She'd discovered that the previous owners had farmed rather than run cattle, but disaster after disaster had befallen them, the worst having been the death of their only child from snakebite. Three bad years of drought and then an infestation of grasshoppers the following year had stolen the last of their stamina.

Mary Jo soon realized the future lay in running cattle, but she needed cowhands for that. This was open range; ranchers branded their cattle and then set them loose. She and Jeff didn't have the combined strength to rope, hogtie, and brand angry half-wild animals.

She'd started so optimistically, only to hear, time after time, that sometimes apologetic, sometimes rude snort when prospective hands learned they would be working for her. Only Tom Raylor had agreed, and later she discovered everyone else had fired him because he was shiftless and careless.

How long would Wade Foster stay?

She opened the one window in the small room, to air it out. Tomorrow morning she would sweep and put fresh sheets on the bed. She couldn't help thinking how small the room was for someone like Wade Foster. He dominated space; everything seemed to shrink around him.

She finally left, hoping that the object of her thoughts had retreated back into the bedroom for the night. She couldn't think clearly when he was around; she had to avoid him as much as possible if she was going to make her plan work.

Mary Jo had brought a carrot with her. She broke it in fourths and fed a portion to each of the horses, ending with her own mare. Her husband had bought Fancy for her on her twenty-fifth birthday, and he had taken pride in the gift. He hadn't been much for presents, so Fancy was special. She was surprisingly fast for her small size, mannerly, and sturdier than she looked.

The horse liked attention, caresses, and Mary Jo needed that at the moment.

She put her head to the mare's. "Am I making a mistake?" she whispered, and received a soft whinny in reply.

"Big help you are," she told the mare, then straightened her shoulders and left.

She was halfway across the yard when she saw Wade Foster. He was sitting on the corral fence, looking off in the distance, toward the mountains. The moon was bright and she could see the loneliness etched in his face.

It touched her heart. She knew loss and grief. But his ran so much deeper. *She* had Jeff.

She hesitated a moment, wondering whether she should intrude, then walked over to him. He didn't acknowledge her presence, although she sensed he knew she was there.

Mary Jo looked up. The sky was crowded with stars, some seeming so close she could almost reach up and pluck one out. It was enchanting, particularly after the week of heavy storms and dark nights.

"It's so peaceful," she said.

His hand tightened around the railing, but he said nothing. Mary Jo felt awkward. Unwanted. She started back to the house.

"Mrs. Williams." His voice was low, and she thought she heard a note of pleading in it. She turned back to him.

He hesitated. When he finally spoke, his voice was low and full of hurt. "You have a lot here, especially Jeff."

"He keeps me going."

Finally he looked at her. "I think you would keep going anyway."

It was a compliment, pure and simple. Mary Jo felt pride welling up inside her, even though it wasn't justified. She had endured, because she'd had to endure, not out of choice. "Sometimes, there's nothing else to do, Mr. Foster."

"Isn't there?"

Mary Jo didn't know how to answer. She changed the subject, instead. "Where will you go when you leave here?"

"It's better if you don't know."

Distrust tinged his voice now. She felt as if he'd plunged a knife into her.

"I won't betray you, if that's what you mean."

"Why shouldn't you?"

"Why should you care, if you meant what you just said?"

"I don't, not for myself. But there are others . . ."

"Indians," she said flatly.

"People," he corrected. "Human beings who know the meaning of loyalty and promises a great deal better than most whites," he said bitterly.

Silence hung heavily between them, but Mary Jo wasn't going to apologize. She kept remembering her sister.

"Hell," he said. "Why should you be any different?"

She wanted to be. She suddenly didn't want to be like all those others he regarded with such disdain. "Tell me about them," she said.

He had turned his face away from hers. He had dismissed her as if she were nothing more than a bothersome fly. She had failed in an important way, and she felt that connection she'd had with him fading. He was willing it away.

She bit her lip. "Mr. Foster—"

His cold glare stopped her. "Not Foster, if I'm to be your almost brother-in-law. What was his name?"

Mary Jo felt uncomfortable, as if she were desecrating Ty. "Smith," she said slowly.

He laughed, but there was no amusement in it. "That's easy enough. I've been Smith before. I had a few other names, too. Curious, Mrs. Williams?"

"No."

"Good," he said, obviously not believing her.

She nodded, not sure how to respond. "Thank you for agreeing to stay."

"You aren't giving me much choice, are you, Mrs. Williams?"

"I think you're a man who makes your own choices," she shot back.

"Really?" He drawled out the word. He slowly put his two feet down on the ground and limped over to where she stood. "I think I'll make one now."

He leaned down, his good arm going around her, drawing her close, so close her body fit into his, and she felt every hard plane of his body. She looked up. She was tall, but he seemed to dwarf her.

His mouth pressed down on hers, and sensations

ignited in her as his tongue seduced its way into her mouth. It was a hard kiss, demanding and challenging and defiant. Angry.

She knew she should pull away. It would be easy enough, as weak as he still was, yet her legs wouldn't obey. Instead they inched nearer until she felt the swelling within his trousers, and she knew a yearning so deep and bittersweet that she didn't know whether she could bear it.

Her lips moved against his, responding with an intensity that seemed to spur his own, and his tongue played inside her mouth, searching so masterfully that he awakened every nerve ending, sending ribbons of tingling warmth surging through her.

Don't, a part of her screamed inside. *He's trying to frighten you again.* But he wasn't frightening her. He was awakening, stirring, bringing something long dormant alive again.

She felt herself tremble as his tongue gentled, as his lips caressed instead of plundered, as his need grew to match her own. Her arms went up around his neck, her fingers playing with tendrils of hair. He stiffened, as if startled by the gentleness, displeased by it.

And then his kiss grew hard again, his tongue withdrawing, and his mouth punishing, bruising. He was trying to hurt her, but it was too late. She had never really feared him, except for what he had done to her emotions, and he could never frighten her now. His need was as raw as her own, as achingly real.

She heard his groan, then the catch in his breath as he suddenly dropped his arm and let her go. He stepped back, his face unfathomable.

"Go inside, Mrs. Williams," he said in a harsh voice.

"Mary Jo," she corrected in barely a whisper. Then she turned and tried mightily to walk with some dignity back into her house.

She would always picture him there, tall and lean and alone.

So alone.

8

Mary Jo hesitated at the door. She was stunned by her own actions, confused by them. Humiliated to the core of her being.

Never had she responded to a man like that, or allowed such liberties. And Wade Foster was a stranger. A stranger with an outlaw past, present, and future. A renegade white man who lived with Indians, who had married an Indian woman. A drifter who would stay only long enough to get what he needed to leave.

She shuddered at the thought of Jeff and Ty looking down from heaven and seeing that shameless conduct.

She pushed back a strand of hair from her forehead. What was there in the stranger that touched a part of her she never knew existed?

It was dangerous as Hades, whatever it was. She

needed to tuck it back where it belonged, behind the common sense she usually practiced, the discipline she had confined herself to.

She braced her shoulders. She could survive this temporary madness. For a few weeks. She would stay away from him, see him only when Jeff was around. She would work until she fell, so exhausted that she wouldn't hear the wayward calls of her body.

Mary Jo took a deep breath, hoping her face was back to its normal color, and opened the door.

Jeff was reading in the light of the kerosene lamp, Jake at his feet.

Mary Jo had bought what books she could find for him. For herself too, if truth be told. She had a hunger for learning, for knowing everything she could, and she tried to kindle those same feelings in Jeff. Especially since he'd scoffed at the idea of going to college. According to him, a Ranger didn't need that kind of education.

He looked up with a grin that had a bit of slyness to it. She suddenly wondered whether he had been watching, whether he had seen that kiss.

"Where's Mr. Foster?"

"He needs some exercise," she lied. "And time to himself."

"I sure am glad he's going to stay a while."

Mary Jo wished she was just as glad. "Why don't you take Jake outside, then get some sleep?"

"But it's early."

"We have a lot to do tomorrow. Go to town, spread the word we have a foreman and need some hands, then clean the room in the barn."

"Why can't he stay here? He can share my room."

She shuddered inwardly at the thought. He would

be near enough in the barn. Just the thought of what had occurred a few moments ago brought a flush to her cheeks. She hoped the light was dim enough to hide it.

"He's a hired hand, Jeff," she said, her tone sharper than she intended. Even Jake shook off his after-dinner lethargy and peered up at her with narrowed, puzzled eyes. "He won't be here long."

The excitement in Jeff's face didn't fade, and a wave of apprehension snaked through Mary Jo. She didn't have time to emphasize Wade Foster's temporary place in their household. Her son had already bounded up and headed out the door, Jake barking behind him.

That kiss had been a mistake.

Wade still tasted her. Would he always taste her?

He had intended to offend, to frighten, but instead had been burned himself, bewildered by the gentleness that inexplicably replaced the harsh attack he'd planned.

He couldn't stay here. He'd been crazy to even consider it. Even if it weren't for the damnable attraction between the woman and himself, he was too much of a danger. There had been too many wanted posters for him not to still be remembered.

No amount of hiding would ever get rid of those memories. Nothing would ever cloud the viciousness of those years. It had lasted longer than the war itself, starting years before and extending past the surrender. There had been no rules of war in Kansas or Missouri, none that anyone paid any mind to.

When would he ever look at the ground again and not see blood?

After all the horror, he had been given twelve years of life he didn't deserve, eight of them lit by twin flames of hope, yet all the while shadowed by death, by a past that never left him.

And then that hope had been quenched when his wife and son died.

He wished they were, at least, in peace, that there really was a life up there in the sky with game running free and the breeze blowing fresh.

He wanted to believe that, but he'd stopped believing in any god when he was fifteen.

"Mr. Foster?"

Wade looked down at the boy standing there, the dog next to him. He wished like hell he could look at young Jeff Williams and not think of his own son.

"I'm really glad you're staying."

Wade unwound himself from the fence and set his feet on the ground. "I won't be staying long, boy."

"Long enough to teach Jake some tricks?"

No, something inside him screamed. He'd said he would stay, but he had broken his word before. Too many times. He'd said he would take care of Chivita. And there had been other promises, best not considered, best not remembered.

He looked away, across to the mountains; his mountains, his sanctuary. But they weren't anymore. Never again. They too were bloodied now.

"Mr. Foster?"

"You don't need me, boy," he said. "Just time and patience. That dog's a smart one. He wants to please. Just let him know what you expect of him."

"But we do need you," Jeff said earnestly. "Ma needs you."

"You need me like you need the pox," he said rudely. "My arm's no good. I'm useless now." He started limping away.

"You won't change your mind, will you, Mr. Foster?" Wade pretended not to hear the boy's plea.

He *had* changed his mind. A horse wasn't worth the torment and danger of staying. Two more days and he could walk. He could live off the land; he'd done it before. He could probably still rig a snare. There would be berries, plants. Mary Jo Williams could keep her horses, her bargain. They would be better off without him.

He would be better off without them.

Wade kept walking, leaving the bewildered boy far behind, hating himself for disappointing the boy. But now was better than later, before the boy started to care.

He wanted to keep walking forever, away from the ranch house with its welcoming light from the kerosene lamps, the homey curtains, and the acceptance based on ignorance. One step, then another.

He stumbled, fell, his leg folding up under him. He cursed softly, listening to the words drift on the breeze, futile and weak.

Just as he had been after he'd buried his family in Missouri.

For two years Wade looked for their killers. He even went up into Kansas, changing his name and joining a group of violent free-staters to learn the identity of those responsible for that raid on his parents' farm.

He'd learned to meld into the background, to keep his rage hidden behind bland eyes. That rage had continued to build as he failed to find the murderers. Then he began to consider all the free-staters his enemies. He had learned to smile at them, to drink with them, all the while planning their destruction. He had learned to be a liar, a thief, and a killer.

When he was seventeen, he met John Quantrill, whose hatred equaled his own, and he became a willing lieutenant in Quantrill's ruthless war against the North, often slipping back and forth across the border gathering information. But instinctively he avoided the worst of the violence. While others in the troop were burning farms and killing families in retaliation or to frighten others away, he restricted his activities to destroying railroad tracks and telegraph wires, and spying.

Until 1863. He had become friends with Bill Anderson, another officer whose father had also been killed by the Jayhawkers, and Wade had courted Anderson's sister, Josie, with the fervent passion of a twenty-year-old soldier. Josie was taken hostage by federal authorities in Kansas City, along with the sisters and mothers of other comrades—Cole Younger, Jesse and Frank James. Josie and the other women were killed when the warehouse in which they were imprisoned collapsed.

Wade's rage became white-hot fury that knew no boundaries, no control. He no longer restricted himself to military targets. The Federals made war on women and children, on civilians. Only one thing would stop them, sudden and sure retaliation. No longer merely scouting and spying, he joined Quantrill when he rode into Lawrence with four hundred men and destroyed the town.

He still saw the flames in his mind, the cries of

women as men were dragged out of homes and shot. His anger had spurred a blood lust that continued through the next year as he rode alongside Anderson, the most ruthless of the border guerrillas. It lasted until a day in September 1864, when Anderson raided a town called Centralia in northern Missouri . . .

Wade groaned as he remembered every hour of that day. It was burned into his heart and soul, like a brand he was condemned to carry the rest of his days.

He owed Mary Jo Williams, no matter what he'd claimed. He owed it to her to get out of her life, hers and the boy's, before he did irreparable damage.

He started back toward the house, damning the fates for showing him what he'd given up years ago. But he'd traded his soul to the devil during the war, and there was no reneging on the bargain.

Mary Jo Williams was sitting on a chair on the porch, obviously waiting for him. Moonlight shadowed her face. "You've changed your mind, haven't you? About staying?"

"It won't work, Mrs. Williams," he said bluntly. "That kiss proved it. Even if I thought I could help, and I don't think so, I'm no good for you or the boy. It's real plain to see he wants a father, and I have no interest in filling that role."

Her color paled, and her jaw jutted out stubbornly. Anger tinged her next words.

"You arrogant jackass. Believe me, Mr. Foster, you would be my last choice for that role. I just thought our needs—mine for some hands and yours for a horse—coincided." She paused, swallowing deeply as if trying to control her temper. "I also thought you might be a man of your word, if nothing else. I see I was mistaken there, too. If you think you can leave tomorrow, I'll pack you some food, and wish you—"

"Good riddance?"

"The sooner the better."

He nodded. "I'll sleep in the barn tonight."

She shrugged. "As you wish."

Her coldness was piercing, painful. Wade was surprised at how much he suddenly cared about what she thought of him. But it was better this way. Contempt was better than pity. Disappointment better than disgust if she ever discovered his past.

She went inside but returned shortly with bed linens and started down the steps.

He reached for her arm. "I'll do it," he said.

She stared at him for a long moment. He felt like shrinking under her steady perusal, but he only drew himself straight. "Thank you for—" He stopped, the words nearly choking him.

"Forget it, Mr. Foster." She turned around and went inside, closing the door firmly behind her.

Wade was not very successful at putting sheets on the cot. He'd barely managed to cover the lumpy mattress before falling on it.

The poor effort made him realize how totally helpless he was at the moment. He would have to learn to make better use of his left hand. He had known men during the war who could shoot with both hands, but he'd never seen the sense in it. Not until now.

Uncomfortable in the clothes of a dead lawman, he started to unbutton his trousers, then changed his mind. He'd felt so helpless without clothes earlier, and he didn't want to be put to that disadvantage again.

Though he'd made sure Mary Jo Williams wouldn't come here.

He thought about that kiss, and how it had made him strike out at her. He'd had no right using it against her. He wasn't sure why he'd taken her offer and her trust and thrown them in her face.

Wade closed his eyes, telling himself to get some rest. He needed it in order to strike out tomorrow.

But too many memories crowded his mind, keeping sleep at bay. Memories of the bright crimson of blood.

Jeff had heard the conversation outside and reached his own conclusion. Mr. Foster was leaving because of him.

He didn't know why he felt deserted again. Mr. Foster hadn't been here that long. Yet there had been something about him, something that had drawn Jeff to him.

It's real plain to see he needs a father and I have no interest in filling that role. The words kept echoing in Jeff's head.

He felt such shame and disappointment, he was sick to his stomach. Then came resentment and defiance. He didn't need Mr. Foster. He didn't need anyone. He would show both Mr. Foster and his mother that he didn't care if their guest left or not.

Jeff got out of bed, found his small box of treasures, and took it over to the window. Light from the bright moon spilled over the contents once he opened the top. A Texas Ranger badge that had belonged to his father. A gold Mexican coin. A belt buckle. A tintype of his mother and father taken when they were married. And finally a fishing lure that Ty had given him the last time they went fishing. It was better than worms for catching trout, Ty had said. The lure was hand carved and decorated with little feathers. "Odd-looking bug," Ty had told him, "but fish don't know any better."

Jeff missed Ty. He tried not to, but he did. He missed the other Rangers, too. One day . . . one day, he would be a Ranger, too. He wished the thought made him happier, but it didn't. He just felt unwanted. Well, he wouldn't be here in the morning to see the stranger leave. Mr. Foster obviously didn't want anything to do with him. No one did. Everyone kept leaving him. Everyone.

Jeff got back in bed. He would get up early, before dawn. He would take Jake and go fishing. He and Jake would be just fine on their own. They didn't need anyone.

The bed seemed big. Bigger than ever before, Mary Jo thought, after sleeping for a week on Jeff's small bed. And lonely. So lonely. Even though she'd changed the linens, the bed still smelled of the stranger. Or was it her imagination?

She couldn't sleep, couldn't stop thinking of how much she would miss having a man to do for, even a man who resented every single offering.

Finally she did manage to close her eyes. Even then she didn't rest very long. Dawn had just broken when she woke.

Mary Jo quickly dressed, leaving off the corset as she usually did these days. For a while, she had kept to her upbringing. A lady always wore a corset, no matter what. But it had seemed too foolish here on the ranch.

She checked Jeff's room. He was gone, but she expected that. He was probably out with Mr. Foster.

Mary Jo started a fire in the stove, then hurried outside. No one in sight. The door to the barn was open, and she hurried over to it.

Wade Foster was awkwardly sweeping out one of the stalls. He was dressed, and his hair was wet. He straightened up when he saw her. The rising sun had followed her inside and lit his face.

"You see," he said, looking at the mess at his feet. "I can't even rake out a stall." He was trying to prove a point, and Mary Jo was surprised he felt he needed an excuse for leaving.

"I didn't want you to rake out a stall," Mary Jo said. "Jeff can do that."

"I wanted to do something to repay—"

"That's not necessary," Mary Jo retorted sharply. "You've already made it clear you wish I'd just left you alone."

The shadow in his eyes seemed to grow deeper. "I'm sorry for that," he said.

She wasn't sure what "that" meant: his sullenness or her saving of his life. And she was too angry to want to know. She ignored his apology. "Have you seen Jeff?"

He shook his head. "Not this morning."

"Or Jake?"

"No," he said, puzzled.

"That's strange. He's always ready for breakfast. So is Jake." She looked toward his horse's stall. King Arthur was there, munching on oats Wade Foster had apparently provided.

A rush of apprehension flooded Mary Jo. Jeff had been so eager to spend time with Wade Foster, and she had expected him to be the man's shadow, particularly since he knew Wade Foster might leave soon. Worried, she hurried back to the house, to Jeff's room, barely aware that Wade Foster was behind her.

In Jeff's room, she found an open box on the table next to the bed. She assessed the contents, taking out the badge, holding it for a moment, then riffling through the other treasures. She knew them all. She had been there when Jeff had carefully packed them for the move to Colorado, his small hands touching each reverently.

Ty's lure. It was missing!

"Mary Jo?" The fact that he was using her given name for the first time registered dimly in her fear-clouded mind.

"The creek," she said, turning to him. "He's gone to the creek. It's been flooding. Yesterday the sheriff said a calf was swept away. Jeff can't swim. He knows he's not to go there alone when it's like this."

"Where along the creek?" Wade Foster's words were clipped.

"There's a place he likes . . . a quarter of a mile from here. We've picnicked there occasionally." She started running. It would take longer to saddle a horse than make it on foot. Fear was smothering her. Jeff was in danger. She sensed it.

She heard Wade Foster's steps behind her, but she paid them no mind. Only Jeff mattered.

Dear God, she couldn't lose her son.

·   ·   ·

Jeff realized quickly that the water was running too fast for good fishing. But the hurt and emptiness inside him had become sheer determination. A goal kept the sickness at bay, the sense of abandonment he'd felt each time he'd been left, starting with his father.

He walked down the bank, Jake following him, his tail like a flag in the wind, whipping back and forth with happiness at being outside.

The morning was golden and glorious, but Jeff barely noticed that fact. The hollowness inside was too overwhelming.

Jeff remembered Ty telling him to look for a quiet place. Trout loved the seduction of a shaded rock where insects buzzed and the water was still. But the water wasn't still anyplace. It was roaring down the sides of the bank, sometimes climbing over them. Branches, even a tree, were being swept down, tumbling over each other.

He looked around. There were no still, quiet holes, not today. But he found a branch anyway and used his knife to fashion a fishing pole, then tied his lure and hook on the string he'd brought. He set it down on the bank, then walked closer to the rushing water, regarding it with disgust.

Shuffling his feet, he tried to figure out what to do next. One of his boots tipped the pole, and it started to slide into the water. Jeff reached out to grab it. He couldn't lose the lure.

His foot slipped in the mud. He threw out his hands to grab something, but there was nothing but mud, and he felt himself sliding, sliding. And then he hit the cold water, swirling with it, going under it. Something hit his shoulder, and pain jolted through him.

A rock. He managed to grab hold of the rock that had stopped his progress downriver. He lifted his head up and drew deep breaths of air.

The currents kept pushing at him, and he held on for dear life. He looked around. He was in the middle of the rushing, overflowing creek. Jake was running back and forth along the bank, barking excitedly.

Jeff wasn't sure how long he could hold on. He tried to stand, but he couldn't get a sure footing. A branch stabbed him in the back, then was pulled into the main current.

"Jake," he yelled. The dog stopped moving, looking at him curiously. He put a paw in the water, then another, but then drew back as if aware he too would be swept away. He whined plaintively, then tried again. This time, the current caught him and threw him into the middle of the stream. Jake battled frantically to get to his master, but the current was too strong. The dog went past Jeff, far out of reach.

"Jake," Jeff screamed. And screamed again.

It was Wade Foster who heard him.

"This way," he told Mary Jo, his legs moving faster than he'd thought possible. He sped ahead of her through the sparse trees that lined the stream.

The voice came again, hoarse and desperate, and Wade felt the boy's despair reach into his gut. And then he saw Jeff, one hand barely holding onto a large jagged rock that divided the creek.

He stopped, grabbing hold of Mary Jo as she started for the water. She swung around, anger and fear pinching her face. "Let me go."

"Can you swim?" he asked, knowing that even if she could, she had little chance in that water.

She shook her head.

"Go back, get some rope. Fast," he said. "I'll try to reach him." She hesitated. "If you want to save him, do it. Neither of us can get him out alone."

She turned around and started running. Wade calculated in his head. Mary Jo should be back in fifteen minutes at the latest. Could the boy hold on that long?

He walked to the water's edge, picking his way carefully. "Jeff," he said. "Can you hold on?"

The boy nodded, but Wade saw the fear in his eyes. "Jake . . . Jake's gone," Jeff yelled, his voice trembling.

"I'll find him," Wade said. "You just hold on real tight. I know you can do it. Tell me if you feel yourself slipping." Wade forced confidence into his voice. That was the secret, Jeff believing in himself. Fear could panic him.

Wade moved closer to the edge of the stream, talking to Jeff, trying to keep him calm. "Can you touch the bottom?" he asked.

The boy shook his head. His face was white with strain. How long before the floodwater swept him away?

Then Wade heard Mary Jo's running footsteps. She was holding a circle of rope. "Tie one end to a tree," he said. "Make sure the knot is strong. Then give me the other end."

He walked to the bank, pulled off his boots, and stepped into the water.

"Mr. Foster." He turned around. Mary Jo was

clambering down the bank, her dress already muddy. "I should go. You're still too weak."

"You don't stand a chance," he said bluntly. "I do, even with this arm." She hesitated, and he knew he had to give her something to do. "Tear some cloth from your dress or petticoat and wrap it around your hands. You'll have to do some pulling on that rope."

She nodded. After she handed him the rope, he plunged into the water. The water tugged at him, and he fought with everything inside him to stay upright. He hadn't been able to save his son, but he could help Jeff.

He *would* save Jeff. He just had to get the rope to him. He couldn't throw it; Jeff might let go of the rock with both hands to catch it.

A dead log rolled into him, nearly knocking him down. He was able to keep his balance, but only a short distance from Jeff the bottom started to suck at his feet. Quicksand! He started to swim, using his left arm. But the water kept swinging him away from the rock, and Jeff.

He gripped the rope tightly and kicked as hard as he could toward the boy. Water washed over his face, blinding him. But then he felt Jeff's body, and his left hand went around the rock, anchoring him.

He rested for a moment, then struggled to plant his feet again. This time the bottom seemed solid.

"I'm going to put my arm around you," he told Jeff. "When I do and you feel secure, let go of the rock, then tie the rope around your waist. Can you do that?"

Jeff nodded.

"It will be all right," Wade said. "I'm not going to

let you go until the rope is around you, and then your mother will pull you out."

"I-I'm all right," Jeff stuttered. Wade smiled, hoping he appeared more confident than he felt. "Good boy." Some of the fear left Jeff's face.

Wade put his good arm around Jeff, holding him tightly. For a moment, Jeff still clung to the rock, but then suddenly let go. Wade felt the pull of his body as the current caught it. He tightened his grip.

"Take the rope from my hand," he said, "and tie it real tight around your waist." The boy did as he said. Even with his hands shaking, he managed to tie a good knot.

"Good boy," Wade said. "That's just fine."

He looked up toward Mary Jo. "Can you pull him up now?"

She nodded.

"Take hold of the rope, Jeff," Wade said softly. "Try to inch yourself up as your mother pulls."

Jeff nodded, and Wade carefully released him. The boy followed directions completely. His hands moved forward on the rope as it started to tug him through the water. At times, his body started spinning but then Jeff would straighten himself out. Finally, he reached the bank, and Mary Jo Foster was pulling her son up.

Now *he* had to get back, Wade thought wryly. Easier thought than done. Getting to Jeff had taken all the strength he possessed.

Mary Jo Foster threw the rope out to him. He reached for it, missed, and she reined it in. She was preparing to throw it again when a log hit his wounded shoulder and he doubled over in agony. The current caught him and started tossing him along. He struggled to stay above water, but it kept sucking him under. And it was hurtling him fast downstream, sending him crashing against rocks and flotsam.

He closed his eyes, too weak to fight back. Maybe he was getting his wish, after all.

9

Mary Jo looked on in horror. Jeff, who was still coughing up water, had glanced up just in time to see his rescuer go under.

"Mr. Foster!" he yelled. "Mr. Foster!"

"You stay here," Mary Jo said after making sure he was all right. "I'll go see if I can find him."

"I'll go, too."

"No. I can't worry about you both. Stay. Just please stay."

"Jake . . . ?"

"I'll look for Jake, too."

She was untying the rope, gathering it up to use again. *Please Lord,* she pleaded silently, *please give him another chance.*

She couldn't bear it if he died for her son.

She started running along the bank, her eyes darting over the rushing water, along the sides. She prayed that he had caught hold of a branch, a rock, anything. She saw something moving swiftly away, some small animal. Not Jake, thank God.

Her heart was frozen with dread. How much more death could Jeff take? How much more could *she* take? The thought moved her legs faster.

She stopped once, when the trees grew thick. And then she saw him, his blue shirt vivid against the dark muddy brown of the water. He was sprawled on a large branch hooked on a rock. She had to get him to shore before the branch dislodged and sent him back down the swollen waterway.

Mary Jo couldn't tell whether he was conscious or not, whether he was even alive. He wasn't moving. She remembered everything he had told her. She tied the rope around a tree and then around her waist.

Wade Foster wasn't as far toward the middle as her son had been. A few feet, that was all. But it was a few dangerous feet. There was no bank left, and the area bordering the water was slick with mud.

"Mr. Foster?" she yelled out as she approached. "Mr. Foster."

He didn't move.

"Dear Lord, let him live," she said, this time aloud. If He hadn't heard her last time, she wanted no mistake now.

She inched closer to him. "Mr. Foster. Wade!"

His eyes fluttered open. His face turned. He groaned.

"Wade!" she said again, then reached out and touched him. The current was strong here, very strong.

"Go," he whispered. "You might—"

"I have the rope around me. Can you take my arm and hold on?"

His eyes closed, and Mary Jo felt that suffocating fear again. She wished she had more strength. She couldn't pull him out on her own. She had to have his help.

"Ma?" She looked up and saw Jeff. He was clearly anxious, and she had no heart to scold him for disobeying her. An idea occurred to her. Could she send him after another rope?

"Run back to the house," she said, "and get another rope. And a horse." If she did manage to pull Wade Foster out of the water, they would need a horse to carry him back to the house.

Jeff nodded, then turned and ran. Air whooshed out of Mary Jo's lungs before she started talking again. "Mr. Foster—Wade—don't let Jeff think you died for him. Don't do that, please. It will kill him, just as if he had drowned today. Please help me. You have to help me."

His eyes opened again, slowly, as if against his will. As if he were drawing on some superhuman reserve.

"Can you take my hand?" she said. "Give me your left hand."

She took one hand off the rope and found his, hoping he had the strength and consciousness to clasp it. "You can do it," she kept saying. "You can do it for Jeff. Not for yourself. For Jeff. Jake is gone. You matter to Jeff. He can't lose everything. Not again. Please . . ."

His left hand took hers. There wasn't much strength in it, but then the fingers seemed to tighten.

"Just a few feet, Mr. Foster. Just two or three steps, and we'll be safe. Can you touch the ground?"

She could. She knew *he* could. If he had any strength left in that body, in his legs. Dear Lord, what a beating that body had taken.

"You can have that horse, Mr. Foster. You can ride out tomorrow if you want. You just have to take a step or two." She felt hot tears mix with the muddy water on her cheek. "Please, Wade. Please help me." His name came easily to her lips now.

His hand tightened around hers. Agony was etched in his face, but his eyes were focusing. Blood from a reopened wound mixed with the dark brown of the water.

"One step, Wade. Just one." Slowly, he pulled away from the branch holding him, and again she felt the tug of the current. Her hand tightened around his. She was strong, but she wished herself ten times stronger. She was pummeled and battered by the water and had to fight to keep her footing. With one hand on the rope and the other clasping his, she took a step. She heard his labored breathing behind her, the low curse that she knew was a disguised moan.

But he was moving with her. One step. Another. Then she felt the ground, but it was so slippery, it was almost worse than the water. One misstep, and they both would go tumbling back into the water.

Another step. She was on solid ground. Then Wade. Dry ground. He collapsed there.

Mary Jo said a prayer of thanksgiving as she dropped next to him.

His eyes had closed again. The sling that held his wounded arm to his shoulder was dark with dirty water and blood. Mary Jo hastily amended her prayer to make one more request. "Protect him," she pleaded.

"He saved Jeff. He's a good man. I know he is, no matter what he says."

She tore a piece of cloth from her petticoat and wrung it out, then wiped the water from his face, her fingers hesitating along the new beard forming on his cheeks. She then gently wiped the creases around his eyes.

Mary Jo didn't know what to do. She was reluctant to try to bring him back to consciousness. Dear God, how he must hurt. Just as he had days ago. But she hadn't known him then, hadn't felt so . . . confused by him. Then, he had not yet risked his life for her son's.

She had hurt then for him, a stranger, as she would have hurt for any wounded thing. But now the hurt ran so much deeper.

She rubbed her own face with the rag, now encrusted with mud and sweat, then with her hand took a swipe at her eyes. This was no time to become maudlin. She needed to think.

Jeff would be back any moment with his horse. Somehow they would have to get Wade Foster onto its back. It had been difficult enough to get him on the wagon. And now the arm wound had been opened, and exposed to the muddy water.

Exhausted from her physical efforts, from the fear she'd felt for both her son and the stranger who had become so important to her, she slumped beside him, taking his good hand in hers and just holding it.

Forcing life into him.

She heard Jeff's approach, his shout. Then he was on the ground next to her. He looked up. "He's not . . . ?"

Mary Jo shook her head. "No," she whispered. *Not yet.* "We have to get him back to the house."

Jeff looked up at her, wonder widening his eyes. "He saved my life, didn't he?"

"I think he did, love."

"He said—"

Mary Jo waited for him to continue.

But Jeff clamped his lips tight as if he regretted speaking. "Nothing."

Mary Jo knew it wasn't nothing, but now was not the time to discuss it. They had to get Wade Foster back to the house, get his wound cleaned out again. Maybe she should send Jeff for the doctor this time.

She would never forgive herself if their stranger died.

Mary Jo thought about bringing the wagon here, but there were too many trees. He would still have to walk a certain distance to reach it, and she wasn't at all sure he could do that. If only he could get on the horse. "Mr. Foster," she said again.

He moved slightly, and her heart jumped.

"Mr. Foster . . ."

His eyes opened reluctantly. He glared at her, and she suddenly felt wonderful. He was alive enough to glare! She knew she was smiling foolishly. His glare deepened.

"Can you help us get you on a horse?"

"You just can't let things be, can you?" he grunted.

"No," she said happily.

He sighed in resignation and tried to move. She watched him bite back a curse. His face, streaked with dirt, went tense and white, so white she felt her own body stiffen. His hand was still clutching hers and it squeezed her fingers so tightly she almost screamed herself.

After a moment, his body relaxed. "I can make it," he said.

And she knew he would.

Dammit. It was one thing to owe a woman when she'd helped him as she would help any stray dog. It was an entirely different matter when she risked her life for him.

In the two days that followed the near drowning, Wade didn't mention her desperate offer of a horse, though he remembered it very well. Nor did she remind him of it. He took some satisfaction in the fact that she hedged her honor some.

He didn't believe the debt had been settled when he'd helped young Jeff. It would have been settled had she not interfered again.

Wade didn't like thinking about those days after his re-injury. He still wasn't quite sure how he got on the horse. He just knew that Mary Jo Williams and the kid prodded and poked and pulled until he did. They just plain weren't going to let him die, even if they had to kill him to prevent it.

And then she stripped him of his clothes again, and there was damn little he could do about it. He did, though, insist on using the cot in the barn. It had been the only battle he'd won.

The first two days had been little more than a blur of pain. The wound in his arm had reopened, and she had resewn it and poured copious amounts of sulfur into it. She'd done the same with his leg. On the third day, his natural resiliency, or maybe Mrs. William's cooking, took over, and he had to start considering the future again. Or lack of one.

Or at least his next step. If he had choices.

He did, he kept telling himself. He had several choices; foremost was getting the hell out of here. He even had a horse now . . . if he was bastard enough to take her up on an offer she made while trying to save his sorry hide.

Ethics hadn't bothered him in a very long time, but Mary Jo Williams and Jeff were a different matter altogether. They had helped him without thought of consequences, even when they knew he had killed. No one did that. No one in his experience had ever done what this small family had done for him. Even the Utes. They had taken him in after he had saved a chief's son.

The parallels suddenly struck him. The Utes had taken him to repay a debt. He could do no less now.

Mary Jo Williams wanted little enough. Stay long enough to hire some responsible men for her and get a horse in repayment. He would feel a hell of a lot better taking a horse that way. He had damn little to feel good about now.

If he was discovered, if someone recognized Brad Allen, well, hell, then he would get caught. He'd already lived years longer than he had any right to expect.

He worked at getting well with new purpose. The sooner he got the ranch going, the sooner he could leave and find a place in the mountains to nurse his wounds.

Jeff mourned Jake quietly. He tried not to show his mother how much he cared. He tried to be a man.

But guilt wouldn't let him be. Mr. Foster was al-most killed because of him. And Jake—Jake was dead because of Jeff's disobedience. How many times had his mother warned him about going to the creek alone?

He couldn't even bear to look at Mr. Foster. He couldn't bear to see the censure or blame in his face. He kept hearing Mr. Foster's words that night, over and over again. *I have no interest in filling that role.* Now, after what happened, Mr. Foster would have even less reason to like him.

When his mother had asked him whether he wanted to take over some soup, Jeff had said no, and his mother had taken one look at his face and gone herself.

He went about his chores woodenly, trying to do his mother's too, so she could spend more time nurs-ing their stranger back to life.

And he missed Jake. He missed him terribly. He used to tell Jake everything, all he couldn't tell his mother. Jake had been his only friend after leaving the Ranger station. Jeff bit down on his lip to keep from crying. Men didn't cry, he reminded himself.

He had tried to look for Jake, but he didn't have much time now. There had simply been too much to do. Taking care of the stock, milking their cow, feeding the chickens, helping with the cooking and cleaning chores. But at evening time, he would take his horse and go up and down the banks, calling for Jake.

It had been three days since the dog disappeared. He knew it was fruitless to continue, but he decided to try one more time. He entered the barn, trying to avoid the closed door to the room Mr. Foster occupied.

But now it was open, and though he tried to sneak by, he heard the man's voice.

"Jeff?"

Jeff stopped in his tracks. He thought about pretending not to hear. He thought about it very seriously. But he knew he couldn't. If he was ever to be a man, he had to face up to the consequences of his actions. He turned and reluctantly, shyly, entered the small room.

Mr. Foster was sitting up on the cot, his arm and chest swathed in bandages. He was clean-shaven, and Jeff guessed his mother had shaved him earlier.

He shifted his weight from foot to foot. "I'm sorry, Mr. Foster . . . about causing so much trouble."

Mr. Foster's mouth was twisted into a half smile. "Are you all right now?"

Jeff was struck dumb with shame. He should have asked that. He should have done it two days ago. He should have come in then and apologized and thanked Mr. Foster, but he'd been too . . . embarrassed. He nodded.

"That's all that's important."

"But you were . . . hurt again."

The hard face relaxed ever so slightly. "Nothing worse than a number of other times," Mr. Foster said, "and for a far better reason."

"Jake—"

"I know," Mr. Foster said. "Your mother told me. I'm sorry."

Jeff couldn't stop himself. He felt a tear running down his face. "It's all my fault."

A muscle flexed in Mr. Foster's cheek. "Jeff, you were being a boy. Bad things happen sometimes. You learn from them. But don't take all the blame yourself. It was an accident."

"But Ma told me—"

"There's never been a boy yet who always did what his mother told him," Mr. Foster said.

"Did you ever . . . ?"

He nodded, much to Jeff's surprise.

Jeff didn't have the nerve to ask any additional questions. "I'm glad you're better," he said shyly instead.

Mr. Foster smiled again, some of the warmth back. "I'm glad to see you. I was worried about you."

Jeff hesitated. "I didn't want to bother you."

"You don't bother me."

"But you said—"

Mr. Foster's brows knitted together. "I said what?"

"That night . . . you were going to leave, I heard you say—" Jeff couldn't force any additional words from his mouth, but he could see Mr. Foster was trying to remember. Then the man's eyes glittered with understanding.

"My God, is that why you left so early in the morning? So you wouldn't have to see—"

Jeff shifted his weight again nervously. He hadn't wanted Mr. Foster to think he had spied on him.

But Jeff's very silence seemed to answer Mr. Foster's question for him, and Jeff heard a long, quiet curse. Then the man's mouth snapped shut as if remembering where he was.

"That had nothing to do with you, Jeff," the man said. "I didn't mean that I don't like you. It's just that I'm poison for people like you and your mother. My God, it was never you. It was me. I was afraid I might bring harm to you and your ma."

Jeff stood a little taller, some of the bleakness leaving him. Still, his eyes must have revealed a little doubt, because Mr. Foster continued after a moment, his voice low and harsh. "You remind me some of my own son. I . . . let him down. I can't do that again."

Jeff swallowed hard, a lump thick in his throat. He knew Mr. Foster was a private kind of man. He knew instinctively it cost him dearly to say what he just did. "You saved my life," he finally said.

Mr. Foster's lips quirked up in a crooked smile. "You wouldn't have been there if you hadn't heard me say something stupid. Let's call it even."

Jeff shook his head. "No, I can't do that. Pa taught me—"

The smile disappeared from Mr. Foster's face. "Friends," he said softly, "don't ever owe each other anything."

Jeff stood still for a moment, then broke into a wide grin and nodded. "I'm going to go look for Jake. Maybe he was just hurt, like you."

"Maybe," Mr. Foster said. Jeff liked the fact he didn't discourage him, didn't say it was useless. Mr. Foster seemed to know he had to do it, regardless.

"I'll see you later," Jeff said hopefully.

Mr. Foster nodded.

"I can tell you some Texas Rangers stories."

Something flickered in Mr. Foster's eyes, but he merely nodded again. "You do that, boy."

Jeff grinned again, then whirled out the door. He saddled King Arthur and led him outside the barn. He was just about to mount when he heard a weak bark. His heart jumped. He knew that bark. He scanned the rolling hills. He thought he saw something black moving among the tall grass.

Another bark.

"Jake!" he shouted. "Jake." He disregarded the horse and started running.

Mary Jo heard Jeff's shout.

It can't be. It's been too long. But hope darted through her just the same. Jeff had been so quiet the last few days. She knew he was holding in his grief, and it had nearly killed her. So many losses for a boy.

She went out on the porch and watched Jeff run toward the high grass beyond the plowed ground.

Please let it be Jake, she thought. Please God, answer one more prayer.

Then she heard the faint bark. She looked toward the sound, then she heard another noise near the barn and she turned around. Wade Foster was standing there, his eyes following Jeff. His chest was bare, his arm in a sling, and he was wearing another pair of her husband's trousers she'd provided him. He was holding King Arthur's reins as he watched Jeff stoop down next to a black form. Wade Foster looked at her, a grin on his face. He looked years younger. And handsome. Incredibly handsome.

He tied the horse's reins to the fence and started limping toward Jeff. He was moving slowly, but determinedly. Mary Jo started after him, walking swiftly until she caught up with him.

They reached Jeff. He had dropped to the ground and his arms were around a thin, dirty, bloody animal that was gingerly holding one front paw up in the air as his tongue licked Jeff's face.

Jeff looked up at them, his face beaming. "He came back."

"So he did, boy," Wade Foster said. "You were right not to give up."

"He's hurt, though."

"Nothing we can't fix," Mr. Foster said.

Wade Foster looked at Mary Jo with pleasure in his face, pleasure for her son, and Mary Jo felt tears in her eyes again.

She had already acknowledged her attraction to Wade Foster. But now, at this moment, she realized with bittersweet anguish, she was also losing her heart. Losing it to someone she knew would break it.

10

Jake had cuts, bruises, and probably a broken leg, Mary Jo thought as she dropped to the ground beside Jeff. He looked dehydrated and hungry, but then he was always hungry. His coat was matted, his breathing labored, but he growled in greeting and his tail thumped, though not as energetically as usual.

"What happened to you, Jake?" she asked, wondering whether they would ever know. But it really didn't matter. He was home.

She looked at Jake's leg, felt it, heard Jake's whining objection. "I think it's broken," she said. "I don't know how he got from wherever he's been."

"Can we put a splint on it, like on Mr. Foster?" Jeff asked.

Mary Jo smiled, and Wade felt bathed in its light.

"Of course we can," she said. "He got here on three legs, didn't he?"

She ran her hand along his thick, dirty fur, and found a bloody wound. She recognized it immediately. "He's been shot." She looked toward Jeff. "Maybe that's why he didn't answer you when you went looking for him. Maybe he was unconscious."

"Who would shoot Jake?" Jeff looked up at Wade appealingly.

"He does look a little like a wolf," Wade said. "If someone didn't know he was a pet . . ."

"Everyone around here knows Jake," Mary Jo said. "He goes to town with us."

"A drifter, then," Wade said.

But Mary Jo wasn't satisfied. Most of the ranchers around here had dogs. None of them would shoot someone's dog, not unless it was going after stock. And Jake loved everyone, nearly everyone, and most other critters. Now, though, the why wasn't important. Taking care of Jake was.

She looked at Jake. He had lain down. She wished she could pick him up, but he was a big dog, too large for her to carry all the way to the house without possibly injuring him more.

Mary Jo rubbed under his chin. "Can you walk home, Jake?" His tail wagged slowly in assent, and he stood, putting his weight on three legs.

She looked toward Wade, noticed his frustration, and she knew it was because he couldn't help more. But his frown smoothed out as he looked at Jeff. "He'll make it," he said. "He has a strong heart."

So do you, she wanted to say, but held her tongue.

Jeff walked next to Jake, his hand buried in the dog's fur as the animal limped along on three legs.

Mary Jo looked at them, a lump in her throat. Jeff was still bruised from his own struggle in the water, and Wade Foster was swathed in bandages. Her ranch was fast becoming a hospital.

Her gaze turned upward and met Wade's, and his mouth quirked in that half smile that revealed no emotion. He was a puzzle, and Mary Jo reminded herself that she wouldn't have time to sort him out completely. *He won't be here long enough. Remember that. Don't forget. Don't let Jeff forget.*

Yet Jeff was looking back up at their stranger with eyes that shone with admiration. She felt a cold chill go up and down her back. They reached the porch, and Wade Foster hesitated, as if trying to decide whether he should stay.

Mary Jo knew he must be hurting. She was surprised he'd lasted on his feet this long, but she didn't want him to retreat back into the loneliness of the bare room in the barn. Not now. Jake returning was a triumph for them all. "I think we need to wash Jake, clean that wound of his. Maybe you can help," she said to Wade Foster, more tentatively than she'd intended. "He likes you. He might stay still for you. You can sit there with him."

He nodded curtly, his eyes wary again. Mary Jo wondered whether she had imagined that brief pleasure in his eyes just minutes earlier.

Wade sat, and Jake settled down awkwardly between him and Jeff, licking his injured leg and whining softly. Mary Jo went to the pump in the kitchen and filled a pan with water, then fired the stove. As the water heated, she went to the door and looked out.

Jeff's arms were around Jake's neck again, his head buried in the dog's fur. Mary Jo shook her head, but had no heart to say anything. Wade Foster was also watching them, his head bent at an angle where she could see his expression. A small smile, a hint of wistfulness, that odd vulnerability that had stabbed her several times previously. His face was naked with a longing she sensed was for his own son. He leaned over, placed his left hand on Jeff's smaller one reassuringly, and said something Mary Jo couldn't hear. She did, however, see Jeff's grateful smile.

She moved from the door and waited until the water had heated. She found a piece of cloth and tucked it in the pan with some soap and went outside. She thought wryly that she was becoming very good at nursing.

She set the pan down on the porch and turned to Jeff. "Can you find me a nice strong branch and whittle a splint for Jake?"

He nodded but left only reluctantly, his face turning frequently back to Jake as if the dog might disappear once more. Mary Jo bent her head to study the bullet wound along Jake's neck. "Thank you for helping," she told Wade.

Wade didn't say anything, just ran his hands down the dog's back, calming him. Jake's body twitched as Mary Jo's hands found the bullet wound again, cut the hair away and washed it. She flinched as the dog's body shuddered, but Jake obviously knew she was trying to help. "I could kill whoever did this," she muttered to herself.

"You don't think it was an accident?"

She shook her head. "I don't know. As I said, people around here know Jake. And he wouldn't attack anyone, not without reason." She looked up at him anxiously. "It couldn't be anyone after . . . ?"

He shook his head. "I don't think so. That . . . man they found was the last of three."

Mary Jo swallowed hard. "Jeff has lost so much . . ."

"He's a strong kid," Wade said. "He'll do all right."

"He felt so . . . guilty."

Wade hesitated a moment, then looked into her eyes. "He heard what we said that night before he went to the creek. He thought I . . . didn't like him. I think that's why he disappeared that morning." He turned away from her.

Mary Jo heard the raw pain in his voice. "Is that why he was avoiding you?"

"Partly. And partly what you said. Guilt." His hand held Jake as another shudder rippled through the dog's body when Mary Jo applied sulfur to the wound. Damn, but he knew how the dog felt. "Guilt," he said, "can eat you up inside."

He was talking more than he had since she'd met him. Warning her in a mild, nonjudgmental way. Revealing something of himself to help her son.

"I know," she said. Her eyes met his. "And I don't want guilt to make you stay if you don't want to."

"You think you read me pretty good, lady."

"No," she said. "Not good at all."

"I'll stay long enough to hire you some men. But not because of guilt. I'm not twelve. I got over guilt long ago," he added roughly as if sorry he'd said anything at all. "I just figure I need a horse."

She nodded, not reminding him that she'd already offered him one. She turned all her attention back to Jake, washing the thick fur with what remained of the water. Then Jeff was back, holding a small but sturdy splint.

Wade Foster stayed long enough to keep the dog still as she and Jeff tied the splint to Jake's leg. After they were finished, Wade rose, his own broken arm held in a sling. He regarded Jake sympathetically for a moment, then turned and limped back toward the barn.

"Why is Mr. Foster leaving?"

"I expect he needs rest just like Jake does," she said softly. "He shouldn't even have left that bed." But it wasn't weakness that had forced him back to his lonely place in the barn. Mary Jo knew that. He had been angry he'd revealed so much about himself.

"He sure was pleased about Jake, wasn't he?" Jeff said, and Mary Jo heard that rough need for a man's attention in his voice. Her heart pounded with anguish for him, and not a little bit of fear. A few words had shattered him a few days earlier, had made him do something he ordinarily would never have done. Did she dare risk more exposure to Wade Foster, for Jeff's sake? For her own?

But she was so grateful for his happy grin after the past three days of gloom. "Yep," she agreed. "I think he was."

"He's going to stay, isn't he?"

"For a little while."

Jeff's smile grew wider. "I knew it."

"Don't get to liking him too much, Jeff. He will be leaving before long. Those mountains are his home."

"We made a new home," Jeff pointed out.

"That's different."

"How?"

Mary Jo shook her head. "Why" and "how" were

Jeff's two favorite words, and she was only too good at painting herself into a corner. "It just is," she said. "Now let's get Jake fed."

Jeff frowned, but for once Jake was on her side. His tail thumped frantically at the words "Jake" and "fed."

Jeff reluctantly got to his feet to fill Jake's dish and water bowl, but his eyes told her he wasn't yet satisfied with her smugly inadequate motherly explanation.

But Mary Jo couldn't explain any better. She couldn't tell him that his Wade Foster had killed three men in cold blood, nor that he clearly had even worse secrets in his past, secrets he believed would catch up with him someday. He wasn't afraid they would. She suspected he was afraid of very little. He was simply waiting for the day.

Everyone who ever relied on me is dead. He'd said the words with so much anger. So much hopelessness. She had seldom heard those two emotions combined, especially with such explosive poignancy. Two more words that didn't exactly fit. Except with him.

I'm damned good at killing. One of the best, they used to say. She was well acquainted with men who killed. She knew them. She had been married to one, nearly married to a second. She had lived with them. She knew what killing did to them, the way they blocked away emotions, even when they killed for what they considered a righteous cause. From what Wade Foster had said, what he'd hinted at, she doubted that he considered all his transgressions righteous. He was a haunted man who doubted his worth, both as a man and as a human being.

He was, quite simply, the last thing she and Jeff needed in their lives.

A few weeks. A month. Then he would be a memory.

Wade Foster sat down on the cot in the barn. The walls were closing in on him, like a prison would, he thought. He tried to flex the fingers on his right hand, willing them to do as he instructed, feeling the pain as his injured arm strove to obey. Nothing.

He leaned back against the wall, exhausted from the effort, from the pain it had stoked. He tried again, welcoming the waves of agony that came with the attempt. He had to fill his mind with something other than the woman, the boy, and the dog.

He couldn't afford to feel again.

But he did. The depth of the feeling astounded him. He had fought to keep from touching the boy in shared jubilation, from smiling in companionship with the woman at the return of Jake. He had no right to do either. This wasn't his family.

He kept seeing them, though, in his mind's eye. Mary Jo Williams. So damned capable, so . . . composed. Never any fuss or feathers, no matter what happened. Not when she found a near dead man near her house, not when he'd admitted killing in cold blood, not when she lied to a posse, not when her son nearly drowned.

It must really have stuck in her craw when she couldn't find men to work for her. She was probably ten times as smart and capable as those who felt they couldn't work for a woman. And pretty. Too damn pretty when that auburn hair was burnished by the sun, and those green eyes flashed sparks.

He had no business thinking that way. He'd had

no business kissing her, tasting her. Getting her in his blood. He'd meant to scare her off, to show her he was both unscrupulous and untrustworthy. It had backfired. It definitely had backfired. He had ignited flames that were consuming him now.

Wade tried to think of Chivita, and the tranquillity of the mountains. He'd thought he had peace then. And he had, of a sort. His son had been a gift he'd never expected, Chivita's quiet devotion and acceptance of him a balm to his wounds. Some of the nightmares had disappeared.

Don't think of them. Don't think of Drew. But the claws were in him now, memories like talons of a hawk. He buried his head in his good hand and felt his body shudder.

Mary Jo had just rebandaged her human patient's arm when Jeff came running. "The sheriff's riding in."

Mary Jo straightened. "Are you ready?"

Wade Foster's gaze met hers. She had already told him what she had told the sheriff. He was Wade Smith, the brother of the man who'd left his ranch to her. He'd been hurt in a railroad accident, and would be recuperating here while he helped her with his brother's ranch. "Are you sure you want to do this? If someone finds out, you could be in trouble, too."

"If I don't, I might lose the ranch." There was not the slightest hesitation in her voice. She had gone over the problem too many times, had kept reaching the same conclusion.

"I don't know a damn thing about railroads." That wasn't true. He knew something about wrecking them.

"I don't think he'll pry too much. He has no reason to. He knows Ty was a Ranger, and so was Jeff's father."

"And you would be the last person to protect a killer?"

He'd lowered his voice so it was audible only to her, not to Jeff who had retreated back into the barn to watch the sheriff's progress.

"Yes," she said defiantly, knowing he was baiting her again. He seemed to get some satisfaction out of doing that.

"What about Jeff?"

"He understands."

"I wish I did."

"Did what?"

"Understand," he answered, "why you're protecting me."

"I explained that. I need you."

His eyes challenged her until they heard another voice outside the barn.

Mary Jo retreated under that steady gaze. She knew why he kept questioning her. He still didn't think he had anything to offer her. Even saving Jeff's life hadn't changed his thinking. The electricity that sparked so dangerously between them didn't help, either.

But then she didn't have any more time to think. A tall, rangy man was walking in the door, his hat in his hand. He nodded to her, but then his gaze went quickly to Wade.

"I'm Matt Sinclair," he said, "the sheriff in this county. Jeff told me you'd arrived." His dark eyes were cautious as they obviously and quite thoroughly took measure of Wade.

And he was no fool. Wade sensed that immediately. "Wade Smith," he said. "My brother asked me to look out for Mrs. Williams if anything happened to him." He paused and looked down at his arm in the sling. "It turns out she's been kind enough to look after me."

Mary Jo listened to the calm, even lazy tone. His eyes never wavered, never dropped from the hard gaze of the sheriff, who continued to study him intensely.

"When did you get here?"

Mary Jo answered for him. "A few days ago. In time to save Jeff from the creek. I'm afraid he hurt his arm again."

Matt Sinclair turned to her. "What happened?"

"Jeff went fishing, lost his footing, and went into the creek. If it hadn't been for Mr. Smith . . ."

The sheriff tensed, but his gaze went back to Wade, settling there, studying every feature.

Is anyone after you?

I expect so.

Mary Jo prayed there weren't any posters, and then wondered at herself. She looked at Jeff's face, staring up at her so earnestly. She flinched at the thought of how many lies they now shared. Wade shifted his weight, and she wondered if any of her thoughts were reflected in her face. If so, his own didn't change expression.

Just then, the sheriff's glance shifted down to Jeff, softened slightly. "You all right, Jeff?"

Jeff nodded. "Jake got hurt, though. The creek took him downstream, and then someone shot him."

Matt Sinclair swore before he caught himself, then apologized. "Begging your pardon, Mrs. Williams, but there's been several heifers slaughtered too, about four miles downstream. We found the remains. I've been wondering whether it had anything to do with that dead man we found. Still no strangers around?"

Mary Jo shook her head no. "Just Wade, and he's not a stranger. And Jake's going to be all right. I just couldn't understand why anyone would shoot him."

"I don't think anyone who belongs around here would." The sheriff's eyes turned back to Wade, and Mary Jo wondered whether she'd been wise to mention him again. But he just nodded. "Glad to see you have a man around for protection."

"Perhaps if you hear of anyone looking for a job . . . ?" Mary Jo asked.

"I'll send them out here. Mr. Smith got any experience ranching?"

"Some," Wade said, moving a few paces closer to Mary Jo. Mary Jo saw the sheriff's eyes narrow slightly and a frown turn down the side of his mouth.

Matt Sinclair turned to leave. "I just stopped to see if there was anything I could do to help. You'll let me know?" The question was directed at Mary Jo.

She felt her face flush. There was antipathy between the two men. She knew the sheriff had been interested in her, and now he sensed a threat. Wade's face was closed, expressionless, but she had an odd, fleeting impression of a buck shaking his antlers in warning. Which was ridiculous. Their arrangement was purely business. She kept telling herself that.

"Yes," she finally said. "And thank you."

"And keep your eyes open for strangers," he warned. "I don't like some of the things going on around here." He turned toward Wade. "I haven't seen you before, have I? You look a little familiar."

Wade shook his head. "I come from up north. Never been south of Denver."

Matt Sinclair shrugged. "My mistake." But his gaze lingered on Wade's face as if he were memorizing it. "Jeff," he acknowledged. "Glad your little swim didn't do any lasting damage."

"Thanks to Mr.—" Jeff stopped suddenly.

"Smith," the sheriff said. "Real easy name to remember."

"He looks just like his brother," Mary Jo said. "Sometimes Jeff slips and calls him Ty. He has a hard time getting used to saying 'Mr. Smith'."

The sheriff just nodded and put his hat back on as he started toward the door. He turned suddenly, his gaze hidden by the brim of his hat, but Mary Jo felt as if it were boring into her. Then he took two fingers and touched the brim of his hat in salute. "Don't forget, Mrs. Williams, you have any trouble, see any strangers, you send for me."

Mary Jo nodded. "Thank you."

He went through the door and the three of them stood waiting until they heard hoofbeats. Mary Jo breathed again.

Jeff looked stricken. "I almost—"

"But you didn't," Wade said gently. "You did real good. Why don't you go see about Jake?"

Jeff hesitated as if he sensed there was a reason for the request, there was something he wasn't supposed to hear.

"Go on," Mary Jo urged. They had put Jake in Jeff's room and closed the door, so he wouldn't be tempted to use his injured leg, or roll in the dirt. The dog must be going crazy now, after hearing the hoofbeats; he always welcomed guests.

"You don't want me to know something," Jeff accused.

"Jeff." Mary Jo's voice held an authority she seldom used, and Jeff's rebellion folded. He went to the door, looked back in one last mute appeal, and then disappeared.

There was silence for a moment. "He's sweet on you," Wade finally said. "He doesn't trust me."

"You said once there might be posters on you?"

"Not recent ones, not in the last ten to twelve years."

"What were the posters for?"

Wade's face tensed. "Shouldn't you have asked these questions earlier?"

"I want to know if there's any chance he might find them."

"Could be, if someone kept one, but I looked a lot different then." He didn't elaborate, even though she looked at him with that same challenging, questioning look.

"You aren't going to tell me, are you?"

"No," he said softly. "But I'll leave if you want."

"You would like that just fine, wouldn't you?" she replied angrily.

"Ask me to leave," he invited her. They were no more than inches apart, and the heat between them could have ignited the barn.

Her hand reached up and touched his cheek. She had shaved him this morning, and his skin was still smooth. She remembered how rough it felt earlier.

His body shuddered at her touch and then his good arm went around her, bringing her close to him, so close she could hear the thunder of his heart. "You're playing with fire, Mrs. Williams," he whispered in her ear.

She couldn't think of a single retort. She was only

too aware of that particular fire, of the blazes that enveloped both of them.

His eyes closed, and then with a heavy sigh, he leaned down and his lips brushed hers. Not with the rough anger of several nights earlier, but with a sweet, lost wistfulness that grabbed her in its spell. Her mouth opened to him, seeking, comforting, wanting comfort of her own.

Buried in the exquisite poignancy of his touch, of his mouth on hers, she wasn't prepared for the sudden, raw violence as his lips hardened against hers. His arm pulled her so tight against him that she felt every muscle of his body, including the swelling, hardening member that reached out toward her, startling tremors in the core of her, tremors that spread a fiery craving throughout her body. A craving she'd never experienced before, not like this. Not so fierce and needy. Not so uncontrollable.

Even through their clothes, her body played with his, making movements that shocked and shamed her. It was inviting him, seducing him, just as his was seducing hers. Still, she couldn't seem to stop.

His tongue invaded her mouth, just as his body was blatantly seeking hers. A moan ripped from his throat, and then he seemed to tear himself away with such violence that she stumbled back, almost falling.

But any hurt she might have felt was lost as she saw the screaming agony in eyes usually so closed to emotion. He turned away from her, but she saw the bunched muscles in the shoulders, heard the labored breathing. She didn't move, couldn't move. She wanted to go to him. She wanted to touch him.

She didn't. She knew it was the last thing in the world he needed. She didn't know the cause of those demons in him, but she knew they were eating him alive, and there wasn't anything she could do.

Mary Jo swallowed hard against her own craving, her own desire, her own need to touch and comfort him. Instead, she backed away, out the door, closing it behind her with a small click. Then she leaned against a wall, and buried her head in her hands, wishing with all that was holy that she could absorb a portion of his pain.

11

Wade damned himself for being a fool and a bastard.

But Mary Jo Williams had looked so appealing, so pretty, yet so resolute. That strength and courage to do what she thought had to be done had attracted him from the very first.

Why in God's name hadn't he learned his lesson from the first kiss he inflicted on her? Why had he ignored that lesson, succumbed to that brightness that always enveloped them when they were together?

When all he had to offer was darkness?

Perhaps he should have told her everything. That would take away some of the light. All of it.

Right now, she thought he'd killed to avenge his wife and son. She could accept that. He knew she couldn't accept the rest of it. No decent person could.

He slammed his fist against the wall. Why in the hell couldn't he stay away from her?

But he'd made her a promise, made Jeff one. Of all his sins, breaking promises hadn't been one of them. Nor not paying debts.

It was dangerous for him to stay. He'd seen the speculation in the sheriff's eyes, the recognition of what he was, if not who he was. He also sensed the sheriff's own interest in Mary Jo, and that would only increase his suspicions. He would bet all he had that the good sheriff had gone straight back to his office and started looking through wanted posters.

Wade doubted he would discover anything. Too many years had passed. But the sheriff was the kind who might start sending out inquiries, who might keep looking, who might somehow link the recently discovered murdered man with a newcomer. He might just check Wade Smith's credentials, or lack of them. Wade wondered exactly how long he had.

He sure as hell didn't know that much about running a ranch. But he did know about farming and horses, and some about cattle. He had helped bring a herd up to the Utes last year. He knew exactly how ornery and difficult beeves could be.

And he knew men. Hard experience had taught him to tell the good from the bad, the honest from the cheats.

If he could find a few good, reliable ranch hands, he could leave with a clear conscience—in this matter, anyway. And that sure as hell would be something.

That meant, though, he had to stay away from the woman. And the boy, too.

.   .   .

Wade drove into Last Chance with Mary Jo and Jeff a day later. It was fifteen miles northwest, which meant an all-day expedition by wagon. They left at dawn. It would be evening before they returned.

Wade was handling the reins. Mary Jo had given them to him without comment before climbing up on the buckboard, and Wade had taken them. He was damned if he would let her see any uncertainty about handling them with one arm. Jake reclined regally on a blanket in the wagon bed. The dog had complained bitterly with soft, insistent whines when he sensed he was going to be left behind, and it was Wade who finally suggested they take him so he wouldn't try to follow on three legs.

Mary Jo had packed enough food for lunch and supper and filled canteens with lemonade and water. They had to buy seed to replace the plants washed away by the heavy rain and purchase grain for the horses. Wade would try to hire some hands.

Going into town was risky, Wade realized, but even being at the Williams' ranch was dangerous. No one would suspect a murderer, a wanted fugitive, to brazenly show himself in town. Both he and Mary Jo had decided that gossip and speculation would be best fought openly.

They'd discussed it after supper last night, after Jeff had taken Jake out for a few moments. Dinner had been quiet. Wade had been a reluctant guest at the table, steeling himself against uncontrollable emotions. But it wasn't fair making Mary Jo or Jeff bring his supper out to the barn, and neither did he like the notion of hiding from his own stupidity.

The silence, though, was uncomfortable and even Jeff had been quiet, sensing that something was wrong.

He'd confined most of his conversation to comments on how Jake was doing, and squirreling away small bits of stew for the animal. Wade was beginning to understand it was more a game between Jeff and his mother than any real need to pilfer treats.

Damn, but he'd felt awkward, like an outsider everyone was trying to convince belonged. But he didn't belong, and he never would. Eventually, even Jeff was affected by the pall, because he left the table quickly, of his own volition.

"I'm sorry for today," Wade had told Mary Jo. "It should never have happened." He didn't have to explain what "it" was. "It" was like a horse rearing on the table. Too big and dangerous to be ignored.

"I'm not," she said with that damnable honesty of hers. He wished she was like other white women he'd known. Less forthright.

"What would your husband have thought? Or the man who left you this place?" Wade struck out viciously. "Lying to a lawman, protecting a murderer?" He ignored what he considered the worst of it: that kiss that had robbed them both of any common sense.

Her eyes clouded for a moment, the bright emerald-green dulling for a fraction of time. "My husband would have been grateful," she finally said. "You saved his son."

Wade felt his good hand clench into a fist, and he asked the last question he should ask. He shouldn't want to know anything about her dead husband. Nor the man she'd almost married. Yet he needed to know. Some devil inside compelled him to discover what kind of men had helped shape her into the woman she was, to show her how wrong he was for her. "A lawman? Grateful to me? Jeff never would have gone to that

creek if it hadn't been for me. If he hadn't heard—"
He stopped.

"Jeff's father was a fair man," she said quietly. "He
understood a great deal."

"You miss him?"

"Yes," she said. "And I missed him when he was
alive. He was gone most of the time. Both he and Ty."
There was grief in her eyes now, and Wade regretted
being the cause of it. He also felt something like jealousy. He had his answer. And it hurt like hell, even
though he knew it shouldn't. She'd had her own share
of pain, both during and after her marriage.

He started to rise and leave.

"Wade," she said, his name coming easily to her
lips. Wade wasn't sure how he felt about that. "We have
to talk about tomorrow."

His eyes questioned her.

"I need seed for the garden. I think you should go
into Last Chance with me. Let people see you, explain
your presence. Try to hire some men."

"You still want to go through with this?" He
couldn't believe it, not after this afternoon.

Her gaze was steady. "Yes."

"I can't promise what happened this afternoon
won't happen again."

"I'm not sure that I want you to."

Damn, he was beginning to fear that directness.
"You should. I'm nothing but trouble, Mrs. Williams."

She sighed. "I know."

"You're crazy."

"Probably," she said affably, but her eyes were
sparkling, even teasing now. She confounded him.
Again and again, she confounded him. "We'll leave at
dawn. It's a five-hour drive."

She had left him little to say. He couldn't think of anything. She had overridden every one of his arguments, his objections . . .

And now they were on their way into town, the sun hiking upward into the sky, spreading its soft morning glow across the golden hills and snow-tipped blue mountains.

Wade was only too aware of Mary Jo, who sat on the end of the bench, Jeff between them. He'd made sure of that. Being with her all day would be torture enough, without having her body thrown against his every time the wagon hit a bump in the rutted road.

She was wearing a daisy-yellow dress. He'd never thought yellow flattered redheads before, but it suited her. The dress was simple, the color faded slightly with use, but it molded her slender form with grace. It had a high neck and puffed sleeves, and she clutched a lacy shawl around her arms to keep them protected from the sun and dust. Her back was straight, but not rigid, just proud, and a few escaping tendrils from a no-nonsense bun under her hat framed a face lightly dusted with freckles.

Jeff chatted next to him, full of information about Last Chance. Wade considered the picture they must make. A man, a boy, a pretty woman going to town. Normal. Except nothing about this was normal. For one long, wistful moment, he almost wished it was.

They stopped at mid-morning to water the horses in the Cimarron Creek, which wound along the same route they were taking. Mary Jo put the canteen with the lemonade in the cool running water and tied it with a rope. Jeff and Jake both kept a respectful distance away from the water, although the creek had receded and was now babbling softly. The ferocity of several days ago was gone.

The sun felt good to Wade. Healing. He could almost feel himself grow stronger in its rays as he stood watching the horses drink. His arm didn't hurt quite as badly when he moved it, and the wound in his leg was now only a nuisance.

He shifted in the too-tight clothes. He hated wearing a dead man's clothes. He longed for his own comfortable deerskins. He was, though, wearing the eagle that his son had worn. It rested underneath the blue cotton shirt, hidden from view.

Just before they resumed their journey, he ate some fresh baked bread with cheese and took a long swallow of lemonade. The meal was sweet with old memories from his childhood. Until Mary Jo and Jeff had found him, he'd not had lemonade since his mother died, since his family had sat around on the porch after finishing the day's chores. He'd been so restless then, so eager to escape the farm. He hadn't realized how much he would miss it.

With Mary Jo's help, he hitched the team back to the wagon and watched Jeff boost Jake up on the bed. He felt a now familiar heat crawl into his groin as Mary Jo lifted herself gracefully up to the buckboard seat, the calves of her legs showing as she did so.

Wade stepped up to the wagon seat. Jeff had chosen to sit in the wagon bed with his dog, and Wade became only too aware that Mary Jo Williams and the sweet scent of flowers were inches away. He snapped the reins in his hand and the horses hurried their pace. Last Chance couldn't be close enough for him.

·   ·   ·

The town of Last Chance obviously had been established with the hope of luring money from would-be miners headed up into Ute country in search of silver and gold. The town consisted of one bank, a blacksmith, two saloons, a lumber yard, a small hotel, a sheriff's office, and several general stores loaded with miner's goods: picks, shovels, pans, heavy clothes, guns, ammunition, maps.

Wade picked up one of the latter, and noted that trails led right into land given the Utes in the last treaty. He knew how much those treaties were worth, particularly with maps like these purporting to show likely sources of gold and silver. He also picked up a copy of the *Rocky Mountain News* and scanned it quickly.

Mary Jo had given him a little money, enough to buy some clothes, and he selected two dark-colored cotton shirts and sturdy denim trousers along with a cheap hat. An advance on his salary, she'd said. He hated accepting it, but he hated wearing her husband's clothes even more. Once he returned to his mountains, he would make sure she was reimbursed with one of his horses. Still, it galled him to take her money.

Then he helped her select seeds that still might have a chance of growing this late in spring.

"We need a brand for the cattle," she said.

"Jumping the gun a bit, aren't you?"

"We won't get back here for a while, and I have faith in you," Mary Jo said.

A large lump constricted Wade's throat. He didn't want anyone to have faith in him. But now was not the time to argue about it, so he merely shrugged. "Do you know what you want?"

"The Circle J," she said. "It's Jeff's future."

"The blacksmith can make it for you. Why don't you go tell him what you want, and I'll scout out the saloon. Maybe I can find some men."

"The saloon?" Her voice was full of doubt and even some disapproval. Then he remembered what she'd said about the hired hand who'd almost burned down the barn.

He shrugged. "It's the place you generally find unemployed hands or hear about some who might soon be." He stopped. "Look, it's not going to be easy. Everyone's gold and silver crazy." And he needed to find men quick. He needed more people around the woman and himself. He needed to get the ranch going, and get the hell out of this valley.

She seemed to read his mind. That infernally appealing mischief fluttered around in her eyes again. His reluctance, his struggle against doing what he promised, always seemed to amuse her. He wished to God it amused him. He just felt damned all over again.

But she didn't say anything. He'd discovered she picked her battles, refusing skirmishes she didn't think really mattered. He wished he hadn't noticed that. He wished he didn't like her more and more. Hell, lust was one thing, but mixing it up with liking was something else altogether. He pushed his new hat down to shadow his eyes and watched her carefully, waiting for her approval, forcing her to voice it.

"The saloon it is," she finally said, her mouth turning up in recognition of his tactic. "Jeff and I will go to the blacksmith's and then to the lumber yard. We'll need material for a bunkhouse."

He just nodded, no longer startled by that incurable optimism and, even worse, that confounded faith in him, believing that he could pull off miracles. Dammit, he was getting more and more sucked into her quicksand, and that, he thought, was a lot deadlier than the quicksand that lay at the bottom of the Cimarron Creek.

Whether Mary Jo Williams had willed it, or whether it was just plain damn luck, Wade would never know. But he found two men that afternoon he thought might do. They had lost their jobs after spring roundup at a neighboring ranch and were at the Last Chance Saloon, trying to decide whether to head north for a cattle job, or west to try their hand at mining.

Wade listened with interest as they discussed what to do. Going north and trying to find another job seemed to be winning. They had no money to buy supplies, and they weren't too anxious to tangle with Indians. There had been recent tales . . .

Wade had nursed a beer, listening to the discussion. The faces looked honest enough and their callused hands spoke of hard work. When one of them glanced around, his eyes met Wade's and didn't waver. He liked that. He also watched the way they drank. Two beers, no more, and they drank slowly, like savoring a treat after long denial, rather than fast like a hard-drinking man.

After listening a while longer, Wade approached them. "Couldn't help but hear," he said as the two men turned to him, looking him up and down. "I'm looking for some men . . . it'll be year-around jobs. Ranching."

One of the men put down the beer he was holding. "How many cattle?"

"Just a few now, but the owner plans to develop a large herd."

"What ranch?"

"The Circle J, some fifteen miles south of here."

"Never heard of it."

"You will," Wade said. "Pay's good. Thirty-five a month and keep."

The second man had been silent, watching, studying Wade. "We be working for you?"

"I'm foreman. The owner's a woman. Widow." He might as well get it out now. "First job will be building a bunkhouse. You'll have to sleep in the barn until that's done."

The second man who spoke looked at the other, then turned back to Wade. "Name's Durant. Ed Durant. This is Tucker Godwin. Everyone calls him Tuck."

"Wade Smith," Wade replied.

"What happened to your arm?" They were all weighing each other, and it was a fair question.

"Railroad accident."

"You gonna marry the widow?"

Wade shook his head. "Just helping out. She was promised to my brother before he died." God, he hated that lie, but he kept a bland look on his face. "She's a good cook."

Their faces brightened. "Hell, why not?" Ed Durant said, turning to his friend. "We could try it."

The other one—Tuck, Wade remembered—hesitated. "We were working for the Bryant ranch if you want to check us out."

Wade shook his head. He'd learned quickly during the war how and who to trust, but he eyed the man called Tuck with renewed interest. A possible foreman?

His eyes were intelligent, steady, though he might be a drifter, like so many cowhands, unable by nature to stay anyplace long. "When can you start?"

Tuck shrugged. "Today? Our gear's in front."

Wade nodded. "Good. We'll go down to the lumber company and find Mrs. Williams. You go ahead, and I'll follow on foot." He started out the door with the two men, then hesitated as he looked out at the street. He'd learned to be careful years ago.

Two men were riding into town from the east. Something about one of them caught Wade's attention. He pulled his new hat farther down on his forehead and stepped into the shadows as he studied the rider.

Like Wade's, the man's hat was pulled down, and his face was turned away, but he seemed so damn familiar. Then Wade's eyes caught the glitter of silver on the saddle and the man turned just enough for Wade to see his face. Bitter, violent memories came flooding back. He faded into the doorway until the two men passed, hoping that Mrs. Williams' new hands weren't noticing. They weren't. They were already mounting their horses.

Wade waited until the two men passed him, and then he headed for the lumber yard, which was in the opposite direction from where the two men were headed. Still, he felt . . . trapped, and wished like hell he had a horse. He wished even more he had a gun, that he could use one.

With his hat still pulled down, Wade limped down to the lumber yard, following his two new hired men.

Mary Jo was dickering with the lumber-yard man over prices, and she smiled when she saw him, her eyes opening wide as she saw the two men with him. The smile widened into something wondrous. "I knew," she said, "we would need some lumber."

Mary Jo looked toward the silent man next to her as the horses pulled the wagon toward home. Two men now rode horses behind them. Quiet men who had looked at her with curiosity and respect. She had been right about Wade Foster. He *was* her solution.

Jake was riding up on the seat, squeezed between her and Jeff. The wagon bed was filled with lumber. Her leg touched Wade Foster's, touched and burned.

He had tried hard to put her on the other side, but she had scrambled up, somehow not wanting Jeff between them. She wanted to share their success with him. But he was in no mood, apparently, to do that. He had retreated to whatever closed world he usually inhabited. There was no smile, no sharing, no anything. He might as well be a piece of wood.

Not for the first time, she wondered what she had done, forcing him into her life, hers and Jeff's. He was clearly uncomfortable there, and she knew she was already in water way above her head. She had told herself repeatedly that she was doing this for Jeff, for Jeff's future, but truth be told she was also doing it for herself. She needed the Circle J.

She refused to believe she needed Wade Foster for any reason other than to get the ranch going. She kept telling herself that. Yet every time they touched, every time their bodies were thrown against each other, she knew it was more than that. Every time she dared look in his eyes, she knew. He did too, and he hated it. She should, too. She couldn't afford to care about someone like Wade Foster.

A means to an end. Heaven-sent or hell-sent. She wasn't sure which. But she knew he could never be more than that to her. More than that to Jeff.

Just a means to an end.

12

They arrived at the ranch well after dark that night, and the next morning work started on the bunkhouse. It wasn't much, just one room large enough for ten bunks, but it was progress. It was the beginning of the Circle J.

All of them worked on it, the two new hired hands hardest of all. But Jeff did his share pounding nails and so did Mary Jo, who did double duty as cook. Wade did what he could with one arm, helping to carry and fitting boards into place. But frustration was written all over his face. It was the only emotion she had recognized since leaving the town of Last Chance. He had sealed himself off from Jeff and herself as if he'd gone to another country.

He drove the men, and he drove himself, and she knew it was because he wanted to leave. She had invited the men to eat supper with them the first full day they had worked, but Wade had declined.

"I would like to see more of the land," he said. "There's about three hours before dark." He already knew she owned five hundred acres and much of the surrounding land was open range. Ranchers branded and turned their stock loose, rounding them up in spring. Calves stayed near their mothers, thus making ownership easy to determine as long as trust remained strong between the ranchers.

Mary Jo searched his face, but it was blank, as if he'd taken a towel and washed all feeling from it. She nodded. "Jeff knows it well. He can go with you."

"No," he said sharply. "I want to get my own impressions. I can do it better alone." He hesitated. "But I will need a horse."

She nodded. "My mare's a little small. You can take Jeff's. One of the men can saddle him."

"I'll do it myself," he said, rejecting the offer. "They've worked hard enough without nursemaiding me."

There was an edge to his voice and though his face still showed nothing, she felt the seething frustration in him. "All right," she said without comment. She wanted to offer her own help, but he would hate that, the implication that he couldn't do something simple like saddling a horse for himself. She also knew he wouldn't attempt it unless he thought he could do it. She just hoped he wouldn't do more damage to himself.

She watched him limp from the porch, sensing he wanted to be alone. She suspected that was his real reason for leaving, not the one he'd given. He'd had little privacy the days he'd been here, and he was a man who cried out for that privilege. She'd wondered whether he had been that way with his wife, whether he'd been as alone as he seemed to be here. And then she wondered what she had been like, the Indian woman who had, if not tamed him, at least held him to her for years. She wondered whether Wade Foster had kissed his wife as he had kissed her, with that fierce hunger that melted so briefly into tenderness.

Jeff bounded up on the porch then, and she heard him ask Wade where he was going.

"For a ride," Wade said shortly.

"I'll go with you."

"No," she heard Wade say, and then he hesitated a moment before adding, "You need some rest. Tomorrow will be even busier than today." He strode off then, leaving Jeff standing there. He'd turned too quickly to see Jeff's face fall with disappointment. But Mary Jo did, and she felt stirrings of anger. *She* knew he was staying only out of obligation, but Jeff, for all he considered himself a man, was only a boy who didn't understand.

She couldn't bear to see him hurt. Mary Jo knew what she was doing, knew she was playing with fire, but she was convinced she could handle it. But Jeff . . .

She held her tongue during supper, tried to draw out the two new hired men. Both were experienced, both drifters following work wherever it led them. They were reticent around her, saying little directly to her but taking to Jeff who never stopped asking questions about trail drives. One of the men—Tuck—had actually followed the famed Chisholm Trail. But though Jeff seemed interested, he kept glancing at the door, obviously waiting for Wade.

He didn't come, and she began to fear that maybe

he'd taken Jeff's horse and was returning to the mountains that were calling to him. He had every right. She had promised a horse; he had hired two men. He had never said how long he would stay.

The two new hired men excused themselves. They were staying in the small room Wade had occupied. He had said he preferred to sleep out in the open.

Jeff, exhausted from the day's physical labor, took Jake into his room. Mary Jo wandered around the house for an hour, then went out on the porch. The moon had turned into a sliver. She thought about saddling her horse, and going to look for him, but that would be useless. If he was going to return, he would. If not, he would be halfway to the mountains and she couldn't do anything about it.

She'd better get used to the idea, in any event.

Still, she sat on the porch. Waiting as she had years ago.

Wade had saddled the horse, taking satisfaction if not pleasure, in the act. He didn't feel quite so helpless. But it took a long time. Hell, everything did.

When he finally mounted, he felt free for the first time since he'd been wounded. King Arthur was a fine horse, well trained, and he wondered if Jeff's father— Mary Jo's husband—had worked with him. But Wade missed his own pinto. Sage had served him well; he had been intuitive, sensing Wade's commands before they came.

He tightened his knees and the horse gathered speed, racing across the hills toward the mountains. Wade threw back his head and let the wind whip his hair, burn his skin. His years with the Utes had taught him a great deal. They had riding contests between the warriors, and it wasn't unusual to see them running alongside a galloping horse, jump to its back and down again, the horse never breaking stride. While he'd never quite mastered that skill, Wade had learned to control a horse with the slightest of leg movements, a turn of his body.

He finally pulled up. The sides of the horse were heaving, foam flecking its mouth.

Wade dismounted on the crest of a hill. He couldn't see Mary Jo's ranch from here, but he could see the shining mountains. If he was smart, he would make a run for them. They were his future, what little he had.

A rock had settled in his stomach when he'd seen the man in town. He could never forget Clayton Kelly. Never. He and Kelly had ridden together with Bill Anderson during the war, and after the war Kelly had carved out a reputation for being as ruthless as the James brothers. Banks, railroads; Kelly had robbed them all. And he didn't mind killing. He just wasn't as flamboyant and clever about it as Jesse and Frank. No cryptic self-serving messages, no justification. He'd simply gotten used to killing, and he'd never drawn the line at women and children.

What was he doing in a little town like Last Chance? Who was with him?

Memories had gnawed at Wade since he'd seen Kelly. He kept thinking of the missing cows Sheriff Sinclair had mentioned, of the bullet in Jake. Were Clay and his men hiding out around here someplace? Running from the law or planning a job? Whatever the reason, it meant trouble for this area. And Wade couldn't do a damn thing about it, not without revealing who he really was.

And then there was that Denver paper inciting the government against the Utes again. It had reported an upcoming meeting between the Utes and the government to renegotiate the treaty giving the Utes land in the San Juan Mountains. It was another blatant attempt to push the Utes out of Colorado to the arid Utah mountains.

It reminded him of his obligation to Manchez and his people. Christ, he needed to get back, to tell Manchez that his sister and nephew had been avenged. Wade felt sick inside, and tired. Long ago he had decided he never wanted responsibility for human beings again. And now he felt torn between two groups: Manchez and his people, and to Mary Jo Williams and her son, Jeff.

And he felt woefully inadequate to protect either.

Mary Jo watched Wade ride up. His shoulders were slumped. That was all she could see in the dim light. Yet he sat the horse easily, riding with a natural rhythm that Jeff, who had grown up with King Arthur, still hadn't quite achieved.

Wade had given his room in the barn to the two cowhands. He preferred, he'd said, to sleep outside and had folded several blankets along the outer side of the barn before he'd left on his ride.

Mary Jo walked down to the corral outside the barn and waited until he'd dismounted. He managed to unsaddle the horse, slinging the saddle on a fence post with his good hand.

He didn't acknowledge her presence until he finished, then he turned the horse loose in the corral and walked over to where she stood.

"Afraid I would steal your horse?" His tone was ironic, but not accusing.

"I've told you," she said steadily, "you can have any of the horses you want. You can turn around and leave this minute."

"Is that an invitation?"

"I don't know what it is," she said, and she heard the desperation in her voice. She wanted him to stay. She wanted him to go. She didn't know which she wanted most.

He turned away from her. "This is good land. Good grassland. The buffalo used to roam here in the thousands. They're gone now."

Mary Jo allowed a moment to go by. "You're thinking again of the Utes, the people you didn't want blamed for—"

"For what I did." He turned back to her, his face still impassive. "They used to hunt these lands. Twelve years ago, there were still so many buffalo you could ride for days and never stop seeing them. And then the buffalo hunters came, and they were all gone in a few years, shot for hides with the meat left rotting on the ground."

"You've been with them that long?" she whispered.

"Almost." He looked away again, back toward the mountains.

"How? Why?" She had wanted to ask those questions for a long time.

"How? I was living up in the mountains. A band of Utes had camped not far away. I used to trade with them," he said, "and I found them a hell of a lot more civilized than most whites. Before long, I seemed to be adopted by them." His eyes avoided hers, and she knew he was leaving something out. He was leaving out a lot.

"Chivita?"

"Chivita is none of your business." His voice suddenly turned cold and he moved away from the gate. "I think I'll turn in now."

"Wade."

He stopped, his body seemingly frozen. He didn't turn back toward her, just waited.

She went to stand next to him. "Jeff, well Jeff, he was hurt tonight."

"I'm sorry," he said, but his voice was cool. "We both know this is temporary. It's best that he knows it, too."

"Best for whom?"

"Don't push me, Mary Jo."

It was the first time he'd used her given name. "Why didn't you ride away tonight?"

He turned around then and faced her. "My own reasons, Mrs. Williams." Mary Jo didn't miss his reversion to "Mrs. Williams," as if he regretted using her given name earlier.

"As long as you *are* here," she said carefully, "take care you don't hurt him. He's vulnerable now. He's lost so much."

"So have you."

"There's a difference. I made choices. I chose to marry a Ranger. I chose to stay at the Ranger station where Jeff could be hurt again. He didn't make those choices, but he had to live with them."

"I don't think he would have had it any other way," Wade said slowly.

Mary Jo knew that was true. Jeff never stopped talking about his father, about Ty, about the Rangers. She'd given him that world, and it was the only one he'd known. He'd never known safety and security and peace. That's what she wanted to give him now, and it was pure irony that she was trying to do it with the help of a man so obviously dangerous, as deadly as the men she'd chosen before.

Not for the first time, she wondered if she was drawn to that kind of man forever.

She didn't have to give in to it, though. She could take his temporary help, and then let go. She could!

Mary Jo turned back to the house, and walked the hundred steps to the porch. It took all the will she had not to turn around and look back.

The bunkhouse went up faster than Mary Jo thought possible.

On the second day after they returned from Last Chance, several of the neighboring ranchers drove up in wagons to help them. Matt Sinclair had informed them about Wade, his rescue of Jeff, and then mentioned the building project.

The Abbots, the Evans brothers, and the Green family came with tools and food. Mary Jo wondered why they would help now. But she knew. The surrounding families hadn't thought she could make it on her own. Now that there was a man around, they were willing to pitch in. Her gratitude struggled with resentment.

She carefully observed their reaction to her new foreman. There was curiosity, and then respect as Jeff told how Wade Foster had saved his life, handicapped as he was with his own recent injuries. None of her neighbors were overly curious men, relying on their own ability to judge a man. Personal questions were considered bad taste, and though they threw occasional glances toward the man they knew as Wade Smith, they kept comments to a minimum and appeared to respect his reticence.

About mid-morning, Wade disappeared into the house and Mary Jo suspected he had taken off his eagle necklace; she didn't see it when he shed his shirt later in the day to wash with the other men. She knew he was doing that for her, not himself, for she had learned only too well he had no apologies for his Indian wife.

Joe Abbot, whose wife, Jane, had brought a ham, came over at the end of the first day. " 'Pears you have a good man there, Mrs. Williams," he said. "Talked to me about buying some calves. You send him over to my place when we finish here, and we'll talk business."

Mary Jo nodded and thanked him, though resentment choked her. She had asked him six months ago about buying some stock, and he'd said he had none to sell.

"Heard tell about your dog," Abbot continued, sending a glance toward the porch where Jake sat, his leg still trussed in a cast. "None of us would shoot that dog. Been strange things happening, and we're real pleased you have someone here to help now. Mr. Smith, he seems like a fine man, and those two hands —hell, we can use them at roundup come spring." He touched his hat before taking his leave.

Wade Smith had been accepted. He'd accomplished in one day what she hadn't managed in a year. What would happen when he left?

She wouldn't think about that, she couldn't. She watched him wash sweat from his face, remembering how hard he had worked, as hard as the rest of them, doing what he could with only one hand. Carrying lumber, balancing boards with one hand, working them into place, holding them while someone else pounded the nails. But nonetheless he had been frustrated by his inability to do more.

Within a week, the building was habitable if not exactly comfortable. Bunks had been constructed of wood and rope and Mary Jo made mattresses out of hay and several layers of cloth and blankets. Real mattresses would be purchased on the next trip into town.

Wade's strength was returning quickly, and he said he was gaining some feeling in the fingers of his right hand, but he still couldn't ball it into a fist. Mary Jo watched him try to work his hand repeatedly, saw the pain and despair on his face as the fingers didn't do as ordered. Those fruitless efforts made her heart crack.

He was also trying to do more with his left hand. He'd turned down her offer to shave him the last few times, and his face grew bristly again, as it had been the first day she'd seen him. Then it was clean again one day, although there were small nicks marring the rugged planes of his face. Their number, though, lessened as the days went on. He went riding at suppertime each night, wearing his gunbelt, and she was sure he was practicing with his left hand.

It was also an excuse to stay away from her and Jeff. She felt certain of that, too.

She saw the puzzlement in Jeff's eyes, and she felt

his hurt. Yet Wade was right about avoiding them. The knowledge was bittersweet.

The night they finished the bunkhouse, Mary Jo met him at the barn before he could ride away. "Stay for supper," she said. "I need to talk to you afterward."

He hesitated a moment, then nodded.

Jeff's eyes brightened when Wade walked in and took a seat. He talked to the other two men about what needed to be done, particularly repairs to the fences. There were also a few head of cattle on the range that carried the C brand of their previous owners. Ed Durant and Tuck Godwin would search for them, while Wade purchased a few more head. They also needed several more horses.

Wade stayed, reluctantly, Mary Jo thought, after Ed and Tuck left. He kept glancing at the door, anxious to leave as soon as possible.

"Joe Abbot said he would sell me—you—some cattle," Mary Jo finally said as she sat down at the table. "Will you ride over with me tomorrow?"

He gave her a brief nod.

She hesitated. "I don't have much money."

Wade's eyes met hers. She knew he didn't want to ask any questions. He hated them himself. And yet he had to know, if he was to help her.

"I started out with two thousand dollars and the ranch," she said. "Now, after supplies, seed, and the lumber, I'm down to eighteen hundred. That's going to have to last me until next spring."

She saw disbelief flicker in his eyes. "Don't forget about the men you've just hired," he said.

"And you."

"I don't want anything," he said abruptly. "But even then you're stretching it."

"I know," she said. "I hope I can get a loan at the bank once they see we have the ranch going."

His eyes turned glacial. "The bank in Last Chance?"

She nodded.

"You keep your money there?"

She nodded again, wondering about the question. He never asked questions without a reason. Why wouldn't she keep her money there?

"What happens if you can't get a loan? If you don't have any cattle to sell come spring?"

It was a question she had asked herself over and over again. She had been banking everything on making this ranch go, and she'd refused to consider failure even when everything looked so bleak, and she couldn't so much as hire a decent hand. Then Wade Foster appeared, almost like a guardian angel.

A very dubious guardian angel, she reminded herself, and a very reluctant one. "I don't think about that," she finally said. "I can't. I already love this valley. I want Jeff to grow up here."

He sighed, as if admitting failure, but his mouth was bent upward in a small smile. "We'll see what we can do tomorrow," he said, rising as if the discussion were ended.

"You need a horse of your own," she said.

He hesitated for a moment. "If you trust me with Jeff's horse for a couple of days—if Jeff does—I can get several good horses in the mountains."

She knew where he was going. It hurt unexpectedly. That faraway look was back in his eyes, the longing for something he'd lost. For his wife. His child.

Jeff had been listening to the conversation avidly. Mary Jo saw no reason why he shouldn't. The Circle J was his future as well as hers. "Can I go with you?"

Mary Jo saw Wade's eyes rest on Jeff. "Someone has to take care of your mother."

"She could go, too."

"There aren't enough horses," Wade said.

"I could ride one of the team horses," Jeff said hopefully. "We have an extra saddle."

Wade's face hardened. "I'll be going into Ute territory. I'll be staying with them."

"I don't care," Jeff said bravely, though there was the slightest flicker in his eyes. He too had grown up on tales of Indian raids.

"I do," Mary Jo said suddenly. This had gone far enough. Wade Foster might trust Indians. She didn't. She certainly wasn't going to risk Jeff. "Mr. Smith can travel faster without us."

He nodded. "I'll leave for the mountains in the next few days, after I'm sure Tuck and Ed will be staying."

Mary Jo again felt an odd disquiet, as she had several times during their conversation. Wade Foster wasn't saying something that was very much on his mind, that was obviously worrying him.

But when he stood to leave, she didn't know how to stop him, how to get him to tell her what was wrong. He simply nodded to her and left. Mary Jo watched Jeff slip out behind him.

After several moments, Jake whined and awkwardly rose on his three good legs, moving toward the door. Mary Jo followed and opened it, watching as Jake limped out.

She stepped outside, to get away from the heat of the stove inside, and she took a few steps toward the barn. The two hired men had disappeared into the new bunkhouse, and Jeff and Wade were talking earnestly. She wasn't spying intentionally, or maybe she was.

It was sunset; there was light enough to see Wade's features in the soft glow of twilight. He was saddling Jeff's horse, and now he was wearing his gunbelt. Her throat tightened as she overheard some of the conversation between their new foreman and Jeff.

"Will you take me with you sometime," Jeff said, "to practice shooting?"

Wade hesitated; she knew he wanted to escape.

"I don't think your mother would approve," he finally said.

"Sure she would," Jeff replied. "Ty taught me to shoot a rifle and six-shooter, but I want to learn to draw fast."

Wade looked down at him. "Why?"

"I'm going to be a lawman."

"I thought you were going to be a rancher."

"Naw. Ma wants me to be a rancher, but I'm going to be a Ranger. Like my pa." He looked up at Wade. "Have you ever been a lawman?"

Wade shook his head. "No."

"A soldier?" Jeff said hopefully.

Wade hesitated a moment, then seemed to sense Mary Jo's presence. He looked up, and for a moment, their eyes met. Mary Jo waited for an answer, just as Jeff had. There was so much mystery around Wade Foster. She wanted every answer she could get.

"No," Wade said, but something flickered in his

eyes. He didn't lie easily. He usually ignored questions he didn't want to answer, but this time Mary Jo knew he was lying. She felt it deep in her bones. And she wondered why. Being a soldier wasn't something to hide, no matter which side he had favored.

But he didn't give her time to ponder his short answer. He centered his attention on Jeff. "Don't be so anxious to do either. You might have to kill, and killing, Jeff, changes you forever. You can never go back once it happens. You can never be what you once were."

"But you—"

"Me?" Wade said bitterly. "I killed, Jeff, because it became easy for me. Too damn easy. Because I lost my soul a long time ago. I don't want that to happen to you." His voice was rough with feeling.

Jeff's face filled with consternation. "Everyone has a soul."

Wade smiled. "Maybe, but if I do, it's in bad shape."

"Like our ranch?"

"I think it will take more mending than that."

Jeff considered that for a moment. "But it can be fixed?"

Wade shook his head as if he had no more answers to Jeff's incessant questions. "Some things can't be fixed, Jeff."

Jeff's attention was drawn to Wade's holster. "But you're still wearing a gun."

Mary Jo, listening, wondered herself. He hadn't touched his gun until they'd returned from Last Chance.

But now he only shrugged and finished tightening the cinch with one hand.

"I still want to learn to draw fast," Jeff persisted.

"Then you'll have to learn it from someone else," he said shortly and placed his foot in the stirrup, swinging himself up easily despite his injuries. He turned toward Mary Jo. "Don't wait up for me."

13

Wade held the six-shooter with his left hand, aimed and pulled the trigger. The bullet went to the right of his target. Considerably right.

He cursed his clumsiness. And he cursed the damn gun. He hated the damn thing. At one time, he thought he would never use a weapon against a human being again, but then he had killed three men. Coldly. Purposely. And he had learned he hadn't truly escaped his past, that the devil had continued to hover inside his soul, waiting for the right opportunity to show himself.

He had taken up shooting again to avenge his wife and child, telling himself that anyone who had killed an innocent child deserved to die, that they would do it again and again. But it had really been revenge, the return of a blood lust he thought he had purged years ago.

And with the death of that final miner and the injury to his right arm, he'd thought it over at last, the killing. But then he'd seen Clay Kelly, and he knew it wasn't. Death followed Clay just as it followed Wade, and the moment Mary Jo had mentioned the bank in Last Chance, he suspected he knew why Clay was in the area.

The bank held Mary Jo's future. And Jeff's.

And their future was now vitally important to him, even if he had no place in it.

But he could say nothing without revealing his own past, and seeing the horror in the woman's and boy's eyes, without sentencing himself to an ignominious death. There was only one solution. Find Clay Kelly. He was out here someplace. The slaughtered heifers and Jake's bullet wound had been Kelly's work. Wade felt it, just as he'd learned to sense danger years ago. That instinct had been dulled in the mountains, when he'd found a measure of peace, but it'd returned now.

Wade had only a few minutes of dim light remaining. He glared at the offending tin can that continued to sit rakishly on a rotting log.

He aimed again, concentrating with all his power, willing his left fingers to do what his right had been able to do such a short time before. Wade slowly squeezed the trigger. The can remained in place, mocking him.

He didn't know if practice would ever help. He'd known men who could shoot with both hands, but during the war one fast one had been enough. More than enough.

Wade aimed one more time. The gun clicked. Out

of bullets, and it was damn hard reloading with one hand. Damn hard doing anything with one hand. He holstered his gun in an awkward movement. The holster still rested on his right thigh, and there was no easy way to get to it.

If he had to face Clay Kelly, he had few doubts about the outcome. How long did he have, he wondered, before Kelly struck? He was waiting for something or he would have hit the bank that day Wade and Mary Jo were in Last Chance. More men? A gold shipment of some kind?

Wade returned to his horse, running his good hand down its shoulder and feeling the animal shudder in contentment. He wondered whether he would ever know contentment again.

After going to the Abbots to buy cattle tomorrow, he would go looking for Clay Kelly. Perhaps he could convince him that Last Chance could be exactly that. Wade knew how to look for him. He knew what Kelly required in a camp. They had made one together enough times.

The thought was not a pleasing one. Somehow he didn't think that summoning back memories of old times would work. They hadn't parted the best of friends.

But as he mounted Jeff's horse, Wade could think of no reasonable alternative. He could ask Mary Jo to withdraw her money from the bank, but she would want to know why. And he would have no reason, none he could give her.

The three of them—Wade, Mary Jo, and Jeff—rode to Joe Abbot's the next day. Mary Jo wore a split skirt and green blouse and looked uncommonly pretty to Wade. Unlike most women, she had the sense to ride astride rather than use a sidesaddle, something he'd always considered dangerous in this country.

To Mary Jo's obvious surprise, Wade had urged both her and Jeff to go. "It's your cattle, your ranch," he said, "and Jeff can learn something about herding cattle."

He tried not to notice Jeff's face, the delighted grin that spread across it, the freckles that appeared to pop out as he did so.

He also tried to dismiss Mary Jo's smile, the sudden brightness of those green eyes.

"It won't be easy," he warned them, hoping he wasn't making a mistake. But if Mary Jo and Jeff were to stay here, and he was becoming more and more convinced they would, they had to learn to move cattle. They could farm all right, and they weren't shirkers. He had seen the garden, what was left of it after the rains. But Mary Jo had been right; they couldn't make it farming. Not the two of them. They had an even chance with ranching if they could keep a couple of good men.

Jeff nodded. "I know," he said. "You can take King Arthur," he added generously. "I'll take old Seth." Old Seth was one of the wagon horses, broad and steady and slow.

Wade nodded, feeling guilty as hell. He hadn't explained his reasons, that he would leave soon, and Mary Jo and Jeff needed to watch him bargain for cattle and to help him drive them back to the ranch. He had herded cattle back on the farm and later during the war when Anderson was raiding the pro-North farmers. He'd read enough about cattle prices to bargain adequately enough.

Wade had always been charmed by Mary Jo's smile, by the quiet humor that usually hovered in her eyes, but on the way to the Abbots, her smile was open and happy, and his own spirits lightened. She was so confident everything was going to work out exactly as she planned, so pleased with him. She almost made him feel he could accomplish anything. Almost.

She was one reason, he knew, they reached such a good bargain with Joe Abbot. Once the rancher believed she was here to stay, he couldn't say no to her any easier than Wade had been able to.

They picked out forty head at four dollars each, all that Mary Jo and Wade had decided they could purchase.

Abbot watched how carefully they chose, then grinned at the end of the haggling. "I'll throw in a couple of them young heifers. And I got a damn good bull. I'll loan him to you for a month."

Mary Jo flashed him that smile that had always set Wade's nerve endings on fire.

At the end of the bargaining, Joe Abbot held out his hand. "Been a pleasure doing business with you, Mr. Smith. Hope you stay around a while."

Wade felt the firm grip, the friendliness in the man's manner, and he was surprised at his own reaction. A measure of pride was creeping back into him, pride that had been missing for a very long time. But then he tamped it. Joe Abbot didn't know who the hell he was talking to. He sure as hell wouldn't reach out a hand to one of Anderson's raiders or to a man who'd lived with the Utes for years and had taken a Ute wife.

He nodded. "We're indebted."

He watched as Abbot's men cut the animals out of the herd, and they started back to the ranch without more conversation.

Wade was hard-pressed on the way back to keep them together. Neither King Arthur nor old Seth had been trained for herding and cutting stock. But Wade had always had a way with horses, and King Arthur was a fast learner. So was Mary Jo, on her neat little mare, and young Jeff, despite his obstinately slow mount.

Still, it was late when they arrived back at the ranch. Ed and Tuck had repaired the fence, and they would keep the cattle in the corral until the new branding iron was ready.

The two new hired men admired the stock. They'd found eight head with the old Callaway brand on them, and had brought them in. Fifty animals.

"The beginning of the Circle J," Mary Jo said proudly when they'd finished.

Wade tried to ignore the glow in her face. As ranches went, hers ranked near the bottom, but he was aware of her sense of accomplishment and it warmed him. She was building something. So was he. He swallowed hard, admitting for the first time the emptiness of the past years, even when he'd had Drew. He'd been avoiding life, avoiding people, avoiding real commitments. He'd grown close to the Utes for many reasons, not the least because they were nomadic people, picking up an entire camp at a day's notice. But now he yearned for something more.

"What's wrong?" Mary Jo asked, her face crinkling with concern, some of the pleasure in her eyes fading.

He was surprised at the question. She asked so few of them. "Nothing," he said shortly, turning away from her to unsaddle the horse. Tuck and Ed had disappeared into the bunkhouse and Jeff had hurriedly unsaddled his horse and gone to see about Jake, who'd been left behind.

Wade hated Mary Jo seeing him try to unsaddle King Arthur, hated her seeing his awkwardness, his difficulty in doing so simple a task. But when he turned back to her, she had moved away, and was unsaddling her mare. He didn't know whether to resent that thoughtfulness or appreciate it. He chose to resent it.

When he'd finished, he stalked across the yard toward the barn. He'd moved back into the small room now that the hired men were using the bunkhouse. He'd wanted the privacy.

"Wade."

Her voice was soft but it carried. He turned.

"Will you be up for supper?"

"No," he replied.

Disappointment spread over her face but was quickly gone, hidden with a blankness of her own. The rebuff had hurt, he could see that, but he wasn't going to apologize. He was suddenly angry. He couldn't quite figure out why, but it had something to do with that brief surge of pride, and the realization that he had no right to that pride. He couldn't afford to feel that, or feel anything else where Mary Jo Williams was concerned.

He started toward the barn.

"Thank you, Wade. Thank you for today."

He didn't move. Not toward her, not toward the barn. He felt rooted to the ground with no safe place to turn. "No need to thank me. I'm repaying a debt, that's all." His voice would have frozen most people where they stood.

"Maybe," Mary Jo said. "Not everyone would have done it so well."

"Buying cattle when you have money isn't that hard, Mrs. Williams. Tuck could have done it just as well."

"I don't think so," she said. "Joe Abbot liked you. He trusted you from the beginning. And I wouldn't have Tuck or Ed without you."

"You have them now, and that's all you need."

There was a silence, long and painful. He wanted to tell his feet to move, but they were still fastened to the ground. He felt, rather than saw, her move closer. Smelled her. The scent of flowers still clung to her despite the long day, the dust, the hard ride. Flowers and woman. Moisture had plastered her blouse to her body, outlining the swell of firm breasts, the trim line of her waist. A curl had escaped the long braid that had confined that fine auburn hair, falling alongside her cheek.

He felt his loins tighten with need. He wanted to touch that hair, rub his hand down the slightly flushed cheek, lock his arm around the damp body. He wanted to feel her and taste her and revel in her womanliness. Christ, he wanted to bury himself in her.

Her gaze held his. "Does that mean you're leaving?"

"I never intended to stay. You know that."

"But so soon?"

"You don't need me any longer."

But she did. In more ways than one. "Tucker and Ed won't stay if you leave."

"I'll talk to them."

"A month," she bargained.

He couldn't take a month of this, and he knew it. He wouldn't be able to keep his hands off her that long. His eyes met hers. "I'm going up to Ute country for a couple of days. There's things I need to do."

"When?"

"I want to check out the country tomorrow. If everything looks all right, I'll leave the next day. I'll have to borrow Jeff's horse."

She stood there, biting her lip, looking vulnerable. She rarely looked vulnerable, but now she did, and tenderness swept through Wade like a tidal wave. He softened his voice. "You have to have more horses. I'll bring some down."

"That's not the only reason," she said. There was the barest note of accusation in her voice. And something else he couldn't define.

"No," he replied. "I owe them, too."

"They're Indians," she said flatly. "They're burning out farmers, ranches. The paper—"

Wade felt her words like a blow to the stomach. He'd never met a woman as compassionate, as accepting, as Mary Jo Williams. If she felt this way, there was damn little hope for his friends.

He turned back to the barn, walking away from her.

"Wade!" He ignored her voice, but then her hand was on his arm, and he couldn't stand her touch. It burned him. He turned back, and he knew he looked angry. He could almost see her flinch.

"I want to understand," she said. Her face was earnest, pleading. But he recalled the abhorrence on her face when she'd first seen his eagle necklace. His son's treasure. Wade's one memento.

"Then go with me," he said recklessly, the words leaving his lips before he'd considered them. "See these . . . savages for yourselves. Isn't that what you called them?"

A stunned look crossed her face, and he immediately regretted that strange impulse. Why in hell did he care what she thought?

But he did. It astounded him how much.

He watched her struggle with herself. He remembered her telling him about her sister, the neighbors in Texas. Part of him understood. God knew, he had certainly reacted when someone had killed those he loved. But another part of him kept thinking about Chivita's gentleness, Manchez's fairness and generosity. Manchez, who was like his own brother, who *was* his brother.

"All Indians are not alike. Just like all whites aren't alike," he said softly. "I've seen whites that put Indians to shame in their ferocity." *And I was one of them.*

I am one of them. He couldn't forget the last months, his deliberate hunting of the miners.

"What about Jeff?" Mary Jo finally said.

"He'll enjoy it."

She stepped back, fear flitting across her face. "I . . . can't."

"The Utes love children."

"He's all I have, Wade."

"And he'll grow up hating people he doesn't understand just like everyone else around here," Wade said bitterly. "It was a bad idea, Mrs. Williams. Forget I mentioned it."

He started toward the barn and this time he didn't turn around and she didn't stop him.

•   •   •

"Where's Wade?"

Mary Jo wondered when her reluctant foreman had become Wade to Jeff.

"He needed some rest," she said, as she put beans and bacon in a skillet. It wasn't much, particularly for the two new men, but she would add some fresh bread and preserves, and a pie she'd baked yesterday.

It was an effort to cook. She wasn't hungry. In fact, the thought of food made her ill. She tried to believe it was the meal she'd had earlier at the Abbots. But deep down, she knew that wasn't true.

She kept seeing that last expression on Wade's face. A mixture of resignation, disappointment, and even something close to rejection. The disappointment had hurt the most. But she couldn't help her feelings toward Indians. She couldn't put Jeff in danger.

"He was great today, wasn't he?" Jeff said. "I've never seen anyone ride like that before. King Arthur never did those things for me."

"King Arthur has to learn, just like you need to learn your sums," she said.

"Aw, Ma."

"Off to your books," she said.

"I want to go see Wade."

"No," she said sharply. Too sharply. He looked as if she'd just hit him.

She went over to him, put her hand on his shoulder. "I'm sorry, Jeff, but he needs some rest. This has been a hard day for him. His shoulder still pains him a lot."

"Jake will cheer him up."

"I think Jake would rather eat."

"No he wouldn't," Jeff demurred. "He missed Wade."

Jake's tail thumped heartily as if in agreement.

"When did he become Wade?"

Jeff shrugged, just as Wade always did, and a pang struck Mary Jo anew. Consciously or unconsciously, her son was picking up Wade Foster's mannerisms.

"In the morning," she said with finality, and Jeff reluctantly dropped the subject.

Wade left at daybreak, before anyone else was stirring. He didn't want to answer questions.

He saddled King Arthur and led him out of the barn, then mounted and walked him out the worn gate just as the first rays of sun hit the hills and bathed them in golden glory. Ordinarily, he might have appreciated it, but right now he had only one thing in mind: finding Clay Kelly.

Kelly would be camping near water, he knew that. He didn't like dry camps. Kelly was a man who enjoyed comforts, and that meant coffee in the morning, plenty of fresh, cold water to drink, and a place to bathe. Kelly was somewhat of a dandy.

Jake had been shot downstream, and so had the calves. That meant Kelly was probably upstream, closer to Last Chance. He wouldn't have left evidence close to his camp but would have killed, taken what he could carry, and then gone back to his camp using the Cimarron to cover his tracks. Kelly had always been careful.

Perhaps, Wade thought, he had just moved on. Maybe he'd just stayed a few days on his way farther west. Maybe he had no plans for Last Chance or the people of Cimarron Valley. Wade's instinct, though, told him otherwise. He felt trouble deep in his bones.

Over the years, Wade had left his mountain lair

occasionally and gone into small towns for supplies. He'd always listened to gossip, listened for the sake of the Utes, and for his own safety. He'd read newspapers, though often they were a week, even a month old. It was through the newspapers—and wanted posters— that he kept abreast of Clay Kelly, as well as the James gang.

He'd liked Frank and Jesse James and Cole Younger. Perhaps because they'd taken up arms for the same reasons he had. But Kelly had gone to war for the gold and booty and women. When Wade had ridden with him, they'd seldom exchanged words. Wade had avoided him, except for one occasion in Lawrence when he'd stopped Kelly from rape. Kelly might have killed him then. Sometimes, Wade had wished he had done just that.

The sun climbed in the sky, and Wade stopped briefly to water his horse. Kelly would have picked a heavily wooded site on a hill or incline where he could more effectively look for intruders. One near the Cimarron, or another nearby stream.

It was noon before he saw a likely-looking place. A hill with a ridge of trees. If Wade knew Kelly at all, there would be a trail on the other side. Kelly never trapped himself.

He stared at the hill for a long time. There was no sound. No wisp of smoke. No movement in the brush. Yet he felt human presence.

Wade had left his gun at the barn. He was still too ineffective to use it, so he figured it was better to leave it, and the threat or challenge it carried, back at the Circle J. He hesitated a moment longer. But he had come this far, and he might as well play out the hand.

He whistled, a long, clear note, then two short ones. He waited. Then repeated the signal.

The very air seemed to still with tension. The few lone buzzards visible in the sky circled, as if waiting for a particularly tasty dinner.

Then he heard a return whistle. Two long notes, a short one. He answered with three short ones.

A rider appeared on the crest of the hill, a rifle in his hands. He rode slowly toward Wade, pointing the barrel at him. Wade raised his one good hand, keeping the reins in them, and using his legs to control King Arthur, who was now skittish.

As the rider approached, Wade saw he was the man with Kelly the other day in town. But he didn't recognize him from the war days. The man drew abreast. The gun was leveled at Wade.

"I don't have a gun," Wade said.

The man leaned over and patted his saddlebags, then eyed Wade's arm in a sling. "Who in hell are you and what do you want?"

"I want to see Clay Kelly."

"Don't know no Kelly."

"Then whoever it was you were riding with in town."

Dark soulless eyes stared at him. "You tell anyone what you saw? Or thought you saw?"

Wade shook his head. "No."

"What do you want with . . . him?"

"We used to ride together eleven, twelve years ago."

"Do tell," the man said. "What name you go by?"

"I've changed names."

The man chuckled. "Haven't we all." He lowered the gun slightly but it would take only a slight movement to bring it back up. "You still haven't told me what you want."

"It's between him and me."

"And me. He told me to check you out."

Wade sighed. Kelly was as cautious as ever. No doubt he had a rifle aimed at his heart right now. Would he remember Wade's face? He doubted it. Wade had sported a youthful beard then. "Allen. Tell him it's Sergeant Brad Allen."

"I'll do that. In the meantime, you stay right here and don't move a finger. There's several rifles pointed at you right now."

Wade nodded. He lifted one of his legs and hooked it around the saddle horn. He wished he knew what in hell he was doing. Maybe he should have gone for the sheriff when he'd spied that hill, but then he would have a lot to explain. How he had recognized Kelly. Why he hadn't gone directly to the sheriff. Too many things.

If Clay Kelly was just passing through, this would be the end of it. They would drink to old times and old comrades, though it would curdle his stomach to do so. If Kelly had plans for the bank, then Wade would face more difficult decisions. If, indeed, he rode away alive.

He waited for what seemed hours. And then he heard the whistle again, and a man on a bay horse appeared and signaled him to ride up.

Wade tightened his knees, and King Arthur started up the incline. Wade made sure his good hand was visible. The climb was short but rough, and it took several minutes before he reached the lone rider at the top.

Clay Kelly looked older, gray flecking his dark hair,

but he wore the same jaunty smile that Wade remembered. "Allen?"

"It's Smith now," Wade said. He endured Kelly's searching gaze, the sardonic twist to his lips, as he noted the arm in the sling.

"There's a lot of Smiths around. What happened?"

"Someone was a better shot than I was."

"Is that someone still alive?"

"No."

"Then I guess he wasn't a better shot."

Wade shrugged.

"How did you find me?" Kelly asked.

"I saw you in town. I remembered how you used to think."

"For old times' sake?" Kelly said with a trace of a sneer.

"No," Wade said. "Self-preservation. Something happens in this valley, the law will come looking for newcomers. I can't afford that. The sheriff found a body not too far away from here, but they haven't associated it with me. I don't want them to. Not until I'm ready to leave."

"In other words, don't hunt your woods."

"Something like that."

"Brave words from a cripple."

"I could have turned you in, and rode away before they knew who I was."

"But you wouldn't do that, would you, Allen? You're too damn squeamish."

Wade felt the fingers of his left hand tense as he struggled to keep emotion from his face. "No one with Anderson was squeamish."

Kelly shrugged, and Wade wondered whether he

even remembered the episode in Lawrence. Kelly had been drunk that day. A lot of them had been.

"What happened to you after Centralia? We thought you were dead."

"I was injured," Wade said. It was no lie. He'd been badly injured that day, though not physically.

"I wondered," Kelly said. "There were posters out on you. But you just seemed to disappear from the face of the earth. The rest of us were hunted." He eyed Wade suspiciously. "You wouldn't have your eye out for a reward?"

"And exactly how would I collect it," Wade asked, "without swinging next to you?"

"That's right," Kelly said, and some of the hostility left his eyes and his legendary charm appeared. But Wade knew the charm went skin-deep and no further. "Come have a drink to old times and Bloody Bill. He was killed, you know, not long after Centralia."

"I heard," Wade said.

"Rode right into the midst of Union Cavalry. He had guts."

"Where were you?"

"Running like hell. I never pretended to be a martyr."

Kelly had already turned his horse, and Wade followed him up through the brush to a stand of trees. Two men, one of them the man who had come down to meet Wade, were standing there with rifles in their hands.

"Meet Perry Jones and Johnnie Kay," Kelly said. "This is Brad Allen, used to ride with Quantrill and Anderson."

Wade was glad he didn't have to shake hands with them. They both looked as if they would sell their very mother to the devil. Kelly didn't, but he was just as apt to do that very thing.

"Kay, you keep watch." Kay was the one who had escorted Wade. He was too young to have ridden with Anderson, though his hard eyes looked ageless. Young and dangerous as hell.

Kelly dismounted and went to a rotting log under a tree. As Wade dismounted, Kelly leaned down to poke around in some saddlebags and came up with a bottle in his hand. Kelly threw the bottle to Wade, who caught it with his good hand.

"Still good reflexes," Kelly said wryly. "I think I would like to see that wound."

"Don't trust me?"

"I don't trust anyone, not with a price on my head. Maybe you got a pardon, turned to the other side of the law."

"Maybe, but I didn't. I'm hoping Brad Allen is dead." He leaned against a tree. "Go ahead and look."

Kelly gave him a cold, mirthless smile. He took the few steps to Wade's side and his hands applied pressure to the still bandaged wound and splint. Wade had to swallow deep to keep from crying out. It had been three weeks since the episode in the creek, when the wound had been reopened, but it still hurt where the bone had been hit. "Goddamn you, Clay," he said.

"Just making sure," Kelly said, apparently satisfied. "Good place to carry a gun."

"I was also hit in my leg. Want me to drop my britches?"

"I don't think I can stand such an ugly sight. Sit down and have a drink."

Wade gave him back the bottle, watching as Kelly sat down, cross-legged. Kelly took a long pull from the bottle. "Not many of us left, you know," he said, apparently nostalgic now.

Wade felt absolutely no nostalgia for those days, only abhorrence and self-disgust.

"Can't find men like that anymore," Kelly was saying. "These two . . . they would betray me in a minute." He didn't bother lowering his voice.

"Why don't you get rid of them?"

"I'm on the run. I get who I can." He looked at Wade speculatively. "What are you doing in these parts?"

Wade decided to tell the truth, without telling too much of it. "Someone took something from me. I evened the score, but got a couple of bullets doing it. I'm just resting here before going back up in the mountains."

"Want to join us?"

"With this arm? I'll never be any good with a gun now."

"You could do other things."

Wade debated his answer. He didn't want to antagonize Kelly or alert him. "I'm tired, Clay. I know a place up in the mountains. I plan to lay low up there for a while."

"Where you staying?"

Wade knew that question was coming. If Kelly had any idea that someone with Mary Jo's looks was within fifty miles, and had so little protection, he'd be at the ranch in a split-second.

"Squatter took me in," he said. "Hasn't been feeling too well, and I promised to stay on a few days, look after him."

"Always did have a conscience, didn't you?"

"No skin off my back. I don't have anything to get

back to, and it was as good a place as any. But I'll be heading out if you have plans here. I can't afford to stay.''

Kelly shrugged. ''Relax. I'm just waiting for an old friend who's being released from prison. Should be here next week. It was too hot for us to wait down in Texas, so we agreed to meet here.''

Why here? Wade wanted to ask the question but hesitated. Curiosity was not usually welcomed among Kelly's acquaintances. *His* acquaintances, Wade reminded himself. He'd been no better than any of them.

''Anyone I know?''

''Barry Shepherd. He says he has a debt to pay someone around here.''

Wade remembered Shepherd. Like Kelly, he'd been a man without conscience, a man who enjoyed hurting. ''How long has he been in prison?''

''Five years.''

Wade quietly sighed. Couldn't have anything to do with Mary Jo. He hoped the same applied to the ranchers who had helped her several days ago. The thought surprised him. A few weeks ago, he could have cared less about people like the Abbots.

He wanted to ask more about Shepherd, but questions would raise suspicions. He had the information he needed. There were apparently no plans to rob a bank, not here, not now. He took another draw on the bottle. ''Guess I'd better be getting back before dark. I'm not all that familiar with this ground.''

''Sure you won't consider riding with us?''

Wade shook his head. ''I can't shoot anymore. I'd get us all killed.'' He got up, half expecting a bullet to go ripping through him.

"Allen," Kelly said, stopping him in mid-stride. "We won't be here after today."

"Don't trust me?"

"I don't trust anyone."

Wade hesitated. "My word mean anything to you?"

"No."

Wade smiled. "What do you want?"

Kelly smiled, but it was a chilling smile. "Don't cross me, old friend. A lot of people think Brad Allen's dead. They would be happy to know otherwise."

Wade nodded. He'd gotten what he wanted. He walked slowly to his horse and mounted. He turned to Kelly and nodded again. It was all the civility he could manage. He turned King Arthur and started slowly down the hill, still surprised he was leaving alive. Kelly had mellowed in the past years.

Or had he?

The doubt stayed with him. What did Clay Kelly want? He turned upstream, away from the Circle J, aware that a man on horseback was following at a careful distance. He would have to lose him.

He wasn't particularly proud that old survival instincts were resurfacing again, that his mind was working as it had years earlier, that Clay Kelly wanted him, and saw in him a man like himself.

In fact, it scared the hell out of him.

14

Mary Jo had spent nearly all her married life waiting. Waiting to see whether her husband came back dead or alive. And then there was Ty. And friends. So many friends who had ridden off one day and had never come back.

She'd sworn she would never go through that again. Not only for herself, but for Jeff.

But here she was pacing the porch at twilight, just as she had so many other times. Her stomach was in knots. Her heart was in her throat. Where was he?

He hadn't recovered from his wounds yet. What if the horse had stumbled? What if whoever was responsible for the recent rustling shot him?

What if he'd left for good?

Jeff had been bitterly disappointed this morning to find him gone. She'd suggested that he take her mare and go into Last Chance with Tuck and Ed to pick up the new branding iron and some fence posts.

She had tried to convince herself last night that she would go with Wade up into the mountains.

He'll grow up hating people he doesn't know or understand. Those words, and the intensity behind him, had echoed in her mind all night. *All Indians are not alike. Just like all whites aren't alike.*

By daylight, she'd known that she couldn't go with Wade, couldn't give up her fears, couldn't risk Jeff. She kept hearing her sister's screams, seeing her father's weary face after one of his endless searches. She saw her friend's body, mutilated in terrible ways, along with her mother and father and brother. She remembered the nights her family had huddled inside their small house, terrified of every noise. She could still feel the fear; she shivered even now. The Utes were no different. Everyone around here had a horror tale about cattle thievery and massacres. One massacre had taken place twenty years ago near this very ranch, and there were tales of more recent atrocities.

She'd trusted Wade with the ranch. She wasn't ready to trust him with her son. She'd already lost far too much.

But she couldn't forget his disappointment in her. She felt she might have lost whatever trust had been building between them.

Jake, who had been lying next to her, struggled to his feet and emitted a long, low growl that became a frenzy of barking as a lone rider came into view, shadowed by the late afternoon sun. Her heart pounded a little faster, her blood quickened. She had to force herself to remain still.

She watched as he guided the horse toward the

corral. She was in the shadows of the porch, and if he saw her he didn't take notice. His shoulders were bent, he seemed tired, and she wondered where he had gone.

As he unsaddled the horse, she saw the side of his face, the rigid set of it. The lines in it seemed even deeper, as if some event today had hastened the passage of time. She hurt as she continued to watch him struggle with the saddle, unwilling to leave it for someone else to do. She was familiar with pride, the kind of pride that killed men, and she hated it fiercely for a moment.

But then he was done, and he started to lead Jeff's horse into the barn. Jake moved off the porch and limped off to greet him, his tail wagging fiercely. Wade stopped and waited for the dog to catch up with him, leaned down, and rubbed an ear. He glanced up, saw her, and hesitated a moment. He nodded respectfully, nothing else, then disappeared into the barn with King Arthur.

Mary Jo went inside. Nervous and restless all day, she'd put her energies into cooking as she used to do when Jeff's father and Ty were gone. Fresh bread. An apple pie. Gingerbread. She'd basted a ham in honey and cooked it. She sat for a moment and wondered what to do. Jeff was gone to town with Tuck and Ed; they would be gone for hours. She wanted to see Wade, to talk to him, but he obviously wanted nothing to do with her. Then she spied the gingerbread.

Hands shaking, she cut a large slice of gingerbread, plopped it on a plate, and poured a glass of milk. Bounty in hand, her legs shaking, she walked out to the barn, wondering whether it was the biggest mistake of her life.

Wade had apparently just filled a bucket of fresh water for King Arthur. He swung around at the movement behind him as if he expected trouble. She watched him visibly try to relax. Where had he gone? Why did he look so troubled?

She ignored her silent questions and tentatively held out her offerings. "I . . . thought you might be hungry."

He smiled then, one of those rare smiles that lit his face. "I am." His nose wiggled as if to prove the statement. "It smells good."

"Gingerbread," she said as she handed it to him. She had kept it on top of the stove and it was still warm.

The smile spread into his eyes. "Hot gingerbread," he said, with an awe that made her smile. "I haven't had that since I was little more than a tadpole." He took a bite, and he looked almost boyish in his pleasure.

Mary Jo wished she had made it before. Her Rangers had always enjoyed her cooking, particularly her sweets, but never had anyone reacted as if she'd given him a gift of inestimable value. She leaned against a stall and watched him finish it, wiping his fingers like Jeff did. She was enchanted at his enthusiasm, at the way a lock of hair fell on his forehead, making him look even more like an errant boy.

She silently handed him the glass of milk and he gulped it down. Had he eaten at all today? Where he had been?

"There will be more at supper," she said.

The smile disappeared, but rare amusement sparkled in his eyes for a moment. "You do know how to tempt a man."

"Do I?" she replied wistfully. She hadn't meant it to sound the way she instantly knew it did: The air was suddenly still with implication, with a thrumming, electrical tension that had nothing to do with gingerbread but everything to do with raw, naked desire.

His face changed, the mischief leaving his eyes, and something dark and brooding took its place. She felt her body move toward him, smelled the man scent of him, soap and sweat and leather, and then she felt swept into a whirlpool of feelings that were uncontrollable. Her face turned upward, inches from his.

Mary Jo heard his low curse, but then his lips were on hers, tasting of gingerbread. She had never liked it quite so much. Thoughts of gingerbread disappeared as his kiss became more and more demanding, desperate even, as if he were drowning again and grabbing for a line. She felt the desperation in every touch, in the way his lips possessed hers.

Her body leaned against his, her mouth opening eagerly for him. She'd never felt anything like it, not this wild, mindless elation. Tremors of pleasure ran through her body as his tongue entered her mouth and caused a flood of heady sensations.

She felt his arousal pressing against her, as his tongue searched, loved, seduced, until she felt her legs might collapse under her with her need for him, with her craving to be closer and closer to him, to be one with him. Everything about him was intense, and that intensity flowed into her, wiping away every vestige of caution, of common sense. She wanted to be a part of him, to share pain and joy and laughter and desire. She wanted him, needed him the way she needed the sun, or food.

Her arms went around his neck, and she felt his

left arm drawing her close as he took his mouth from hers and his lips burned a trail down the side of her face. He then just held her cheek next to his heart, and she heard his quickened breathing.

"I want you," he said in a voice hoarse with emotion. "You should run like the devil was after you."

"I can't," she whispered.

He pulled back, his eyes burning into hers, as if seeking answers. "I can't stay."

"I know."

"Do you, Mary Jo?" His voice seemed to croon her name. It was deep and husky and sensual.

She realized suddenly she didn't. Some part of her had hoped one day would stretch into two, and two into seven and a week into a month and . . .

But now it didn't matter, nothing mattered but feeling the warmth of him, easing the aching loneliness in her. Nothing mattered but his touch, and the craving he always ignited deep inside her, reminding her she was a woman.

"Where're the others?" he asked, the huskiness even deeper.

"Jeff . . . Jeff, Tuck, and Ed went into Last Chance to get the branding iron and some fence posts."

He closed his eyes for a moment. "This is crazy, for you and me."

She knew it. She knew she was risking everything, most importantly her heart. But she would take these minutes, this promise of magic.

Mary Jo felt his hand take hers and he led her into his tiny room in the barn. He closed the door and looked at her, his hand moving from her hand to her cheek, his fingers running up and down it, lightly, gently, as if touching something precious and breakable. His fingers hesitated as they reached her chin, and then dropped to her blouse, to the opening at the neck. Again he hesitated, and she found herself unbuttoning the top buttons, welcoming the feel of his large hand as it moved inside her chemise and rested on her breast.

She felt it swell and grow tender under his caress. The craving inside her quickened, became more demanding, searing.

Their lips touched and although they had met before there was a new exploration, a savoring of feelings, an enchantment that spun her into a world without boundaries or rules or fears. His mouth ignited a warmth that seeped throughout her, settling into the core of all her feeling, both contenting and exciting her.

She wanted more. More of the cascading sensations he created, more of his strength. She wanted to give and she wanted to take, and she wanted them both in the most terrifyingly urgent way.

He was trailing kisses down her throat, and she shuddered with spasms of desire and pleasure. Every nerve was so alive, every part of her responding in wanton, hungry ways. His lips dropped down to her now bared breasts, caressing, arousing until she thought she would go mad with wanting.

He guided her to the bed and finished unbuttoning her shirt with his left hand. Every touch seemed to burn right through her, fueling the fever that was sweeping up both of them. He dropped next to her, and she found her own hands unbuttoning his shirt, her fingers catching in the hair that formed an arrow down toward his waist. It was still damp with perspiration from the ride.

She felt his hand move behind her, and then her hair was falling away from the braid and down her shoulders. "You always smell like flowers," he whispered. "I'll always remember that, that and your damn stubbornness."

Mary Jo felt pain so deep she almost doubled over with it. He was telling her again he wasn't staying, no matter what happened now, or in the next few minutes. He was warning her one last time. She was beyond warning, though. He had already become a part of her heart, her soul. She knew she would take whatever he offered.

His mouth plunged down on hers, hungrily now, his tongue entering it with primal intent. He plundered her mouth, his tongue ruthlessly exploring every tender, sensitive spot, then gently, inviting her to journey with him, to taste all the sensations humming through her. Her blood felt hot in her veins as her hand went to the back of his head and her fingers danced seductively along his skin. She felt him shudder, tremble even, and she knew he was caught in the same hot whirlwind as she, both of them tumbling along without will, carried by instincts so strong they overpowered all sensible emotion.

Her hands went to his trousers, unbuttoning them quickly as he groaned, a low cry of pain escaping him. Her breath caught in her throat at the need in that cry, and she felt a tightening at the back of her eyes, a sorrow such as she'd never felt before. She'd never needed to give like this, never felt this aching tenderness, a desire to heal wounds she couldn't even comprehend.

She wondered why she sensed his errand—whatever it was—had only served to deepen them. Where had he gone? Why had he seemed so troubled when he returned? Her hand went up to his face, her fingers touching the curves in it, following the crevices that began at the corner of his eyes, the lines she knew had little to do with laughter, and everything to do with a darkness that was never far from him.

His mouth caught one of her fingers and nibbled at it, his gaze now holding hers. Another question. Another challenge.

She answered it with a kiss, a long, lingering one with no reservations.

She heard him curse under his breath, but then her skirt was being pulled up and her underdrawers down, and she felt his warm hand touch her, stroking her until she felt she could bear it no longer.

"Wade," she whispered, her hand pulling him down to her, aware of his awkwardness. Even so, his body fit hers so well, the hardness of him meeting the soft, welcoming crevice between her legs. He hesitated, then moved slowly before entering, seducing what was already seduced. She felt him enter, slowly, carefully, at first, but then his body assumed a rhythm of its own as his mouth rained kisses across her cheek and down her throat. Heat surged, and passion, and glory. Glory splendid and strong and tender and healing. She felt her body respond to his in every way, moving with his in such complete harmony that it seemed to her they were born to this, to this melding, to this wonder.

He plunged one last time, and she felt his heat, his seed, in her, and then waves and waves of pleasure so deep and strong she thought she might explode.

Wade collapsed on her, and she knew it had taken

all his strength to hold himself above her with his one good arm. Now she felt him against her, his body wet from the coupling, his breath harsh, his cheek resting against hers. Warm contentment bubbled inside her, as she felt the shuddering aftershocks of their lovemaking.

Wade felt as if he'd been struck by a thunderbolt. It was as if she had reached inside him, baring a heart he thought unbreachable, sharing something with him he instinctively knew was also new to her. He had cared for Chivita, had been grateful for his son, but this . . . it had been a piece of heaven. For the first time in nearly twenty years he felt as if he belonged, that he had somehow reached home after an agonizing journey. It was exhilarating, terrifying—and completely puzzling, as if she'd taken some healing balm and spread it across wounds he'd thought would fester all his life.

For a moment, he wanted to take it all, to think it could last, but awareness, bitter and intrusive, fought through that moment of hope. He was who he was, and the past didn't allow for a future. The appearance of Kelly had reminded him of that. There would always be a Kelly, reminding him of shadows and darkness and death.

He moved away from her, turning over on his back, but the narrow bed forced them together. She managed to squirm up a bit, and rest her head on her hand, to watch him. He couldn't meet her eyes. Of all the despicable things he'd done, this had to be the worst.

Her voice was soft, uncertain suddenly. "Are you . . . is your arm—"

"My arm is fine," he said. Then his mouth

crooked in a small, wry smile. "Don't you ever think about yourself?"

Mary Jo hesitated, as if afraid to say anything, and he realized he didn't want her to answer. He saw what was in her eyes, and it was too damn painful to bear. He turned his face away.

"I *was* thinking of myself," she said. "I know you didn't want this, but . . ." Her voice trailed off.

Her hand was moving across his chest now, making it difficult for him to think, much less speak. "You made me feel alive again," she said.

"I've never met anyone more alive," he replied huskily. "Since the first day, when you were so damned determined to save me."

Her fingers stopped moving but rested on his heart. "Not inside, not where it counts," she said. "Not since . . . Jeff's father died. Even Ty . . . I . . . he was such a good friend, so wonderful with Jeff, but I was afraid to love him. I've been afraid of ever caring again." She stopped, afraid she was saying words he didn't want to hear, but they were welling up inside her. She'd never talked about her feelings before, not to her husband, not to Ty. She'd never expressed her fears or loneliness. They wouldn't have understood. She knew Wade would, even if he didn't want to.

He was still, his body rigid. "You have Jeff."

"Oh yes, I have Jeff. And I love him more than life itself, but . . . another part of me was closed off."

"Don't care about me, Mary Jo." His voice was gruff.

"It's too late for that," she said. She put her fingers over his mouth to stop him from replying. "I know you feel you have to go. I'm . . . not asking you to stay. I'm not asking for anything. But I do care, and I always will.''

He closed his eyes to shut out her image, the glow in her eyes, the huskiness of her voice, the courage it took to say what she'd said. He owed her the same honesty, the truth about what he was, had been, the reason he couldn't stay. She saw him as the man who had saved her son, not as the man whose name to this day was a curse word in parts of Missouri and Kansas. But he couldn't do it. He couldn't bear the horror in her face. Even if he tried to forget it himself, to put it behind him, there would always be someone or some event to remind him.

He forced himself to move, to get her to do the same. "Jeff and the others will be back soon," he reminded her, closing himself off again, making his face blank, hoping his eyes didn't reveal his despair.

She gave him a level stare, then rose slowly, leaning over to take her chemise and slip it over her head, then her blouse. He wished it wasn't so damn awkward pulling up his trousers and trying to button them with one hand. Still, he was grateful she didn't try to help.

They dressed in silence, a silence so leaden that he thought it would suffocate them both. He didn't bother with his shirt. It felt stiff with perspiration from the ride. Mary Jo finished and walked over to him, her hand going to the eagle on his necklace, taking it in her hand.

"It suits you," she said. "You remind me of an eagle. Free and untamed." She fingered the seven points that surrounded the eagle. "What do they mean?"

"It's Indian," he said roughly. "Do you really care?" He suddenly wanted to hurt her.

"Yes."

He hesitated, but her face was so damn earnest. He shrugged. "Four of the points are for north, south, east, and west. Two are for the sky and earth."

"And the seventh?"

"Self. It's for your self. Utes believe the individual is at one with the land. They have deep respect for the sky and the earth, the plants and animals. They kill only when necessary for survival and then murmur apologies to the plant or animal."

She was silent. She wanted to tell him she would go with him, but she couldn't. She wanted to tell him she understood, but she couldn't do that, either. She didn't. She was afraid she never would.

"I want to understand," she said.

"You can't," he said. "I was wrong in even asking you to come. You can't understand what has been taken from them. Their land, their hunting grounds, their buffalo, their dignity. And they *have* dignity, and honor, more honor than I've seen among whites. The Utes have tried so damn hard to live with the white man, ceding more and more land, and still the government pushes. And it continues to push and take, and men like those three miners kill without worry, knowing the government won't do a damn thing. Indians are nothing more than animals, something to be eliminated, slaughtered like the buffalo." He stopped, then continued softly, "Like my son."

She stepped back, as if burned by the intensity of his words. But before she could say anything, they both heard Jake bark, signaling the return of Jeff and the two cowhands.

Mary Jo looked down at her blouse as if to make sure the buttons were in place. She pushed her hair back, tying it with the ribbon. But her face was flushed, her lips swollen. Wade saw it. He didn't know whether the others would.

"Wade?" He heard Jeff's voice outside, and he felt an undeserved pleasure. The death of his son had left a hole in him that could never be filled, but Jeff's natural affection and enthusiasm lessened the grief, made it more tolerable.

He opened the door, and Jeff came flying into the room. "I was afraid you'd left us."

"I wouldn't do that without telling you," he said gently. "And I couldn't take your horse."

"I know, but—" Jeff stumbled as his eyes went to his mother, seeking help. But she had none to give. She had apparently thought the same thing, Wade realized wryly, that he had just taken off, that he had disappeared like every other man in their lives. But then neither of them had much reason to trust him. And they shouldn't.

Mary Jo broke in. "Did you get the branding iron?"

Jeff broke into a big grin. "Yep. The Circle J. Tuck said I can watch tomorrow, maybe even help." He was beside himself with excitement.

Mary Jo's smile tightened. "I'm not sure . . ."

Wade watched Jeff's smile fade. "Tuck's a good man," he said, breaking his rule about interfering. "He won't make mistakes."

"It's dangerous."

"Everything out here is dangerous," Wade said. "I'll stick around tomorrow and make sure he's safe."

"But you said—"

"I'll go the next day."

Jeff's face glowed as he turned to his mother for permission.

"All right," she said. "Are you hungry?"

Jeff's grin was back in place, broad and happy. "Am I ever."

"Then wash, and come up to dinner." She looked at Wade. "Are you going to join us?"

"Please," Jeff pleaded.

He nodded. "I have to wash, too." He also needed to think, to get control of his feelings, to harness them as he had years ago—until that day he had come back to the cabin. Since then, they'd been on a rampage.

Jeff grinned, whirled around, and disappeared out the door.

Mary Jo turned to him. "Thank you for not disappointing him."

"And you?"

She smiled, and it was as if the sun had appeared from under heavy clouds. "And me."

He put his hand to her face, caressing it. "You're a remarkable woman, Mrs. Williams." Her face leaned against it for a moment, and he savored the gesture of trust. Even if he didn't deserve it.

When he looked at her, he thought how easy it would be to forget Manchez and Clay Kelly. But he knew his blood-stained past would always taint him. And he refused to have it taint—worse, destroy—those who cared for him.

"I'll be there shortly," he said.

She hesitated, reluctant to leave his touch. "You were planning to leave tomorrow . . . for the mountains."

He shrugged. "Jeff's horse needs some rest. I'll leave at daybreak the next day." It would give him a

chance to see Tuck and Ed work, to judge their exper-
tise. And he needed rest as much as Sir Arthur. He still
wasn't up to full strength; his arm ached and so did his
leg.

But he did need to return to the mountains. He
had to get the horses and come back quickly, in case
Clay Kelly started any trouble. It would be easy for Kelly
to discover where he was staying. Gossip seemed to be a
big business in Last Chance, and apparently, the talk
recently had been about the new foreman at the
woman's ranch.

Feeling torn apart by responsibilities, he turned
away from Mary Jo. He hadn't wanted any, and
now . . .

He couldn't figure out how this had happened.
Hell, his whole damn world was going crazy.

15

Supper was agony for Mary Jo.

Her body had been awakened, and so had her heart, and she didn't know what to do about either.

The two hands had disappeared quickly after eating a meal best remembered for its lack of conversation, she thought wryly. Ed and Tuck, and even Jeff, couldn't shovel in food fast enough. Wade, on the other hand, had been quiet, watchful.

As soon as they finished, the two hired hands left, obviously ill at ease in the house.

Wade too wanted to make an escape, but Jeff stopped him.

"They were talking in town about the Indians, how they should go to Utah."

Wade's eyes narrowed and his mouth thinned slightly. "What do you think?"

Jeff looked up at him. "I don't know," he said earnestly, his thin shoulders hunching up. "You like 'em, don't you?" It was obvious to Mary Jo that anything Wade liked merited consideration with Jeff, even though her son was familiar with the Indian wars in Texas.

"Yes," Wade said simply.

"Why?"

Jeff's standard question caused Wade's tight-lipped expression to ease some. He looked up at Mary Jo, as if expecting her to object. He knew only too well how she felt. But Mary Jo held her tongue.

"My son," he said slowly, "wasn't so different from you. He always asked why, too. He liked to fish, and he liked to play, and he wanted to know how things worked, and why the sky was blue and the grass was green."

Pain edged his eyes as he spoke. The deep, painful sorrow never went away, but now it was exposed for everyone to see, something he'd seldom allowed since that night when he'd been so ill. She suspected that night was the first time he'd allowed himself to really feel the loss. Perhaps because he'd refused to talk about it, to admit his grief, the loss remained a suppurating wound that would always be raw. She felt it bleeding now.

"He was half Ute," Wade continued softly, almost as if he were alone. "His mother was one of the gentlest people you would ever meet, and his uncle, Manchez, loved him dearly." He hesitated again, then looking straight at Mary Jo as if in challenge, he added, "Manchez is my brother."

Jeff's eyes grew wide. "Your real brother?"

"My blood brother as well as my brother-in-law,"

Wade said, his tone changing, reacting to Jeff's sudden enthusiasm, once more submerging that grief. "He rides like the wind. He rides without a saddle and he can lean down and pick up an object from the ground at a full gallop."

"Jumpin' Jehoshaphat," Jeff said. "I sure would like to see that."

Fear arched down Mary Jo's back. She didn't know why, but she felt it. A shudder shook her body. She rose from the table. "I think it's time for bed, Jeff. It's been a long day."

"But—"

Wade rose, too. His expression had eased somewhat as he talked, but now his face was closed. His gray-green eyes were blank again, curtained against intrusion, and Mary Jo's heart dropped with the sudden and immediate sense of loss. But she didn't want Jeff enraptured by tales of Indians. It was like that river. Jeff had too little fear and much too much curiosity and any challenge attracted him.

"I'll be leaving," Wade said. "It's late, and tomorrow will be a big day."

But Jeff wasn't to be mollified. "Will you take me to see Manchez?" he asked.

Mary Jo stilled, waiting for an answer. She didn't want to be the one to say no.

"You're needed around here," Wade replied gruffly. "There will be a lot to do with those new cattle."

"But—"

Mary Jo wanted to shake him. Next to "why," "but" ranked second in Jeff's vocabulary.

"You want to hold up your end, don't you?" Wade prodded.

Put that way, Jeff didn't have an argument. He nodded glumly, obviously unconvinced that his help was of great value.

Wade gave him one of his rare smiles. "It's rough growing up," he said, and Jeff's frown disappeared in that moment of manly confidence. He reluctantly said good night and under Mary Jo's expectant eyes finally went into his bedroom, followed by Jake.

Mary Jo followed Wade to the door. "Thank you," she said.

He looked at her levelly for a moment. "He's your son," he said noncommittally, his eyes curtained again. It was as if he regretted this afternoon, regretted those few remarks at dinner. He was distancing himself again, and she felt a deep hole opening up inside her heart. She wanted him to touch her, to say something . . . anything.

But he just touched his forehead in a gesture of impersonal farewell, turned and left. She bit her lip and swore she wouldn't cry. She didn't have to worry. The hurt was too deep for tears, the loss so much more than she'd expected.

Mary Jo watched apprehensively as the branding continued throughout the day. Jeff was given the job of tending the fire while Tuck and Ed wrestled down the steers. It didn't take long to discover they needed two men to do that, and Wade was enlisted to apply the brand, something he could do with his left hand, albeit awkwardly.

Mary Jo also had another chance to admire Wade's skilled handling of a horse. King Arthur hadn't been trained as a cutting horse, but Wade, using his knees and one hand, easily guided him between the penned cattle, cutting away the calves found with branded Callaway cattle, along with the cattle bought from the Abbots. The calves would be branded for the first time, the Abbot cattle with a second brand, the new Circle J design.

The sun was hot, the air still, the smell and sound of burning hide sickening, the bawl of the cattle heart-rending. But the three men and boy worked perfectly together, their shirts clinging to their bodies with sweat. Words were rare; they communicated mostly by gesture and instinct.

Mary Jo couldn't take her eyes from Wade. Every muscle in his body was outlined by damp clothes. He had asked Jeff to roll up his left sleeve, revealing a length of tan skin between the cotton and a leather glove he wore on that hand. He would frequently reach up with that hand and wipe his brow, pushing away an errant lock of hair.

Remembering last evening, her heart thundered, her body hummed, tingled, and did other rebellious things as she looked at him.

Even with his right arm still in a sling, he was remarkably effective and efficient. He was one of those rare men who seemed instinctively competent at nearly everything they did. Despite his own feelings to the contrary—caused, she felt, by circumstances he couldn't have prevented—he had a natural assurance and ability that couldn't be learned or taught. It was obvious that he was winning the strong respect of the two men he'd hired. They jumped when he made the merest suggestion.

And Jeff. Dear God, every time he looked at Wade, his eyes fairly glowed with hero worship, just as they had last night when he'd asked Wade about the mountains just beyond their range.

Was she losing Jeff as well?

She knew she'd never had Wade to lose. She'd had a taste of something wonderful, no more. She'd tried to convince herself she needed no more, that a taste could last her. She'd tried to tell herself she didn't want another man in her life, one she most likely would lose, just as she had lost others. She tried to tell herself all that, but none of it worked. She did want him. She wanted forever. She was so tired of minutes. Of small pieces.

A woman's lot, another woman had said at Ty's funeral. Well, she was damnably tired of it.

The sun beat down unmercifully. She went inside to prepare a midday meal. Something cool. Sliced pieces of the chicken she'd cooked earlier. Cold water from the well. Keep busy. Don't think. Not about today, nor tomorrow when he would leave.

That night, Jeff made preparations to follow Wade. He'd never been so tired, but he felt good. He had done a man's work today, and he'd noticed the approving glances Wade had sent his way.

Jake eyed him sorrowfully from the floor as if sensing his friend was not only leaving, but leaving without Jake. Jeff was sorry about that. Three weeks ago, he would have taken Jake as protector and companion, but Jake was still healing, the leg splinted, and he couldn't possibly follow on foot.

Today had given Jeff confidence. He could do anything. Well, almost anything. He could certainly follow Wade. Everyone in town had been discussing the Utes and where they had settled in the mountains. They shouldn't be hard to find if he just followed the trails, even if he did lose Wade. But he wouldn't. His father and Ty had both taught him something about tracking, had even taken him out and taught him how to recognize certain signs and to tell how old campfire ashes were. He'd also been reading one of the dime novels about an Indian tracker. It seemed easy enough, and Wade said the Utes were peaceful. His friends.

Wade wouldn't have friends he didn't trust. And if Wade trusted them, then Jeff could. Blood brothers, Wade had said. Even the sound of it made Jeff's blood stir.

Jeff had seen Indians in Texas. Apache scouts, mostly, since Comanches never came close to the Ranger station. Tame Indians, the Rangers had called them. They had often accompanied the army on punitive expeditions, and various army units had stopped at the Ranger station, sometimes for information, sometimes to enlist more manpower. Everything else Jeff knew about Indians had been bad—until he'd met Wade.

Jeff had heard tales of terrible things, especially massacres committed by the Comanches. He knew about his aunt, and knew about other raids, too. They'd been discussed behind closed doors to keep him from hearing, but he'd listened avidly at keyholes. He'd learned to be very good at that, since there was so much grown-ups believed only they should know. He'd also read about General Custer and the Little Big Horn. But all that seemed a long way away, little more than stories.

And now Wade talked about Indians with liking and respect, and Jeff wanted to know more. Not only that, he wanted to be with Wade, and he realized their new foreman wouldn't be here much longer. He'd said as much. But maybe . . . just maybe, he might stay if he had a . . . reason. Like a son. Not like his real one, of course. Jeff knew he could never be a substitute for him, just like Wade would never take his pa's place, but . . .

He left the "but" up in the air. He didn't know what he expected. He just knew he didn't want Wade to leave them. His ma didn't, either. He knew that too, though she would never say so.

So it was up to him. Jeff knew his ma would never let him go up to the Utes, to show Wade that he was worthy of his friendship. And Wade would need help if he brought fresh horses back with him. Jeff could show him how much help he could be, almost like a son. How much help he would continue to be if Wade stayed with them. And his ma worried too much. She didn't realize he was old enough to take care of himself. Most of the time, he thought wryly, as he remembered his near drowning. But this was different. He merely had to catch up with Wade.

And despite what Wade had said, he knew he wasn't needed here. The big job—branding—was done, and Tuck and Ed had only a few cows to herd out to the range.

He finished gathering what he thought he needed: a spare shirt and pair of trousers. A knife. Some matches. Three cans of fruit and some bread. Also some jerky his mother had made for the hands when they were out all day. He rolled everything up in a spare blanket to make a bedroll.

He had thought everything through. He knew Wade would leave early. He always did. Jeff would invent some excuse not to accompany Tuck and Ed as they took the newly branded cattle out to graze. And when he'd finished that chore, he would tell Ma that he was going out to meet them. That should give him more than half a day before anyone discovered his absence. He would ride hard and try to catch up with Wade. He knew the road his friend would take, and he hoped to catch sight of him before Wade headed up into the mountains, so he could follow. Jeff had already written a note, telling his mother not to worry, that he would be with Wade. He knew she trusted him.

He looked out the window, scorning the bed, too excited to sleep. He thought for an instant of his earlier mishap at Cimarron Creek, but then forgot it. He wouldn't be crossing any creeks or rivers, and he would be near Wade. Wade could do anything, could protect anyone, even with his wound. He was almost as good as his pa had been. And Pa had been the best. The very best.

He heard his ma moving around. She came in each night to say good night and smooth the covers. He liked it, though he tried to act as if he didn't. Baby stuff. Jeff made sure the blanket roll was well hidden before scooting between the sheets just as she opened the door. She came over and sat on the edge of the bed and cocked her head just a little. He thought how pretty she looked for someone that old. Her eyes sparkled, and they hadn't done that in a long time. She smoothed down the sheet and put her hand to his cheek. It felt cool. Nice. He pushed aside the guilt that suddenly rushed through him. She would miss him. But it would just be a few days, and she would know he was with Wade. She trusted Wade, just like he did.

She touched his cheek with her hand. That was all

he would allow now—anything more was mushy. She smiled wistfully at him. "You're growing up, Jeff. I watched you today. You did a fine job."

Guilt swamped Jeff, and he became defensive. "I told you I could take care of myself."

"Of course you can," she said. "I'm just not sure I'm ready for it."

Jeff switched tactics. "You like Wade, don't you?"

"Yes," she said. "But he'll be leaving for good, I think, after this trip. Remember that, love."

"I do," Jeff said and faked a yawn. "But I don't want him to go."

"I know. I don't, either. But his home is in those mountains, just like our home is here. I think Tuck and Ed will stay."

Jeff wanted to ask her if he couldn't go with Wade. Help him out with the horses he'd said he would bring back. But he knew his mother would say no. He knew she didn't like Indians, even ones that might be friendly, although she had never said much about it. He could tell by the expression on her face, the fear he never saw otherwise. Indians, he thought, were probably the only thing she was afraid of. Jeff had seen her shoot rattlesnakes, ride half-wild horses, help fight a prairie fire that had come close to the Ranger station. He'd been real proud of her. But if anyone mentioned Indians . . .

"Good night," she said reluctantly, as if she didn't want to leave. He yawned again and nodded.

His mother started toward the door, reached it, then hesitated. "I love you, Jeff," she said softly, then left, closing the door behind her.

He wished he didn't feel lower than a snake's belly.

·   ·   ·

Everything had worked out just as he hoped, Jeff thought with something akin to dismay as he urged his horse into a faster gait.

Once on the way, he started having second thoughts, but he couldn't go back now. Everything had been so easy, it was scary, and once on his way, he realized that part of him had expected someone—or something—to stop him.

If you start a task, finish it. Ty had told him that. So had his father. *Never leave anything undone.* He wouldn't quit now, even if his horse wasn't terribly cooperative, or fast, or . . .

He nudged the animal again, his knees tightening, and old Seth cooperated, but just barely. He would never catch up to Wade at this pace.

Jeff looked at the sun. It was early afternoon. His mother wouldn't expect him until late since he'd told her he was riding out to meet Tuck and Ed. That heady excitement, the anticipation of adventure had dulled, leaving misgivings in their wake. What if he didn't catch up to Wade?

He was still amazed at how easily his plan had worked. Wade had left early, as had Tuck and Ed. Jeff had declined to go with them, saying he would follow after finishing his chores. He had eaten a big breakfast, pocketing some biscuits and blaming their disappearance on Jake. After feeding the chickens, milking their one milk cow, and cleaning the stable, he'd made his escape, saying he would meet the two hired hands. Ma was washing clothes, and he'd been able to smuggle out his bedroll by dropping it out the window. He'd taken his rifle with him.

He dug his heels back into old Seth's side, wishing he was riding King Arthur, but Wade had taken him, and old Seth was the best of the two wagon horses. The horse reluctantly speeded his pace into a canter.

Hours went by and Jeff's apprehension deepened. The rutted, dusty ribbon of road that headed through Black Canyon and up to the San Juans was empty as far as he could see. One day, two days, three days? He wasn't sure. Last Chance was to the north, and this road went south.

In late afternoon, he started climbing upward. The road narrowed into a trail. He saw fresh horse droppings and his spirits rose. He wasn't so far behind Wade, after all. He didn't even consider the fact it might not be Wade. He couldn't.

Jeff stopped at a stream to water the horse and fill his canteen. He figured he would keep moving until dark, hoping to catch up with his quarry. But then the trail split into two, and he had not the slightest idea which to take. The sun was falling quickly now. He took the left trail, looking for signs of a recent rider, but he found none, not a track in the rocky terrain, not any sign of passage. The trail divided again, and he tore a scrap of cloth off his shirt and tied it to a branch as he guessed again.

Darkness and trees closed in on him at the same time. He stopped and dismounted when he saw a small opening in the trees, overhung by rocks. Some shelter. An owl hooted, and he heard the faraway cry of a wolf. He swallowed hard. He didn't dare go on and risk getting totally lost.

His father wouldn't have been afraid. Neither would Ty, or Wade.

Jeff started a fire, huddling near it for safety. He heard the comforting snort of old Seth. At least he wasn't totally alone. In the morning, he would find Wade's trail again.

He chewed on some biscuits, but they were dry and tasteless and stuck in his throat. Another owl hooted, and one answered, and the night was full of sounds that grew progressively scary.

He was afraid to go to sleep, afraid the fire would die, afraid of what roamed in the night.

And he wished he was home, in his own bed. He would have given anything, at that moment, to hear the door of his room opening, his mother's footsteps. He wouldn't even mind a kiss.

Mary Jo was frantic when Ed and Tuck returned without Jeff. She searched Jeff's room and found the note.

I'm going with Wade up to the mountains. He will need help with the horses. Don't worry about me. I'll be fine.

If it was meant to be reassuring, it failed miserably.

How could Wade do that? That was her first thought. And then she realized he wouldn't have, not the Wade she knew. Unless Jeff told him she'd approved. She wouldn't put that past him.

But even then . . .

Wade knew how she felt about the Utes. He would know she wouldn't have consented. Or would he? Did she know him that well?

Fear squeezed her heart. She told herself not to panic, to think it through. Tuck and Ed were standing at the corral, puzzled, not quite sure what to do.

"You haven't seen Jeff at all?"

Tuck's shoulders seemed to squinch together. "No, ma'am. Not since this morning. You want us to go look?"

She considered the offer. But she knew it probably wouldn't do any good. Jeff was accompanying or following Wade. She would have to go after him, and the two men had to stay here with the animals. She didn't particularly want to tell the two newly hired men that their foreman was a friend of the Utes'; that might lead to more questions, more speculation. She couldn't risk it. They had known only that Wade was going to obtain some additional horses.

No, she had to go. She knew a name: Manchez. From talk in town, she knew the Utes sometimes camped along the Uncompahgre River, and she'd heard tell of a mountain man who lived near there. He might be able to lead her to the Utes. She swallowed her own fear. Nothing mattered but Jeff.

She wanted to leave that evening, but it would soon be dark; the moon was new now, only a small slice, and clouds spun like webs across the evening sky. It would be very dark and riding up into the hills would be foolish. Crippling her mare would not help Jeff. But she would leave at first light. Her mare was swift, and Jeff's mount old and out of shape. In the meantime, she could only hope that Jeff had somehow caught up with Wade, and she would meet them on their way back. The alternative left her stiff with terror. She couldn't lose her son. That would be one loss she knew she wouldn't survive.

She thought about going into Last Chance, and to Matt Sinclair, for help, but that was to the north, and Wade, and therefore Jeff, would be heading south. She would lose too much time.

Mary Jo didn't understand why she had so much faith in him, believed he could do the impossible. But he had done it once before when he'd saved her son. She had to believe he could do it again.

At first light, Jeff mounted old Seth and turned to retrace his steps. He tried to pay attention, but he was tired after a sleepless night. His eyes sometimes closed, and then he would jerk awake again.

He kept looking for the piece of shirt. He didn't find it. How, he wondered, could he have missed it? He didn't remember going so far after the trail split. But then the trail was leading upward again, and Jeff knew that was the general direction Wade was taking. A trail, after all, had to lead someplace.

He took a sip from the canteen, then splashed some water on his face to keep himself awake. His horse plodded along as the trail became steeper and steeper. Pines mixed with aspens, their branches overhanging the trail and shadowing it. The farther he went, the more the trail narrowed, the path nearly obliterated by needles. He looked behind him, and he couldn't see it anymore. The forest had closed in around him.

A squirrel darted from one tree to another, making Jeff wince before he realized it was simple play. He fought down his growing fear and wiped the sweat that drenched his face despite the cool mountain air. What would his father have done? What would Wade have done?

He found a place wide enough to turn around and he did that, lightening his hold on the reins. Maybe old Seth could find the path again, maybe he knew the way home. The horse snorted, obviously displeased that he was not in the stable munching oats.

"Let's go home," Jeff said, ready to give up his attempt to follow Wade. All he wanted now was the Circle J. Home.

Old Seth plodded back down, foam flecking at his mouth. He wheezed, and Jeff's guilt escalated. He stroked the horse's neck. "It's all right, old boy," he said. "We're going home, you and me." He hoped his tone conveyed more confidence than he had.

Mary Jo pushed back a lock of hair as she approached the ramshackle cabin. She'd been riding hard for long hours, following the road until it became a trail and started climbing upward. She had a sack of supplies, food, matches, oats for the horse, two extra blankets, her rifle and a pistol.

When several trails split off from the main one, she tried to puzzle out which to take, wondering whether she should head toward Last Chance after all. But then a lone miner and mule approached from one of the trails. He'd not seen a boy, nor a man with an arm in a sling, but he told her where she could find Tom Berry, the reclusive mountain man she'd hoped could help her. He was famous in these parts, having once explored with Kit Carson. Mary Jo obtained some vague directions and headed for Tom Berry.

After hours of searching, she found a faint trail leading to a small clearing and cabin. A mangy-looking mule glared at her from where he stood, a tether around his neck.

Mary Jo knocked on the door, waited, then knocked again. There was noise inside, but no one answered. She knocked again, louder.

"Goddammit," someone roared from inside. "Can't a man be left alone?"

Mary Jo just knocked louder.

The door banged open, and she stared at the sight in front of her. Tom Berry was a tall, solid man, and he stood there in dirty long johns. A black beard, just slightly laced with white, fell several inches past his chin. His age was impossible to determine. Though his body seemed fit, his face was like a well-traveled road, jutted and rocky and crisscrossed by dozens of trails. Pale blue eyes stared at her with enmity.

If she hadn't been so worried about Jeff, she might well have lost her nerve.

"Mr. Berry?"

His eyes narrowed. "I'm not in no mood for a woman."

She caught his meaning. She felt her face flush. "I need a guide. My boy, my son, is gone, and—"

"I ain't no shepherd." He started to shut the door.

"I'm looking for a man," she said desperately. "Wade Foster. I think he might have gone up to the Ute camp."

The door stopped moving. The man seemed to hesitate a moment. "Foster? Why?"

"He's been staying with us . . . I think he went to get some horses from the Utes, and my son . . . decided to follow him."

"Foster's got a family of his own." His eyes looked her over shrewdly. "But then he might not have told you that."

Her back stiffened at the implied insult to both Wade and herself. "Of course he did. They're . . . dead," she said, before stopping suddenly. Had she made a terrible mistake? But she'd hated the man's insinuation.

"Chivita? The boy?"

She could have bit her tongue. Had she just condemned Wade? She didn't make any response.

"How long ago?" Berry asked.

"I'm not sure."

"How?"

She kept silent. It was Wade's business, not hers to reveal. Tom Berry's eyes seemed to be boring through her. "Foster sure set store in that kid of his." He stopped. His eyes narrowed again. "Why was he staying with you? I didn't think he would ever come down out of those mountains."

Mary Jo wanted to answer, explain that Wade had been wounded. Jeff's life might depend on it. But she couldn't tell whether this man was Wade's friend or enemy.

The man suddenly cracked a smile, showing slightly yellowed crooked teeth. "You know him, all right," he said. "You'll do, I guess. First woman I met who kept her mouth shut when she should. How long your kid been missing?"

"Since yesterday morning."

"You say he's with Foster. He'll be all right." He started to close the door. "Foster likes kids. I don't."

"You don't understand," Mary Jo said desperately. "Wade . . . Mr. Foster didn't take him. My son followed him. I think . . . Mr. Foster would have brought him back if Jeff had caught up with him. He knows how I feel about—"

Those damned pale blue eyes impaled her. "You an Indian hater, too?"

She squirmed under his gaze. She felt herself

shrinking. *Indian hater.* It sounded ugly, put like that. "I just don't trust—"

"How in the devil did you ever get mixed up with Foster?"

"It doesn't matter," she said. "Just my son. Please, I'll pay you anything. Just help me find Wade Foster."

He hesitated.

"Are you afraid?"

"I've been trading with them Utes for fifty years," he growled. "They ain't nothing to be afraid of. Now them damned pilgrims, they're something else again. Can't leave a man in peace. Takin' what ain't theirs to take."

From the glower on his face, Mary Jo figured unhappily she qualified as a pilgrim. She suspected that any settler who came to these mountains did.

"Wade . . . Mr. Foster—"

"He fits into these mountains. " 'Preciates 'em for what they are. Doesn't try to dig 'em all up."

For the first time, she detected a note of approval in his voice. Hope filled her. She tried again. "Please . . . he would want you to. He and Jeff are friends."

"Hell, you ain't gonna give me any peace till I do," he mumbled. "Planning to go up there, anyway. Got some goods to trade. But you better keep up with me, missy, or I'll leave you flat-out."

"I will," she promised, relief flooding her. Then she felt renewed impatience after clearing that hurdle. "How soon?"

He scowled at her. "When I get my trousers on. That all right with you, missy?"

She nodded.

"And I'll want a couple bottles of good whiskey in payment."

"As many as you want," she swore.

He didn't say anything but went back into the cabin, banging the door shut behind him, leaving Mary Jo outside, wondering again whether she was doing the right thing. Tom Berry looked as if he would cut a man's—or a woman's—throat as easily as look at him. There had been no warmth in his eyes, only irritation and dislike. And now Jeff's life depended on him.

Jeff couldn't lie to himself any longer. He was totally lost. So was old Seth. He realized it when they passed the same rotted log for the second time.

If he continued, he might just go farther from the trail, from where someone might find him. He looked up at the sky. Mid-afternoon from the position of the sun. He should get some sleep now, before night, when he needed to stay awake. He thought about his food. Enough for two more days if he ate sparingly and added berries to it. Water was no problem. It dripped from any number of rocks, and the horse could find enough grass to survive. He tried to remember everything his pa and Ty had told him about survival. The first was not to panic.

That, he thought, was easier said than done. Fear kept tugging at him. He found a small clearing and dismounted. He had watered Seth just an hour earlier at a small waterfall and pool, but he knew not to linger there. There had been too many animal tracks. Jeff unsaddled Seth and staked him out near a patch of grass, then gathered wood for a fire. After he had finished that, he spread out his blanket and ate the last of

the remaining biscuits. He eyed some nearby mush-
rooms hungrily, but he was afraid to try them, not being sure which were poison and which weren't.

His stomach growled, and he took some swallows
of water. His rifle was next to him, the horse several
yards away, securely fastened. He was so tired. He shut
his eyes and, despite his fear, felt sleep closing in on
him.

— 16 —

Tom Berry was the quietest man Mary Jo had ever met. She'd thought Wade Foster was until that morning. Did the mountains do that to a man? Or was it the character of the men who chose to live in them?

Mary Jo followed the man silently. She was afraid too many questions might make him change his mind. They'd exchanged only a few words as Tom Berry saddled the mule. She'd watched with astonishment as the animal tried to bite him, and he twisted deftly out of range. He hit the mule on its side, and quickly tightened the buckle as the mule released air that had bloated its stomach.

The bearded man glanced up, and Mary Jo would have sworn she saw a twinkle for a moment before it disappeared in the flat blue of his eyes. "Don't like horses myself. Too dumb. Now Rachel here, she's right smart, smart enough to know she don't want no one on her back.''

"Rachel?" she said.

He gave her an irritated look. "Rachel's as good a name as Sam," he said with as much explanation as he was apparently going to offer for giving a woman's name to an animal that was obviously not of the feminine gender.

That odd conversation was the last, and puzzling enough to keep her mind off Jeff for the first several miles, but Mary Jo soon discovered Rachel's appeal. They seemed to go straight up into the mountains, and Rachel never faltered on the steep trail, never blew hard, never slowed, while her own Fancy struggled for footholds, and was breathing hard. The trail was narrow and overgrown, seemingly leading to nowhere, and she questioned several times how wise she was to follow him. But after several hours, she had no choice. She had absolutely no idea where she was.

He called a halt only once before they stopped for the night, and that was to give the mare a few moments of rest. He did that begrudgingly, looking at both of them with disgust. "Want to make it by nightfall," he growled. "Won't do it if we have to stop every few moments."

Since this was the first stop in hours, Mary Jo wanted to protest, but she held her tongue. Instead, she ran her hand comfortingly down the mare's neck and poured some water from a canteen into her hat for Fancy to drink as she pushed back tendrils of her own hair.

She was filthy. It had been hot below, and sweat had trickled down her face, her back, and between her breasts. Now the air was cooling fast as they ascended into the mountains. The sweat had cooled, and grit clung uncomfortably to her body. She was stiff and hungry and afraid. Fear for Jeff wiped out any concern for herself. She only prayed that her son had somehow met up with Wade, that he was safe. He was still just a boy, no matter how much he thought otherwise.

They mounted again after the mare had rested and traveled until it was dark. He stopped again and dismounted. "We stay here tonight," he said.

"But—"

"You've got grit, missy. I'll say that for you. But that damn horse of yours could break a leg on this trail at night. We'll leave again at daybreak." He turned away from her, taking some food from a pouch and eating by himself, obviously expecting her to do the same.

"A fire?" she asked tentatively.

He shrugged. "If you want one. You'll have to stay up all night tending it." The thought quickly killed any desire for one. Her mind was willing, but her body wasn't. Her eyes kept closing, and her arms and legs felt like dead tree limbs, ready to snap with the slightest breeze. She thought of Jeff. She prayed he wasn't alone out here.

She looked at Berry. He had already spread out his blanket. He was smoking a foul-smelling pipe.

She heard a coyote and flinched.

"Ain't within miles of here," her companion said disdainfully.

"I'm not worried about me," she said sharply. "But Jeff, he'll be frightened."

He eyed her with indifference. "Not if he's your get, I'm thinking."

It was approval, nothing else, and she felt a certain

pride in it. She'd tried all her life to be useful, and after her husband had died, she had to be self-reliant. And then when they'd moved here, she was so sure she could handle everything. That it hadn't happened that way, that she needed Wade and now this man, shamed her. But with those few words, Tom Berry restored something important to her.

She didn't reply, just sort of savored the words, hoping with all her heart he was right. And then knowing she needed her strength, she snuggled down in the blankets she'd brought and closed her eyes.

It was around noon the next day when they reached a plateau. A rich green valley dotted with tepees spread out before her. Women and children gathered to look when they spied the visitors, and then men, their hair plaited into braids decorated by beaded bands, started to appear.

Mary Jo stifled her apprehension. It looked peaceful enough. The tepees were made of animal skins and richly ornamented with beads. Dogs barked in greeting, and Mary Jo saw the women's faces reflect curiosity and concern, even some fear, while the men's faces were stoic, as blank as Wade Foster's had been so many times. There was no war paint as she'd seen on Comanches, no angry scowls.

She sat straighter, her back stiff, as she looked for Wade's blue trousers and shirt. She looked for a redheaded boy with freckles spread over his nose. She saw neither. Then Tom Berry approached two of the men, bending over to speak to them quietly. One nodded, looked at Mary Jo curiously, then retreated back into the tepee from which he'd emerged.

In another minute, she saw Wade coming out of the tepee, his back bent as he stooped through the flap. He looked defiant in his deerskin clothes and beaded eagle necklace, and his feet were encased in leather moccasins that reached nearly to his knee. He appeared so savage and primitive that Mary Jo wondered whether she knew this man.

He walked over to her. "Mrs. Williams," he said, eyeing her as warily as the others.

"Is Jeff with you?" she asked, refusing to waste time with preliminaries.

His brow wrinkled and his eyebrows knitted together. "Jeff? Why would he be here?"

Her heart sank. She had hoped against hope he would be here.

"He left a note three days ago. He said he was going with you. He left several hours after you did. He told me he was going to find Tuck and Ed. I didn't find out until they returned that night. He never came home."

Wade's sun-bronzed face paled. "What did the note say?"

Mary Jo searched in a skirt pocket, retrieving the wrinkled piece of paper she'd read and reread so many times. She handed it to him silently and watched his face change as he skimmed it once, then read more carefully. *I'm going with Wade up into the mountains. He will need my help.*

"I never saw him," Wade said hoarsely, pain in his voice. "If I had I would have brought him back to you."

Mary Jo swallowed. "I know . . . I just hoped—I knew he would be safe with you."

He held out his hand to her, helped her down,

holding her just a moment longer than necessary. She felt herself trembling as her body leaned against his. She needed his strength.

"We'll find him," he whispered, his voice sure again. "He must have followed the road, then taken a wrong trail."

"We?"

"Manchez, his friends, they'll help search."

Mary Jo backed away, searching his face.

"Don't worry," he said. "They're all good trackers, great trackers."

"But why should they—"

"Because," he said gently, "they're my friends and they value children." His eyes warned her not to object, not to insult the men standing around him.

They were not as tall as Wade, but their bodies were sturdy, compact, and their piercing obsidian eyes difficult—if not impossible—to read. They were foreign to her, and therefore frightening. Most were wearing dusty deerskin shirts and leggings; some wore bright plaid cotton shirts.

"I would be grateful," she said, trying to ignore the lump of fear in her stomach, trying to be grateful to anyone who would help. Still, she didn't feel reassured by the idea of these warriors tracking her son. *They value children.* Comanches had valued her sister at one time, enough to risk their lives to kidnap her.

Wade's eyes narrowed slightly, and his hand left her. He turned to the man next to him. "Brother," he said, and Mary Jo wondered whether that address was meant particularly for her ears. "How many can you send out?"

Mary Jo had also turned her gaze to the Indian. So this was Manchez, brother of Wade's wife. He reciprocated her perusal, his eyes unblinking. But not hostile. That surprised her.

"Ten and eight," Manchez said. He put his hand out to Wade's arm, guiding him away from Mary Jo, lowering his voice and speaking in a language she didn't understand. She heard Wade answer in the same tongue. They spoke for several moments, then Wade turned back to her.

"Manchez saw the fear in your eyes. He wants to know if you trust him to hunt for your son." His own voice was empty of emotion, forcing her to make a decision, forcing her to trust.

She swallowed her protest. Wade trusted them. She had to. She had no choice. She took a few steps to Manchez. "Please find my son," she said.

He studied her face, then nodded. "You stay with my wife."

She opened her mouth to protest, then saw Wade's mouth form the word "yes."

"I want to go with you," she said instead.

"We will all go separate ways and we will move fast. We cannot spare time for you." Manchez's tone was adamant. "You stay."

Wade caught her arm and guided her several feet away. "This is no longer their land," he said abruptly. "They will be risking much to help you. Do as he says."

"What about you?"

"You'd slow me down, too. You don't know these mountains. You'll be safe here. They think you're my woman."

Her eyes opened wide with questions.

"I told them that because I knew they would be more willing to search. After being robbed of most of their land, all their best land, do you think they would risk what little they have to find a white child? If they run into some soldiers or liquored-up whites . . ."

"They value children," she reminded him.

"They value their own children too, and helping yours could injure theirs," he said bluntly. "We don't have any more time to waste. You can return with Tom Berry and get help in town or you can stay here and trust them, trust me."

Mary Jo was defeated, and she knew it. Jeff had been out here three days now. She didn't have time to go back, summon a search party of white men. Jeff may have somehow gotten back home, but she didn't think so. Deep in her heart, she knew he was in these mountains. She nodded.

"Her name is Shavna," he said. "She is a good woman who has two sons of her own." He turned, nodding to Manchez and leading Mary Jo to the tepee he'd left. He stooped to go in again, and in a moment was back out, a pretty young Ute woman following him.

The woman smiled shyly at her and held out her hand, inviting Mary Jo in. Mary Jo hesitated once more. Wade took several steps toward her, and put his hand on her shoulder, squeezing it gently.

"We'll find him," he said with one of his rare smiles, and for the first time since she'd known Jeff was missing, Mary Jo felt hope welling inside, drowning out all the misgivings, the fear and distrust of those warriors now springing to the back of horses that had been grazing among the rich mountain grasses. She nodded and followed the Ute woman inside.

Jeff's stomach rumbled and ached. He'd been eating berries, too many of them. He just hoped they weren't poisonous. He had little food left, only a piece of jerky he'd been hoarding.

He'd tried to go hunting today, but he missed two squirrels and he'd been afraid to use any more of his ammunition. He'd only had six shells and he thought he'd better save the remaining four for varmints. He'd seen tracks earlier today, several of them, and he thought they might be wolves.

He'd already collected lots of wood for the fire tonight, to help him stay awake.

His fingers shook as he prepared the fire. The sun was setting now, red streaks coloring the sky. He'd never been so lonely or scared in his life, not even when his pa didn't come home years ago, or when Ty was killed in Harmony. He'd had Ma then. He'd never felt so awfully alone. And Ma. He knew she must be going crazy now, and guilt weighed on him.

The bloody crimson of the sky dissolved into the dark blue of night. The darker it got, the scarier it seemed. And more dangerous. Every sound now was enough to make him want to jump out of his skin.

Old Seth stamped nervously where he was tethered, and Jeff heard a faraway cry of something terrified, a cry like a baby's. An eagle grabbing a rabbit? Whatever it was, it ran a chill through him. Wind brushed the tops of the tree, and he drew his blankets closer. The temperature was falling fast now, as was the last light. He struck a match and lit his precious pile of kindling, fanning it with his hands. He knew he had to keep this fire going, not only to keep the animals away but because he was running out of matches as quickly as he was running out of everything else, including courage. He wanted to cry, but that wouldn't help.

An owl shrieked as the night turned entirely black.

He wished Jake was there with him. Jake would miss him, too. He was a one-man dog, at least he had been until he found Wade Foster. He prayed. At least he tried. He was too scared, and he didn't really think God was listening to him. He hunched his shoulders against the darkness, the night, and snakes and coyotes and other animals he knew prowled these woods.

He reached out and touched his rifle. He had to stay awake. He had to.

Shavna did not speak English, but Mary Jo sensed her sympathy, her worry, and she found herself responding to it.

The inside of the tepee surprised her. There was a strong odor, but everything was neat and clean. Buffalo robes were folded in a corner, and gaily decorated pottery and intricately woven baskets edged the circle of the elkskin that covered the frame. A baby gurgled happily as it lay in a hide cradleboard, elaborately and apparently lovingly decorated with laces and fringe and beads. Another child, no more than two, played happily with a small drum.

Shavna leaned over and touched her hair, as if it were something wondrous, and then smiled shyly again. She pointed to what appeared to be a doeskin dress she'd been beading. Mary Jo touched it, wondering at its color and softness. It was lovely, the skin exquisitely tanned and ornamented with beads. Shavna handed it to her and smiled.

Mary Jo, not knowing exactly what was expected, smiled back, her fingers touching the softness of the garment. Worry kept her from concentrating. Her mind was far away, riding with Wade. But her fear began to fade as the little boy toddled over to her, his fingers catching in her braid, as fascinated by her hair as his mother was.

He said something she didn't understand, and his mother smiled with the kind of pride that all mothers knew. The boy was irresistible, his dark eyes glowing with curiosity and fascination as his small hands touched Mary Jo's mouth and gave her a big baby grin.

Mary Jo had to smile back, her arms going around the child, and he cooed with pleasure and laughed. In minutes, she was teaching the boy a little game she used to play with Jeff, riding a horse to market, and taking pleasure in the shrills of delight that accompanied it.

Later, when the boy was sleeping, Shavna pushed the dress back in her lap, and Mary Jo then realized it was a gift. Already emotionally battered, she fought to hold back tears at the generous gesture. The woman had obviously worked on the garment for days, if not weeks, and Mary Jo had never felt quite as humbled.

Wade rode off with Manchez and eighteen other warriors who had volunteered to join the search. Even Tom Berry surprised everyone by accompanying them. Wade had tried to thank his brother-in-law, but they had never needed words between them, and Manchez had shrugged off his halting words. But Wade knew the possible cost of the search to Manchez and his people.

The Utes had been pushed farther and farther west and now lived on the western slope of the Colorado Rockies, having given up much of their land in the San Juans in a succession of treaties. They had done so under the leadership of Chief Ouray, who'd devoted his life trying to ensure that the Utes wouldn't be forced on a reservation as other tribes had. He had signed treaty after treaty with the white man, each time seeing the treaty broken by greed. Now there were renewed calls to completely displace the Utes from the new state of Colorado.

Any incident, any at all, would strengthen the pressure for all Colorado Utes to be moved to the semiarid mountains of Utah, away from the rich grass of their centuries-old homeland.

Chief Ouray had been one of the few Indian leaders to see early on that the Indians could not win a war with the whites, that they had to find some way to satisfy the increasing lust for Indian land while keeping some for themselves. It had not always been easy to control the Ute warriors, who found their buffalo gone along with their grazing lands. But he had managed to keep the peace, except for a few isolated incidents.

Wade was keenly aware of the quiet, hopeless rage that often affected his friends. He had known he had to avenge the deaths of his wife and son, or Manchez would, and that would have meant disaster for his band, and possibly for the Ute nation.

And now they were risking a great deal for this white child, because he'd asked them. Although supposedly they had hunting rights in these mountains, the establishment of a summer camp went beyond the treaty. The Utes had taken care to keep far away from white settlements and new mines, but now they would be searching in areas where whites could be encountered, in the areas where Wade had killed three miners.

The Utes, though, could move like shadows. They'd always been hunters, had controlled these mountains for hundreds of years, and for years had fought the Arapahoes and Navahos. If anyone could find Jeff, it would be these men.

Manchez had asked only one thing when Wade had returned two days earlier. "The men who killed Chivita?"

"Dead," Wade had replied, and Manchez had nodded in approval.

Wade had told him about the last miner, his own wounding, and the white woman and boy who had saved him.

"I owe them for my brother's life, as I now owe my brother once again," Manchez had said.

After several hours, the Utes separated into groups of two and three, to cover more ground and to better fade into the forests if they encountered miners or troops. Wade went with Manchez, heading down toward the main trail to Black Canyon. They spoke very little; Wade's thoughts were focused on Mary Jo and Jeff. He couldn't banish her from his mind; it amazed him that she had come to him for help, and not only, he knew, because she thought her son might be with him. He had seen the hope flare in her eyes when she'd first seen him, and he'd felt both pleased and unworthy. He'd also known gut-deep fear for the boy. He hadn't realized until this morning how much he cared about Jeff, how much he cared about Jeff's mother, how much he'd been trying to deny those feelings and how badly he was failing.

He only knew he couldn't lose Jeff. He couldn't stand another loss in his life. His gaze met Manchez's, who watched him with compassion. "We find the boy," he said.

Wade nodded. He only hoped it wouldn't be too

late. Night was only hours away and these forests were filled with killers, human and animal alike. He kept remembering Drew, his crumpled body, his cut throat, and he dug his heels into his horse.

17

Jeff huddled next to the fire as dawn came slowly. Very slowly. The fourth morning. But last night had been the worst. He'd felt surrounded by the night, enveloped by it, haunted by the continued calls of the wolves.

He thought he'd seen a pair of eyes staring at him at one point, and he'd fired his rifle twice in panic. He'd barely restrained himself from taking more shots, and now he had only two left. There had been a rustle in the bushes, and then stillness. His horse had neighed and pawed the ground frantically, and Jeff had brought Seth closer to the fire and rubbed his neck until the trembling stopped.

But his own trembling hadn't stopped, not at any time during the long dark hours.

He watched the first morning glow widen and

spread across the sky in pinks and golds, wishing he could take pleasure in it. But he was tired and hungry. The fire was almost out, and he didn't try to keep it going any longer. But he did lean against a tree trunk and close his eyes, wondering whether he dared sleep now, or whether he should try looking for the trail again. Just a few minutes sleep. No more, and he would start looking again. Just a few minutes. He felt his head nodding, and even his hunger started to fade under his immense exhaustion.

Jeff wasn't sure how long he'd slept when something awakened him. He just felt heavy all over. His head hurt, his stomach ached from emptiness. He tried to shake the shadows from his mind, tried to figure out what had awakened him.

And then he heard the cry of his horse, its frantic thrashing against the rope that tethered him to a tree. In one sudden lunge, he broke free, rearing up, his front hoofs pounding against the hard, rocky terrain. Jeff reached out to grab the rope, but then had to duck to avoid the horse's hoofs as it reared once more, then turned and fled through the trees.

He heard something, or sensed it. His back stiffened and he grabbed the rifle, just as there was a movement above him, the smell of animal, and he saw the large cougar perched above him on a rocky ledge, its eyes fastened unwinkingly on him.

Jeff swung the rifle up, trying to take aim. Two shells left. The large cat was in a crouch, obviously ready to spring, and Jeff fired. The cat roared in fury and sprang. Jeff tried to twist out of the way, but he felt

the full weight of the cat on him and everything went
black.

Wade was tired but he wasn't going to rest. Neither was
Manchez. They had traveled fast during the afternoon,
then slower during the night hours, moving down
toward the main trail from the San Juan mountains to
Black Canyon. They had stopped only to rest the
horses, using what little moonlight there was to pick
carefully through the woods. Manchez had always been
able to see at night, a talent Wade had envied.

Just past daybreak, they heard the insistent call of
an owl, and Wade knew one of the warriors had found
a trail. He and Manchez quickened their pace, soon
meeting Cavera, a cousin of Manchez's. Cavera had
found a piece of cotton cloth and picked up horse
tracks. The three of them followed the trail as it led
upward. Before long, those tracks had crisscrossed, and
crossed again. The rider had been traveling in circles.
They found the remnants of a fire, then a cartridge.

Suddenly there was a thrashing sound from the left
and a horse burst from between trees, a rope trailing
behind it. Wade spurred his horse in that direction and
saw the boy just as he fired at the large cat. He couldn't
reach his rifle tucked in the saddle scabbard fast
enough with his wounded arm, but Manchez's hands
quickly aimed the rifle he'd been carrying and fired
just as the cat leapt from its ledge.

The horses were going crazy with the cat smell, but
the two Utes had no trouble controlling them. Wade
was riding one of his own Indian-bred ponies since it
was more surefooted than Jeff's, and it danced nervously as Wade slipped off and hurried over to where

the cat and Jeff lay in a deadly embrace. Wade took his pistol from his belt with his left hand, but the animal was still, dead, one of its paws resting on Jeff's chest, its claws stained now with blood draining from the boy.

The two Utes were next to him, pushing the animal off Jeff, kneeling next to him. Wade knelt on the other side, leaning down to place his ear next to the boy's mouth, then his chest. Jeff was still breathing, but he was bleeding profusely and there was a large jagged scratch in his side. His head had obviously hit the ground, knocking him out.

Hampered by his bad arm, Wade moved aside and watched as one of the Utes cut a piece of cloth from Jeff's shirt and pressed it against the wound to stop the bleeding. Wade felt so damned helpless as he knelt beside the boy, his hand touching the now pale face. The freckles stood out more than ever. This was his fault. He'd allowed himself to care, allowed the boy to care, and he'd once more been the instrument of disaster. If Jeff died . . .

"We take him back to camp," Manchez said. "Shavna will care for him."

Wade hesitated. He knew only too well how Mary Jo felt about Indians, but he also remembered she had said the only doctor in the area was none too competent. He knew that Shavna often tended to the ill, that she filled in when the medicine man wasn't along. And he wasn't now, which was just as well. Sickness and its cures for the Utes were related to spiritualism and religion. Sometimes the medicine man or shaman went into long trances or would press the top of his own head against the sick spot on the patient's body, then ceremoniously spit from his mouth to the source of the

sickness. Their herbs and poultices, though, were usually very effective.

And Mary Jo herself was good at healing. Wade was
alive because of her.

Manchez waited for his reply, and Wade nodded.
The wound was deep but Wade didn't think it was fatal.
Blood poisoning, though, could be. And Wade trusted
his Indian friends more than a drunken white doctor.

Because of Wade's bad arm, Manchez lifted the
boy and handed him carefully to Cavera, who cradled
him in his arms. Wade mounted his horse as Manchez
gracefully leapt on the back of his, and they headed
toward the mountain valley.

Mary Jo had spent a tense day in the Ute camp, despite
Shavna's efforts to distract and comfort her. She was
invited to join the women in tanning several deerskin
hides, and she did so because she *had* to do something
or go crazy, just as she used to wash floors over and
over again when her husband had been late from an
assignment.

Despite those moments of shared motherhood
with Shavna, she felt awkward and out of place among
these women dressed in deerskin dresses. Her skirt and
blouse were hot and dirty but she couldn't force herself to wear the dress with its short skirt that would
reveal most of her legs. Not here, not among . . .
people she didn't know. She tried to erase the word
"savages" from her mind. She held on to Shavna's
kindnesses, to the fact that these Indians were looking
for her son, that they were so obviously Wade's friends.
"Brother," he'd said.

But it was hard not to want to slide away, to close

her ears to the melodic language she didn't understand, to close her eyes to the differences she didn't want to fear but did. So she kept her hands busy, using a large bone scraper to rub the flesh and hair from the skin, as she watched others work the skins in various other stages. One woman was stretching a drying skin by placing one end between her feet and continually pulling over and over again. Others were tending small fires, smoking hides propped over them.

While the other women worked, one of them tended to the children laughing and playing with sticks and balls covered in hide. It was the children who made her relax, who gave her a feeling of normalcy. She'd always wanted more children, and it had been a matter of sorrow that there had been no more after Jeff.

Her hands kept moving, but she felt herself smiling at one of the children, a little girl of three or so, who followed one of the older boys who was running. She fell on her bottom and chuckled, her face full of pure joy at being young and free. The other women nodded and smiled, and suddenly there weren't any differences anymore, none that mattered.

If only she knew that Jeff was safe—

Just then the camp dogs started to bark, and the children stopped playing. The camp suddenly became still, except for the woman pulling the hide, and the two tending the fires. Everyone else turned toward the opening in the mountain that led to the valley, and Mary Jo knew the men were returning. Mary Jo stiffened, her fear returning. What if they hadn't found Jeff, or what if they had, and he was—

But she couldn't think of that. She would know. Somehow she would know that her heart was gone.

She saw Wade first. He was riding as easily as the others, but he had a saddle, and his height and lighter hair made him stand out. And then she saw the others. Four of them, one of them holding something, another leading an old chestnut horse. Her chest seemed to burst with pain, with raw anguish, but then the riders were almost upon them, and Wade had slid off his horse and taken two quick steps toward her. "He's alive, Mary Jo," he said. "Hurt some, but alive."

Her gaze went immediately to the Ute lowering her son to another man. Mary Jo recognized Manchez, and she saw the gentleness in the way he took her son and moved toward Shavna's tepee. She followed, frantic to see some sign of life, kneeling next to her son as soon as he was laid down on the ground. She saw the blood-soaked cloth first and looked up toward Wade, who had also entered the small, compact space.

"Cougar," he said. "Manchez shot him just as he sprang on Jeff. If he hadn't . . ."

Mary Jo looked up at the Ute. "Thank you," she said brokenly. "Thank you for my son."

He gave her a nod and left, while Mary Jo unwrapped the cloth from the wound, wincing at the raw meanness of it. Shavna had entered and kneeled on the other side. Jeff was so still, his face pale. She put her palm to his face, willing her strength into him, willing life into him. She looked up at Wade, looking for reassurance.

But he was looking intently at Jeff, his face expressionless.

Mary Jo looked back at her son. Her hand hadn't left his face. "Jeff?" Then louder, "Jeff."

Shavna looked up at Wade and said something Mary Jo didn't understand.

"She said it's better he sleeps while she tends his wound."

"I'll tend him," Mary Jo said, more sharply than she intended.

The Indian woman looked up at Wade questioningly.

Wade reached over with his good hand and touched Mary Jo's arm. "Come with me," he said gently.

She shook her head stubbornly.

"You want him to die?"

She looked at his face. The gentleness was gone, and a hardness had taken its place. "I can't leave him," she said.

"Do you have medicines with you?"

She didn't. She didn't have anything but her heart.

"The Utes are good at healing. They have herbs and poultices that work. I've seen it. But they won't do it with you questioning everything. Come with me, just for a few moments. He'll be all right, I swear it."

Mary Jo looked at Shavna, saw the compassion in her face, the desire to help. She reached up and took Wade's hand, letting him pull her up. She looked back at Jeff for a moment, reluctant, so reluctant to leave. She looked again at Wade. He nodded.

She had trusted him again, had sought him out, and he had found Jeff for her. She had no choice but to trust him again. But it went against everything she knew, everything she believed. She leaned against him, feeling his strength, his confidence, letting it seep into her. His arm went around her. "He'll be all right," he whispered. "A scar, no more."

She looked up into the green eyes, so deep and intense. And she believed. She believed he could move the moon if he tried. She let him lead her outside, into the sun.

"Thank you for finding him."

"It was Cavera who found the trail, Manchez who killed the cougar. I . . . couldn't reach my gun in time." Agony slid across his face.

"They wouldn't have done those things if it weren't for you."

"And Jeff wouldn't be in there, cut by that cougar, if it weren't for me," he said bitterly. "Every person I touch is . . . hurt." Mary Jo knew he started to say something else, perhaps "dead," and a shudder ran through her.

"No," she said.

He looked away from her.

"I need you now." Her voice was little more than a whisper.

"They'll take good care of him."

"I know," she said.

"No doubts?" he asked, bitterness still in his voice. "No fear they might scalp him instead of heal him?"

"No."

He spun around and faced her. "You were damn sure they might a few days ago."

Shame coursed through Mary Jo, shame and chagrin. She knew now what he'd tried to tell her, and she'd refused to hear. Shavna was no different than she. She loved her children as Mary Jo did, loved her husband as Mary Jo had, had taken a stranger, one obviously suspicious, to her heart because of a friend and a shared love of children.

"I was sure of a lot of things a few days ago, a few weeks ago. Now I'm not sure of anything," Mary Jo said.

His lips quirked slightly in a half smile that disappeared almost immediately, replaced by the despair that had enveloped him seconds ago. She touched his good arm. "It wasn't your fault. None of this was."

"He was following me. He thought . . . godammit, he thought I needed help. And I do. I always will with this arm. I couldn't shoot that cougar, I couldn't even carry Jeff. I'm no damn good for anything except—"

"Except . . . ?"

"You don't know anything about me, Mrs. Williams," he said in a hoarse voice. "You think you do, but you don't. Everyone I've ever cared for has died, everyone who has ever cared for me. It's like a damn shadow that follows me wherever I go."

"Jeff isn't going to die. You said so."

"Only because of a miracle," he said flatly. "Only because Manchez was there. Jeff came too damn close. That's twice now, both times because of me. There won't be a third time."

It was as if a cold wind blew through Mary Jo. In just a few weeks, he had become so important to her, to Jeff. While part of her realized he wouldn't stay, she'd never really admitted it to herself. Until now. His eyes were cold, like the death he'd spoken of. His jaw was set, the lines in his face more pronounced, like ridges in a mountain, unyielding and stubborn.

"You'll take us home?"

"Tom Berry can do that better than I."

"And the horses you mentioned? He can't drive them back with Rachel. Besides, he doesn't like me."

"He wouldn't have brought you here if he didn't like you," Wade replied, although the set of his chin eased some, perhaps at the thought of Rachel the mule driving the horses.

"He doesn't like children," she continued to argue.

"Jeff's no longer a child. It took a man to survive out here for four days." There was approval in his voice. "If it hadn't been for that cougar . . ."

"He cares for you a great deal."

Wade turned away. "I don't want him to care about me," he said in that hoarse voice that Mary Jo now recognized as emotion he wouldn't, or couldn't, express in any other way. It was meant to be harsh, a warning, but it had the opposite effect. Mary Jo heard the need in it, the raw desperation in the denial.

She started to say something, but then Shavna poked her head from the tent, and gestured to her. She turned and hurried inside, kneeling once more next to Jeff.

His eyes were trying to open, and his thin body jerked with pain as he moved. There was a poultice, something that looked like moss, on the wound, but she also saw tiny little stitches at its edge. She placed a hand on his uninjured shoulder. "It's all right, Jeff. You're safe. You're all right now."

Jeff looked frantically around, noting first the tepee and then finally Shavna, who was also kneeling next to him. "This is Shavna," Mary Jo said. "Wade's friend. She's been taking care of you."

"Shavna," he whispered and tried to smile, a terribly lopsided smile that was half grimace. Mary Jo felt her heart jerk around inside.

"I'm . . . sorry," he said, his gaze returning to her. "It was . . . dumb leaving, but—" He stopped.

"But what?" she asked gently.

"I thought . . . maybe if I could help Wade, he would . . ." His voice trailed off again.

"Stay?" she asked.

He nodded miserably. "I . . . just showed how much trouble I was."

She put her hand to his cheek. "It's all right, Jeff. I don't think he cares about that now that you're all . . ." She hesitated, unable to finish the sentence. After a moment, she started again. "How do you feel?"

He tried to smile again, but his heart obviously wasn't in it. "Not so good. My head hurts, and I—" He looked down at his chest, then up at Shavna. He tried to move, but he fell back down with a groan.

His eyes seemed to cloud. "A big cat . . . a cougar. I saw it come at me."

Mary Jo took his hand, clasping it tight. "Shavna's husband killed it just as it came down on you. Your head hit the ground, knocking you unconscious."

His gaze searched behind her. "Wade?"

"He's outside. He helped bring you back."

"I knew he would," Jeff said. "I knew he would find me. Can I see him?"

"Not now," she said. "I think you should get some rest."

"Is he angry?"

"No," she said gently. "He's grateful you're alive, just like I am."

"I didn't mean to worry you." His face flushed as he realized the foolishness of his words.

"Just promise you won't ever do anything like that again," Mary Jo said.

He moved slightly, and pain flashed across his face. Shavna leaned down and held a cup to his lips. He took a sip and shook his head, but the Indian woman pressed it against his lips again, and Mary Jo nodded at him to drink. Wincing at the taste, he did.

Manchez had been sitting cross-legged in the back of the tepee. "He will sleep now," he said. He and his wife exchanged looks, and Mary Jo saw the affection dart between them. And love. She suddenly felt envy.

She looked down at Jeff. His hand was still clenched in hers, but his eyes were already closing. His breathing was regular, his color not quite as pale as when he was brought in. Gratitude welled up inside her. She gently unraveled her hand from Jeff's and both of hers took Shavna's. "Thank you," she said, hoping she understood.

Shavna gave her a shy smile and nodded, her hands briefly tightening around Mary Jo's before letting go.

Cavara, the Ute who had found Jeff, insisted that Wade and Mary Jo use his tepee that night.

After they had taken the evening meal—fresh antelope meat and dried cake made, Wade said, from the root of the yampa plant, and piñon nuts—Wade asked Mary Jo to take a walk with him. Jeff was still sleeping peacefully.

It was a beautiful night, soft and gentle with streaks like rivers of peach and pale gold stretching across the sky. The wind was low, and the temperature unusually warm for these mountains. Children's laughter echoed across the rich green grass, the sound enriched by the soft call of night birds; the evening air smelled of smoke and roasted meat. The world seemed at peace here in a valley cradled like a gem between snow-covered peaks.

"It's so beautiful here," Mary Jo said after several moments of silence.

"The Utes have lived here for hundreds of years," he said, his voice full of regret and sadness. "Their shining mountains."

"The name fits them," Mary Jo said. "They *are* shining."

He swung around on her. "It's not fair. They're being taken away, piece by piece, and soon they will have nothing. They're being forced to move to some piece of arid ground like all the other tribes, forced to give up everything meaningful to them."

Mary Jo didn't know what to say. Until now, she'd approved of efforts to move the "savages" away from whites. Today, she'd learned just a little about the harmony between these people and the land.

"There's nothing on God's earth anyone can do," Wade said. "One incident, one hothead, and they'll be shipped away, just like the Apaches have been, the Cherokees, the Creeks, the Sioux."

"That's why you wanted me to get your gear."

He nodded.

"You can't help at all? You can't go to the governor or—"

"Hell, I can't help anyone. If I tried to protest and anyone discovered who I really am—" He stopped, aware that he was about to say something he'd regret.

She had stopped. "Who are you, Wade? It won't make any difference to me."

He laughed bitterly. "Believe me, you don't want to know. Isn't a cripple who killed three men enough to scare the hell out of you?"

The darkness was back in him. For a few moments, he'd seemed almost relaxed, comfortable with these people and his surroundings, but now those terrible shadows were once more shrouding him, pulling him away from her again.

"No," she said softly. "You'll never scare me."

"I will, lady. Give me the chance, and I will." He walked on, not waiting to see whether she was following him. She almost had to run to keep pace with him.

He stopped again in the shadows of a tree. The moon was up now, fragile and luminous. "Cavera has given his home to us tonight," he said. "They will be insulted if we don't use it."

She didn't understand at first, then slowly comprehended. They were expected to stay together in a tepee. And Wade didn't like it at all, but he didn't see any way out.

"Why?"

"They think you're my woman. That's why they went after Jeff. It would hurt them deeply if my woman didn't, wouldn't, share their hospitality."

"But you were married to Manchez's sister."

"Utes are very practical. They mourn as we do, but they believe in family, in the need for children. They would want me to find a new woman."

His woman. Wade's woman. A shiver ran down her back. A shiver and something else, something warm and thick and sensuous, like molasses flowing through her body. She hadn't ever wanted to be someone's woman again. She hadn't wanted the pain that went with it, the dependence, the waiting, the hurting.

But she wanted him. She wanted to bring a smile to his lips, to hear him chuckle. She wanted to feel the tenderness of his hands, the excitement of his body, the joy of his mating. She wanted all that, and she wanted more. She wanted to dissolve his ghosts, the bleakness she so often saw in him.

"What will they do?" she said finally.

"Cavera's not married. He'll sleep outside tonight. Shavna will continue to care for Jeff. She's the healer."

Mary Jo hesitated.

"He will be well taken care of."

"I know, but—"

"They will be hurt if you don't trust them." He said it reluctantly, and she knew he didn't welcome the prospect of spending the night alone with her. But then he had made it clear he didn't want any further involvement.

She thought about lying next to him. Heaven and hell. Could she do it without touching him? Without him touching her? After that afternoon several days ago, which now seemed so far away, her body ached for him. "What about you? What do you want?"

"It doesn't matter what I want," he said curtly. "I don't want to offend Manchez. If you can bear it, for one night, I promise not to touch you. I had no right before. It was a mistake."

She swallowed hard. He didn't want her. She nodded miserably.

"I'm sorry, Mary Jo," he said quietly. "I'm sorry you found me. I'm sorry I've brought you so much trouble. I'm not going to make it worse." He turned then and walked away, making it clear, very clear, that he wanted to be alone.

She watched him move through the trees until he disappeared into the shadows. Alone. Wounded in so many ways. Yet proud. Always so proud. Too proud to share the hurts and the pain and the loneliness.

Mary Jo felt ice touch her heart. Sometimes he

reminded her of a wild and graceful animal. One with courage and heart and endurance. There was something she remembered being told about animals like that. They usually went off someplace alone to die. He seemed to be preparing to do that, if not literally, then in all the important ways. His soul was dying, and she didn't know what to do about it.

18

Mary Jo spent the rest of the evening with Jeff, just watching him as he slept. Whatever Shavna had given him to rest worked.

A small fire flickered, casting a glow over his face, over the freckles that seemed more pronounced than ever. But his breathing was easy and only occasionally, when he moved, did a small moan escape his lips.

He was a man, but he was also a boy. And he looked so young and vulnerable with the poultice on his chest and the many bruises and cuts that ringed the flesh around it. She had been so lucky it wasn't worse.

Only Shavna sat with her, her two children nestled in buffalo robes. The men sat outside, smoking pipes, talking. Mary Jo wasn't sure whether Wade was with them, or whether he was roaming the valley, expelling demons. He would return tonight, because it would be a discourtesy not to. And she knew now that while courtesy had not been supreme in his relations with her, it was with these people.

As she looked at Jeff, she wondered about the younger Wade, the boy he'd once been. He couldn't be that much older than she, and her life had not been easy, yet he had obviously been marked by events she couldn't even comprehend. The war? He would have been very young, but many boys fought in that war. She knew a few, including some who had later become Rangers. Their eyes had been haunted, their faces marked forever. Her own husband had missed it; his company was one that had stayed in Texas, and she used to thank God that it had.

She leaned down and brushed her lips against Jeff's cheek, wanting to guard him against death and horror and hopelessness. She loved him with every ounce of her being, and the last two days had shown her that she too might give up if he were taken from her.

Was that why Wade appeared so alone, so lost? His son? His wife? Or was it more than that? How many references had he made to the past, a past he obviously abhorred, one he felt made him an outcast forever? She couldn't imagine him doing anything dishonorable. She understood why he had gone after those three men he'd said he killed. She too would have gone after anyone who had killed her son.

So she just stared at Jeff's face, still young, still innocent, wishing it could always be thus, knowing it wouldn't. And then Manchez returned to the tepee, and she knew it was time to leave. She knew that Wade would join her soon, not because of desire, or want,

but because he didn't want to offend those who had
helped her son.

She felt terribly unsure. She had been so frightened these last few days, she just wanted to be held.
Comforted. Reassured.

Loved.

Wade delayed his return as long as possible. When he
finally went back to the camp, the men were discussing
the upcoming talks with the government in Washington. Some Utes, knowing what would happen, knowing
they would lose even more land, advocated fighting.
But fighting, others argued, only meant that the end
would come sooner. Look at the Sioux and Cheyenne.
They had been virtually destroyed in the year after
their one great victory at Little Big Horn. Chief
Ouray's negotiations had kept the Utes among the last
of the tribes not yet forced onto a reservation. It was
best to follow him.

When asked his opinion, Wade reluctantly con-
curred. To go to war with the whites meant only death
and annihilation of a people. Give as little as possible,
keep the young warriors in check. Don't give whites
the reasons they wanted so badly to remove the Utes
from their spiritual home. Manchez watched his friend
from across the fire, nodding. He knew Wade had
risked his life, had probably given his arm, to avenge
his sister and nephew, partially so blame wouldn't fall
on the Utes. The tie between them had pulled even
tighter these last few months.

When the last of the men went off to their sleeping
places, Wade had little choice but to join Mary Jo. He
went first and checked on Jeff. The boy was sleeping

peacefully and there were no alarming streaks of red around the wound. He was a damned tough kid, he thought with affection. Hell, his mother was a damned tough woman under that prettiness.

He was still surprised that Tom Berry had brought her up here. He didn't even want to think about the way his heart responded when he first saw her yesterday. Realizing full well how she felt about Indians, he knew how much courage it had taken to come here almost alone. Berry certainly hadn't provided much reassurance. She could have gone into Last Chance, raised the countryside, brought in troopers from Fort Wilson. It would have meant no little trouble for Manchez and his band, and for Wade. She had chosen, instead, to trust him when he'd given her damn little reason to trust, to go against all those lifelong fears for him.

That trust had felt too good. For a few moments yesterday, he'd even allowed himself to hope, to believe that something could be salvaged from his life. But then he'd seen that cougar and had been unable to do anything about it. Manchez, not he, had saved Jeff's life with that shot. That moment had deepened his conviction that he couldn't take care of those he cared about. Nor could he forget Kelly, or others who knew of his past, of the price on his head, of the scars that were being rubbed open again in a soul he'd tried to lock away. That damned shining trust in Mary Jo's eyes was misplaced.

He wanted to cry. He wanted to rage at the demons in him, the demons that had made Mary Jo Williams a dream he could never have, the demons that put her within touching range and then told him he would destroy her if he did. He lifted the flap of the tepee and allowed his eyes to adjust to the darkness. The night had turned cooler in the past several hours and she was wrapped in a buffalo robe. He listened for a moment to her breathing, hoping she was asleep. He would move to the far side, shiver in the cold, for there appeared to be only one robe and his bedroll was in Manchez's tepee where he'd been staying.

He willed himself to sleep, but he couldn't. He lay awake, rigid and hurting, knowing full well that release was only a short distance away, a smile, a hand touch from him. Even through the not-too-clean smell of the buffalo robe, he caught the scent of flowers, or perhaps it was his imagination. He always thought of her that way. God, how he wanted to hold her, pull her to him.

He didn't know how long he lay there when he heard the first sound of distress, the quiet whimpering sounds and then the small plaintive cries. He caught the word "Sally," and he wondered whether that was the sister who had been taken.

Wade's body tensed as the nightmare continued, and then she was jerking, crying, and he couldn't bear it any longer. He moved over to her, putting his good hand against her cheek. He felt wetness, tears, those very rare tears. His heart swelled with compassion, personal gut-deep caring, the kind he'd tried so hard to avoid. He would have given his life to take away the pain and the memories that still haunted her, and he realized again how much strength it had taken for her to come here alone, to give up her son to Shavna's care.

"Mary Jo," he said softly. The buffalo robe moved slightly as she seemed to struggle, and then she slowly sat up. Even in the darkness, or perhaps it was just in his mind, he could see the green of her eyes, the waves of hair falling alongside her right breast. He couldn't see, but he could imagine, the expression in her eyes: the fading of terror, confusion, then the softness that so often came into them when she looked at him. Softness and trust. That was the worst of it.

She sat there for a moment. "Jeff? Is Jeff all right?"

"I just looked in on him. He's fine."

"I waited for you. For a long time."

His jaw clenched. "You were having a bad dream."

"I don't know why. It's been so long . . . since I had it last."

"Your sister?"

She nodded, her hand taking his and holding on tight, as if the images still were real to her.

"You were tired. You've been scared half to death."

"I knew you would find him. Jeff was sure, too. He said he knew you would come." It was so simple a statement. So positive.

Her hand was trembling in his. It made her vulnerable, so very vulnerable to him, and he found himself doing what he promised he wouldn't do: he wrapped his arm around her, holding her tight to him. "It's over," he whispered.

"Don't leave," she pleaded. And he knew she was asking him more than not to leave the shelter.

"I have to," he said.

"Not tonight."

"Not tonight," he agreed. He felt her body shiver and he knew it wasn't from the cold, but he pretended it was. He moved next to her, pulling her close and wrapping the buffalo robe around them. And then he found his lips touching her cheek, her eyes still wet with tears that clung to the lashes.

"I thought I was strong," she said in a low voice. "But I'm not, not where Jeff is concerned."

His arm tightened around her. She was the strongest woman he'd ever met. The most independent, and that independence made her current surrender dear beyond measure. He supposed that was where Jeff got his gumption. Nothing seemed to daunt them, not a nearly dead man lying in the prairie who said he was a murderer, nor a rundown ranch without hands, or even Indians she'd once feared. The woman and boy just met each obstacle the best they could.

It was folly, this touching her. But he couldn't stop himself. He wanted to absorb all the fear she'd felt in the past several days. Hell, he wanted to take it all away. He meant to hold her just until the shivering stopped, but her lips reached up and touched his. Searching. Questioning. Needing.

And he needed her, God, how he needed her. He had from the day he'd left the ranch and realized how much she and the boy had come to mean to him in those few short weeks. He'd stayed with Manchez longer than he'd intended, trying to work out a way to solve the problem of her need for horses and the threat of Kelly without returning to Cimarron Valley. But there were no solutions. He could completely abandon them, and leave them and everything they had unprotected, or he could risk not only his physical survival but what was left of his soul.

But he couldn't turn down what was being offered now, to the damnation of that very soul. His tongue licked her lips, and her mouth opened to his. They were suddenly engulfed in a whirlwind, a wild, sweet lunacy as their mouths opened to each other. Their bodies moved together and they reacted and hungered, carried by needs so great they transcended every screaming warning in him.

His good hand touched her hair that was part fire, part sun. He tasted the dried tears on the side of her lips, and relished the woman scent of her. He felt the passion in her, and it made him feel invincible.

Wade closed his eyes and drank in the essence of her, savoring every sensation she aroused in him. He hadn't done that before; their lovemaking had been too sudden that day in the barn, and he'd been stunned by both his recklessness and the emotions he'd felt. But now he knew he wanted to capture these memories and keep them forever.

Her hand was touching his face, slightly bearded now since he had not shaved since he came here. It had been too difficult with his bad hand and there had seemed little purpose.

Now he felt rough and dirty. Her hand didn't leave his skin, but played around the bristle, hesitating here and there as if to place it forever in her mind. There was such tenderness in her touch, even as it conveyed a desperate urgency.

Then her hand moved, going down to his manhood, and her fingers hesitated on the outside of his tight deerskin trousers. He felt the swelling, the need, the deep ache for release. Her hand went to the laces, somehow undoing them under the buffalo robe, and he sprang free. Her touch was like cool rain on a heated rock, sizzling and welcome. He'd never felt such tender passion as she explored every part of him, making him quiver with need. He felt like a fiery volcano ready to explode.

Her hands left him for a moment, and then he felt her bare skin against him, and he moved over her, hesitating just a fraction of a second before plunging in, feeling her intimate channel close around him, dance with him, love him, consume him. Her legs went around his, drawing him even closer to her, until he was so deep in her that he felt he was touching her heart.

She leaned up, her lips touching his face, kissing its rough exterior, then met his lips again and the kiss deepened as he plunged again and again into her, and small whimpering sounds came from deep in her throat. Her body moved with his, arching against him as they sped toward the zenith of sensation, cherishing each star-step along the way. Then the shattering explosion came, and he knew she experienced it at the same splendid moment as he. He felt her quivering inside as waves and waves of pleasure washed through them, soothing, comforting, healing.

He bent his head, holding his cheek next to hers, hoping that his rough skin didn't abrade her. At the same time, their hearts seemed to touch and pound in concert. He'd never known this kind of exquisite bond with another, not even with Drew. He had been so terrified of caring and losing again, of burying people he loved, that he had pushed Drew away.

That was part of the immense guilt he felt. If only he had taken Drew hunting with him on that warm summer day when the birds were singing and the squirrels were playing . . .

Mary Jo, awash in rippling aftershocks of pleasure, suddenly realized she was losing him again. His cheek still lay next to hers, his hand still wound in her hair, and yet . . . part of him, the important part, was like a ghost leaving the body, drawing away from its shell. It terrified her. She'd always known he felt he couldn't stay, and these last few minutes, when they so naturally became one, made her realize how much she would lose.

She moved her hand to the back of his neck, playing with the thick hair and tracing circles on the golden skin. She wanted to bring him back to her, but how? Words wouldn't do it. She could only hope that he would come to believe, as she had, in the magic of faith and love. For now, all she could do was relish being with him.

He was still inside the core of her, and she tightened around him. He groaned, and she wasn't sure whether it was protest or renewed need or something else altogether. She knew parts of him so well, yet others remained aloof and alone and elusive.

I love you. The words were locked in her heart, unable to be spoken aloud, for fear that he might leave her in body as well as mind. But she hoped that somehow they might filter into his consciousness as the gift they were meant to be, as the acknowledgment of that enchantment between them.

He rolled over on his side, easing his weight from her but tightening his arm around her as if indeed he had understood those unspoken words. She felt his tenseness, the struggle inside him, and then she heard the curse, low and desperate, as she felt him hardening inside her again, felt the first rhythmic movements stir and tease the ever so sensitive core of her. The exquisite electricity, that stimulation of every nerve end, ran through her body again, racing and heating her bloodstream with expectation so strong she trembled with it.

She felt herself moving a half turn until she was on

top of him. He became so strong inside her, so large, so compellingly . . . complete. His smallest movement ignited such incredible feelings, she felt like an eagle racing toward the sun, toward a golden glory so splendid she'd give everything for it. He moved slowly at first, and then with an urgency that met her own, and that sun came nearer and nearer until the world as she knew it exploded in thousands of radiant streaks, each one sending glorious sensations surging through her body. She felt his warmth flood her, his seed rush into her, and then his hand, which had been holding her, dropped, and she heard his deep sigh. She fell down next to him, their bodies now separating. She lay next to him, her hand on his heart. She felt its beat, rushed, hurried, as was his breathing.

He was still now, so still. She wished they could whisper to each other, exchange soft expressions of love, but those words didn't seem to exist for him. So she clasped them to herself and waited. Waited for the self-condemnation she felt in him, the dismay, the reluctance.

It didn't come. He pulled her close to him, as close as they could get without him entering her again, and he just held her. It was suddenly as if the world held its breath for her. She kept expecting him to say what he had expressed several other times. This was wrong. This was a mistake. He didn't. Instead, it seemed as if he clung to her for his life.

She wanted to turn and look into his face, but it was too dark to see his eyes, and she didn't want to do anything that would make him take his arm away, that would break the closeness that cloaked them so snugly. She didn't dare shatter it with words, or movements, or promises, or pleas. She closed her eyes instead, relishing this wonderful sated contentment that settled around her like a beam of sun on a cool day. Wrapped in that glow, she closed her eyes and, cosseted by his warmth, she allowed sleep to settle gently around her.

Wade didn't move for what seemed like hours. His shoulder ached some from leaning on it when he made love to her, but that was a minor ailment. His heart was a major one.

He'd discovered tonight that he loved Mary Jo Williams, that somehow she had crawled into his heart and soul and gut. He suspected she would stay there forever.

He'd loved Chivita, but it had been different. It had been like loving a friend who was good to you. It had none of the passion and wild sweetness and need that he'd just experienced, none of that incredible oneness he'd just shared. He'd felt as if two people had become one, that they'd exchanged fundamental parts with each other.

He lay awake the rest of the night, nestling her against him, wondering how he could leave her, knowing he must. In his mind's eye, he saw those thick brown lashes shielding those eyes that were so damned honest. Why couldn't he be as honest with her?

Because then he'd lose her sooner than he was prepared to do.

Mary Josephine, he uttered in his mind, caressing each syllable. If only it wasn't too damn late for him.

He was gone when Mary Jo woke the next morning. She looked with dismay at the empty place he had occupied and prayed that he did not regret those moments last night. She stretched, her body still glowing. The memories lingered in her mind, then she remembered Jeff, and she shook her head to remove the remaining lethargy.

She shook away the buffalo robe and took stock of herself. Her split skirt and shirt were sitting in a wrinkled pile. Her hair, unbound by Wade last night, was a mess of knots. She was glad she didn't have a mirror. Dear Heaven, she was the thirty-two-year-old mother of a twelve-year-old son who thought he was a man, and she'd acted like a wanton last night.

Still, she thought lazily, being a wanton felt rather nice. Wonderful, in fact, as she remembered the delicious warm sensations that had filled her last night.

She groaned at the stiffness in her body as she managed to get to her knees and then up on her legs. She wasn't sure whether it was the lovemaking or sleeping on the ground, but she suddenly felt twenty years older.

She found a comb among the few belongings she'd brought with her and raked it through her hair, then braided it carelessly. She had long ago lost her pins. She tried to smooth out her shirt and then the divided skirt.

She found herself increasingly anxious to see Jeff, and she wanted to try to find Wade. She was full of questions: When could she return home? How soon Jeff could ride? Would Wade accompany them? He'd said nothing about the horses that he'd used as an excuse to leave them days ago.

But now Jeff was the most important concern.

She stooped and lifted the flap and faced the bright sunshine.

The camp was fragrant with smoke. There was the rich smell of meat roasting and another more astringent smell of curing hides. The women seemed to be in perpetual motion. Only a few men were around, and she wondered whether any were still looking for her son. She prayed no harm had come to any of them.

She walked swiftly over to Manchez's tent, and hesitated, but then Shavna appeared and smiled happily at her, holding open the flap. Mary Jo leaned over and went inside. Jeff was sitting up, and now he wore a deerskin shirt. His face had some scratches but he managed a painful grin.

"Jeff?"

"Manchez and Shavna gave me a shirt."

"I noticed," she said seriously.

"It feels real good."

"How do *you* feel?"

His grin faded. "All right," he replied. He tried to sound brave and adult, but his effort was undermined by the faintest quiver of his lips. "Manchez says there'll be a horse race tomorrow. Can we stay?"

"Tuck and Ed will be worried," she said.

"Oh no. Wade said Tom Berry would take them a note."

"Tom Berry?"

He nodded. "He's a famous mountain man."

"I know who he is," she said dryly, not mentioning her less than comfortable journey up here. She couldn't imagine him doing a favor for anyone, particularly a "pilgrim."

"He's a friend of Wade's," Jeff explained, then winced as he moved slightly.

Wade was becoming more and more of a mystery. The more she knew about him, the less it made sense.

He had seemed so much a loner, yet these Utes had put aside everything to find her son. For him. Because he had asked. A man who indicated he had few if any attachments appeared to have more than most, and some of them most unlikely ones.

"Let me see your shoulder," she said, and he obediently lifted his treasured shirt. His obedience, she thought wryly, probably stemmed from his desire to stay to see the horse race. She didn't undo the poultice tied to the wound, but she inspected the skin around it. It looked pink and healthy, at least the area that wasn't blue and purple with bruises and abrasions. He would be hurting for a few more days.

"If you ever do that again . . ."

He looked sheepish. "It wasn't very smart, was it?"

"About as smart as going fishing after a rainstorm."

The sheepish smile deepened. "I didn't get scared."

"Not even a little?"

He hesitated, obviously torn between bravado and honesty. "Maybe, just a little, but—"

"You knew Wade would find you," she finished wearily. She fumbled with his shirt, pulling it back down. "You can't always depend on him," she said carefully. "What if I hadn't found him?"

"But you did," he said with childish logic.

She sighed. "He may not be with us long," she said. The words hurt, but she needed to say them. For herself if not for Jeff. "You have to start taking some responsibility for yourself. I depend on you, you know," she added, softening her tone.

"I just thought he needed some help . . ."

"I know what you thought," she said. "But he

never would have gone off by himself if he didn't think he could handle it. How would you feel if you started to do something, and someone secretly tried to help you even though you didn't want any help?''

"I wanted to see the Indians," he said after a moment's consideration.

"You've done that well enough," she said with the slightest smile.

"I like 'em." He looked at her almost defiantly.

"I do, too," she said. "They saved your life, and I'll always be grateful."

"They're not savages," he persisted.

"No," she agreed, feeling regret now that she had ever used that word in front of him. But she hadn't been the only one; everyone used it. Except Wade. Guilt stuck in her throat; she would never rush to judgment again.

Before she could say anything more, Shavna came back in with a pitcher. She poured some liquid into the pottery cup Mary Jo had seen the night before and kneeled before Jeff, urging him to drink. He made a face but took some swallows. Mary Jo watched as his face relaxed, the little indications of pain around his mouth vanished. He gave her that devil-may-care grin of his, but with a sheepish edge to it, and then he closed his eyes.

Mary Jo just watched him for a while, thinking of the transition that was going on, that treacherous journey between childhood and manhood. Part of her dreaded the time the transition would be complete. He was still her baby, her child, and he wanted so much to be something more. She wasn't sure she could let go.

Then she felt Wade's presence behind her, and suddenly she felt as if she were floating on air.

"He's going to be fine," he said.

"I know. Thanks to you and—"

"Friends," he said simply.

"Friends," she confirmed, looking up into those haunted eyes, wanting something more than the friendly tone he was offering. But his face was shuttered, as usual. "I have some horses for you to see," he told her.

That had been his original purpose in coming here. Or had it? Had he been running from her, from Jeff, from what had been happening between them? Would she ever know?

She ached to take his hand, but he strode toward a copse, leaving her to follow or not, as she wished. She stiffened her back. She wouldn't plead. She could act as indifferent as he.

Then why did she ache all over with need for him? Did he feel even a fraction of that yearning? His stiff back gave her no answers.

19

Wade felt as if he would shatter into a million pieces. He wanted to touch Mary Jo so badly, to pull her to him and claim her forever. He needed every ounce of self-control he had not to do exactly that.

He tried to mask that need as he led her to where he'd separated his twenty horses from the others. He knew each one of them: the mountain ponies he'd bred from the wild herds descended from those brought by the Spaniards hundreds of years ago. He had no use for them now. With a useless arm, he couldn't take them alone into the mountains as he'd planned. The horses had been his wealth when he was married to Chivita, her prestige, her security, if anything happened to him. They would have secured a place for her in the tribe, made it easier for her to find a good husband. Now they meant little to him other than what they could bring to Mary Jo and Manchez. His farewell gift to both. Even his pride in them, he told himself, was gone, crushed in the anger and despair of the last months.

He heard Mary Jo's exclamation of delight. He turned to see her face awash with pleasure as she looked at the sturdy, swift animals. She clearly knew animals, but then she was from Texas and had been the daughter of a rancher and wife of a Ranger, both of whom depended on good animals for survival.

She ran her hand down the neck of one of them, the best one in fact. It was a gray, the horse he'd ridden yesterday in the search for Jeff. Fast and intelligent, it could move over these mountain paths like a goat. She turned and her eyes met his. "This is the one you rode."

He nodded.

She went to another, and then another, her hands running over their sides, down their flanks. "They're fine horses."

"Pick out ten," he said.

She hesitated, meeting his eyes. "I can't afford them."

"Yes you can," he said. "You've already paid the price in full. You saved my life. Not that it was worth saving."

"No. Only one," she said. "And thirty dollars each for three more."

"My life's only worth one horse?" he teased. "That's even less than I thought."

She appeared startled by his gentle barb. "I can't," she said miserably. She was being stubborn again; he'd come up against that stubbornness before.

"Ten or none at all," he said implacably. "You will

need them all, and more, if the Circle J is to survive. The ones you don't take go to Manchez. I have no use for them where I'm going."

He saw her swallow hard before speaking. "Where is that?"

"Where I can't hurt anyone," he said.

"You're leaving Manchez?"

He nodded. "If the sheriff ever learns the truth about me and those miners, he and his people would be the ones to pay for it."

"You could tell them what happened," she said desperately.

He smiled that sardonic half smile again, all the brief, gentle humor gone. "Three whites killed for an Indian and her half-breed kid? Hardly even, in the eyes of civilized society. Nits make lice, the army is fond of saying. Hell, those miners did a public service." His bitterness made her shudder, but he ignored her reaction. "Take your pick."

"You do it," she said, "but I insist on paying you."

"You saved my life, lady," he said. "There's no price on that."

"Mary Jo, dammit," she said. "Don't you dare call me lady again." Anger kept the tears from flowing.

"Mary Jo," he said softly. "Prickly Mary Jo who would risk a posse to save a man she didn't know and take on an Indian band she didn't trust to find her son. Is there anything that daunts you?"

Losing you. The words hung between them, unspoken.

When he couldn't bear to look at her anymore, couldn't bear to look at what he was giving up, he turned away. Every moment he spent with her was dangerous. If he were smart, he would let Manchez guide

Mary Jo and Jeff back to their home. But he couldn't ask that of his brother, nor could he let Mary Jo go alone, not with Kelly back there.

Kelly had to have something more in mind than he'd mentioned, and that something was probably the bank. He wished now he had asked Mary Jo to withdraw her money. He could still do that. But then knowing Mary Jo, she would probably want to protect her neighbors too. Questions would be asked, the sheriff would get involved, and the truth would come out about Mary Jo shielding and protecting a murderer.

Goddammit, Kelly was *his* problem.

The silence between them lengthened. Their eyes clashed, their wills engaging once more, their wills and so much more.

"Will you return with us?" she finally asked.

"For a short while. Until I know things are working out."

"How short?"

He shrugged. "A week, ten days."

She turned and he couldn't see her expression. "Which horses do you suggest?"

He was relieved that she changed the subject. "The smart ones. Speed doesn't matter much in a cow pony. Learning how to cut, to respond to its rider, is. On the other hand, speed is important to the Utes, so you won't be taking what's most valuable to them."

"What about you? Will you keep the gray?"

He nodded. "We're getting used to each other." He walked over to a short, stocky bay. "This one has a lot of endurance, and smarts. It would make a good second horse for Jeff." He continued on, making quick assessments of each horse until together they had selected ten. He was pleased she hadn't argued more

about the gift of horses, but then she might just be
waiting. She was good at that, waiting and then springing something on him. He started to turn away.

"Wade."

He stopped, hesitating at the sound of his name on
her lips. Damn, he wished it didn't have such a strong
effect on him.

"Is there a place to take a bath? In private?"

His hand touched his scratchy face. Hellfire, it was
time he did something about his own bathing. The
Utes didn't place much value on cleanliness and when
he was with them he didn't, either. At first he had
bathed as usual, but they all thought it was rather
funny and foreign, and before long he'd adapted to
their ways. A bath now, however, seemed inviting. He
knew it was yet another mistake, but the temptation of
bathing with her was too strong for someone of such
low moral character to resist, and at this moment his
moral strength was very low indeed.

"There's a spring a thirty-minute ride from here,"
he said, hoping she might object. Part of him hoped,
anyway, the sensible part.

But her face lit up with delight. "I'll get some
clothes and soap."

His throat tightened, knowing he was every pound
a fool. "I'll saddle your mare."

She didn't give him a chance to take back his offer.
She was gone in a second, leaving him to saddle her
horse and ponder his idiocy. Still, his pulse raced and
his body tingled with anticipation.

It had been so long since he'd gone swimming
with a woman, and never in a spot like the one he had
in mind. The pool was fed by both a waterfall and one
of the many hot springs in the area. The Utes used it

for medicinal purposes, and years ago, they had built a hut next to it to warn off invading tribes.

He had gone there once with Chivita, but she had been shy with him and had waited for him inside the hut. He knew she had always been somewhat in awe of him though he hadn't the damnedest idea why. He sensed, though, that Mary Jo would love this place. He had discovered she was a deeply sensuous woman, relishing the taste of the wind against her cheek, delighting in the quiet beauty of a summer evening.

She was back almost immediately, as if afraid he would change his mind. She had a small bundle with her that she tied to the saddle. "Jeff is still sleeping," she said as she easily mounted without any help from him.

He, on the other hand, was far from sure he was going to make it. He'd tried several times in the Ute camp to mount without a saddle, failing on the first two tries. It used to be as easy for him as with a saddle and stirrups, but his wounded right arm threw off his balance. Still, he preferred riding without a saddle. It gave him a sense of freedom, of being one with the animal, and now he wrapped his left arm in the horse's mane and swung up with an ease that pleasantly surprised him.

Wade wrapped his legs around the animal, using them to signal his instructions. It was late morning and the sun's rays drifted through the trees. He loved these mountains as much as the Utes did, and now he was sharing them with a woman he knew was learning an appreciation of her own. He fought the warm contentment that knowledge stirred in him. She moved her horse abreast of his, and his eyes met hers. She smiled, and shadows lifted from him—for this day, anyway. It was such a glorious smile, full of quiet happiness and anticipation. She always made his heart hum when she smiled like that, made him dream impossible dreams.

The pool was empty, as he knew it would be. He slipped down from his gray and went over to her, holding his left hand out to help her dismount. He held it a moment longer than necessary, reluctant to lose that warm touch, the pull on his fingers, the closeness of their bodies.

He finally let go, moving away. He watched as she approached the pool, which was surrounded by tall pines, the ground carpeted by aged needles, softened by elements and time. The pool was below a high cliff, and a steady but thin stream of water tumbled over jagged rocks and down into it. An eagle soared over them, circled and cried out, and he was certain there was a nest above.

"It's beautiful," she said.

He remembered what she had told him weeks ago about not being able to swim. He didn't dare allow her to go in alone. God, he wanted to teach her, both her and Jeff. But there wouldn't be time. If he made time, he would be irretrievably lost. Every minute he spent with them drew him closer, tightened the web trapping them together.

"It can also be dangerous," he warned. "You're safe enough if you stay on the ledge, but toward the middle it drops off."

"You'll be with me?"

That damned trust again. Some help he would be with his bad arm. But he nodded.

She opened her bundle and took out some soap. She went to the edge of the pool, sat down, and started to undress. He liked the way she did it. No fake mod-

esty, no darting glances toward him. But he appreciated more than the efficiency of her movements. He
had never seen her completely undressed, just bits and
parts. She was even more desirable than he'd imagined.

He'd known she worked hard. He'd watched her
around the ranch, and he knew feeding a station full of
hungry Rangers must have been wearing. Whatever the
cause, her body was firm and slender, though rounded
enough that she always felt soft to him.

He wanted to discard his trousers, but he'd already
done enough damage. If he did that, they would make
love and he'd be risking a child once again. The bastard child of a fugitive and killer. The thought cooled
some of the growing heat in his groin, and he decided
to wait to wash until she'd finished. But he would be on
the side, ready to help if she needed it. He could
watch, even if he couldn't touch.

Wade carefully took his arm from its sling to en-
able him to slide the shirt from his body. He replaced
the sling, then folded his legs, Indian style, at the edge
of the pool as she slipped in, wincing for a moment at
the chill, and then taking a step and finding the heat
below. That mischievous gleam danced in her eyes.
"Ahhhh," she murmured and held out her hand to
him.

God, how he wanted to take it, to strip off his trousers and join her, sliding his body next to hers, feeling
her bare skin touching his. He could almost hear the
water sizzle with the electricity sparking between them.
He wanted his arm to be whole again, he wanted no
past, he wanted to be young again without dark, haunting shadows. He ached to slip into the water and play
with her as if they were two kids, and then love her,

slowly and sensuously, and lie next to her to dry lazily
in the sun.

He wanted all that. He wanted it with an intensity
that fought with whatever small piece of honor and
decency he had left. With a strangled groan, he shook
his head, trying to croak out a refusal, taking several
seconds to do it. "Someone needs to keep watch," he
said, knowing it was a lie. There was no danger of inva-
sion here, none except his own. He looked enviously at
the icy water falling from the rocks. Never had he
needed it more.

Disappointment appeared momentarily on her
face, but then that smile came back into her eyes. It
had always enchanted him, right from the beginning,
that imp of a smile, that suggestion of humor that
tugged at her lips. Even when she was being practical
and efficient, as she was when she first cared for him,
he'd sensed an inherent joy in her. It had been tem-
pered by grief and tragedy, but still it lurked in her,
and that, more than anything, fascinated him, gave
him hope, stirred life in him, and made her so irresistible. He wanted to share it, to grab something so long
gone from his own existence.

Now that smile promised that she hadn't given up.
But she moved to the edge and took the soap. She
leaned back, dunking her hair completely in the water,
and then vigorously started washing it. He watched her
every move, memorizing the sight of her long hair as it
floated in the water. When wet, it was a dark, lustrous
auburn . . .

He forced his gaze away, staring off into the trees
on the far side of the clearing, but he was unable to
stop from darting quick glances back. To make sure
she was safe, he told himself. Every splash tested his

will. Every glance, every movement, shook his conviction.

Then at last she was finished and she held out her hand for him to help her up. She climbed up on the bank next to him, limber and lovely. Drops of water on her skin caught the sun and reflected like diamonds. She didn't relinquish his hand, but held on to it, braiding her fingers with his. "It was wonderful," she said, her voice breathless with a kind of awe. "Now it's your turn. I'll keep watch." Her eyes glittered with mischief, and he knew she understood his dilemma and was ready to tempt him every inch of the way.

He handed Mary Jo her clothes. "Lookouts have to be dressed," he said. It sounded ridiculous and he knew it.

The very pomposity of the statement made her grin. "It's in the instruction book?"

"Of course," he said wryly. "I read it myself."

"You didn't write it?" she retorted suspiciously.

He didn't answer, just eyed her clothes with suggestion. After a moment, she reluctantly took them and pulled on her chemise. "The sun feels too good," she protested.

And it did. It was a perfect day in the mountains, the sun's rays sparkling off the snow of nearby peaks, and burnishing her auburn curls with fire. He turned his head away, and considered briefly whether he should rid himself of his trousers. They would be uncomfortable wet, but he knew he would feel a great deal more uncomfortable if he shed them. Every time he looked at her, his loins began to pulse and swell. Hellfire.

He slipped into the water, into the cold part, welcoming its freezing impact. After a moment, he moved into the warmer area, swimming, using his good arm and legs. After several moments he moved to the bank, taking the soap Mary Jo had used, and started scrubbing himself. He didn't linger after that. It was too dangerous. He saw the gleam in her eye, and knew it was a matter of time before she slipped back into the water. He pulled himself out and stretched out on the pine needles, letting the sun dry him.

For several moments, he watched her comb her hair dry in the sun, then plait it into one long single braid. It was so intimate an act in this quiet place, so tender, he wanted to reach over and touch her. Instead, he steeled himself and closed his eyes, but still that warm intimacy seemed to stretch between them. There was a lazy sensuousness in the air. The water, the soap, and now the sun conspired to wash contentment over him. Yet every one of his senses was only too aware of Mary Jo's presence, her nearness. He didn't know whether the clean smell of her soap came from him or her, but it was intoxicating mixed with the sweetly pungent aroma of pines.

Her hand touched his and finally he turned slightly and opened his eyes. She was on her side, her hair falling along the line of her right cheek, her mouth gentled in a slight, wistful smile. Her other hand went to his cheek, still heavy with beard, and her fingers ran down it. "If I had a razor, I'd shave you," she said. "You look like a brigand."

"I *am* a brigand."

"No you're not."

He started nibbling on her fingers. "You have too much faith, Mrs. Williams."

"No, I don't," she denied. "I've learned to be suspicious. But you're different."

"Why?" He was truly curious.

"I don't know," she said honestly. "I would have taken in anyone hurt as you were, but . . . I might have gone to the sheriff. You were just so . . . gentle with Jeff, I suppose. You were hurting so much because of your own son. I know how that feels, to lose someone you love."

He was silent, but he kept nibbling on her fingers. They tasted very nice, irresistible in fact. He sighed, then said what was worrying him. "What if there's a child?"

"I think that would be lovely."

Her answer astounded him. He stopped nibbling.

"Don't worry. I know you plan to leave, and I won't try to dissuade you. I don't understand your reasons entirely, but . . . I won't try to hold you. But I would love to have your child." Her hand traced the indentation in his chin. "I want him with your face, with this dimple." She swallowed hard. "And I want him to be happy, ever so happy."

"What if it's a girl?" He heard himself ask the question, as if a stranger were saying it.

"Then I don't think I want her to look like you," she said teasingly as she studied him again. "Except maybe for your eyes. I would take those."

He shook his head. "Your neighbors . . . ?"

"My neighbors would just have to mind their own business," she said. "I always wanted more children, but I really didn't want to marry again."

"Why?" It was a question he'd asked himself over and over again. Jeff had told him the sheriff was sweet on her, that she could have had the pick of the Rangers.

"I didn't think I could ever love again," she said slowly. "I didn't want to. It hurt too much."

He was suddenly very still. Her words about a child had quietly, ridiculously, foolishly pleased him; but these last words were like a jagged knife in his gut. Of all the things he'd done in his life, hurting her would be the one to haunt him most. And he would hurt her, especially if there was ever a child. No matter how she dismissed the issue, he knew the condemnation that came to women with children out of wedlock. How could he ever have risked it?

He must have frowned because she continued slowly. "Don't worry, I'm very used to taking care of myself. If it didn't work out here, we would go someplace else."

That thought didn't help a damn thing. He suddenly thought of her, of his child, moving beyond his reach, beyond his knowledge. It couldn't happen. No matter how difficult it would be, he couldn't make love to her again. And he could only pray that a child hadn't already started to grow because of his stupidity. He sat up. "I think it's time to leave."

She nodded. "I want to see Jeff." She hadn't wanted to be away from him for several hours, but she knew now he was in good hands, and that rest was the best thing for him.

"He's a strong kid," Wade said, glad that the subject was changed, even as thoughts unsaid hung in the air. "Damned resourceful."

"He was excited about the race tonight."

"He'll never see riding like this again," Wade said.

She hesitated. "Can we leave in the morning?"

"I think so, if we take it slow and easy." His eyes questioned her.

"I know that you said Tom Berry would tell Tuck that Jeff was found, but . . . still there might be a search."

Wade stood, hoping his face didn't reflect his reaction, didn't give away how much he was affected by her decision. But he felt pleasure, pure and simple. And a certain amount of pride in her. Mary Jo, who days ago had been so mistrustful of Indians, any Indians, now wanted to protect them as he did. It wasn't easy to conquer prejudice and fears. He knew that better than most. It had taken him long, hard years to learn that.

He awkwardly pulled on his shirt over his wounded arm and walked over to the horses, untying her mare from a branch and stooping to unhobble his gray.

"Wade?" He hesitated at the sound of her voice but didn't turn around. "Thank you for bringing me here."

He tried to steady his hand as he laid it on the gray's mane. He nodded. It had been such a small thing, especially after all she'd been through in the past weeks.

He held the reins of her horse while she mounted, then mounted himself. Without any more words, they started with a fast pace back to the Ute camp.

20

Jeff's eyes widened as the two Utes moved from one side of their horses to the other, running alongside them and leaping on their backs as the horses ran at a full gallop. Then they were under the horses, on top, clinging to the sides.

Mary Jo watched Jeff's expression with pleasure. His cheeks were flushed with excitement, and he was grinning. Though occasionally he winced when he moved, he shrugged off the pain.

Then her gaze turned to the riders again. She too was full of astonishment. She'd thought there were no better riders than the Rangers who practically lived in saddles, but she'd never seen riding like this before. Her awe was as great as her son's as she watched man and beast become one. Mary Jo looked toward Wade, but his eyes in the late afternoon sun were impenetrable once more, his face carved in stone.

He had distanced himself almost immediately on their return, freeing their horses to graze with the others, then sitting with the men. A newcomer had appeared while they were gone, and she was told it was Chief Ouray, the greatest chief of the Utes and the man almost solely responsible for the peace still existing between the whites and Utes.

Wade had joined him and the other men, who had been sitting, smoking pipes, their tones serious and gloomy as they spoke in their own language.

Mary Jo had stayed with Jeff, who had been sitting up when she returned. He'd been talking to an Indian lad and admiring his dog. Love and admiration of animals, she surmised, was universal. Her son was now dressed in deerskin trousers, just like Wade's, and was shirtless, much like the young Indians; only his reddish-blond hair and freckles and the bulky bandage on his chest differentiated him from the others.

He still looked a little pale to her, but his eyes were full of that curiosity she'd learned to live with. He was asking questions, exchanging a few words he'd learned and letting sign language do the rest.

In late afternoon, preparations began for the race. The camp had grown in size, and Wade told Mary Jo and Jeff that Utes, including Chief Ouray, had come from several other camps in the mountains for this race. Mary Jo had watched during the afternoon as Wade was greeted with affection and respect by the newcomers, including Chief Ouray. Curious faces had turned toward her and studied her. But they had shown no resentment, no hostility, and she wondered why. Wade had been married to one of their own.

She had eaten with the women and children, and Wade with the men. It had been a lavish meal this time. Game had been plentiful and there was roasted venison and antelope, piñon nuts, and a strange type of vegetable Wade identified as camas bulbs. Jeff had eaten enthusiastically, as if, in fact, he hadn't eaten in a week—which was about true, from what he'd said.

"Great grasshoppers," he now exclaimed as one Ute, holding on to his horse's mane with one hand, leaned down and picked up a knife on the ground without the horse slowing so much as a fraction of a second. He looked toward Wade who had moved over to sit with them. "I bet you can do that, too."

A muscle flexed in Wade's cheek, and Mary Jo knew then that he could, at least he once had. He glanced down at his right arm, and Mary Jo saw bitterness flash across his face before he fought it down, and turned to Jeff. "No one can ride like the Utes," he said in what was a precise nonanswer.

But it was enough of an answer to satisfy Jeff, though he looked unconvinced.

She was, too. She had seen what he'd done with Jeff's untrained horse. Wade was a master horseman, whether or not he could now hang on the side of a horse with one hand woven in its mane. She looked at his lean, hard body, his long legs folded in front of him, and she sensed his frustration, could almost feel it as if it were her own. Over the past several days, she'd watched as he tried to move his fingers and flex his hand, and though he was having some success, she knew it was not nearly enough to satisfy him.

He was watching the riders avidly now, and the wistful look on his face told her he'd probably have taken part in this race if it hadn't been for his arm. She wanted so badly to walk over to him, to tuck her hand in his, to balance his longing. But she had learned long ago that everyone had to deal with grief and loss in their own way.

She swallowed hard. She would have to deal with loss again herself. She knew that objectively, intellectually, but she also knew she wasn't prepared, would never be prepared, for Wade Foster actually leaving. She couldn't bear to think of it except in the abstract, and she hated being such a coward.

The horsemen were racing back now, riding low on the necks of their horses. They had been showing off their skills earlier, but now it was all seriousness. Their horses were pounding toward the feather tied to an arrow in the ground, and then a black and white Appaloosa inched forward, pushing its head in front of the others, and it was over. Manchez had won. He accepted congratulations and took possession of a horse that was obviously a prize, then came over to Wade, sitting down cross-legged next to him.

"You see, brother, I don't need so many of your horses."

Wade smiled. "If I had—" He stopped suddenly.

The Ute sighed patiently and continued Wade's sentence with surprising gentleness, at least surprising to Mary Jo. "If you'd had your paint, you would have won." He paused, then added, "Maybe."

Wade grinned. "You never could admit defeat." It was the first real grin that Mary Jo had seen and she reveled in it. She only wished she could bring a smile to his lips more often.

Manchez turned to Mary Jo. "He can ride nearly as well as a Ute."

Wade raised his eyebrows. "Nearly?"

Mary Jo heard the bantering between them, almost like real brothers. Now that she'd met Manchez, it didn't seem nearly so strange as it had before. The affection between the two men was tangible, thick and real. Yet it had that friendly combativeness and competition she'd encountered among the Rangers. Men, she was discovering, were apparently the same everywhere, whether they were red or white. That realization made her feel even more comfortable where she was, even as something in the back of her mind rebelled at the swift change in her thinking. She had understood Wade's hatred for his family's killers, because of her own feelings. But his had been narrowed to the specific offenders while she'd broadened hers to include all Indians. Shame suffused her as she looked around at proud and laughing faces. Faces not that much unlike her own.

Wade was a mystery to her because he kept so many of his thoughts and feelings to himself, and yet now she felt she understood him better than she had. She recalled her revulsion at the eagle he'd worn, at the braided gear on his horse, and now she partly understood some of his reticence. She wondered even more about his wife, Chivita, about the son he'd lost so brutally. But Shavna didn't speak English and there was no one else she could ask.

She could only try to guess what was going on in his mind, and that course led to perdition. At times, the shadows in him were so deep and black, she knew they could swallow her, and with her, Jeff. He had hinted several times that there was more to those shadows than the deaths of his wife and son, that there were reasons he'd fled to the mountains, away from his own kind. As she watched him now, a smile on his face but that reserved wariness still guarding his eyes, she wasn't sure she really wanted to know.

But she couldn't lie to herself. She did! She wanted to know everything about him. Dear God, how badly she wanted that, even if it did lead to disaster. She wondered whether anything could really affect the way she felt about him, the way her heart speeded when he approached, or her blood heated when he looked at her, or the way her limbs turned liquid when he touched her.

Just thinking about him now was arousing her. She turned her attention to Jeff, forcing her thoughts away from the enigmatic man who was capable of extreme violence and also such compassionate gentleness with her son, with Jake, with his horses. A chill made her shiver suddenly, and she tried to contain it as Jeff turned to her.

"I want to learn to ride like that," he said. "Do you think Wade can teach me?"

"I don't know if he'll be with us that long," she said, trying to keep her voice steady. "He told me he plans to leave in a week or so."

"But . . ."

Mary Jo saw the hope in his eyes fade, and it broke her heart. In a very short time, Wade Foster had invaded both their hearts as well as their lives, leaving a painful impact she knew neither of them would ever forget. She couldn't help but wonder whether they had made a similar impression on his. But then, if they had, he would consider staying. He'd made it plain his life was here in the mountains. Because of his wife? His son? Because he could never replace them? Nor wanted substitutes of any kind?

"Don't try to change his mind, Jeff," she said

softly. "I don't think we can, and it will just make it more difficult for him. We owe him more than that."

"You'll miss him, too, won't you?"

"Of course. He saved your life twice. I'll always have that."

Jeff looked over at Wade, who was deep in discussion with Manchez. Mary Jo could hear, but couldn't understand. Once Manchez's eyes roamed in her direction, and she wondered whether they were talking about her.

But Wade kept his eyes on Manchez. Darkness had crept over the camp, and his face was highlighted by the flickering flames of the fire. They shadowed the gray-green of his eyes, deepening the crevices in his chin and the hollows in his cheeks. Even in deep conversation with his friend, he looked alone, his face carved in stone, his emotions locked within that same stone. The brief smile was gone, so was that momentary relaxation when Manchez had first approached. His good hand was stiff, stretched out along the ground, and she could almost feel the tension radiating in him.

She saw Jeff bite his lip. Perhaps it would be better if Wade left soon. She was in too deep already. So was Jeff. And more days would only deepen the loss.

She placed her hand over Jeff's. "We'll have a lot to do with the ranch. And Tuck and Ed will be there."

But Jeff was inconsolable. "Why does everyone go away?"

Everyone. His father. Ty. Now Wade Foster. Her hand tightened around his, and the depth of his unhappiness was evident because he didn't pull away, but clung to her as she clung to him.

·   ·   ·

Wade stayed away from the tepee that night. He'd taken a blanket and found a spot out under the trees near the horses. He liked hearing their movements, the soft clop of hoofs on the needle-carpeted ground, the soft blowing as the animals rested. He understood them. They asked damn little of him, about as little as he had to give.

He was worried about Manchez and Ouray and their people. There was to be another conference, more demands for land. Ouray was prepared to give up some more for peace. The question was how little would temporarily appease white greed. Some of the younger warriors were making war sounds and Ouray wasn't sure how much longer he could control them. Utes in northern Colorado were also restless, and Ouray had little influence over them, though trouble from them also meant trouble for the southern and central Utes. Few whites distinguished between the bands, which were separate, much as people in Kansas and Missouri were different from each other.

Utes had never had strong chiefs or centralized leadership. They were a nomadic people, wandering at will over their shining mountains, moving their camps frequently as they followed the buffalo herds and other game or grazed their horses. It was only the force of Ouray's personality that had kept the southern Utes united in a search for peace. Wade had been asked for his advice, and he had given it, as little as he thought it was worth. He agreed with Ouray that the Utes must do anything they could to avoid war. War meant annihilation. They could only play for time now, hope that no more gold or silver was found on the western slopes of the Colorado mountains.

He had said his farewell to Manchez last night. He

doubted whether he would return. He was a liability now to a people who already had too many liabilities. Manchez had finally agreed to accept the ten horses, but he said he would hold them for his brother, those or ten others. Wade finally nodded, knowing it was the only way Manchez would accept them.

It had been a difficult parting. It was yet another loss for Wade, and they were becoming far too many. After Manchez had left the fire, Wade had stood uncertainly for a time. He wanted to go to Mary Jo. Christ, how he wanted it. He needed her, especially now, especially after taking his leave of Manchez. He needed to hold her tight, to feel life next to him, to warm this cold, lonely emptiness that was suffocating him.

He might gain temporary relief, but it would only deepen the later pain, for both of them. He'd done enough damage already to both Mary Jo and Jeff.

He forced himself away from the tepee, but he ached in vulnerable places. He would take Jeff and Mary Jo home tomorrow, settle accounts with Kelly. And then . . .

Wade couldn't think beyond then. It was simply too agonizing. For a little while, he hadn't been alone. For a few hours, he'd allowed himself to feel, to dream, to hope. But the past was like a corpse thrown in a river. It rose to the surface, refusing to be forgotten.

They left just after dawn. Jeff was much better. His color was back, as was his appetite. And he was eager to ride his own King Arthur again, especially after watching the Utes. He already wanted to learn to ride without a saddle, to turn a horse with only the slightest pressure from a knee.

Wade's body was stiff, his face set, as he insisted on saddling the horses and stood waiting for Mary Jo as she said her own farewells. She hugged Shavna and wished she had something to give her; she thought of a colorful silk scarf Ty had given her last year, and she vowed to send it here, via Tom Berry. In the meantime, she hoped her eyes and hands conveyed her gratitude.

She found Manchez and thanked him, too. He studied her for a moment, his face as stoic as Wade's usually was. "Thank you for taking care of my brother," Manchez finally said.

Mary Jo found herself blushing. This was Wade's wife's brother. She nodded. "He has more than repaid us."

His eyes bored into hers. "He needs you, you and your son."

"I need him, but he says he must go."

"Sometimes he is a fool. He pushes people aside so as not to hurt them. He doesn't realize he hurts them more by doing that."

Mary Jo smiled at that very apt observation. "Does he do that to you?"

Manchez didn't answer.

She tried again. "How did he come to be your brother?"

He returned her gaze, but now there was emotion in his face. "He saved my life, and took me back to my people. I think he was very lonely then, and sad. As he is now."

Manchez's face closed then, as if he'd said too much. "You are welcome to come back," he concluded before turning and disappearing through the trees.

She walked to the horses and mounted her mare,

watching carefully as Jeff mounted gingerly, and then Wade. He led the way out without looking back. She saw Jeff look back though, his face wistful as he waved at the boy with the dog.

Wade stifled his impulses and set a slow pace, partly to accommodate Jeff's still raw and painful wound and secondly because of the ten horses that trailed them on a lead rope.

They were mountain ponies, however, bred in the mountains and trained to maneuver their steep paths, and he had few worries about them. Jeff worried him more, and he feared the boy might try to be too brave and not call a halt when he should. He was one hell of a gutsy kid.

Wade felt comfortable on his big gray rather than Jeff's smaller King Arthur. He was back on a saddle, and he had belongings now: a bedroll, a set of clothes in addition to the deerskins he was wearing, his rifle—even if he was damn poor at using it. Saddlebags were filled with dried meat and yucca roots.

He hoped to make the base of the mountains by late afternoon, depending on how well Jeff managed. They could be back at Mary Jo's ranch by late tomorrow night.

The three of them didn't talk much, partially because the trail was often narrow, too narrow for more than one horse at a time. Wade and his string of horses would go first, then Jeff and finally Mary Jo, whose gaze seldom left her son.

Wade stopped at noon alongside a waterfall. Insisting that Jeff lie down and rest, Wade and Mary Jo watered the horses. They worked well together, Wade observed. He seldom had to tell Mary Jo anything; she followed his lead with a minimum of questions. But then her efficiency had always impressed him, as had her grit. He would never forget the way she retrieved his gear from a days-old dead horse in a rainstorm.

They finished watering the last of the horses and sat down next to the fall. Wade had shaved this morning. The chore was still difficult for him, and he had several small cuts, but he felt a hell of a lot better. She had glanced at his face this morning, her eyes softening as she noted his improved appearance. She had looked tired, and he suspected she'd had as little sleep as he, that she had waited for him just as he had lain awake wanting to go to her.

Jeff was asleep, apparently more worn out than he'd thought. Mary Jo leaned down to the shallow small pool and splashed some water on her face, then rinsed her hands in it. "You didn't have to sleep outside last night," she said awkwardly.

His eyes met hers, and he felt his blood heat again. Christ, would she always make him feel like a volcano ready to erupt? He turned away. "Dammit, one of us has to have some sense."

"We didn't have to—"

"Make love, Mrs. Williams? Of course we did. If we get within two feet of each other . . . Goddammit." His voice was low, so as not to wake the boy, but he heard the raw desperation in it, and he hated it. "You don't know what you're doing," he continued in what he hoped was a more dispassionate tone. "You don't know anything about me."

"Manchez says you saved his life. How?"

He was completely thrown by the unexpected question, even more by the fact that Manchez had mentioned it to her, to a white woman. Manchez didn't like whites very much. In fact, he hated most of them for the land they'd stolen, for the beggars they'd made of his people.

He shrugged. "It was little enough. He was going through his manhood test. They send a boy out with only a knife for a week. He'd come up against a grizzly and had been badly mauled. I found him, that's all. I bandaged him and took him back to his people. I knew where they were camping."

"How old was he?"

"Thirteen."

She wondered how long ago that was. Manchez was a man now, with a child of his own. And Chivita was his sister. Why couldn't she stop thinking about Chivita? Because of what her death had done to Wade?

"Is that how you became brothers?"

He nodded.

"Before you married his sister?"

His lips drew into a thin line, and for a moment she wondered whether he would answer. "Yes," he finally said in a curt voice that effectively silenced any more questions. He stood. "We'd better get moving again if Jeff feels well enough."

Mary Jo nodded. She went over to Jeff and stooped down, her hand gently waking him. He looked confused for a moment, and then grinned sheepishly. "I went to sleep?"

She nodded. "How do you feel?"

He moved slightly as if testing himself. "I'm all right."

"Sore?"

He looked sheepish. "Maybe a little."

She looked inside his shirt. The bandage was dry,

the skin around it still pink and healthy-looking. "You'll tell us if you get too tired?"

He nodded, giving her that "I'm not a baby" look. She suspected it would come more frequently in the next months, the next years.

"Jake's going to be glad to see you."

His face suddenly lit up. "I miss him. He would have gotten that old cougar."

She smiled, hoping Jake would never be put to that kind of test. "I think he would have tried."

Jeff stood, wincing a little but walking normally to King Arthur and mounting easily enough. She was proud of him, proud of that spirit.

She looked over to Wade, who nodded his own approval. His eyes appeared darker than usual, but he had a slight smile on his face. For Jeff, she knew. Not for her.

She mounted and waited as Wade mounted his gray. She waited for him to start out, leading the string of horses that were now hers, then allowed Jeff to pass her. She had wanted to be last so she could keep an eye on her son. But she felt lonely, left out of that momentary flash of masculine approval and pride that had passed between Jeff and Wade. She wondered for a moment whether she was jealous of her son, and how preposterous that would be. She knew, though, it wasn't that. She didn't begrudge her son one moment of that acceptance. She just wished that Wade would open his heart to her too, shed that armor he thought he needed for protection.

Perhaps tonight. Perhaps tonight, she could break open that shell. Tomorrow, she feared, would be too late. There were too many ways for him to avoid her at the ranch. And she suspected he would do exactly that.

He needs you. Manchez's words. They had given her hope, until this morning. Wade didn't seem to need anyone, much less her. And he'd alluded again to secrets, to shadows she didn't understand.

But she *did* know him. She knew he was a good man. Not only had he twice saved her son, but long ago he'd saved a young Indian boy he didn't know. He had been instantly accepted by Tuck and Ed, and her neighbors. He had the respect of a people who had no love for his people.

Everything she learned of him only reinforced her certainty that he was a special man, no matter what he thought. But however could she convince him of that? How could she convince him that he didn't have to leave, that he had a place here? How could she light those dark places?

It was dusk when they finally stopped for the night. Wade had suggested stopping earlier, but Jeff had objected. He wanted to get home to Jake. So they had continued.

The path had widened. Mary Jo rode alongside the first of her newly acquired horses, behind Jeff and Wade. She watched the two of them, her son almost a miniature of Wade. Jeff had been watching and imitating everything Wade did, even his relaxed seat on the horse. He even held the reins in one hand, exactly as Wade did.

It touched her, and hurt her. She wanted so badly to shield Jeff from hurt, from caring too much about the man who had become a hero in his eyes, who was ten feet tall and had no faults.

As they dismounted, Jeff insisted this time on helping with the horses. He couldn't unsaddle his own, for it could pull the stitches, but he led the new horses by their rope halters to water and helped Wade establish a picket line as Mary Jo found wood for a fire. Mary Jo had wanted to stop him several times, but the flushed look of pride and determination on his face kept her tongue in check. She remembered the words from his note: *he will need help with the horses.* The thought that had sent him on his ill-fated journey. Her son needed to help now, to recoup some of the self-respect he'd lost, to try to make up for some of the trouble he knew he'd caused. Even if it hurt her to watch, even as she felt some of the pain and exhaustion she knew he must feel.

Consequences of actions. She would be paying for her own, too.

She'd tried so hard after her husband's death to rein in her own impulsiveness, to discipline her own naturally passionate nature, those headlong flights into trouble. Jeff's father had been so controlled, so very disciplined, she'd often felt like a wayward child when she'd wanted to race the wind or dance in the mud when it rained after a drought. She accomplished a certain measure of self-control, for Jeff's sake, and her own, but now those hidden longings were taking wing again, the common sense she'd tried so hard to cultivate in shreds around her. And every time she looked at Wade Foster, those scraps of sense became even more tattered. It had been a fraud, all of it, all those vows to herself that she wouldn't love again, couldn't love again. She had been able to close part of herself off only because there'd been no temptation, no Wade Foster.

She finished preparing the makings of a fire, and

searched in her saddlebag for a match, striking it against a dried piece of wood. It flared in her hand, and she watched it for a moment before placing it next to the kindling. It seemed to waver, almost go out, and then the small flame caught, and flared, suddenly greedy.

Her sense of impending loss, of almost overwhelming loneliness, flared with it. She felt weakened by the impact of her feelings. She took several deep swallows of air, staring into the golden fire as it ripped through its fuel, consuming it. Like her need for Wade was ripping through her, consuming what remained of a heart already wounded.

How could she bear losing him? And she was losing him, with every step toward the Circle J. She and Jeff were losing him. And she didn't even know why.

Dusk had turned into night when Wade and Jeff had finished with the horses, and washing themselves, and joined her at the fire. She had not brought coffee on this trip, packing only essentials, and wordlessly she poured them water from the canteens while Wade passed out the dried meat and fruit supplied by the Utes.

Jeff, though his eyes were drooping, had a million questions as usual, most of them about the Utes. How long would they stay in the valley? How long had Wade known them? How did they live in winter when the mountains were cold? How did Utes marry?

Wade kept his attention on the boy, rarely looking at Mary Jo, and answered each question carefully. They would stay in the valley until the game was gone, perhaps another month. During the winter they retreated to another slope of the Colorado mountains, taking with them dried and boiled meat from the summer hunting. Utes married by consent and could divorce just as easily. A courting warrior would kill a deer and hang it on a tree branch near the girl's tepee. If she wished to accept him, she would skin and dress the animal, then build a fire and prepare her future husband a meal.

"Is that what you did?" Jeff asked, curiosity outweighing Mary Jo's earlier warning not to ask personal questions.

Mary Jo was prepared for the usual dark look when Wade was reminded of the past, but he surprised her with a small grin. "No, I just traded some horses for her."

"She was Manchez's sister?"

Wade nodded.

"Was she pretty?"

Mary Jo held her breath, stunned that Wade seemed to be speaking easily of something that had been so difficult for him earlier. She wondered whether his visit to the Ute camp had eased a little of his grief.

"Yes."

"Was she as pretty as Ma?"

Mary Jo went stiff with embarrassment, but she should have expected the question from Jeff.

Wade was silent for a moment, and she thought he wouldn't answer. But finally he looked at her, his mouth twisted in that strange little half smile that said so little. "You'll find, Jeff, that each woman is pretty in her own way. You can't compare two, for each is special in her own right. Chivita was the most gentle person I ever met, and that alone made her beautiful. Your mother—"

He stopped suddenly, and Mary Jo found herself holding her breath.

Jeff was waiting anxiously for an answer.

Wade's mouth twisted again with a bit more of a smile. "Your mother is embarrassed, and I think it's time for you to get some sleep."

"Awwww."

Mary Jo could have echoed that, but then she didn't want to hear lies from him, or flattery. She knew she couldn't compete with the woman Wade had once loved so well, for whom he'd killed, but she couldn't help the hurt that welled up inside her. "Wade's right," she said, trying to keep her voice steady.

Jeff gave a disgusted snort, but he finally lay down on his blanket. Wade and Mary Jo waited minutes in silence, then Mary Jo stood. "I'd better wash up."

Wade stood with her. "I'll go with you. No telling what's out there."

She shook her head. "I can take care of myself."

He hesitated a moment, as if debating with himself, then sat down again. Reluctantly, she thought.

And reluctantly, so very reluctantly, she walked away from him, keeping her tears inside and her pride intact. She just wished it didn't cost so much.

21

Wade lay awake all night, fighting every natural impulse he had. Occasionally he sat, watching Mary Jo and Jeff sleep, wishing they were his, both of them. He frequently fed the fire, both to have something to do and also not wanting a repeat of Jeff's night of horror. But mostly he fought the temptation to move to Mary Jo's side, to pull her to him. Not to make love, but just to share warmth, to feel her next to him, to break the loneliness.

Now it was overwhelming. He had been able to tolerate it when he was alone. He had grown used to it, had even taken some satisfaction in it. A repentance of sorts for a past that still haunted him.

There was nothing, though, worse than being among those he wanted to care about, wanted to be part of, and couldn't. Never could.

He hadn't missed the hurt in Mary Jo's eyes earlier when he talked about Chivita. For the first time, talking about her and Drew hadn't been like driving a burning brand into his gut. The pain was still there, and so was the ache that would never quite go away, but it was becoming tolerable. He could remember good times with his family without the hot, fierce heat forming behind his eyes, without that white rage that consumed every human part of him.

He could look at a sunrise again and feel life fluttering inside instead of that dead weight he'd borne so long, surviving another day because there was nothing else.

He didn't want to die anymore, and that was most surprising of all. Even when Chivita and his son were alive, he'd not cherished life, had always felt that he didn't really deserve to live, deserve any happiness or contentment. Because of that, he'd pushed away the two people who loved him, and when they were gone that had hurt most of all.

And now he had to do it again, this time not for his sake, but for theirs.

Someone was laughing in the heavens, or in the lower regions.

He finally rose, stretched, and after making sure the fire had sufficient wood, walked down to the mountain stream where Mary Jo had gone earlier. He scooped up a handful of freezing water and splashed it across his face, feeling the new beard again on his face, and he cursed softly. Shaving was such a goddamn task with his left hand, yet to stop it would be admitting defeat.

He was not a little surprised that he didn't want to do that. He flexed his right hand and had more movement than before. He wished he could throw off the sling and try his arm, but it was too soon. He could do even more damage to it. A month at the very least, probably two, before he could even try to learn whether it had healed enough to be of any use. And if it hadn't . . .

He stayed there by the stream, by himself, away from the others he wanted so badly. He watched the first silver light filter over the horizon, trailed by layers of pink as the sun tipped the mountains. He splashed some more freezing water on his face and hands, then went to wake the others.

About mid-morning, Jeff saw where he missed the trail. He marked it in his mind. Someday, he would go back. Someday he would visit Shavna and Manchez and thank them. Someday he would learn more about their horses, and their magical soft deerskins, and their ways. He really liked their way of life. It was so free. No feeding chickens or milking cows. Or pulling weeds from the garden.

He hoped he could go with Wade, but although his friend had said more yesterday than usual, Jeff wasn't blind to the tension between him and his mother, nor did he fail to sense a kind of wall between them that hadn't been there before.

His chest itched and he wanted to scratch it. Manfully, he resisted, stretching back in the saddle as he'd watched Wade do.

Wade turned and gave him a brief smile. "Tired?"

He was. He shook his head no. Jeff watched as Wade turned around and looked at his ma questioningly. They exchanged a lot of looks, his ma and Wade. If only . . .

He settled back in the saddle and started plotting. They were only hours from home, from Jake. He moved his horse closer to Wade's. "Can I take the horses for a while?" he said.

He watched Wade hesitate, then nod his head. He undid the rope to the string of horses and handed it to Jeff, watching as Jeff tied it to his saddle horn and started moving slowly. Jeff felt the pressure of the rope, the momentary balking of King Arthur. He looked at Wade, who merely raised an eyebrow in question.

Wade wasn't going to help him, and Jeff felt pride surge inside him. His friend obviously felt he could handle it, that he was a good enough horseman now to pull his own weight. Jeff tightened his legs around King Arthur and the horse moved forward, nickering in protest but doing as told. A new kind of confidence seized him. He grinned up at Wade, and received a small half smile in return. Despite the smile's small size, Jeff felt as if he'd caught the granddaddy of all trout.

Jeff waited until that afternoon, until after they had stopped to rest the horses and eat some more of the dried meat. Then, as they started again, he felt confident enough to maneuver King Arthur and the trailing horses behind Wade Foster and his mother, forcing them to ride together.

Part of him concentrated on the lead rope, part of him on the two people in front of him. Wade's body had stiffened. His ma's back was so straight, Jeff thought it might break. Jeff wanted to kick them both. Instead, he just waited.

.   .   .

Why did she have to look so goddamn pretty?

Wade thought about Jeff's question last night. *Was she as pretty as Ma?* Of Mary Jo's expression when he hadn't really answered.

God, she was beautiful, but he didn't have the right to say it.

And he could never compare the two, Chivita and Mary Jo. Chivita was what he had needed ten years ago, a soft, gentle acceptance of what and who he was. She'd never asked for more than affection, had never asked questions, had never searched inside him.

Mary Jo would always search inside him and couldn't help but be appalled as to what she found. She was passionate in all things, while Chivita had been . . . quiet and undemanding. He had no doubts that Chivita had loved him, but she'd never demanded his heart and soul, and Mary Jo would never take less, no matter what she said. And his soul already belonged to the devil.

But now she looked so damned irresistible. That auburn hair was caught again in a long braid that hung down her back, little curly tendrils escaping and framing her face and those green changeable eyes. He couldn't believe that she didn't realize how completely desirable she was, how lovely when her lips smiled and her eyes sparked and her face lit up with that indomitable spirit that never ceased to amaze him.

She'd needed reassurance last night, and he couldn't give it to her, because it would reveal how much he really did care, how much he wanted to risk everything to stay with her and Jeff for weeks, months, years. It wasn't his to risk, though. Kelly's appearance had demonstrated only too well how fragile his existence, and identity, was. He wasn't going to brand Mary Jo as wife to a killer, a marauder, a war criminal.

Still, he couldn't help responding as she gasped in sudden delight at a doe and its fawn standing, suddenly alert, in tall grass on a ridge not far from them. Their scent must have been downwind, for now the doe did sense their presence, arching its graceful neck before turning and sprinting away, the small fawn behind it.

Her eyes smiled at him and he couldn't help but smile back. Her face had softened, her lips creasing into a delighted smile. He had noticed before she loved young things. She should have had more children, a lot more. Maybe the sheriff—

The thought was a godawful one. Unaccustomed jealousy ran through him like snake's poison.

"They're beautiful," she said, breaking the awkward silence that had accompanied them most of the morning.

He nodded, not speaking, that snake poison cutting off a civil response. He heated with anger at the very thought of her with anyone else, of her having a child with someone else.

Her back stiffened again, and she bit her lip, her face flushing a little under the golden glow dusted there by the sun. She turned her head away.

Clearly, he'd hurt her, and he couldn't bear that. "Mary Jo?"

She looked back at him.

"Don't ever lose that . . . joy." He didn't know why he chose that particular word. It wasn't one he usually used. But it was what he wanted to say. She had a quiet but heartfelt appreciation of life that was almost hurtful for him to see.

She seemed as stunned as he felt, then gave him a searching look. "Are you ever going to let yourself have any?" she finally said.

The question ripped into him. He'd never thought he had a choice. Joy, happiness—whatever you called it —had been torn from him when he was fifteen, when he'd found his family slaughtered. Subsequent events, both of his own making and of others', had robbed him of any capacity to bring it back. Once you'd experienced murder and terror, and participated in it, there was damn little left of the soul. Joy required a certain amount of innocence, and he had none. Oh, he'd had moments of pleasure, particularly recently when he'd made love to her. But joy? That was gone forever, like so many other things. But he didn't want her to lose it. Or Jeff his wonder of all things new and different. Christ, he couldn't bear that.

He felt the muscles tensing in his face.

"Wade?"

There was such concern in her voice, he wondered what his face was showing. He hoped to hell it didn't reveal everything he was thinking.

"We need to move faster," he said curtly, "if we're to reach the ranch by nightfall." He nudged his horse into a slow canter, hoping it would silence her questions and his own unwanted answers.

They reached the Circle J at dusk. Tuck was pumping water for the water trough and his face lit up as they approached. Mary Jo saw his gaze move from one to the other, and rest on Jeff, a smile on his face.

"An old codger stopped by to tell us you found Jeff, but it sure is good to see for myself," he told Mary

Jo, who reached him first. Wade had gone directly to open the corral gate.

Mary Jo dismounted wearily. Jeff, she knew, should be even more tired. "He's fine. Tired. We all are."

"I'll take care of those horses. Looks like a fine lot."

Mary Jo looked toward the string. "It is."

"Are they broke?"

She nodded again. "Anything happen while I was gone?"

"That sheriff was here asking for you yesterday. I wondered if I should tell him about your boy being missing, but that old man said it was best not to say anything. I wasn't sure, but I just said you were off buying horses." He looked anxiously for approval.

"You did just right," Mary Jo said, profoundly thankful for Tuck's unsure discretion. Matt had never said much about the Utes, but she could only suppose he felt like others in the community: the Indians should all be moved away, far away. He would probably have taken an armed posse up into the mountains and God knew what would happen. She wondered if there was anything she could do to change opinions. She knew she would try.

"Anyway, ma'am, we took care of everything. Ed's out looking after the cattle. There was a lion come down from the hills and killed one of the younger beeves. Ed's out hunting for it now."

Jeff had dismounted and was walking unsteadily toward them, his face dusty and tired. Mary Jo wanted to grab him and hustle him off to bed, but you didn't do that with a man, and Jeff had come close to becoming one in the past few days.

Tuck seemed to recognize that. He thrust out his hand. "Good to have you back, Jeff."

Jeff looked sheepish. "I'm sorry for causing so much trouble." Then he looked toward the house. "Where's Jake?"

"We had to keep him locked up. He kept trying to go after you. He's in your room. Didn't want you to come home and have him gone, and the barn just wouldn't hold him. Hope you don't mind none."

Jeff gave him a grateful smile and started for the house, the exhaustion disappearing in eagerness.

Mary Jo thanked him with a smile. "Thank you," she said quietly. "Both you and Ed."

"No need for that, ma'am. We like this place. I'd better go help with the horses."

She nodded and headed for the house. She'd fix something quick for supper. She hoped Wade would join them, but she doubted it. He'd been silent all afternoon. She wished she hadn't asked him that question about joy, and yet his comment had been so wistful, so unusually personal for him.

Jake was on his back, baring his stomach for scratching, his left leg moving ecstatically, and his tail thumping the floor, as Jeff rubbed him. Growls of pleasure met her, and she smiled. It was a ridiculous sight. Jake's tail moved faster as he noticed her, and his growl became a whine of welcome.

She stooped down and rubbed his ear. "We're glad to see you too, Jake," she said, and was answered by another fierce growl.

Jeff buried his head in the dog's fur and Mary Jo thought, and not for the first time, how much Jeff needed more human companionship. She wished he had a brother, or two. Maybe a sister.

But that thought hurt. It was too unlikely. She went to the kitchen and used the kitchen pump to wash her hands then checked the food shelves. There were canned tomatoes she'd brought from Texas, beans she'd harvested from their garden before the flood. Potatoes from town, and eggs from their chickens. That would have to do. She was too tired to make bread or biscuits.

"Jeff. Take Jake and see if the men want to join us for supper. In about an hour."

He nodded, and started out. He turned. "How long will Wade stay?"

"I don't know, love," she said.

"He likes you," Jeff said wistfully. "Maybe you can get him to stay."

"I don't think so," she said softly.

"But why?"

"I don't know," she said. "I just think he's very sad about his family and wants to go back to the mountains. He belongs there."

"We could go there, too."

"Come here, Jeff."

He left the door and approached warily. She put her arms around his neck and hugged him to her. "He's already given us lovely presents," she said softly. "And now you have to let him do what he thinks he must."

"You don't want him to go, either," he accused.

"No," she said. "I don't want him to go."

"You can make him stay."

"I don't want to make him stay," she said. "He has to want to stay." She could tell by his face he really didn't see the difference. One day, he would.

"I love him," Jeff blurted out, his face suffusing with embarrassment and frustration.

I do, too. But her hands just tightened around him. "Then you have to let him go."

His face clouded, but he didn't protest anymore. He gulped once, as if to hold back unmanly tears, then wriggled away from her touch and fled out the door, Jake limping behind him.

Wade helped Tuck water the new horses and told him a little about each one. One was gentle, one cantankerous. The pinto was smarter than the others, the black had more endurance. He took care of his own big gray, then went into his room at the back of the barn.

God, he was tired. He'd had little sleep during the last three days, fighting his attraction to Mary Jo, battling his need for her. Tomorrow he would find Kelly again, see what was happening, hoping against hope that Kelly and his cutthroats would ride out once Shepherd appeared.

He had some dried meat left and he ate that on the side of the cot and gulped some water he'd taken from the pump. He quenched the kerosene lamp and lay down, expecting to go to sleep almost immediately. By all rights, oblivion should have come easily. But his mind wouldn't stop.

There was a knock, and he swore to himself. He leaned over, struck a match, and lit the lamp. "Come in."

Jeff entered hesitantly, but Jake didn't. Despite his still healing leg, he moved swiftly over to Wade and put his big, ugly head on Jake's knee, looking at him imploringly.

"He missed you," Jeff said.

Wade tried to glare at the boy. "Is that what you came over to tell me?"

Jeff ignored the glowering expression. "No, Ma wants to know if you'll come over for supper."

"I already ate."

Jeff's face fell a mile.

Wade felt the size of a flea. He tried to smile. "You did real good today."

Jeff looked up at him. "But you didn't need me at all, did you?"

His voice was so woeful that Wade realized how important being needed was to him. But above all, Wade owed him honesty. "I could have made it by myself," he said quietly, "but you did make it easier. I won't lie to you about that."

"You don't lie about anything, do you?"

Wade had to smile at that. "I've been known to do that."

"But not about important things?" Jeff's earnestness sliced through Wade. He hadn't lied to Mary Jo and Jeff, except about his true name, but neither had he told the truth. It was a fine distinction he didn't like, and they didn't deserve.

He put a hand on Jeff's shoulder and his voice was harsher than he intended. "I'm not a hero, Jeff. I'm not even a good man. Sure, I've lied. I've lied and I've killed, and I'll probably do it again." He looked down at his arm. "If I can."

"But you had a reason. Ma said so."

Christ, but Wade wanted to shake that hero worship out of Jeff's eyes. He didn't deserve it and he was damn scared one day Jeff would learn how undeserving he was.

"Your father was a hero, Jeff," he continued slowly, hoping it was true. "I'm a rotten substitute."

Wade wasn't sure how far Jeff's chin could fall, but it was pretty damn close to the floor now.

"Jeff," he said quietly. "I wish my boy had grown up just like you. You're one hell of a kid. But I'm no good to anyone and I never will be."

"That's not true," Jeff burst out angrily.

"Jeff, listen to me. I'm the worst possible thing that can happen to your mother. To you."

"I would have died if you hadn't been here."

"No you wouldn't. You went to that stream because you were angry at me, and then you followed me up into the hills to prove something to me. You never would have been in danger, were it not for me. I won't let that happen again, dammit."

Jake jerked his head back at the vehemence in Wade's voice and whined. Jeff just stared at him for a moment, then whirled around and ran out without another word. Jake stared at Wade reproachfully for a moment, then reluctantly followed Jeff. Wade swore.

He closed his eyes, opened them, and blew out the light, knowing as he did so it was going to be another godawful night.

And it *was* a terrible, ghost-filled night. Worse, in fact, than usual. As if reminding him of the danger of hope, the nightmare returned when he finally was able to close his eyes. He saw it as clearly as if it had been yesterday. The naked men standing beside the train, all scared to death. They were no older than he, and guilty of nothing other than being conscripted or volunteering to fight for their country.

Their uniforms had been kicked away from them, so blood spatters wouldn't spoil them for future use by the Reb guerrillas. They seemed to sense what was coming. Anderson and Kelly had looks of expectation in their eyes, and then the firing started . . . and he began retching.

Wade woke to the sound of his own retching, to the protest that had lodged in his throat. He opened his eyes, confused at first, and then his eyes adjusted to the darkness and he remembered where he was. He thought he had triumphed over that particular nightmare. He was wrong.

He bent over and was sick again.

How had he ever thought for even the fleetest moment he could hope again? Whenever he looked back, all he saw was death. For a moment, he remembered those sermons he used to be forced to sit through as a boy. Something about beholding the pale rider.

He went to the window. The sky was still dark, lit by millions of stars that looked like candles in the dark. The night, the hills, looked so peaceful, he could almost forget he'd killed a man not far from here a month ago. It seemed a year, a lifetime, ago. And yet it was a month, and blood still covered his hands. Just as it had twelve years ago. Nothing was ever going to change that.

Wade dressed before the sun came up, saddled his gray and rode out into the cool dawn. It was time to meet his past again.

22

Clay Kelly was no longer where he had been, but the man named Kay was.

So Kelly hadn't trusted him, Wade mulled, but he had been willing to sacrifice Johnny Kay. If Wade had talked to the law, it would have been Kay taken, not Clay Kelly. Kay, apparently, was oblivious, though, to being the tethered goat. He was stretched lazily over a piece of grass near where he had been last time, but Wade didn't kid himself. The man's hands were on his rifle, a finger a fraction of an inch from the trigger.

"Clay said you would be back."

"He's a shrewd man."

"Anyone with you?"

"Do you see anyone?" Wade's tone reflected sheer exasperation.

"That don't mean anything. A posse could be waiting back behind those hills."

"Could be, but it isn't. It's my neck, too."

"Not if Clay dies," Johnny Kay said.

"That what he said?"

"Yep. I don't think he trusts you."

"That's between him and me."

"Mebbe."

"You going to take me to him, or do I leave?"

"Going back to that woman?" Wade hid his anger at Kelly's snide tone. He should have known Kelly would discover where he was staying. It was common knowledge in Last Chance that the widow Williams had acquired a foreman.

"Ain't too many men around with broken wings," the man continued. "Clay ain't too happy you lied to him."

Wade shrugged carelessly. "It wasn't any of his business where I stayed."

"He don't see it that way."

"You do all his talking for him? He's changed some if that's so."

Kay shut up at that, and Wade knew he'd hit a bull's-eye. Still, he didn't like Kelly knowing about Mary Jo. It made his stomach churn.

Kay finally stood and stalked over to the horse grazing nearby. "He has a proposition for you."

"Shepherd didn't show?"

"He showed all right. Damn fool. Went right into Last Chance for a drink, got into a fight and killed someone. He's in jail now."

Wade held back any satisfaction. Three men weren't enough to take a bank. Why in the hell did

Kelly want him? He wouldn't be any damn good with a gun.

"Let's go," Johnny Kay said.

Wade shrugged. He had come this far. He might as well find out what Kelly had on his mind. Knowing Kelly, he would find out one way or another, and he didn't want Kelly coming riding up to the Circle J.

"Kelly wants you blindfolded."

"Ah, trust is a wonderful thing."

Kay stared at him. "You're a real smart-mouth, aren't you?"

Wade gave him a menacing smile. He'd become good at it.

Kay started to bluster. "Don't know why Clay wants to fool with you."

Because you're stupid, Wade wanted to say but resisted. "I'm not going anyplace blindfolded," he said instead.

Johnny Kay's eyes narrowed, and Wade knew he was trying to decide what to do next, even as he knew Kelly had probably given him instructions for this, too. Whatever else he was, Clay Kelly was smart.

"We could go after that lady," Kay said. "Heard she had a kid, too."

Wade felt the old rage boil up inside him, that killing rage he knew only too well. But now he was at a disadvantage. He didn't have to see Johnny Kay draw to know he was fast. Kelly wouldn't have anyone with him that wasn't.

He swore to himself. He had no chance going for the rifle, nor for the six-shooter he'd buckled on this morning, not with his left hand. But he didn't allow any of those thoughts to show. He merely shrugged. "If Clay wants to see me that bad . . . ?"

"He said you'd see reason," Kay said, his shoulders relaxing.

"Always glad to help a friend."

"Oh, you can help him, all right."

Wade struggled to keep his face blank as Kay mounted and moved his horse over to where Wade still sat astride the gray. He leaned over and tied a bandanna around Wade's eyes. It was a smelly, dirty piece of cloth, and Wade nearly gagged. Still, this was what he had wanted: to know what Kelly had planned. It galled Wade to play by Kelly's rules.

Wade surrendered his reins to Johnny Kay and relaxed in the seat, trying to concentrate on what direction the man took. He soon gave up and admitted to himself he had no idea. He suspected Kay took him in circles, and he attributed that to Kelly, too. Kay wasn't smart enough to think of it himself.

Wade guessed they rode two hours before coming to a stop. As they did, Wade took the blindfold from his eyes and looked around. It took him several minutes to accustom his eyes to the morning sun as it glared down through pine trees.

Kelly was standing a few feet away. "Get down, friend," he said.

Wade dismounted, and Kelly came closer. "Good to see you again, Allen. No, Smith now, isn't it? I'll have to remember that." He smiled, but there wasn't any warmth in it. "I had a feeling you might come back. Don't know why." His eyes suddenly blazed with suspicion.

"I wanted to make sure you get the hell out of here," Wade said, sensing his way. Lying wouldn't do any damn good, nor would the whole truth. "I don't want anyone around who knows about—"

"Bloody Bill," Kelly finished for him. "You didn't tell that pretty little lady I heard about?" He clicked his tongue in admonishment. "Now why didn't you tell me about her?"

"Just like you don't want me to know where you're holed up," Wade said. "We don't trust each other."

Kelly laughed. "You're right about that. I always wondered what happened to you after Centralia."

"I told you. I got a bullet," Wade said. "And I decided to retire."

"But not entirely," Kelly said as he looked knowingly at the sling Wade was still wearing.

"Let's stop playing games. Your errand boy said you wanted to see me."

"Yep. I want you to help me bust Shepherd out of jail."

"You've got to be crazy."

"Nope. I need him for a certain job, and you're right about your being no damn help in a holdup. But you can do something else for us. You can get into the sheriff's office, being the—what was it?—brother of your lady's poor deceased fiancé."

Bile rose in Wade's throat. Kelly had scouted him out, all right. Probably had sent one of his flunkies to town. And that certain job? Probably that damn bank. "Goddamn sheriff doesn't like me," Wade said. "He was courting Mrs. Williams."

"Ah, the lovely widow. Well, he'll like you a damn sight less if he knows who you are, might even be real grateful to me."

"He'll hang you just as high as he will me."

"Maybe. If he catches me. A rock flung at his door with a note attached. And the lady? Does she know you rode with Bill Anderson, that you have a price on your head just like we all do?''

''I'd be long gone by then, my friend,'' Wade said dryly. ''That's why I rode out today. You go or I go.''

Kelly smiled. ''And leave the pretty lady to me?''

Wade held his tongue, and his temper, though his gut was twisting inside. Wound or not, he wanted to jump Kelly, crush his throat with his hand. But any show of anger would only make Kelly more sure of his one weak spot. Wade shrugged. ''Go ahead. I'm not risking my skin for you or for Shepherd.''

For the first time, Kelly's eyes showed some uncertainty. He was a man who understood that kind of reasoning. Kelly had certainly never risked his life for anyone, not even Bill Anderson whom he'd considered his friend and hero.

''All it would take is slipping him a gun,'' Kelly said cajolingly. ''Those posters of you are years old. No one would suspect you.'' He paused. ''For old times' sake.''

''And get the sheriff checking up on me?''

''The sheriff won't be alive long,'' Kelly said. ''I'm sure Shepherd will take care of him.'' He hesitated, then continued slowly, deliberately. ''There's a lot of cash in there now, since most of the ranchers have banked their money from this year's cattle sale. Heard there's twenty thousand in cash. Your share would take you a long way, particularly with that bum arm. But I need Shepherd. He knows explosives.'' Threats hadn't worked. Kelly was depending on greed now, certain that most men were as corrupt as he himself was, Wade thought. Well, why not? He hadn't been much better than the others during the war. They had robbed, used the money to buy whiskey and women. Damn little ever went to the Confederacy.

With or without your help. And he meant it. Kelly's eyes were glittering with determination now.

"How much?" Wade asked.

"Five thousand if you deliver Shepherd. You don't have to do anything else. Just give him a gun. He can do the rest. No one here will have to know, not even that pretty widow lady."

"Will Shepherd agree to the split?"

"Hell, yes. He could hang this time."

"And how do I get the money?"

"We'll meet you afterward."

"With a posse behind you?" Wade asked, shading his voice with suspicion and doubt, just as would any sane man dealing with Clay Kelly.

Some of the suspicion in Kelly's own eyes was fading now. He understood lack of trust between thieves, Wade thought wryly. He'd found just the right strategy. Wade had to make Kelly think he was with him, that he needed the money as bad as Kelly did. "You could ride with us," Kelly offered. "Hold the horses. You always were real good with them."

Kelly remembered more than Wade thought, but then he'd never underestimated Kelly's smarts, only his total lack of conscience or scruples.

"No," Wade said. "You've been hiding. No one has seen your faces but me. Too many people know me. I don't want a new poster."

"Shepherd?"

"I'll try to find a way to deliver that pistol without raising suspicions, but I want to make damn sure I get my share of the money." He thought a moment. "You'll be going south out of town? Toward the San Juans?"

Kelly nodded.

"When will you hit the bank?"

Kelly's eyes grew suspicious again, and he hedged. "Next few days if Shepherd gets out."

Wade thought for a moment. "I'll be waiting where the trail turns off toward the San Juans each afternoon. There's a big cottonwood there. Drop my share behind it. I won't be far away."

Kelly's eyes looked speculative.

Wade stared at him. "Don't even think about trying to double-cross me. I know who you are. I know your friends. I know how you operate. I've also made friends with the Utes in the area you'll be passing through. If they miss you, I won't. I'll find you someday, and I'll make you sorry you ever drew a breath." His voice was heavy with menace.

Kelly shrugged. "It'll be there. How do I know if you're successful with Shepherd?"

Wade shrugged. "When he shows up. I suppose he knows where to go?"

"We've made plans to meet." Kelly suddenly grinned. "I thought you would see reason. Sure you won't join us? Could use someone else who knows how to think."

Wade looked him straight in the eye. "You're right about this arm. It's ruined. Maybe I could buy a small cantina in Mexico."

Wade turned to leave.

"Allen!"

It took Wade a moment to remember his former name. He stopped, turned back to Kelly. "What?"

"Double-crossing goes two ways. You wouldn't want to do that."

Wade met his eyes. "We both want the same thing: enough money to get the hell away from here. And how can I cross you? I can't shoot anymore. I sure as hell can't go to the law.''

"No, you can't, can you?" Kelly said. "Heard tell a man was found dead around these parts a few weeks ago. Just about when you were shot."

"That right?" Wade said steadily.

"Keep that in mind," Kelly said.

"I keep everything in mind."

Kelly's eyes flickered for a moment, that uncertainty back for a fraction of a second, and then he grinned. "We understand each other."

"We always did," Wade said, his tone so neutral that Kelly could assume any damn thing he wanted.

It was a long ride home. Home. Odd how naturally that thought came to him. He'd never thought of the cabin he'd shared with Chivita as home. A shelter. A place to sleep. But never really home.

He'd been blindfolded again, for about an hour, he guessed. Trust went two inches, then retreated. Wade hadn't protested. In the first place it wouldn't do any good. In the second, it would raise suspicions. So he'd allowed Kay to blindfold him, insisting this time he use Wade's own bandanna. They'd finally stopped about an hour later, at Cimarron Creek. "I 'spect you can find your way from here," Kay said, and Wade merely nodded, wanting to get away from him.

Wade spurred his horse before the gunman could say anything else.

He approached the ranch slowly, noting the cattle now dotting the hills around it, the new fences the two hired hands had fixed or built. A trail of smoke was rising from the chimney. Mary Jo was cooking again.

His stomach rumbled at the thought as he cantered up to the barn.

Jake let out a belated bark, damn useless watch dog that he was, and then the ranch-house door sprang open, and Jeff was there, a wide grin on his face. He sprinted over to where Wade was dismounting.

"We were hoping you would get here for dinner. Ma's making fried chicken."

Wade felt so damn ridiculously welcome. He didn't want the pleasure that snaked through his being, but there it was. He reached out and messed Jeff's red hair. "You doing all right?"

"I went out with Tuck. He showed me how to rope, but I'm not very good at it."

"It takes lots of practice."

"That's what Tuck says."

"Well, he's right. I think he's right about a lot of things." He wanted to put his hand on Jeff's shoulder, but he had no right. In another week, Jeff and Mary Jo would know exactly what kind of man they'd been harboring. He closed his eyes at the thought.

He wished there was another way, but there wasn't. He couldn't fight Kelly and Kay and the man called Jones. Hell, he could barely fire a pistol, much less a rifle.

"Where did you go?" Jeff asked, still filled with questions.

"Just checked on the cattle."

"Can I go with you next time?"

"I think you should take it easy for a few more days. You don't want that cut to open up again."

"Aw, it's nothing," he said.

Wade sat on the corral fence, balancing himself on

the top rung. "Come up here," he told Jeff, who did so, his eyes on Wade.

Wade's heart turned as the boy imitated him, his eyes gazing up at him with such damn worship.

"It's time," he said, "that you start thinking."

Jeff's eyes searched his, but the smile on his lips faded.

"No more creeks," Wade said. "No more running off. Your mother needs you, Jeff. You've shown you can do a man's job, but you have to start thinking like a man. Take a man's responsibility."

Jeff bit his lip, and Wade was reminded that Mary Jo did the same thing when uncertain, when hurt. Yet he had to prepare Jeff. Wade had to know Jeff could be Mary Jo's strength, just as Mary Jo was his strength, at least for now.

"You're leaving, aren't you?" Jeff said.

"Soon."

"Tomorrow?" the boy guessed.

"Yes," Wade said shortly, the curtness of his voice covering the heartache he was feeling.

"But why? I thought you were going to stay longer."

"You'll be all right now, you and your mother. You have something real fine in Tuck and Ed. Listen to them. Learn from them. They're damn good men."

"No one can be as—like—you." Jeff blurted out the words, tears forming in his eyes, and Wade felt like such a fraud. He'd allowed this, allowed Jeff and Mary Jo to care about a man who didn't exist.

"I hope not," Wade said quietly. "You're going to hear some things about me, Jeff, and most of them will be true."

Jeff looked him square in the eyes. "I don't care what anyone says about you."

The earnestness in Jeff's face, the affection in his eyes was almost Wade's downfall. There was more he should say, but he couldn't. The words were caught in his throat.

Then Mary Jo came out. She had washed her hair and the deep red-gold auburn glittered in the sun. She was wearing a green dress, and her eyes sparkled when she saw them, he and Jeff. "Who wants dinner?"

Jeff looked at him, and Wade tried a smile and nodded. "We'll talk in the morning."

"You won't leave until then?"

"No."

Jeff looked at his mother, then to him, and Wade saw hope return to them, and he wished he'd been stronger, been able to tell Jeff the whole truth, to tell him not to hope, not to dream, not to wish. Not about him.

Jeff nodded his trust, then jumped down and jogged to the house, satisfied for the moment. Mary Jo smiled tentatively. "You looked deep in conversation."

"Man talk," Wade said.

She smiled that lovely smile he would remember for a long, long time. That and the green dress that made her eyes the color of emeralds.

"Jeff said you had fried chicken," he said, trying to sound casual.

"And gravy and biscuits and green beans and apple pie."

Everything she knew he liked. Hell, liked? Plain heaven. The ache inside was deepening. Ache, hell. It was more than that. Emptiness was clawing at him. Except emptiness should be painless, and this wasn't.

Hellfire. How much deeper could pain get? He looked at Mary Jo, and his world changed, colored in such spectacular ways. And then he saw Kelly standing there under a tree, and he heard his threats toward Mary Jo, and he knew he'd deflected them only a short time. If Wade didn't deliver, Kelly would go after Mary Jo. He knew it.

"I'd better wash up," he said.

Her eyes searched his, apparently wondering why he'd been gone all day, but she didn't ask, and that surprised him as it always did. It shouldn't anymore, he knew, yet her understanding and lack of questions still amazed him.

"Tell Tuck and Ed. They're both in the barn."

He nodded and turned away. At least dinner would be some easier with the two men at the table. But afterward . . . afterward he would have to tell Mary Jo . . . what? Part of the truth anyway, in case he failed.

Dinner was, thankfully, an opportunity to get his thoughts—and emotions—back where they belonged. Tuck and Ed discussed what had been done while they were away. Ed had tracked the cat that had killed one of the young cows and killed it. The rest seemed to be doing well. Fences had been repaired, stalls added to the barn. Both men apparently were capable of working on their own.

Mary Jo would have the help she needed once he was gone. He was sure of that now, and his mind was partially relieved. He wouldn't be leaving her alone, unprotected. But he would have to drop a word in Tuck's ear, warn him about strangers. Neither man, though, was a gun hand, though they carried rifles, mainly against animal predators and snakes. They'd stand no chance against Kelly and his human predators. Which meant his plan had to succeed, as half-baked as it was.

After supper, Tuck and Ed retired to their own quarters. Jeff, who had watched Wade steadily throughout the meal, took up the dishes. Mary Jo stood and started to help Jeff. Uncertainty showed in her eyes, as if she knew something unpleasant was coming.

"Come outside with me," Wade told Mary Jo.

She stared at him, obviously surprised and wary of the unexpected invitation.

"Please," he said. He rarely used the word.

She set down the dishes she was holding and walked to the door, opening it herself and going out to the porch. She looked out toward the mountains where they'd stayed, and he saw her bite her lip. He would never forget the way she and Jeff did that. He swallowed hard. Whenever he saw her do it, he wanted to take her, hold her, wipe away that nervousness, that apprehension, she tried to hide. He closed the door behind him, and stood next to her, his left hand going to her cheek, his finger running along the lip she'd been biting. There was the slightest thickness. He swallowed hard. He wanted to touch her everywhere, not just stop here. But he did.

He took the few steps down the stairs and waited for her to join him, walking away from the house. He didn't want Jeff to hear any part of what he had to say. They walked out to the far edge of the corral, and he watched the enclosed horses for several moments as he tried to frame words.

He leaned against the top railing, wishing he didn't smell the scent of roses that always hovered around her. "You can depend on Ed and Tuck," he said cautiously. "And now you should have enough horses for more hands."

She didn't say anything, just waited. He turned and looked at her. Her face seemed pale in the moonlight. Her eyes seemed wider than usual, her lips trembled slightly. She looked so damn beautiful and vulnerable . . . and desirable. Yet, he also knew her strength now.

That didn't help one damn bit. It should. But it didn't. He wanted to be there for her, even as goddamn useless as he was. He looked around at the ranch, which had become home in such a short time, the porch where he'd sat talking to her. At the barn where he'd first made love to her.

He turned away. "I'm going to Last Chance tomorrow," he said abruptly, not looking at her. "If I don't return by the following morning, go into town and take your money from the bank."

There was a stunned silence.

He waited for the questions. He knew they would come this time. And they did.

"Why?"

"Because it might be robbed."

The silence grew longer this time. He turned his gaze to meet hers, faced the questions there, the terrible unanswerable questions. "Not you?"

"No."

Something in her face eased slightly, yet the implications of his statement were clear enough. She finally asked the question he knew was coming, the one that would have to be met, if not completely answered. "How do you know?"

His hand pressed down on the fence railing, barely feeling the sliver that dug deep in his palm. "I ran into

. . . some men I used to know. They wanted me to join them.''

The silence again. The awful silence. She was as afraid to ask questions as he was to answer them. ''Friends?''

''No.''

''Then why . . . ?''

''They know something about me . . .''

Silence again. Hard, dead, cold silence.

Then, finally. ''Those men you said you killed?'' The question was asked almost hopefully, and Wade felt part of himself die. Again.

''Something else.''

The silence was even longer this time. He heard her intake of breath, the audible swallow. ''You can't go to Matt then,'' she said. It was more a statement than a question.

He didn't answer. A horse whinnied, stamped his foot nervously in his new, unfamiliar quarters. Wade was grateful for the distraction.

''And if *I* go to Matt, or tell anyone, Matt will wonder how I knew . . .'' Her voice trailed off.

''If you don't, you'll be ruined and so will your neighbors,'' he finished for her in a low, dispassionate tone.

''You're planning something,'' she said in a bare whisper. Her body suddenly leaned against his, and his arm went around her as he felt her tremble against him. Her head lay against his heart, and he felt his shirt dampen. He wanted to tell her things would be all right, but they wouldn't. Not for them. Three fates awaited him after tomorrow: a bullet, a noose, or prison. He preferred the first. Then, perhaps she and

Jeff would never discover what he'd tried to hide for so many years.

His silence answered for him.

"I love you, Wade. I don't care what happened in the past." It was a plea, clear and simple, and it ripped through him. He knew she could tolerate him killing men who'd killed a child, but what if she knew he'd stood silent years ago when farms were raided, men taken and shot, and boys were killed. Oh, they were called men, but they hadn't been; hell, half probably hadn't started shaving. She wouldn't love him then. She would despise him as much as he'd despised himself all these years. He should tell her. He should tell her, so she could let go.

He couldn't do it. The words simply wouldn't force themselves through his teeth.

"Listen to me," he finally said. "If I'm not back by the day after tomorrow, get Tuck to go into town and withdraw your money from the bank. Don't you go. Hide it someplace safe. Then I want you and Jeff to go to the Abbots and stay there. Tell them to withdraw their money too, that you heard some kind of rumor there might be trouble. If I'm in jail, don't come near me."

"No," she said.

"It's Jeff's life, too," Wade said. "Both of you could be in great danger because of me. I won't let it happen again, Mary Jo. Don't make me watch it happen again." His last words were little more than a tortured groan.

Mary Jo's hand caught his good one, pressed her fingers between his with a desperate possessiveness.

"Promise me, Mary Jo. Promise me you won't put Jeff in danger."

"Go to the mountains," she said. "I can talk to Matt."

"And tell him what? Your foreman is not Wade Smith. That you've been harboring a murderer? How would you explain knowing there might be a bank robbery?"

He could almost see her mind working. She was not a devious person, but she was trying to be for him. Dammit, he didn't want to corrupt her as he had been corrupted.

"No," he said. "Don't even think of ways. They wouldn't work, and this is my problem."

"What are you going to do?"

"It's better you don't know," he said quietly.

"You keep telling me that," she retorted rebelliously. "I'm not a child."

"No one knows that better than I do," he said softly, regretfully. "Dammit, Mary Jo, you gave me so much more than I had any right to have. Now give me this. Make it easier for me to do what has to be done."

She looked up at him, and in the moonlight, he saw the tears hovering in her eyes. There was still defiance in that face, but realization, too. She stretched up until her lips met his, and she kissed him with such poignant sweetness, he thought his heart would shatter. He knew better, he knew much better, but his lips responded and the kiss turned fierce and hungry and desperate. She was already leaning into him, but now his manhood responded, growing hard and wanting, and she pressed into him until he wanted to moan with longing for her.

"Oh God," he whispered, his lips moving away from hers as he stared at her.

"I want to stay with you tonight," she said.

No! But the word didn't leave his mouth, and they were moving toward his small quarters in the barn. He wasn't sure who was guiding. He didn't care. He just knew he didn't want to let go, that he needed this night just as she did.

"Jeff?"

She hesitated. She turned to him, putting her hand on his face. "I'll see him to bed, then come to the barn."

"Are you sure, Mary Jo?"

"I've never been so sure of anything in my life," she said and fled before he could make any more protests. Not that he was capable of any.

23

Mary Jo checked Jeff's cuts before sending him off to bed. He was more subdued than usual.

"Ma," he said as she started for the door, "Wade says he's leaving."

"I know," she said.

"Can't you make him stay?"

"I don't think so."

"I'll miss him."

"I know, love. So will I. Good night now."

He turned over, and she sensed he wasn't at all satisfied with her answers. Neither was she. She wished she could come up with a way to change Wade's mind.

She waited a little while until she thought he was asleep. She brushed her hair and left it down and looked in the mirror. Her heart thumped as if she were sixteen with her first beau. Deep inside, she knew what she was about to do was foolish. Going to him tonight would only place him more securely in her heart and soul, only make his leaving worse. Yet it would give her memories, too. She swallowed hard and went out the door, almost running.

Once inside the barn, Mary Jo let her eyes get accustomed to the darkness. There was only a faint light coming from under his door. She followed that slim trail of light and pushed the door open.

He was stretched out along the cot, one knee bent. He wore no shirt, only the white sling against his skin. His chest wasn't as bronze as a month ago, but in the light of the kerosene lamp it seemed to glisten with the golden hair she now loved.

He moved, sitting up and placing bare feet on the wood boards of the floor. There was grace to each of his movements, an easy fluidity that had always captivated her. He'd shaved, she noticed, and changed to the deerskin trousers. They were easier to discard, she'd discovered. She wondered briefly if that was why he had changed, and dismissed the idea. He'd been riding the entire day when he'd come in, had been sweaty and dirty from the horse and trail dust.

"I thought you had changed your mind," he said.

"No," she said in what sounded like a croak to her. "Jeff was wondering whether there was any way to make you stay."

"I'll miss him."

"I'm afraid he might do something foolish again."

"I'll watch out tomorrow, but you'd better keep him in sight."

She nodded, still standing where she was. He stood and walked over to her. "I prayed you wouldn't come."

"Prayers don't seem to be doing either of us any good."

His hand took a lock of her hair and played with it. He smelled like soap and leather. An enticing scent. An irresistible one.

"I like your hair," he said, his voice husky now. "I like it this way, down, where I can run my hand through it."

She wished she could move. She couldn't. His eyes were devouring her. There was nothing blank about them now, nothing secretive.

Mary Jo closed her eyes, memorizing everything about him. The sound of his voice, the scent of him, the way he felt, and the texture of his skin against hers, the soft breeze of his breath against her hair. All these, and more.

She felt his mouth touch her skin with such tenderness she shivered with the wonder of it. And then he trailed kisses down to her throat, and his tongue explored her pulse there, sending desire rushing through her blood.

His left hand was touching the back of her neck, his long fingers kneading the muscles, relaxing her even as his tongue excited. The sensations played against each other, tumbling her emotions along rapids and waterfalls. She heard herself moan with the sheer sensuality of his touches.

And then his fingers moved from her neck to the front of her dress, and she felt the buttons go, and the dress opening, felt his hand touch her breast, felt them swell and ache. He leaned down and his mouth played with her left nipple, sucking on it until she cried out with torment. Then the next as he pushed away the dress and it fell to her hips. She could only stand help-less under the magic of his hand and mouth.

She opened her eyes and looked down. His trou-sers were bulging with his own need and her hand went down and untied the leather laces.

Together they stepped out of their garments. Her chemise came over her head, everything else was dropped, and they were standing there in the flicker-ing light of the kerosene lamp, their bodies touching, then melding, fitting into each other so naturally. He glided his hand over her hair, watching as it tumbled over her shoulder. He buried his face in it with a soft cry, then took her hand and led her the two feet to the bed. She seemed to float, the magic was so strong be-tween them.

His hand guided her down to sit on the bed, and then he moved next to her. She shifted slightly and touched his face, closing her eyes. She was memorizing the feel of it, of every little crease and curvature, every small crevice. And then she did as he had done, cov-ered that wonderful face with kisses, tasting him now as he had tasted her, and when she reached his lips, they met and challenged and consumed.

And loved. Together, they lay down on the bed, their bodies twisting together with a hunger of their own. Because of his arm, almost unconsciously she slid on top of him, and as their lips gentled she felt the hardness of his need below her. She moved slightly, positioning herself, and he came into her, gently at first, both claiming each other in the most intimate and wondrous of ways. They held one another, savored the closeness of the act, but then a familiar urgency took hold. Hot. Intense. Desperate. Even angry. She sensed it in him, that anger.

"No," she whispered. "It's right. It's so right." She moved until he filled her so completely she thought she might break with the sublime joy of it. He moved, beginning a primitive rhythm that swept her along, intensifying until they were both locked into a swaying, explosive world of feeling.

Mary Jo heard her own moan mix with his cry as passion erupted brilliantly. She lowered herself until her bare skin touched his. Sensations continued to ripple through her body. His body was quivering ever so slightly, and his eyes closed as his good arm wrapped around her, and he held her tight. She laid her head next to his heart, heard its loud beat. So strong. So fine. She would always believe that.

Her hand went up to his hair. Thick and damp now, it curled slightly around her fingers.

"I love you," she said.

His chest heaved, and she felt its quake all the way through her.

Wade didn't say anything, but his hand ran down her back, his fingers gently saying things he couldn't say. He couldn't allow more. He couldn't think how much he wanted her, needed her. How much he would miss her, miss that sparkle in her eye, that tentative smile that so often hovered on her lips, that heart that gave so much and asked so little.

He didn't want to move. She felt so fine on him, his chin resting on that mass of auburn hair, her body wrapped so intimately with his.

He would never feel like this again, and he wanted to savor every second of it. He wanted to remember the feel of her breath on his chest, the glazed look in her eyes as she studied him so solemnly. He felt so unworthy. If she knew . . .

But she didn't, and he was too much of a coward to tell her, too greedy for that trust she handed him so easily. He swallowed hard, as he leaned his chin against her head, thinking nothing could be this silky, this intoxicating. But then everything about her robbed him of his ordinary caution and common sense. He had been so damn determined not to spill his seed in her, but that, as before, had been impossible.

I love you. And loving him was the worst thing that could happen to her. All of a sudden, he wanted so much. Part of him had remained numb from years of brutal guerrilla warfare. He'd become afraid to love, and the deaths of Chivita and Drew had nearly destroyed what small thread of hope had survived.

Mary Jo had taken that thread and weaved it into something he wanted desperately. He knew that Mary Jo and Jeff could revive those embers of life he thought he'd quenched so long ago. But it was too late. Much too late.

He held her that entire night. She snuggled in his arms, and they made love again, this time slowly and gently, as if hoarding every tender moment. There was a bittersweet anguish to each touch, each kiss.

They rose, dressed, and went outside to watch the sunrise together, the gold spreading over the eastern horizon. "Don't go," she said. "Don't go because of me."

"It's not for you anymore," he said. "It's for me. I've been running so damn long." He put his hand on her shoulder. "If the sheriff wants to know, just tell him what you did before. That you know me as Wade Smith, your fiancé's brother. Stick to it. Tell Jeff to do the same."

"What are you going to do?"

"Stop running," he said softly. "No matter what you hear about me, remember one thing. You are the best thing that has happened to me." He turned abruptly toward his horse. He hadn't wanted her to watch him go, but she'd stood next to him as he saddled his horse, and now she stood at the barn door as he walked his horse to the gate. He mounted, then looked back one last time before digging his heels in the gray's side and riding toward Last Chance.

Despite what he told her, he knew he wouldn't come back, couldn't come back no matter what happened. He couldn't say goodbye again.

Last Chance seemed even more dilapidated or maybe it was just his mood. During the last two hours, he'd steeled his thoughts to the task ahead. He would be walking a fine line.

One mistake, and Kelly might go after Mary Jo. Another, and the law might go after her.

He wished she'd never spread the story about a Wade Smith, the brother of the man she almost married, but it was too late now to take it back. He could only concoct a tale to cover it, and Mary Jo. He'd met Wade Smith in Denver, heard his tale about going to help out at a ranch, and then the man had been killed. Wade had taken his name and used the ranch as a hiding place.

The number of lies was mounting, as were the number of names. And then there was a second problem: getting a gun to Shepherd and making sure the man didn't kill anyone. Wade had enough blood on his hands without adding that of the sheriff's.

He had two choices. He could tell Matt Sinclair

what was happening and hope the man believed him, or he could free Shepherd and then hope to hell Sinclair would hear him out.

If only Wade knew where Kelly was. He was out there, and he was deadly. Kelly's years as a guerrilla had made him wily and dangerous. The sheriff would never find him.

Wade went into the saloon and was greeted by several men he'd met previously. His eyes skimmed the few daytime drinkers. "The sheriff?"

"In his office," the barkeep said. "Has a prisoner, real desperado, I hear." He eyed Wade curiously. "How's Mrs. Williams making out?"

"Just fine. She found some good hands."

"You staying?"

Wade shook his head. "Getting a little restless. I don't like to stay anyplace very long."

"Sorry to hear that. Abbot said you were real good with horses."

"Not with this arm."

"That's not what he said."

Wade wondered how Abbot knew. He'd been with the man only a few hours that day Mary Jo had bought some beeves. Tuck, maybe?

He drank the glass of whiskey he'd ordered. It tasted bitter. But then everything tasted bitter now. Everything but what he'd left hours ago. But even then, he'd seen Kelly's leering face in his mind's eye, approaching Mary Jo as those miners had approached Chivita—

The glass broke in his hand, and he looked up to see the barkeep staring at him. "Sorry," he said, tossing several coins to him.

"Better get that hand tended, mister," the

barkeep said, scooping up the coins. Wade looked down and saw the blood. Strange, it didn't hurt. Nothing could hurt again.

He nodded and went through the swinging doors to the street. He looked up at the sun. A little after noon. Hell, he might as well get it over with. He took off his bandanna and wrapped it around his left hand. No one was paying him any mind and he slipped into the shadow of a building. He took his gun from his belt and stuck it in the sling he was wearing, and then led his gray over to the railing in front of the sheriff's office. There was a small house next to it, with a bay hitched in front. The sheriff's, he supposed. He hoped.

The door to the sheriff's office was locked, and he knocked. He saw Sinclair peer out one of the front glass windows, protected by bars. Then heard his footsteps approach the door, and a bar opening. The sheriff looked tired, but his blue eyes glanced quickly around Wade, before opening the door wide for him. "Mr. Smith?"

"I wanted to talk to you about Mary Jo."

The sheriff motioned him inside. "What about Mrs. Williams? Is she hurt?"

"I'm leaving soon, and I wanted to make sure someone was looking out for her."

"Leaving?" Matt Sinclair looked none too sorry about the news.

Wade shrugged. "I'm no help here." He looked around the small office. There were two small cells, taking up half the office. The rest contained a desk, a cot the sheriff apparently used, a cookstove with a coffeepot on it, and a locked rifle rack. In one of the cells, a man rose from the cot as Wade came in and was now leaning against the bars, watching. Wade recognized him. He wondered if Shepherd had similar recall, but doubted it. Wade had had a beard then, but none now. Shepherd still had his. And cold black eyes Wade remembered well.

Sinclair had not taken his eyes from Wade, though. He was a competent man, Wade thought regretfully. "There's something else," Wade said. "I saw a couple of men yesterday who looked out of place. I remembered what you said about strangers and thought I might check your wanted posters."

Sinclair nodded. "They're in the desk. I'll get them." He turned his back and that was all Wade needed. He slipped the gun from the sling and struck Sinclair with it, blocking the man's fall with his own body, then lowering him with his left arm to the floor.

Wade looked toward Shepherd. "The keys?"

"Top desk drawer. Who are you?"

"An acquaintance from years ago."

The man's eyes narrowed, concentrating, and Wade put his gun on the desk drawer, found the keys and unlocked the cell. "Consider this a favor from a friend of yours."

"Kelly?" the man said as he left the cell.

Wade nodded. "For a percentage of the bank payroll. Now get the hell out of here."

"I'm going to shoot that goddamn sheriff first."

"And let the whole town hear? Hell, no."

The man glared at him for a moment, then nodded. He took the keys and unlocked a drawer in the desk and took out his gunbelt.

Wade went to the door and opened it slightly. "It's safe. There's a bay next door. Take that."

"I think I'll take that gray in front."

"You try it, and he'll throw you to hell and back. And then I'll kill you."

The man suddenly grinned. "I do remember you. Allen?"

Wade nodded.

"You'd do it too, wouldn't you?" Shepherd asked. "Kill me if I took your damn horse. You always cared more for your horse than any of us."

"They're worth a lot more. Now get out of here."

"What about you?"

"I'll use the knife on your friend. Then slip out quietly. People in town know me. They won't think anything of me riding out."

"You going to meet up with us?"

"In a couple of days. I have my own hiding place."

Shepherd nodded. "I owe you," he said, taking one last look, then sprinting out the door, slinking down a few steps and then quietly unhitching the bay.

Wade watched him ride away. He leaned over the fallen sheriff and unbuckled his gunbelt, then pulled him into one of the cells and locked the door. He tugged down the cheap shade on the window, sat in the chair and picked up the gun, wondering idly how much time he had.

It wasn't long. Within minutes, he heard a groan, a muttered curse. He saw a bucket of water with a ladle on the table in the corner next to a stove and coffee-pot. He filled the ladle and went over to the bars. Sinclair was half sitting, leaning on one arm. He glared at Wade from within the cell. "What in the hell . . . ?"

He looked toward the front door, which was closed again, and then around the room. He took in the fact that he was now in the cell that had previously housed his prisoner. He shook his head as if to clear it, wincing as he did so. "Shepherd?"

"Gone."

"Why?"

Wade had to admire him. Sinclair didn't waste time with curses or threats. He got down to the heart of the matter. There was obviously a reason Wade had remained behind.

"Water?" Wade said as he tried to judge the man inside the cell.

Sinclair rose slowly, painfully, and moved to the bars. He held out his hand for the ladle, took a couple swallows, then used the rest to dash on his face. His hand fingered the back of his head.

"Sorry about that," Wade said. "I didn't think you would let him go on your own."

"Damn right I wouldn't."

There was a knock on the door.

"Ignore it," Wade said, picking up the gun from the desk and pointing it at the sheriff.

Matt Sinclair stared at the gun, then his face. "What in the hell do you want?"

"Your cooperation."

"You have a damn strange way of going about getting it." Sinclair's eyes narrowed to slits. "Mary Jo?" It was the first time Wade had heard him use her given name and that deadly jealously started playing around inside again.

"Mary Jo doesn't know anything about this," Wade said. "But she's why I'm here. She's in trouble."

"How?"

"Because of me. I'm not who you, or Mary Jo, think I am."

"Then who are you?"

"Later," Wade said. "First, your bank's going to be robbed."

Sinclair stared at him, his dark eyes guarded. "Why are you telling me this?"

"I want you to stop it."

Matt Sinclair didn't blink, didn't show any surprise at all. "I suppose you're going to explain."

Wade found himself smiling. He wondered what it would take to ruffle the man in the cell. The sheriff certainly used a minimum of words. Wade nodded. "It's complicated."

Sinclair's eyebrows furrowed in question. "Then start from the beginning. Why did you free Shepherd?" The sheriff was trying hard to focus. His head must hurt like crazy, and Wade felt momentary sympathy for him.

"Because the men with him would have gone after Mary Jo if I hadn't. I can't protect Mary Jo and her son with this arm. Neither can Tuck or Ed."

"Who are they?"

"Their leader is a man named Clay Kelly."

The sheriff's head jerked up in recognition of the name. His hands went around the bars. "Kelly?"

"You know the name?"

"I don't know a lawman around that doesn't. I have a bunch of posters on him, every place from Kansas to Texas to Wyoming. He's a killer."

Wade winced at the word "Kansas." His was probably there, too. He nodded, bracing himself for the next question.

"He's the one who's been doing the killing, the rustling?"

Wade sighed, then decided to let Kelly take the blame for the killing of those miners. There was some justice to that. "He's been around," he said, allowing the implication to sink in.

"How do you know all this?" Sinclair's eyes were on the gun, even as the knocking on the door continued. A gesture from Wade kept him silent.

"I saw him in town a while ago, and went looking. I found him."

"Why aren't you dead?"

"I rode with him twelve years ago," Wade said flatly.

Sinclair's mouth thinned as he obviously thought back. "Where?"

"That's not important now," Wade replied shortly. "Mary Jo is. And your bank."

The sheriff didn't respond. He was too busy thinking. Wade could almost see him trying to figure out where he had seen Wade before meeting him at the ranch. A wanted poster perhaps? He was also wondering how to get out of that cell alive and take Wade.

"Why didn't you just come to me?"

"Because I wasn't sure whether you'd let Shepherd go, and I wanted him to think it was a jailbreak."

"It is a jailbreak," Sinclair said bitterly, his hand going back to the lump on his head again. "And you'll pay for it."

The knocking on the door stopped, and Wade lowered his six-shooter. He shifted his position against the desk, his gaze never leaving Sinclair.

"I fully expect to," Wade said, finally acknowledging Sinclair's last comment.

The sheriff's hands tightened around the bars. "You gonna let me out of here?"

"Maybe. If you're reasonable."

"Damn you. I don't feel reasonable."

Wade grinned wryly at the honesty. Mary Jo had liked Sinclair, had disliked lying to him. Wade was beginning to understand why. He was a direct, honest man. "I don't expect you do," he replied.

"Just what do you want?" The question was low and bitter.

"I want you to listen to me. Try to believe me."

"Why should I?"

"A lot of lives could depend on it. And this whole town."

"I would listen a whole lot better out there."

Wade considered. He would have to trust Sinclair sooner or later. He'd already put his life—and Mary Jo's—in Sinclair's hands. Shepherd would be long gone now. The question was, would Matt Sinclair listen, or would he just lock Wade up and throw away the key? Wade had taken measure of Sheriff Sinclair, and, if nothing else, Wade believed Sinclair would do what he could for Mary Jo and Jeff Williams. It was all Wade could ask for. All he wanted.

Wade nodded. He put down his gun, picked up the keys and unlocked the cell, moving back to allow Matt Sinclair to pass, waiting for the sheriff to order him inside. Sinclair didn't. He did pick up Wade's gun and put it in the drawer, then found his own and returned it to the holster, keeping wary eyes on Wade.

"Sit down," Sinclair said as he took the chair behind his desk.

Startled, Wade obeyed.

Sinclair leaned down and took out a bundle of wanted posters from a drawer in the desk and flipped through them, taking several out. He studied them for a moment, then reached in the top drawer and took out two long, thin cigars. "Want one?"

Wade didn't, not particularly, but he took it, fascinated with Sinclair's reaction. Wary. But encouraged. Maybe he'd underestimated the sheriff. But then he'd never had much respect for the law.

After the sheriff lit both cigars, he leaned back. "Allen?"

Wade was surprised. He had changed a hell of a lot since that old poster. Sinclair had good eyes. Wade shrugged his indifference. He'd known this was coming.

"You're still wanted." Sinclair sighed. "Suppose you tell me exactly what you intended before I lock you up."

Wade's eyes never left Sinclair's, willing him to believe. "I hadn't seen Kelly for twelve years until several days ago when I saw him riding through town," Wade said, sticking to the truth as much as possible. "I heard what you'd told Mary Jo about the slaughtered cattle, and I thought Kelly was probably responsible. That meant he was staying and probably planning a job. And the only thing worthwhile around here is the bank. So I went looking for him."

"Why did you care?"

"Mrs. Williams has been good to me. I didn't want her and the boy to lose everything they have."

"Why didn't you just tell her to withdraw her money?" The sheriff was shrewder than Wade had anticipated.

"I would have had to tell her how I knew, and I didn't want her to know who I was," he said simply. "She thinks I'm Wade Smith."

"We'll go into that later. Tell me more about Kelly."

"I found him. He said he was waiting for Shepherd, and that's all."

"Why do you think differently now?"

"One of his men came for me." Wade changed the facts slightly to suit his purpose. "They found out where I was staying. You'd arrested Shepherd, and they wanted me to help get him back. Kelly told me they planned to rob the bank, offered me part of the take if I would get Shepherd out of jail. He's the explosives man."

Sinclair's eyes didn't blink. "Why didn't you just come to me? We could go after them."

"He moved from the first place I met him, and I was blindfolded the second time I was taken to him. I have no idea where they are now. Kelly was a guerrilla for six years, long before the war started. He knows how to hide and when to strike."

"How does Mary Jo fit into this? You said she was in danger."

"They found out I was staying with her. If they knew I came to you, or if I refused to help with Shepherd, Kelly would go after her. That's why I—"

"Assaulted me and broke Shepherd out." Sinclair's eyes narrowed. "Posters say you both were with Anderson at Centralia."

Wade nodded. There were no excuses.

"You can still hang for that. It was considered a war crime."

Wade was silent.

"You knew that when you came in?"

"I guessed as much."

"I don't get it, mister," Sinclair said, suspicion alive in his eyes. "You walk in here, let a killer go, assault me, and give me this wild tale. You expect me to let you walk out?''

''No,'' Wade said softly. ''I want you to get Kelly. Then I don't care what happens.''

Sinclair studied him for a moment. ''When do you think he'll strike?''

''As soon as possible. He was getting restless. Now that he has Shepherd, I think you can expect him tomorrow. Certainly by the next day unless he suspects something.''

''And if he does, he'll go after Mary Jo and Jeff?''

Wade nodded. ''I told her to go to the Abbots tomorrow if I didn't return.''

''Oh, you're not going to return, Allen,'' Sinclair said curtly. He looked at Wade's arm. ''How did you really get that busted arm?''

Wade had been waiting for that, too. ''A hunting accident.''

The lawman's lips turned down in a frown. ''Mary Jo has no idea who you are?''

''No. I ran into the real Smith in Denver during a poker game. He said he was heading this way to see the woman who inherited his brother's ranch. I heard several days later he was shot in the street. When I was hurt, I decided to head this way.''

''A young widow with property,'' Matt said contemptuously. ''Good place to hide out.''

Wade didn't flinch. He didn't care what Sinclair thought as long as Mary Jo wasn't tainted by him. ''That's right,'' he said coolly. ''But I didn't count on putting them in danger. I don't want anything to happen to the kid.''

''You willing to hang for that?''

''I'm willing to let them try.''

"I still don't know why you think I should believe you. Maybe you want me to bring all the men into town, so your friends could rustle cattle or raid the ranches."

"You have me."

"Yeah, I do, don't I?" Sinclair said, standing. He put a hand on his six-shooter. "And you're going to stay a while. Move into that cell."

Wade stood. "What are you going to do?"

"I'm going to think on it some," the sheriff said laconically.

Wade's good hand clenched into a fist. He would have sworn he'd gotten through to him. Now, he wasn't sure. He hesitated. "If Kelly thinks I've been taken, he might also think I talked."

"I'll consider that, too," Sinclair said. "Now get inside." His hand brought the gun from the holster and pointed it at Wade.

Wade slowly obeyed, knowing there was nothing further he could do, or say. He just hoped to hell he hadn't just condemned Mary Jo and Jeff, that he hadn't failed once again.

24

Matt Sinclair locked the cell, checked the office to make sure everything was secure, then left for the telegraph office.

He needed time to think.

He'd been raised in Kansas, was eighteen when the war started. He'd wanted to join but he was needed at home; he finally joined the Union Army in '64 when his brother was old enough to take care of the farm.

The Sinclair family's farm was in northeast Kansas, and it had escaped much of the violence that splattered blood throughout Missouri and Kansas. He'd heard enough tales, though, and had known men who'd gone through the hell of the border war. He knew about Centralia, how unarmed soldiers had been killed in cold blood, then mutilated and scalped.

He had nothing but contempt for the guerrillas on

both sides, most of whom used the war as an excuse to steal and kill. And it had been his experience that such men didn't change. A conscience existed, or it didn't.

But the man called both Wade Smith and Brad Allen confused him.

Matt Sinclair considered himself a fair judge of character. A sheriff had to be. He hadn't liked Wade Smith when he'd first met him. Something about those cold, guarded eyes had alerted him, and he had the troubling sense he'd seen the face before. He'd tried to ignore the warning signals, afraid that they might be jealousy, resentment that Mary Jo Williams appeared attracted to her foreman. Now he knew the truth.

Leopards didn't change their spots, dammit. The man was pure trouble. Matt had absolutely no reason to believe him.

Nothing but the fact that Brad Allen now sat in Matt's jail when he could have easily killed Matt and escaped.

For the life of him, he couldn't figure what the man had to gain in jail that he couldn't gain outside it. Except Matt's trust. Matt sure as hell wouldn't have released someone like Shepherd on a stranger's say-so.

So Brad Allen, alias Wade Smith, was a smart son of a bitch.

Matt went to the telegraph office and sent three wires, one to the sheriff in Texas who'd sent out the last poster on Clay Kelly, one to a fellow lawman in Lake City for help, and one to the U.S. Marshal's office requesting the status of Brad Allen.

The telegraph operator looked at him strangely, but didn't ask questions. He'd learned long ago he wouldn't get any answers.

Then Matt walked to the largest of the two saloons in town. "Any strangers around?"

"Just that new foreman from Mrs. Williams' place."

"Let me know if you see any others." Matt sighed. He wished he had time to ride out to Mary Jo's, but she was half a day's ride away. He had stopped thinking of her as Mrs. Williams months ago, although he still called her that publicly. In his mind, though, she was Mary Jo, and the stranger's easy use of that name irked him as much as the blow across his head. He shook away the thought and went over to the bank.

Sam Pearson was owner and president of the Last Chance Merchants and Farmers Bank, and he was bent over some ledgers, while a clerk counted figures at the counter. There were no customers.

"You have a lot of cash now?" Matt asked, not bothering with formalities.

"Enough," Sam said. "The ranchers deposited their cattle money here."

"Is there any other place you could put it? Besides your safe?"

"Barton at the general store has a good safe. So do you. Mind me asking why?"

It suddenly crossed Matt's mind that maybe this was what Allen or Smith or whoever he was wanted: the money placed in a more accessible spot.

"I'm not sure," Matt said slowly. "I'm hearing rumors that an outlaw named Clay Kelly's in the area. He likes banks."

Sam blanched. "You know what that would mean to the town?"

"Hell, yes, I know."

"How sure are you?"

Matt hesitated. "Enough that I'm going to put a posse together to guard the bank for the next several days." He surprised himself at the commitment. Until this minute he hadn't been sure he believed the prisoner in his jail. "I've also sent for some extra help, but it might take several days to get here."

"I'll disperse the cash around, make some payroll deliveries early to the ranches."

Matt nodded. "But don't tell them why. I don't want anyone to know but those on the posse. If Kelly comes, I want a surprise." He hesitated, then added as insurance, "And you don't want a run on the bank."

"This doesn't have anything to do with the prisoner you're holding, does it?"

"Shepherd?" Matt said, realizing suddenly that no one knew his original prisoner had been broken out of jail. He shrugged. "I'm not sure. Just disperse as much cash as you can. Starting in the morning, I'll have men posted all over the town. We'll get them trying to go into the bank."

Sam Pearson nodded.

Matt had a dozen questions in his mind now for the man in his jail. Dammit, he believed him. He didn't want to, but he did.

He stopped by the boarding house and picked up two meals, one for himself and one for his prisoner. He wanted answers, lots of them, and then it was going to be a very long afternoon. He wished the ache in his head would go away. He felt the bump again. It was tender as hell. He had Allen to thank for that.

Wade had never been in a cell before. He'd never known how crushing it could be to the spirit, locked like an animal in such a small space. He'd better get used to it, he told himself.

What really made it unbearable was his helplessness. Why had he ever thought he could trust Sinclair?

He kept seeing Mary Jo's face, and Jeff's, and Kelly's leering one. He should have just told Mary Jo to take her money from the bank, and the hell with the rest of the town. She wouldn't have done that, though. He knew that.

Wade cursed Matt Sinclair and he cursed himself. He was too worried to sit down on the iron cot with its inch-thick mattress. He investigated the lock, thinking he should have done that before giving his gun to Sinclair.

How could he have been so wrong? But the man had seemed to be listening, and Wade had so few options. If only his arm were functioning, but that was like wishing the sun was blue. It wasn't, and nothing was going to make it so.

He heard a key turn in the front door of the jail, and he leaned against the bars. He didn't care if he looked anxious or not, desperate or not. By God, he was!

Sinclair entered loaded down with a tray. He put it on the desk, then took a sandwich over to Wade. Wade just stared at it, refusing it.

"Take it," Sinclair said. "We have a lot to talk about."

Wade obeyed reluctantly, taking the food in his good hand, watching warily as the sheriff poured some coffee from the pot on the cookstove and set the cup down on the cell floor. Then the lawman pulled his chair up close to the bars and plopped down in it with his own sandwich. "How many men are with Kelly?"

Wade released a long breath. He started pacing, mindless of the sandwich in his hand. "Four now with Shepherd. Two young gunnies. Seem real eager with their guns."

"Would they go in shooting?"

"These would. Kelly enjoys killing."

"And you, Allen, you enjoy killing?"

Wade stopped in mid-stride.

"I'm from Kansas," Sinclair said quietly. "I know what Anderson did there."

Wade felt the familiar sickness of soul. "Kansas and Missouri were both pits of hell," he said tonelessly. "My entire family was wiped out by Jayhawkers, my mother and sister raped before they were murdered. I did my share of killing. I won't lie to you about that, and I don't excuse myself." He clenched his teeth together. He didn't want to talk about it, but he had to make Sinclair believe him, and the truth was the only damn option. "There was some satisfaction at first," he added slowly, trying hard to be honest with himself. "Maybe even some pleasure. I don't know. I just knew how angry I was, how . . . I needed to avenge my family." He hesitated. "That went away, but not fast enough," he said. "I'll always regret what happened back then. I've tried damn hard to forget it, but I can't and I never will."

There was a long silence, then Sinclair continued his questions about Kelly. How might he strike? From what end of town? How many men would he send inside?

"You don't want to wait until he's inside, or he'll kill everyone there," Wade said. "He doesn't leave witnesses."

Sinclair raised his eyebrows. "You were friends?"

"I said I rode with him. I also rode with Jesse and Frank James, the Cole brothers. We were all with Quantrill and occasionally with Anderson, but that didn't particularly make us friends."

"When is the last time you saw him?"

"I left Anderson after Centralia."

"Why?"

"That's personal."

"Not anymore," Sinclair said. "I don't know how far I can trust you. You're asking me to put a lot of faith in a man on a wanted poster, who walked in here and used a gun on my head."

Wade's hand gripped the bar. He was being asked to expose everything he'd buried inside for so long. He hadn't been able to tell Chivita, nor Mary Jo, hadn't been able to put his capacity for violence into words. Not while that violence still existed inside him, and it *had* lingered, exploding again when Chivita and Drew were killed. It was alive even now. He wanted to kill Kelly with his own hands for threatening Mary Jo. God, he hated admitting what kind of man he was. But he needed Matt Sinclair, and Sinclair wasn't going to accept evasion. "Because I was turning into the same kind of animal as those Jayhawkers who killed my family."

Sinclair rose from the chair and walked away from him. Wade watched as he poured himself another cup of coffee. Wade knew he was thinking, assessing, wondering how far he could trust one of Anderson's guerrillas, a butcher like other butchers. He felt a chill run through him; he could never put that damn past behind him.

"How old were you?" Sinclair finally asked.

Wade was momentarily stunned by the question,

then he shrugged. He'd surrendered his privacy when he walked in here. "Fifteen when they raided our farm," he said.

"That when you joined Quantrill?"

Wade hesitated. "The next year, but I'd been hunting for someone like him."

"And since the war?"

"I've been trying to get away from the war, from what happened then," Wade said flatly, without excuse. "Moving around, mostly in the mountains. Hunting. Rounding up wild horses and breaking them for trade." Then he remembered his lie about Denver. "I went into Denver occasionally for supplies." He wasn't going to mention the Utes, or Chivita. The way most folks felt, that would only condemn him. Ordinarily, he wouldn't care, but . . .

Sinclair's eyes bored into him, and Wade realized the lawman knew he was holding something back. "You wouldn't know anything about a miner found dead a month ago?"

"No," Wade lied, afraid that admission would hurt Mary Jo, hurt his believability, but God, he hated lying again.

Sinclair was good at his job. Very good, a hell of a lot better than Wade had expected. He kept changing the subject, throwing questions apparently at random but boring in, inch by inch.

"Would Kelly expect you back?"

Sinclair was offering him a way out of this cell. Wade wanted to take it. Christ, he wanted to take it. Already, he felt suffocated by his confinement. He thought about spending the rest of his life in a cage, if, that was, he didn't hang.

He locked his jaw together for a moment. "No,"

he finally admitted. "I don't know where he is, and we don't particularly care for each other. He thinks I want a share of the money, but he expects me to find him later."

"Trusting sort, are you?" There was doubt in the lawman's voice.

"He doesn't think he gave me a choice. If I didn't do what he wanted, he was going to find a way to tell you just who I was, and then he would go after Mary Jo. He suggested I just come in and slip Shepherd a gun."

"You could have."

"And you would be dead."

"That would bother you?"

"I told you I didn't want any more innocent blood on my hands." Anger shaded Wade's words now. He was tired of talking, of being forced to talk about matters he wanted to forget.

"I don't think you did say that," Sinclair said, milking him again. "Not exactly."

"Damn it, enough about me. What are you going to do?"

Sinclair just sat back. "What would you suggest?"

"An ambush as they come in."

"More killing?"

Wade swallowed hard, trying to control that anger of his. "Kelly's a coward at heart. They all are. Put enough guns on them and they'll surrender."

"And tell everything they know about you?"

"Hell, you already know."

"Do I?" Sinclair said thoughtfully. "I might just owe you my life. I'm not sure I wouldn't tear up that poster if we save the bank. I can't do that if they're still alive and talking."

Wade stared at him hard, wondering what game he

was playing now. Matt Sinclair wanted Mary Jo. That had been clear the first time he'd met him. And Sinclair was a lawman. He wouldn't give up a catch like Brad Allen. Matt Sinclair would become a hero, just as Jeff so wrongly believed Wade was. But Sinclair would be a real one. "I'm through running," Wade finally said.

A frown crossed Sinclair's face, then disappeared. "Fair enough," he said. "Give me a fresh description of Kelly and the two gunhands with him."

By evening, two of Matt's telegrams had been answered. He now had a lot of information on Kelly, and it matched everything Allen had told him. He also had the promise of assistance tomorrow from a neighboring lawman, but that might be too late. He had to depend on his townspeople, men he'd deputized before. But he worried about them. They weren't killers. He could only hope Brad Allen was right, that Kelly and his bunch were cowards at heart.

He'd stationed men in windows throughout town, coordinating shifts, concentrating on the morning hours but leaving skeleton crews of watchers at night. He wanted to leave little to chance. The banker had dispersed the money to every trusted man with a safe and had left only a minimum amount of money in his own safe. Matt was not, however, going to share this information with the man in the jail. Sinclair believed Brad Allen, but . . .

He had told no one about the change in prisoners. Brad Allen was his own business, and he wasn't sure what he wanted to do with him. Jail seemed to be the safest choice at the moment.

Brad Allen, or Wade Smith, continued to puzzle him. Matt had never met a man like him, one so contradictory to everything Sinclair believed about men like him. Foster, as he called himself now, radiated danger and untamed violence, and yet he was obviously willing to sacrifice himself. Matt still wasn't quite sure why.

Matt wanted to believe him. Hell, he did believe him. He'd known killers, and there was always a blankness in the eyes, a coldness they couldn't cover. His prisoner's eyes were different. Bleak. Sometimes angry. But they weren't empty.

Matt stopped at the hotel and bought supper for both of them, shoving the plate through a space at the bottom of the cell, then poured his prisoner another cup of coffee, which was so strong it almost didn't need a cup to hold it. He met Allen's eyes, but didn't say anything. He wanted the man to stew, to get angry. Perhaps he'd learn more that way than through sweet reason.

He asked only one question before going out again. "Any chance Kelly might come at night?"

"I don't think so. He can't see at night, and he likes to be in total control."

That coincided with all the information Matt had collected from the telegrams he'd sent. Kelly liked to ride in quietly, go into a bank, terrorize everyone there, and then ride out, guns blazing. Matt hadn't yet received a reply to his telegram about Brad Allen. He almost hoped he wouldn't, and several times he'd considered releasing him. Despite that arm in a sling, he might be handy. Mary Jo had said he saved young Jeff's life.

A most unusual man, this Brad Allen/Wade Smith,

but one Matt wasn't ready to trust completely. He was safer where he was.

Matt checked the streets, then returned to the jail, napping on and off in the office, leaving several more times to check the streets, always securing his office before going. Allen was quiet, but he wasn't resting. Matt felt as if he had a prowling tiger back there, and he didn't feel easy about it.

There was no window in the cell. No moonlight. No sky. No breath of air.

Wade tried to force himself to relax. He'd done the best he could, the only thing he could. It was probably the only time in his life he had done the right thing. He hoped to God it was right.

But the silence, the darkness, the closeness of the cell all brought the nightmares to life. Only he wasn't asleep. They weren't dreams, but a succession of memories. Even the most recent—from last night—were cloaked in regret. He prowled the small space, wishing he could take it back for her sake, for Mary Jo.

I love you. He kept hearing those words. They echoed in his mind and heart. They should have healed, but they only exacerbated the wound.

She needed someone like Matt Sinclair. Wade had come to respect him in the last few hours. He was honest, certainly smart and probably brave. He said little to Wade, but it was obvious he believed at least some of his tale, and that preparations of some kind were going on. He wished like hell he could be a part of them.

If he were Matt Sinclair, he wouldn't take a chance on someone like Wade either, even knowing only part of the truth.

The walls were closing in on him, crushing him. He tried to blank out his mind, but he couldn't. A hundred possibilities flitted through his mind. What if Kelly went directly to the Circle J? What if he didn't come here at all? Wade was so damn helpless. Just as he had been before.

Mary Jo didn't sleep at all the night after Wade left. Although he'd said he would try to get back, she knew in her heart he was really saying goodbye.

She wished she knew exactly what he was going to do. Despite the fact that he'd denied doing anything for her, she knew he was risking everything for her and Jeff. She wished she knew what everything was.

What haunted him so? *They know something about me.* She kept trying to think what it could be, what could be worse than his first confession to her, that he'd killed three men in cold blood.

She knew him well now. Or thought she did. He still kept many parts of himself guarded. But she knew everything that was important: his loyalty, his courage, his gentleness with both her and her son.

She had lost before because there wasn't anything she could do. She wasn't going to lose now if she could prevent it. She wasn't going to let him walk away because he thought that was the best thing for her. It wasn't. It never would be.

If he didn't return in the morning, she would take Jeff to the Abbots as Wade suggested. She would go into town herself, ride her mare, which would be faster than the wagon. She would take Tuck with her.

She could fight this time. She *would* fight for him. For all three of them.

Mary Jo rose before sunset. She dressed and went outside and watched the sunset come up, but today its beauty hurt instead of sending a thrill through her. She kept seeing Wade ride off, as he had twenty-four hours earlier, his back stiff and straight until he'd looked back . . .

He'd given himself away then, in that one backward look. There had been a world of longing in that gesture. She wiped away a tear from her face, then went to fix breakfast for Jeff and the two men.

Sinclair took breakfast to Wade. "When do you think they might come?"

Wade wished he knew. It had been twelve years since he rode with Kelly. The man always looked for an advantage. Wade took the proffered cup of coffee and hesitated. He'd been thinking all night and had an idea. He didn't know how Sinclair would take to it. "You wouldn't have some spare men?"

Sinclair looked at him curiously.

"For a posse. Kelly will be expecting a posse to chase Shepherd. And he'll take advantage of that, of you and most of the men leaving town to look for Shepherd."

"You wouldn't be here just for that purpose?" Sinclair asked with sudden suspicion. "Get us out of town and they could hit the bank and break you out?"

"Kelly's not that smart."

"But you are," Sinclair said, a hint of suspicion in his voice.

Wade shrugged. "It was just an idea. Send out a few men, some that wouldn't be too useful here."

"I wouldn't have any idea where to send them."

"South, toward Mary Jo's place. He's somewhere in that direction and it's the logical route for a posse to take. Only figures a wanted man would flee to the mountains."

"You'd know about that, wouldn't you?"

Sinclair was needling him again, and Wade didn't like it, but he wouldn't let it show. He shrugged.

"That's where I found that body a month ago."

Wade kept his eyes level. Sinclair wasn't going to let go of that bone. "I wouldn't know about that."

Matt Sinclair sighed. "You sure you don't know where Kelly is?"

"He let me find him once. He won't do it again, not until he wants to be found."

Sinclair got the coffeepot and poured them both another cup of coffee, handing Wade's through the bars of the cell. "I wish I knew what to make of you."

Wade shrugged. "It's not complicated. If I had the use of this arm, I would have gone after him myself. The only thing I care about is two people who were real good to me."

Sinclair eyed him skeptically. "That doesn't go along with the rest of the package you've given me."

"Let's just say I got religion."

"I don't believe that either, but we'll discuss it later. I'll go see about forming a posse."

After he left, all Wade could do was wait. The hours passed particularly slowly because he didn't know what was going on. Only the growing heat in the jail told him the sun was rising. The shades were still down on the windows and only a little light filtered through.

Time. Christ, he hated this enforced idleness. He wished he was out there with Sinclair. He knew about ambushes. He knew more than he wanted to know about them. Time. So much time to think. So much time to remember. So much time to regret. He swallowed a deep breath to keep from pounding on the barred door. He forced himself to sit, to wait, to blank out his mind. It had worked once. It didn't work now. He heard men ride out, and he wondered about his gray. He would make sure Mary Jo got him.

He heard the lock turn in the front door, and he moved up from the cot where he'd finally sat after pacing for an hour or more. He stood and went to the barred door, expecting Sinclair to come with more questions.

It was Sinclair all right, but Mary Jo was with him. He went still, wondering how much the sheriff had told her. His fist clenched the bar. He didn't want her to see him like this, like a vicious animal in a cage. But he should have known she would come. At least Jeff wasn't here.

"I told you not to come," he said tightly.

"Tuck came with me." Her voice was low.

"Did you withdraw . . . ?"

"The bank's closed."

Wade looked over at Sinclair, who had raised the shades and was now peering out the windows as if he had no interest at all in the two people staring at each other. Wade wanted to jam his fist in the man's face. He'd had no right to bring Mary Jo here. And then he realized the fallacy of that thought. Hell, Sinclair had every right, and that was galling. Wade didn't have any rights now. He'd given them up when he walked in here yesterday and broke Shepherd out. That fact, though, didn't make this easier to take.

She looked so goddamn beautiful.

And Sinclair hadn't told her a thing. He knew that from the look in her face. It hadn't changed since yesterday morning at sunrise. Or was it a year ago? A lifetime? Her eyes still shone when they looked at him, even as he stood behind bars.

"Jeff?"

"He's at the Abbots'. I think he'll stay there this time. At least he promised when I told him he might put you in danger if he came." She looked embarrassed. "It was the only argument that worked."

"It didn't work for you?"

"No," she said softly. "I couldn't let you go."

"You should have," he said bitterly. "It would be better for all of us."

She moved closer to him, almost leaned against the bars and put one hand on his.

"Don't," he said in a strangled voice, tearing his hand from hers and retreating from the bars, leaning against the stones of the back wall, looking at another wall, anyplace but at her, at those trusting eyes. After a moment, he looked past her to Sinclair. "Can't you take her to the hotel?"

Sinclair hesitated, looking from one to the other. "I really think that would be best, Mary Jo. We're expecting a little company. I want you off the streets."

"Why are you holding him?"

Sinclair looked toward Wade, then back at Mary Jo. "Safest place for him at the moment."

"But . . ."

She wasn't going to go on her own. And every moment she stayed here was dangerous. Wade wanted her off the street, safe in the hotel. Hell, safe at home. "Tell her," Wade said suddenly. "Go ahead and tell her everything."

Just then, all three of them heard a number of hoofbeats on the dry-packed dirt street. Matt Sinclair looked out and grinned suddenly, then took the keys to the cell door and opened it.

Wade found himself staring at him.

"Just stay with me," Sinclair said. "Don't say a damn thing."

The door flew open and a tall man entered, flanked by two others. All three wore badges. Sinclair greeted the leader with familiarity. "Glad to see you, Dave."

"When I heard Kelly was down this way, you couldn't keep me away. Been riding all night," the newcomer said. He looked at Wade and Mary Jo curiously. "I'm Marshal Dave Gardner from Lake City."

Sinclair made the introductions. "This is Mary Jo Williams, who owns a ranch about twenty miles from here and Wade . . . Smith, her foreman. He's the one who recognized Kelly."

Dave Gardner nodded at Mary Jo, then fixed a stare on Wade. "You sure it was Kelly?"

Wade had stepped outside the cell. He nodded, wondering what kind of game Sinclair was playing. "I'm sure."

"You think they're going to hit the bank here?"

"That's what he thinks," Sinclair answered for him, cutting off any additional questions.

Gardner looked from one man to the other, obviously sensing something odd, but he didn't pursue it. Instead, he turned back to Matt Sinclair.

"When?"

"Anytime now."

"Where do you want my men? I have six with me. All good men, good shots."

"Thank God. All mine are townsmen. Willing enough, but none are easy with guns."

"Just tell me where you want us."

"I have ten men posted in windows and on roofs above the street. You were probably in their sights when you came in. If your men can replace four nearest the bank, I'd feel a lot better."

The marshal nodded. "I'll do it now."

Sinclair hesitated. "I'd better go out and give a signal. I don't want any accidents. You wait here," he told Wade, "and I'll take Mrs. Williams to the hotel."

Mary Jo looked from one man to the other, then surrendered. At least, she appeared to surrender, Wade told himself. And what in the hell was Sinclair doing, allowing him out of the cell, apparently leaving him free in his office? Free for the moment.

Mary Jo leaned up and kissed Wade, apparently indifferent to the avidly watching observers. The kiss was long, sensual, and . . . loving, so damn loving that all protest fled from him.

"Mrs. Williams?" Sinclair prompted after a moment, and Wade reluctantly let her go, moving a few steps away, trying to quiet the quaking in his heart. She looked back at him for a long moment, then followed Sinclair and the other men, leaving Wade alone in the room.

25

Wade looked at the cell, then at the door. Freedom. It had become more important to him after the last day and night in jail. Infinitely more important.

There were even guns within reach. But he wasn't certain he was good enough at shooting with his left hand to hit a target.

He went to the door and opened it, half expecting an armed guard. There was none. The sheriff was at the end of the street, directing several men. There were men with rifles on roofs, but they were all looking toward the road from the south.

And there were horses within an arm's reach.

Freedom. And just as important, he would never see the disillusionment in Mary Jo's eyes.

Why hadn't Sinclair told her about Brad Allen? Why had Sinclair left him an open invitation to flee?

I'm through running. The words he had spoken so bravely earlier. But that was before he fully realized how he might spend the rest of his life. He'd been prepared to die, even to hang. He wasn't sure he could live in a cage for twenty or thirty years.

And he wasn't at all sure he could face Mary Jo and tell her the truth. Or Jeff. Jeff would try to find excuses, reasons, and that would destroy some of the boy's inherent decency. There was no reasoning away murder.

A horse was seconds away. And then what?

He couldn't join Manchez again. He'd only bring trouble on their heads. The twelve-year-old search would be resumed. He would be hunted again with renewed effort, and he would never stop running. Mary Jo and Jeff would read someday of his capture or death. Another one of Anderson's guerrillas brought down.

Sinclair was no one's fool.

He couldn't figure out why Mary Jo hadn't been interested in the lawman. He appeared to be everything a woman should want: decent, hardworking, honest. Wade was everything a woman should avoid. Perhaps when he wasn't around . . .

The door opened and Sinclair came back in alone. "Still here, I see."

"You told me to wait," Wade said, biting back the smallest of smiles.

"People don't always do what I tell them."

The smile disappeared. "I hope Mary Jo did."

"I think she'll stay put for a while, for your sake. I stressed that point, just as she apparently did to Jeff. It's the only thing that seems to get through to either of them."

"Why did you let me out of the cell?"

"I wanted to see whether you meant it when you said you were done running. If you are, maybe I can help."

"Why?"

"Because I don't see your kind much. Because you might have saved this town. You've been with those Indians up in the hills, haven't you?"

Sinclair had done that before, switched subjects so rapidly he could easily disarm someone just as he fired a shot into their heart.

"Talk is," Sinclair continued, "the Utes found young Jeff. They wouldn't go to that trouble unless they had good reason."

Wade was silent. It was obvious the sheriff was fishing.

Sinclair continued, his voice soft but compelling. "There's also been talk of a white man living with them. He even married one of the Ute women. Had a kid. I was wondering what happened to him?"

So Sinclair had put the pieces together. Wade should have expected it by now. Sinclair's pleasant expression hid one hell of a lot of shrewdness.

"You through?"

Sinclair shrugged. "Just curious."

"So am I. Why didn't you tell Mary Jo about that poster?"

"You're the one who wants to stop running. Seems like you should tell her."

"What are you going to do?"

"Depends on what happens in the next few hours."

"I don't think I like your games."

Sinclair smiled. "Not many people do." He looked

at his watch. "If they're coming today, it should be soon. A telegram from Texas says your friend prefers afternoon. He plans his getaways to the west. Pretty smart. Eyes are blinded by the sun." And then Sinclair switched topics again. "You want to come with me?"

"Where?"

"Inside the bank. I thought about stopping him on the street and shipping him off to Texas, but it would be safer for the town to take him inside the bank now that I have some professional help. I don't like shooting in my streets."

Wade narrowed his eyes. "Why take me along?"

"I got a feeling about you, mister. A real strong one. Damn if I can put a handle on it, but something just tells me to take you along. Of course, you don't have to go."

"I could stay in a cell?"

"Yep."

"I'll go with you."

Sinclair smiled. "Thought you might. Can you handle a gun at all with that left hand?"

"Well enough to crack your skull."

"That's true, though it wasn't too smart to remind me."

"I didn't think you'd forgotten it," Wade said wryly.

The sheriff reached in one of the drawers and took out the six-shooter Wade had handed him yesterday. Wade checked. It was loaded. He didn't say anything, though he wondered at the man's carelessness. He tucked it into the band of his trousers.

Sinclair checked his own six-shooter. "Dave's gonna be the clerk and one of his men the manager. Another will be a customer. You and I will be behind the counter. Our other men will be outside. I figure one of them will wait outside with the horses, so there will be five of us to their three, and they won't expect us."

"I still can't shoot worth a damn. Why do you want me?"

"You know him. You'll know his voice when he comes in. Your face might surprise him. And you want him. Bad enough to come to me. But," he added softly, "I want them alive."

Wade nodded. He wasn't sure how he felt about that. He hadn't lied when he'd said he was tired of killing. That last one, that miner, had demonstrated how much. He'd felt no satisfaction at the man's death. There hadn't even been hate left after the long hunt. He'd only felt empty. Alone. Ready to die himself.

And then Mary Jo and Jeff had come along, and he'd found embers of himself still alive.

They entered the bank. The owner, Sam Pearson, clucked around nervously for a few minutes, worrying aloud about whether he should stay or not, and was finally ejected by the sheriff as more hindrance than help. The lawmen all took their places, Wade sitting on the floor next to Matt Sinclair.

Sinclair was silent for a few moments. "Maybe I'll get my horse back. I sure liked that horse."

Wade was reminded of his role in that piece of horse stealing. He didn't think that was Sinclair's intent. The words had been spoken wistfully. He could think of no reply that wasn't self-serving; he added that slice of guilt to all the rest.

"Heard you're real good with horses," the sheriff continued, and Wade wondered what was coming next. The lawman, he was discovering, seldom said anything just to hear himself talk. Every word, each question, seemed to have some purpose, even if it seemed a little obscure at the time.

"I like horses," Wade replied. "They don't talk."

Sinclair chuckled but fell silent.

There were no customers, and Wade realized the entire town must know by now what was going on. He hoped the silence in the street didn't alert Kelly. Or maybe he didn't. Maybe Kelly would just ride on, go back to Texas or up to Wyoming. Or maybe he would hang around and go after Mary Jo if he suspected Wade had crossed him. If Kelly didn't show, Wade would probably go back to jail, and Mary Jo and Jeff would be alone. Of course, they had Tuck and Ed now, but neither man was a match for Kelly and his gunhands. Neither was he, though, not with his busted arm. Wade took out his gun, and fingered it with his left hand. It still wasn't comfortable there.

He glanced up. Sinclair's steady blue eyes were watching him without visible emotion. "Waiting's always hard," Sinclair said, "but then I guess you know about that."

Wade hesitated, then asked a question of his own. "You in the war?"

"Two years in the Union infantry. Never wanted to walk again." The flatness in his voice indicated he didn't want to say more. Wade understood that.

An hour went by without more words. Wade sensed the tension rising in the room. Waiting always made a man consider the possibility of death. Idle conversation somehow seemed almost foolish.

The skin crawled on the back of Wade's neck as he heard something at the back door of the bank, and the man posing as president went to open it. "Strangers riding in, four of 'em," the man assigned to watch from the roof reported.

The door closed, and Wade heard, and saw, sudden movement. Final last check of guns. His and Sinclair's were out. The others had hidden them in easily accessible places. The three visible men had all picked locations where they could duck suddenly as they grabbed their weapons. They needed only a second and it was up to Sinclair and Wade to give them that second.

A bell on the front door jingled, and Wade heard the sound of boots and spurs on the flooring. The lawman posing as the customer was at the counter window, talking to the counterfeit clerk. Wade, sitting on the floor next to the legs of the clerk, felt the man's sudden tension. He looked over toward Sinclair, whose brow was now creased with concentration.

And then Wade heard Kelly's voice. "I want to make a withdrawal." Wade nodded to Sinclair just as a man sprinted over the gate that separated one side of the customer area from the the back of the bank where the safe was. Wade recognized Shepherd, whose gaze, focused on the safe, missed seeing Wade and Sinclair as they stood.

Wade saw everything in the flash of a second: Kelly becoming enraged when he saw Wade; the other three lawmen reaching for their hidden weapons; Shepherd sensing something and turning, seeking a target for the gun in his hand.

The lawman posing as manager shot Shepherd, and Shepherd went down. The young gunman—Johnny Kay—fired wildly. The bullet plowed into Sinclair, and as the sheriff spun from the impact, three lawmen fired at Kay.

Sinclair was still standing, a stunned look on his face, blood running down his right shoulder, when Kelly jumped over the counter and had Sinclair by the neck, shielding himself with the sheriff's body.

There were shots from outside, a yell, then silence. Kelly held a gun to Sinclair's head. Shepherd was moaning on the floor, and the three lawmen stood motionless watching Kelly and Sinclair.

Kelly's attention, though, was on Wade. It wavered for a moment as his eyes went to the three lawmen. "Put down your guns or I'll blow his head off."

The three did so, slowly. "You too, Allen." He looked around the room. "You know who you have here?" He looked at Wade with hatred. "I could kill you now, but I would rather you hang." Again, he looked around the room. "His name is Brad Allen, and he's wanted for murder. Old and recent." He turned slightly and jerked Sinclair around. "We're going to leave now." Wade saw the sheriff flinch with pain.

"Take me," Wade said. "I planned this, and you can't get far with him like that."

"I think not," Kelly said. "They might not value a turncoat as much as a lawdog, and I think he'll last long enough." He grinned. "You can help, though. Make sure the street's clear." Kelly looked down at Shepherd, who was lying on the floor, groaning. "Can you make it on your own?"

Shepherd shook his head. Kelly shrugged.

"You," he said to Wade. "Get the money out."

"There isn't any. It's all been taken someplace else," Wade said, goading him. He wanted Kelly to turn the gun on him, giving the other lawmen time to sweep up their six-shooters, for Sinclair to drop to the floor. His eyes met Sinclair's, and he knew the lawman knew what he was doing. Sinclair shook his head almost imperceptibly, but Wade didn't pay any attention.

"I planned the whole thing, Kelly, even helping Shepherd get away so you would come into town. There's a man and rifle in every window. You won't get away."

"Why?" Kelly's eyes were blazing.

"Because I don't like you. Because you're a rabid animal, just like you always were."

"So were you, my friend," Kelly ripped out. "You were no better than any of us."

"No," Wade said. "But I know it and you don't. You're a fool, Kelly. A mistake. A snake walking on two legs." His voice lowered. "And a coward. Always a coward."

Kelly's face was livid now with rage, and the pistol in his hand moved from Sinclair's head to Wade's stomach. At that moment, Sinclair pushed hard and went sideways, only slightly deflecting the bullet that plowed into Wade. As Wade went down to his knees, a searing pain stabbing through his middle, he heard more shots, a yell, some cursing.

His eyes remained on Kelly, watching as surprise and pain replaced rage. The outlaw tried to lift his gun again, but blood spurted from his right arm, and he dropped it as he went down. Sinclair reached over and took his gun, and then two lawmen were leaning over Kelly, the third over Shepherd. Other men were now pouring into the bank.

Sinclair moved over to Wade, one hand clenching the shoulder wound to staunch his own bleeding. His eyes, those watchful brown eyes, scanned Wade's body. Wade looked down. Blood was puddling on the floor beneath his left hip, and the pain, momentarily dulled by the shock, was excruciating. He knew from the pain the bullet had hit the bone.

"That was a fool thing to do," Sinclair said.

Wade ignored him and looked toward the lawmen checking Kelly. "Is he still alive?"

One of them nodded. "He'll live. So will one of the others. The other two are dead."

Wade closed his eyes wearily. More death. Wherever he went . . .

Wade woke through clouds of pain. His eyes didn't want to open, and his mouth was dry, as if he'd been sucking a cotton ball. He tried to remember. Shots. Pain. Blood, red and sticky and nauseating. Darkness. He kept his eyes closed against all that, but then other sensations started filtering into his consciousness.

The smell of flowers hovered around him. Her scent. Her essence. The comfort of a bed. Soft. Not hard like the jail cot.

Then he felt a cold nose nuzzling him, heard the comforting thump of a tail.

"He's moving." Wade heard Jeff's anxious voice as if it came from a distance.

Then hands. Her hands. He would know them anywhere. Gentle. So infinitely gentle. He didn't deserve them. He didn't deserve anything. For a moment, he wished himself back in the darkness.

"Wade." Her voice called to him, and he couldn't bear the sadness in it.

He slowly willed his eyes to open and tried to focus on her face. Such a pretty face. So sad. So worried. So caring. She didn't know. She didn't know yet just what kind of a monster he was. Wade understood that from her face. She would soon. Kelly would yell it from the rooftops.

He felt that nose again and dropped his gaze. Jake sat next to his bed, his tongue busily licking his good hand. Jeff was next to him, a big grin on his face. "I knew you would be all right. I just knew it."

"Jake," Mary Jo said severely. "Don't do that!" Jake looked wounded and dropped his head.

For a moment, all of Wade's hesitation disappeared. He felt as if he were home. He belonged to these people around him, the woman and boy, even the dog. And they belonged to him in some inexplicable way.

If only . . .

There was a knock on the door, and Mary Jo went to open it. Matt Sinclair stood there, his arm in a sling; Wade's arm was bound to his chest, apparently so it couldn't be moved. He frowned. "How long . . . ?"

"Two days," Mary Jo said as she returned to his side. "The doctor said you were just plain worn out. He said he didn't know how you were even alive with all those wounds. We couldn't risk taking you all the way back to the ranch, so we put you in this boarding-house in town."

"I told the doctor you were the toughest man in Colorado," Jeff said. "Maybe even Texas." The latter was obviously the highest compliment he could give.

"That the doc you said wasn't any good? The one you were afraid might cut off my arm?" Wade asked.

She smiled, her eyes sparkling, that mouth curved in the easy smile he liked so much. "There was nothing he could take this time."

Wade thought that wasn't entirely true, and from her sudden smile, he knew she read his thoughts again.

He felt his own lips twist, but then he turned his head toward the sheriff. "You all right?"

"Thanks to you. I knew there was a reason I wanted you along. He would have killed me once we were outside. There was no way he could have gotten me on a horse."

"Where are they?"

"In my jail. Dave's taking them to Denver tomorrow for trial."

There was a silence, long, awkward, painful. Then Sinclair turned to Mary Jo. "I would like to talk to him alone for a few minutes."

Mary Jo looked at Wade, who nodded. Her gaze moved from Matt Sinclair to Wade, then back again, and Wade saw a glimmer of apprehension in her face. Then she turned toward Jeff. "Let's go get our patient something to eat."

"I'll leave Jake here for company," Jeff said. "He'll watch out for you." His young eyes were suddenly full of hostility as they looked at Sheriff Sinclair.

Wade nodded solemnly, his stomach churning. He tried to move, to sit up, but the slightest movement sent agonizing pain penetrating his hip. He fell back down.

"Water?" Sinclair said.

Wade nodded, and he watched as the sheriff carefully poured water from a pitcher on a nearby table into a cup and handed it to Wade. Wade's fingers shook as he took it, lifted it to his lips and drank. Then his gaze met Sinclair's. "What happens now?"

"Kelly's gonna yell his head off about you," Sinclair said. "I have to take you to Denver, unless you somehow slip out of town unnoticed." The invitation was there in his voice. It would be real easy to slip out of town unnoticed.

And run and run and run.

The alternative: a possible noose, prison. Kelly would do everything he could to see that it was the former.

"It seems my choices are limited."

"If you surrender yourself, I'll do everything I can to get you a pardon," Sinclair said. "This whole town will be behind you, but you should know there's no guarantees."

"But first I'll have to tell Mary Jo."

Sinclair nodded.

Wade hesitated. There was something else. Maybe days ago, he could have kept lying about it, but not now. Sinclair had been too damn decent. "That dead man you found a month ago . . ."

Something flickered in Sinclair's eyes. He waited.

"I killed him. You were right about me being the man in the mountains. Three miners killed my wife and son. He was one of them."

Sinclair nodded. "Figured it was something like that. Figured you had to be close to those redskins for them to help out like they did."

Wade felt himself bristling at the term "redskins."

Sinclair grinned suddenly. "Now don't go getting your back up. I don't have anything personal against them. They mind their business and don't bother my town, I don't bother them. Maybe next time we have a lost tenderfoot, or a little disagreement, I'll send you to negotiate for me."

"If I'm here."

"Something tells me you're pretty hard to get rid

of. Otherwise I would have tried to run you off in the beginning."

"Because of Mary Jo?"

Regret flashed in his eyes. "I'm a realist. I tried for a year and never got the time of day. You ride in and a week later . . . hell, I saw a light in her eyes I never saw before."

A kind of warmth washed over Wade. It crawled into all the crevices of his heart.

"And about that body," Sinclair continued, a bland look on his face, "I figure no one will ever know who he was or exactly what happened. That's what I wrote."

"Kelly?"

"No one's gonna believe him. He's too full of hate. Your one problem is Centralia, but that was a long time ago. I checked you out and finally got some telegrams back. Centralia's the only thing against you, and a lot of those Rebs have already been pardoned."

It was all too much for Wade's mind; which was still swimming in darkness, in fuzziness, still wrapped in pain. "It can't be that easy."

"I don't think it's been easy. I think you've been punishing yourself for the last twelve years, and it's been a worse judgment than anything anyone else can do to you." He hesitated. "I have my own ghosts, and it took me a long time to get to where I could live with them. But that day does come. And you were only a kid, for God's sake."

"I was twenty."

"And fifteen when that hate started. That's a young age to have to deal with such strong emotions."

"You a sheriff or a preacher?" The confusion inside made Wade lash out.

"A sheriff who thinks you would make a good neighbor."

Wade swallowed hard. "You don't owe me anything. I just wanted Kelly out of my life."

"There were ways of going about it. You picked the hard one." Sinclair stuck out his hand. "I think Mary Jo will understand more than you think. She's that kind of woman."

Wade hesitated, then took his hand. Accepting it was a kind of commitment. "When do we go to Denver?"

Matt Sinclair grinned. "When you can sit in a saddle again. Think it might take some time. Doc says weeks. In the meantime, I think I'll put you in Mary Jo's custody. Jake looks like a pretty good guard dog." Jake, who had been sitting next to the bed, started thumping his tail again as if in agreement. His tongue reached out reassuringly and took a big swipe on Wade's hand.

Another part of Wade started to ache, one that had nothing to do with his physical wound.

"By the way," Matt Sinclair said, "there's a big reward for Kelly. The mayor and I figure you should get it."

"No," Wade said.

"The reward's gotta go someplace."

"Doesn't this place need a school or something?"

Sinclair's grin widened. "Now I really know I want you as a neighbor, but I'd better get the hell out of here before Mrs. Williams takes a broom to me. She's been real protective, just like a mother cougar. Blames me for that gunshot, and she's partly right. I never should have taken you into that bank. I'll never figure out why I did."

He turned to leave.

"Sinclair?" Wade's voice stopped the sheriff, but he didn't turn.

"Thanks," Wade said, knowing it came out as a croak.

Sinclair just nodded and went out the door, without turning back.

26

Mary Jo wanted to touch all those wounded and scarred places on Wade's body and miraculously make them go away. She wondered if some of the hidden ones were too deep to heal.

Kelly knows something about me. Those words kept haunting her; so did the fact that Matt had locked Wade up. No one had told her why.

She felt terribly uncertain, which was just slightly better than how she had felt two days ago when she'd heard the shots and saw Wade being carried out.

She had insisted on caring for Wade herself after the doctor, still smelling of whiskey, had told her Wade had a painful but survivable wound. It would be days before he could sit a saddle, or anything else for that matter. The doctor hadn't understood why he'd remained unconscious for so long, unless it was exhaustion combined with loss of blood.

And Matt had been as closemouthed as ever, though he'd checked regularly to see whether Wade had returned to consciousness. And now Matt and Wade were together in the room, and Mary Jo sensed they were deciding his fate. Which would affect hers, too.

She had sent for Jeff almost immediately after the shoot-out, knowing he would come by himself if he heard. Once Jeff had arrived in town, Tuck had returned to the Circle J to tend the animals.

The door to the room finally opened, and Matt came out. "You can go in," he said.

She hesitated. "What's going to happen now?"

"He'll tell you," Matt said. "Take good care of him now."

There was something about the way he said those words that made her heart flare with hope.

She went in. Wade was lying on his side, three days' growth of beard on his face. He looked like a brigand again. She tried to look inside his eyes, to see some of the hope that she thought Matt had just offered. He moved slightly, and she heard him draw in his breath as pain hit again.

"I have some laudanum," she said.

His gray-green eyes seemed to search hers. "Later," he said. "Where's Jeff?"

"In the kitchen, getting you something to eat."

She moved over and sat carefully on the bed. "Matt said you had something to tell me." She reached over and put her finger on his left cheek. "It doesn't matter, you know," she said. "Nothing matters except you're alive. And you're a hero in this town now."

His good hand took the finger, stopping its movement. "I'm no hero. I never have been." He hesitated a moment, then continued in a low voice. "Have you ever heard of Bill Anderson?"

Anderson. She tried to think, but nothing came. She shook her head.

"During the war, he commanded a group of bushwhackers in Kansas and Missouri."

She'd been in Texas during the war. Fifteen, sixteen, seventeen years old, and in love with a Texas Ranger. She tried to remember Anderson from all the other war news that had flooded Texas, but she'd been more concerned about Jeff and thanking God his Ranger company had remained in Texas. "Bushwackers?"

He shifted again, bringing her hand down from his face, the fingers on his good hand playing with it absently. Or was it absently? His brows were furrowed together, his lips thinned. "Anderson used to like to say he was a Confederate soldier, but the truth is, most Rebs disclaimed him." Wade didn't spare himself. "He and his men murdered, stole, raped. They even scalped some of their victims." His fingers abandoned hers. "I was one of Anderson's raiders."

A muscle worked in his jaw. "I joined after my family was killed by Jayhawkers—Unionists. They were abolitionists for the most part, but they had a lot in common with Anderson. Some of them just killed for the love of killing."

Mary Jo felt the blood drain from her face. He'd never said anything before about a family other than Chivita and Drew. "What happened?" Her voice was so low she wondered whether he could hear.

"My father was a Missouri farmer. He never liked

slavery, but neither did he like being told what to do. When he refused to join a group of Jayhawkers, they came by to teach him a lesson. I'd been sent to town to get some feed, and stayed too long. When I got back, my father and brother were hanging from a tree and my mother and sister had been raped and murdered." He paused. "It was my fault. If I had been home earlier, there would have been another gun, and maybe—"

"And maybe you would have been killed, too," she interrupted gently.

"It would have been better," he said. "I wanted to kill every Jayhawker I could find. So I joined Quantrill and Anderson, and we raided farms just like ours, and killed farmers just like my father. I was sixteen and seventeen and I hated. God, I hated." His fingers had balled into a fist, and her hand tightened around that fist. "That's how I knew Kelly and Jesse James and the Younger Brothers. I knew them all. I pillaged with them all, and everything was justified in my mind. These were the people who killed my people. And then—" He stopped, his voice cracking, and a wetness started to rim his eyes.

"Then?" she asked softly.

"There was a little town in Missouri called Centralia. The Yanks had taken it, but Anderson made a successful raid and we won the town back, temporarily. A train came into the station, loaded with Union soldiers on furlough, and we stopped it." He hesitated. "Both Anderson and Quantrill rarely took prisoners in any event, and just a few days earlier some of Anderson's men were hanged. It was all the excuse he needed. The Yanks were ordered off the train and ordered to strip. None of them resisted. They were so damned scared.

They stood in a line, naked and shivering with fear. And then Anderson gave the order to fire. Some of them tried to run, but they didn't get far. I saw several of them scalped." He closed his eyes, and Mary Jo knew he was there again, seeing it all. She could only hold on to his hand, even as she recoiled against the horror of what she heard.

He swallowed after a moment. "One soldier, no more than a kid, probably hadn't even started shaving, made it behind some trains. Anderson sent me after him. I hadn't fired, but neither had I done anything to stop it. To this day, I don't know why I didn't yell out against it, try to stop the killing. I just didn't think it would happen, though I knew deep down Anderson was capable of it. Hell, he was capable of anything, but most of his men would follow him to hell and back. I was that way for a long time."

"The one he sent you after?" she prompted.

"I went after him. I knew he had a chance that way. I was just going to let him go. But Anderson sent another man, and he reached the kid before I did. I yelled for him to stop, but he shot the boy in the back, and leaned down to finish him. I yelled at him and he turned to fire on me." He paused. "I killed him, instead, killed one of my own kind."

He looked at Mary Jo and saw a single tear rolling down her cheek. "I dismounted and checked the boy," Wade continued. "He was dying. He asked me to write his mother." Wade closed his eyes. "He was naked and ashamed of it, and thinking of his mother. He rambled on about home, his farm. Christ, but he reminded me of my brother. The same earnest face, the same love of home and family. I stayed with him until he died, found something to cover him with, then mounted and rode away. I'd finally had enough killing until . . .''

He hesitated, trying to keep up his own courage. Mary Jo looked devastated, but she had to know all of it. "I thought I could never hurt anyone again. I went up to the mountains not to hide from authorities but from myself, what I'd become." He tried to pull his hand away. "The beast never goes away, no matter how much you want it. When Chivita and Drew were killed, I reverted to what I was twelve years earlier. It was so damn easy."

"That's what Kelly knew?" she said.

"He was with us that day in Centralia. Everyone with Anderson was wanted for . . . what happened that day. *I'm* wanted. Matt Sinclair has a poster."

"Is that why he locked you up?"

Wade nodded, his eyes wary.

Mary Jo felt numb as the last of his words penetrated. Now she remembered talk of the vicious fighting in Kansas and Missouri, even the name Quantrill. But she couldn't even imagine the horror of what he was telling her, and she couldn't believe Wade Foster had taken part in it. She understood the other, the dead miner; she would have killed anyone who harmed Jeff. But this other—raiding, killing farmers, people like her father. Her hand still clinging to his, she battled to keep her emotions from showing on her face. At his next words, she knew she had failed.

"I'm sorry, Mary Jo. I tried to tell you I wasn't what you wanted to believe."

He sounded so defeated; he had retreated behind a wall of defenses once more. He had torn it down a few days before when, risking imprisonment or worse, he'd revealed to Matt Sinclair the truth about his past.

And he had done it for her, for Jeff, for the town she now called home. He'd done none of it for himself.

The numbness started to leave. She felt his pain, and her own. "What is Matt going to do?" she asked.

His eyes were blank as he moved slightly, turning away from her, shutting her out. He shrugged as if it were a matter of great indifference. "He's going to take me to Denver when I can ride. He's going to try to get a pardon." He sounded as if he didn't really care whether Matt did or not, and Mary Jo knew she had drawn some more of his blood, that she had just wounded him as badly as that bank robber had. And all she'd wanted to do was heal.

"Wade?"

"The name is Brad Allen," he said curtly. "And I would like to be alone."

She bit her lip. "It doesn't matter, none of it matters," she started.

"You're not a liar, Mary Jo. At least you weren't until you met me. I corrupt people. I get people killed. And it *does* matter. I saw it in your eyes, and I don't blame you. You *should* be disgusted. I appreciate everything you've done, but I don't need you anymore." His voice almost cracked. "Just get the hell out of here and take the damn dog with you."

She stood there, unseeing.

"Goddammit, get out." There was so much pain in his voice now she found herself shaking.

She swallowed hard. "Jeff—"

"Go home, Mary Jo, and take your kid with you. If you give a damn at all, go home."

"Wade . . ." Jeff's voice came from the doorway. He was holding a tray, but he looked small, uncertain. Mary Jo wondered how much he'd heard. Her gaze went to the man in the bed, the man she'd known so well, thought she'd known so well.

"I—I can't," she said.

His shoulders lifted slightly. "Then stay in town but stay away from me," he said in a low voice. "I don't want you here."

Jeff's lips were trembling. He took the tray over to the table beside the bed and with great dignity set it down. "I want to stay with you."

"If you want to do something for me, go home and take good care of those horses I raised. I've been worrying about them."

"Tuck will take good care of them."

"Never depend on someone else to take care of your animals," Wade chided. "Not if you want to be a real rancher."

Jeff shifted from foot to foot. "I don't want to leave," he said stubbornly.

"Doing things you don't want to do is part of growing up, Jeff."

Jeff hesitated.

"Do it for me," Wade said.

"You're not going to stay with us, are you?"

"I have some business in Denver, then we'll see." It was a lie, and Mary Jo knew it was a lie. She'd just ruined any chance with that one unguarded response she'd made.

Jeff's eyes started to tear, but he simply held out his hand like a man. "It's been an honor knowing you, sir," he said formally. It was the first time Mary Jo had ever heard such words come from his mouth. He'd been taught to say sir to his elders, but the rest . . . ?

Jeff turned and nearly ran from the room, becoming a boy again.

Mary Jo hesitated another minute.

"Please go," he said again, and it was the please that did it. The word seemed to crack in his mouth. He wasn't going to listen to her now. Maybe later. She turned around and left.

Wade had known it was too damn easy, that he'd had no right to hope, to allow Matt Sinclair to dismiss his past lightly. He turned to the wall, ignoring the pain. It was minor compared to how he'd felt when he'd seen the horror in Mary Jo's eyes as he told her about Anderson, about Centralia. She'd tried to hide it, but she couldn't. Just like he could never hide that part of him again.

I love you, she'd said days ago. And because she had, she would have tried. She would have tried hard to love him, to forget that dark side of him. But he would never know when it might surface again.

Laudanum. Damn, but it would be welcome now. But that wouldn't work, either. The ache ran too deep.

He tried to sit. God, it hurt. He twisted back down into the bed. He looked at the tray Jeff had brought. He wanted to sweep it on the floor. But the stronger he got, the faster he could leave. Denver. Jail. A trial. He no longer believed in a pardon. No more than he believed Mary Jo could ever accept what he was.

Six days later, Wade insisted on going to Denver where the other two prisoners had been taken. That's what he considered himself now, though Matt Sinclair had shrugged off his suggestion that he stay in jail. The simple fact was that Wade didn't really care where he was. He just wanted to get away from Last Chance.

He had not seen Mary Jo again although Matt said she'd asked about him.

Had she gone home?

Sinclair had become Matt. A friend, even. And now he shrugged. "You have to give her time," he said. "You threw a lot at her. I didn't like it when you first told me, either."

"You still don't like it."

Sinclair shrugged again. "That doesn't have anything to do with the man you are today."

"I wish I could believe that," Wade said ruefully. "I wanted to kill Kelly."

"But you didn't."

"Only because I didn't have a chance."

Matt gave him a disgusted look. "A lot of people think otherwise, including me."

Wade was eating a bowl of stew Matt had brought him. It didn't taste nearly as good as Mary Jo's. Probably better than what he'd get at the jail in Denver, though.

"When do we go?" Wade asked.

"Tomorrow since you're so eager. We'll take a wagon. I don't think you're up to a saddle yet."

Wade smiled for the first time since the robbery. "Hell of a place to get shot."

"Every other place seemed to be used up," Matt said. "Doctor can look at that arm in Denver."

A barber came later that day. The shave was free, he said. He'd had money in the Last Chance bank. The owner of a general store dropped in to leave a new set of clothes. He'd also had money in the bank. The doctor, the smell of whiskey on his breath again, checked his wound and said there would be no charge.

The mayor came a little later, stood awkwardly, then cleared his throat. "Sheriff Sinclair said you were donating the reward for a school. It'll mean a lot to this town." He hesitated. "Anything you need, you let us know. That bank means a lot to the people in this area. So does Matt," he said as an afterthought as he glanced at the sheriff.

Sinclair winked at Wade. Still, nothing could quite stifle Wade's loneliness, that aching need for Mary Jo and Jeff. Part of him wished they had come back, had defied his wishes. In fact, he'd kept expecting her quick step, Jeff's bright smile, and Jake's rough tongue. He found himself repeatedly glancing at the door.

With every moment that passed without their arrival, his loneliness grew.

The mayor finally left, after saying how much he would like, the entire town would like, Wade to return to Last Chance.

After he left, Wade turned to Sinclair. "Does he know about Centralia?"

"Yep."

"Does he know I took a Ute wife, fathered a half-Ute child?" He couldn't say half-breed.

"Now I was a little bit more, ah, quiet about that. I did say you had lived with them, that because of you they helped find young Jeff Williams."

"I won't hide it." Wade didn't know why he was even discussing this. He would be in prison.

"You got to give them a little time," Sinclair said. "We're throwing a whole lot at them, just like you threw a lot at Mary Jo at one time. It takes a little adjustin' to."

"Mary Jo couldn't take it," Wade said bitterly.

"You're the one who ordered her out."

Wade's eyes narrowed. "What did she tell you?"

Sinclair grinned. "Do you always underestimate everyone?"

"I've found damn few reasons to do otherwise."

Sinclair shook his head in disgust and changed the subject. "You might want to get some exercise. I warn you, though, you go outside and everyone in town will want to shake your hand."

Wade shut his eyes. Christ, he couldn't stand that. He still thought of himself as one of Anderson's raiders, a man without honor. Mary Jo had finally realized that—and hers was the only hand he wanted. Jeff had given him his, but he hadn't known yet about Anderson, about all the killing.

He would start walking in this room. It was a little larger than a cell. He'd better get used to cramped spaces. He went over to the window and looked down. He wanted to see a tall, slender figure with red hair. Just one more glimpse. The man he recognized as the banker looked up and saw him, waved. Wade turned away.

Tomorrow. Tomorrow he would leave Last Chance forever. The name was ironic as hell. He'd thought he might have one, but Mary Jo's absence proved he didn't.

They left at daybreak. Because of the hour, Wade didn't expect to see anyone. What must have been practically the whole town, though, was assembled in front of the boardinghouse. Matt just shrugged when Wade threw him an accusing look.

They all wanted to shake his hand, to wish him well. Several women handed them picnic baskets, one of the men a bottle of whiskey. It was the damnedest thing Wade had ever seen. But Mary Jo wasn't there, and he didn't think he'd ever see her again.

Matt had acquired a sturdy wagon, and had equipped it with a mattress in back and some cushions on the driver's bench. Sitting down, though, still was an ordeal. It was going to be one hell of a long journey. Three days, maybe four in this wagon, Matt Sinclair had said.

He would take the time to look, to experience, to memorize sunsets and sunrises, to fix in his mind the image of an auburn-haired woman with the smiling mouth. He welcomed the first jolt of the wagon, the discomfort it brought. He didn't know whether he could bear four days of those kinds of memories.

Mary Jo and Jeff finished the last of their rounds. They had covered the entire Cimarron Valley, gathering the signatures of every man and woman within a hundred miles. It had taken them five days, but now they had a petition with better than five hundred names, all asking that Brad Allen be pardoned.

She had thought about staying in town, trying to talk to Wade, but she had seen the way he closed himself off. Talk wouldn't do any good. So she'd set off to do something that really would do some good. Until Wade had forgiven himself, until he saw himself as others now saw him, he would never accept his own worth. Matt Sinclair had agreed, and he thought the petitions would help Wade's cause.

It had been ten days now since the robbery, and

she knew Matt had probably started out for Denver with Wade. He had sent word that Wade was insisting on leaving as soon as possible. The Abbots had loaned her two men, and she and Jeff, with Tuck for protection, would ride to Denver, hopefully arriving before Wade.

Mary Jo packed carefully. Wade's necklace, the one that had belonged to his son. Her prettiest dress. The package of notes that some of the grateful customers of the Last Chance bank had asked her to take to him.

She on her mare and Jeff on King Arthur then dropped by the town livery to pick up Wade's big gray, and then with Tuck they headed for Denver. On horseback they could take trails Matt and his wagon couldn't. With luck, they would be in Denver ahead of them and could make their case to federal authorities there. Matt had already sent numerous telegrams to everyone he knew in Washington and Denver.

With luck, with lots of luck, Wade would return with them.

Denver was a bustling town, but Wade was too damn sore to appreciate it. The whiskey had helped some, but it hadn't been able to dull the sharp pang of loss or the constant pain in his hip.

He noted dully the saloons, pleasure palaces, hotels. They finally stopped at one of the latter. Wade stiffly climbed down from the wagon and followed Matt inside the hotel lobby where the sheriff took two rooms. Wade had expected to go directly to a jail, but Sinclair had surprised him often since they met. His eyes met the sheriff's. Sinclair shrugged. "Might as well be comfortable while we can." He paused for a moment, then continued. "I've got some people to see," Sinclair said. "I'll have a meal and bath sent up to you."

Wade just shook his head. A tentative friendship had deepened on the trail, as they shared that bottle of whiskey as well as fried chicken, cookies, and other delicacies prepared by the women of Last Chance. "Wish I had more prisoners like you." Sinclair grinned. "Don't usually eat this well."

But it had all tasted like dust to Wade. He went through the motions of eating, but that was all. And now even the prospect of a bath and a soft bed didn't alleviate that deep, clawing emptiness.

He just turned and headed up the stairs with his bedroll and, he hoped, the oblivion of sleep. He'd had little of that during the journey. The whiskey was gone, unfortunately, even though it had seemed to sharpen his losses rather than dull them. Perhaps he'd just needed more of it.

He fingered the key to the room in his hand, turned and looked back. Matt was already gone. Not for the first time, he thought about turning and running. He'd thought about it a lot. But he owed Matt, and the truth was that without Mary Jo and Jeff, his life didn't hold much interest. Prison was probably as good as anyplace. After Mary Jo's reaction, he didn't share Matt's optimism about a pardon.

Wade reached the room and opened it. It was luxurious compared to the one in Last Chance. He threw the bedroll onto the floor, then tested the bed. It was soft, like Mary Jo's had been. Hell, would everything always remind him of Mary Jo?

He went to the mirror. He was covered with dust

from the road, and his face was bristly again with new beard. There was a bowl of water on a table and some towels. He took a couple of swipes at his face and sat on the bed, tugging at the pair of new boots the boot-maker in Last Chance had given him. It was the best pair of boots he'd ever had. He thought of the people who'd seen him off the morning he left, the good will they had expressed. Momentary gratitude, he told himself. It didn't mean anything.

Still, it had been nice.

Matt left his gear at the front desk of the hotel, then found quarters for his horses and wagon. The next stop was the federal marshal's office. The lawman in charge groaned when Matt introduced himself. "Not Allen again," he said.

"You got my telegram?"

"And about fifty more, and a visit from a very determined young lady, and calls from the governor and two congressmen, not to mention a general at the War Department in Washington."

Matt smiled. "How long has Mrs. Williams been here?"

"A day and a half and it was as if a tornado hit this place."

"Where is she staying?"

The federal lawman mentioned a hotel one street away from where Matt had taken rooms. The lawman squinted at him. "Where's Allen?"

Matt told him the name of the hotel. "He came willingly. Hell, he damned well forced me to bring him."

"Will he sign the loyalty oath?"

Matt's looked the marshal in the eyes. "I can't speak for him, but I would think so."

"We've been wanting Kelly real bad for a long time, and we owe Allen for getting him for us. After getting your telegram and the mayor's and hearing out that young lady, I did some checking on my own. Your boy picked the right time to surrender. The politicians in Washington want the country to heal. They're doing an awful lot of forgiving right now, except for renegades like Kelly. All Allen needs to do is sign the loyalty oath and swear to uphold the laws of this government."

Matt grinned. "It's a pleasure doing business with you. I'll have him over here this afternoon."

"Wouldn't mind seeing that young lady again. Real persuasive. Even the governor wired Washington on Allen's behalf." He shook his head. "Determined woman."

Matt felt a familiar regret. "Yep, she is that."

An insistent pounding woke Wade up. It was the second time. Porters had already brought buckets of water for his bath. He had washed off the dust and dirt and sweat, tried his hand at shaving, making only a small cut with his left hand, and then struggled into a pair of trousers before sinking down into the bed again.

He woke reluctantly. Must be Matt Sinclair. He brushed back a shock of hair and went to the door, opening it. He swallowed, and his heart pounded uncontrollably.

Mary Jo slipped into his room. She was wearing a dress he'd never seen before, and when she looked up at him, a corner of that enchanting mouth tugged upward.

And then her arms were around his neck, and his good arm was around her, pulling her to him. He didn't know why she was here, and he didn't care. He just needed her. He needed her so bad.

There was mist in her eyes, an invitation on her lips, and he bent, capturing her mouth. The kiss was fierce, wanting, uninhibited.

"I missed you," she whispered when their lips parted a fraction of an inch.

His hand caressed that fine auburn hair that smelled of flowers, that felt like silk. He hadn't thought he would touch it again, feel it again. He leaned his face against the top of her head, drinking in everything he loved about her.

"What are you doing here?" he finally managed.

She moved back a step. "I came to see you and bring something to the governor."

"The governor?"

"Petitions from more than five hundred people who want you to come back to the Cimarron Valley."

He stared at her in amazement. He knew the townspeople had been grateful that the bank had not been robbed. But five hundred people?

He looked down at her wonderingly. "You?"

"I had lots of help. Jeff. The Abbots. Matt. And it worked. I just saw Matt. If you take the loyalty oath, you'll be pardoned."

"Just like that?" He couldn't believe the best after believing the worst for the past week.

"Just like that," she confirmed.

"And you? Can you live with what I used to be, what I probably still am?"

"I love what you are," she said softly. "Matt told me everything that happened in that bank. I know how hard it was for you to tell me the rest." Her hand went to his cheek, to the cut he'd made while shaving.

He winced. "I don't know how much use I'll ever have of that arm."

She rose on tiptoes and kissed him. Slowly. Thoroughly. "You seem to get along well enough without it. But Matt said there's a fine doctor here."

He swallowed hard. "I already owe him a lot."

"He's a good man. So are you. A whole town thinks so."

He drew her back into his arm. "I don't think I want to dispute a whole town."

"Jeff's waiting to see you."

"You think he could wait thirty minutes?"

She looked up at him, her green eyes gleaming with mischief. "I think it will be very hard, but I also think he'll understand."

"Matt?"

"He said he'll come back in a few hours. Had some hell-raising to do after that long trip. He said you weren't very good company."

"I thought I'd lost you."

"Never," she said. "I just knew you wouldn't even consider staying with us with . . . that hanging over your head."

"But you—" He stopped suddenly, remembering the horror in her eyes when he finally told her what had happened years ago.

"I hadn't expected it. But that was so long ago, when you were little more than a boy yourself. Matt told me about Kansas and Missouri, what it was like back then, and that you had had the courage to see it for what it was, and leave."

"I ran," he said flatly.

"No, you threw away hatred."

"I don't know," he said, not wanting to let go of her, but not wanting to lie, either. Not anymore. "It came back when—"

"You think I wouldn't have done the same thing, or Matt or nearly anyone in Last Chance if it had been their wife and child? It's over now, Wade. It's really over."

He closed his eyes, wondering whether she was right. A kind of release swept over him, the way a fresh, cool wind erases footsteps in the dust. "I love you," he said. He hadn't said those words in years, not even to Chivita. He'd never felt he had the right to say them, not with a heart half torn away. That heart felt whole now, though.

She smiled at him, humor and challenge tugging at her mouth. "Prove it," she said.

And he did.

Epilogue

Cimarron Valley, Ten Years Later

Wade approached the sprawling ranch house, his heart lightening at the sight of the flickering lights that welcomed him.

He'd been gone five weeks this time, once more fighting for the cause of the Utes. They had won one more minor victory in Washington. The southern Utes wouldn't be pushed into the semidesert reservation in Utah, as many Coloradoans wished, but would be permitted to stay on their own reservation in southern Colorado.

The word "reservation," in regard to Manchez and his other friends, still gave Wade cold shivers. It was so wrong to cage these riders of the wind on a small piece of land. Yet the southern Utes had fared better than any of the other tribes. They still had a corner of their ancestral land and were given occasional permission to hunt outside the reservation.

The trip had tired him, as had the numerous visits to congressmen and senators. He had legally taken the name of Wade Foster, wanting to bury deeper his memories of Kansas and Missouri. His life started, he thought, when he'd met Mary Jo.

They had three children now, including Jeff, and he loved them all with the same intensity. Matt was eight, and as curious and mischievous as Jeff had been. And Hope, at six, was the baby and adored by all. She was as pretty as a rosebud with her mother's auburn hair and green eyes, and she was such a happy little girl. He wanted to give her the world. He wanted to give them all the world.

Most of all he'd wanted to give them love and safety and security. And tolerance. It had taken him so long to learn tolerance, so much time and so much pain. If there was any legacy he wanted to leave, it was to understand and accept people for *who* they were, not *what* they were. He'd been guilty as a young man of condemning a whole group of people for what a few had done, as so many whites now did in condemning the Indians.

And Drew, the son he'd lost, was always in his heart, as was Chivita. Mary Jo had taught him to remember the good, rather than the evil, to protect the fine things rather than discard them with the bad. Mary Jo was his light, the candle of his soul, and his children were its joy.

He stopped his horse and looked out over the Circle J. It was so long since she had asked him whether he had ever allowed himself to have joy. He'd thought then that joy was gone forever from his life.

And now he had so much. Mary Jo and Jeff had given it to him through their love and sheer determination. Mary Jo, he thought with a small secret smile, could move mountains if she wished. And Jeff took after her. Now twenty-two, his eldest son was assistant foreman of the ranch, which had grown to include more than ten thousand head of cattle and a substantial stable of fine horses. Tuck still ramrodded the ranch and would until Jeff was ready, and then Jeff and Tuck would run the ranch together. Tuck had become indispensable, a member of the family in all important ways.

Wade supervised the horse-breeding. Circle J horses had become famous throughout Colorado, and Wade had little doubt Jeff could handle that operation, too. After numerous trips to Ute camps, Jeff had become as fine a horseman as many of the Utes. He had, in fact, won the last race, which had taken place on the Ute reservation just two months earlier.

Jeff had grown as tall as Wade. He was more thoughtful now, though he would probably always have a reckless, adventurous streak. Texas Ranger blood, Mary Jo called it. Wade, however, thought Mary Jo definitely had a part in it.

He nudged his horse into a canter, his right arm falling to the saddle horn. His fingers had never fully regained their dexterity, and his elbow was stiff, but he'd learned to function well despite those two problems. He'd taught himself to shoot with his left hand, though he hoped to God he would never have to use a weapon again against a human being.

He doubted that he would. Civilization was coming

west. Matt Sinclair had moved on five years ago when Last Chance had died, surrendering to dust after a rail line had bypassed it in favor of a more centrally located ranching town. Matt had become a good friend of the family and had stood as godfather to young Matt, but they had heard nothing in the past five years except for a gift on each of the children's birthdays. Wade often wondered what would have happened to him, to them all, if Matt had not been sheriff. He was an extraordinary man. But he had been restless those last years in Last Chance, and then one day he had come by the ranch to say goodbye.

Wade thought of him often and wished him well.

Another light flared up inside the house, and the door opened. Mary Jo always seemed to sense his presence, was always there to greet him when he returned from a trip. Just as she opened the door, Hope darted out and threw herself in his arms.

"Daddy," she screamed happily. "We had puppies."

"You did?" he said with a small grin. "I would have liked to have seen that."

She giggled. "You're silly."

"So are you," he said, then planted a kiss on her forehead as she wriggled down. "And I like you just that way."

The pups would be Jake's grandlitter, and he would be unbearably proud. He was getting stiff in his old age, but he still felt as if he owned the family rather than the family owning him. And sure enough, he too was at the door, the now graying tail thumping as enthusiastically as always.

Wade held out his arms to Mary Jo. "Our brood

keeps growing," he said, nibbling at her lips. She looked just as pretty as she did ten years ago.

"Hmmmm," she said, standing on tiptoes to kiss him with the passion that had not faded with time. It had grown instead, the early desperation changing into something sweeter, everlasting.

"Welcome home," she whispered.

Wade put his an arm around Mary Jo and, filled with a happiness that never ceased to astound him, walked into heaven.

About the Author

Patricia Potter has become one of the most highly praised writers of historical romance since her impressive debut in 1988, when she won the Maggie Award and a Reviewer's Choice Award from *Romantic Times* for her first novel. She received the *Romantic Times* Career Achievement Award for Storyteller of the Year for 1992 and a Reviewer's Choice nomination for her novel RENEGADE (Best Historical Romance of 1993). She has worked as a newspaper reporter in Atlanta and was president of the Georgia Romance Writers Association.

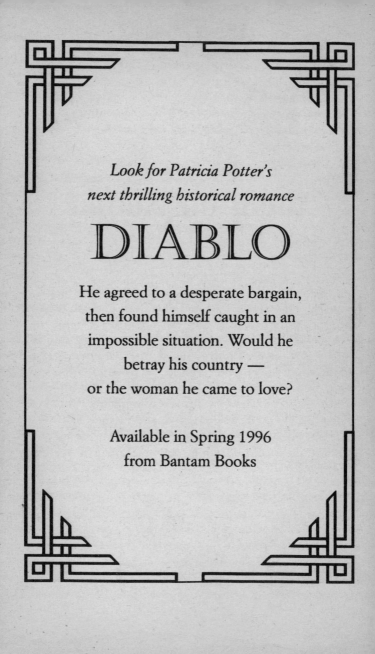

Look for Patricia Potter's
next thrilling historical romance

DIABLO

He agreed to a desperate bargain,
then found himself caught in an
impossible situation. Would he
betray his country —
or the woman he came to love?

Available in Spring 1996
from Bantam Books